THE LATEHOMECOMER

ESSENTIAL STORIES

MAVIS GALLANT

SELECTED AND INTRODUCED
BY TESSA HADLEY

PUSHKIN PRESS CLASSICS

Pushkin Press
Somerset House, Strand
London WC2R 1LA

© 1956, 1963, 1965, 1969, 1974, 1976, 1977, 1983,
1985, 1991, 2025 The Estate of Mavis Gallant

Introduction © 2025 Tessa Hadley

This selection first published by Pushkin Press in 2025

ISBN 13: 978-1-80533-229-9

All rights reserved. No part of this publication may be reproduced, stored in a retrieval system or transmitted in any form or by any means, electronic, mechanical, photocopying, recording or otherwise, without prior permission in writing from Pushkin Press.

The authorised representative in the EEA is
eucomply OÜ, Pärnu mnt. 139b-14, 11317, Tallinn, Estonia,
hello@eucompliancepartner.com, +33757690241

Designed and typeset by Tetragon, London
Printed and bound by Clays Ltd, Elcograf S.p.A.

Pushkin Press is committed to a sustainable future for our business, our readers and our planet. This book is made from paper from forests that support responsible forestry.

www.pushkinpress.com

1 3 5 7 9 8 6 4 2

PUSHKIN PRESS CLASSICS

THE LATEHOMECOMER

ESSENTIAL STORIES

'The irrefutable master of the short story in English. She is the standout. She is the standard-bearer. She is the standard'
FRAN LEBOWITZ

'One of the most brilliant story writers in the language, who deserves to be read as widely as her fellow Canadian Alice Munro'
NEW YORKER

'Gallant's work reminds you to think more deeply about the people you deal with… She reminds us of how fathomless we are, how there is always more to know'
PETER ORNER

'[Gallant's stories] are so much richer, so much denser than so many novels… Her body of work is unique and profound'
JHUMPA LAHIRI

MAVIS GALLANT (1922–2014) is widely regarded as one of the great writers of the short story in English. She was born in Montreal and worked as a journalist before moving to Europe to devote herself to writing fiction. There, Gallant travelled extensively before settling in Paris, where she lived until her death, though she never renounced her Canadian citizenship. Starting in 1951, the *New Yorker* published 116 of her stories. She was the recipient of the 2002 Rea Award for the Short Story and the 2004 PEN/Nabokov Award for lifetime achievement.

TESSA HADLEY is the author of eight highly praised novels, four collections of stories and a novella, *The Party*. She won the Windham Campbell Prize for Fiction in 2016, *The Past* won the Hawthornden Prize for 2016, *Bad Dreams* and *After the Funeral* both won the Edge Hill Short Story Prize, in 2018 and 2025. Her stories appear regularly in the *New Yorker*.

Contents

Introduction by Tessa Hadley   7

In Italy (1956)	17
The Ice Wagon Going Down the Street (1963)	30
Paola and Renata (1965)	57
The Wedding Ring (1969)	69
The Latehomecomer (1974)	74
Irina (1974)	99
The Moslem Wife (1976)	120

(from "Linnet Muir")

The Doctor (1977)	164
Voices Lost in Snow (1976)	186

("Édouard, Juliette, Lena")

A Recollection (1983)	199
The Colonel's Child (1983)	209
Rue de Lille (1983)	219
Lena (1983)	224

(from "The Carette Sisters")

1933 (1985)	237
The Chosen Husband (1985)	244

Forain (1991)	266

Introduction

Mavis Gallant mostly didn't keep her reviews; even when they were kind, she too often felt they were "off the target". But there was one review in *El Pais*, when she was first translated into Spanish, which she liked and kept. The reviewer said that when Gallant came to Western Europe after the war, no one knew who she was and she didn't know anyone—she had lived as anonymously as possible with an exercise book, a notebook and a pencil. She was like Kafka's invisible woman, the reviewer went on, and the invisible woman took note of everything that Europeans thought was of no importance. Now people saw that these things were indeed important.

This seems to describe wonderfully well both Gallant's history as a writer, and the mood and form of her stories. To begin with, there's the uprootedness, and the not-quite-belonging, whose origins she traces very early in her own life. She was born in 1922 and grew up in Montreal, Canada, the only child of restless, attractive, heedless parents; similar figures haunt a number of her stories, like the couple who "drank old-fashioneds and danced to gramophone records out on the lawn" in summer in "The Doctor". For reasons she's not wholly able to fathom, although they were both English-speakers and nonbelievers, they thought it a good idea to send their small daughter, aged four, to board at a French convent school run by nuns, "where Jansenist discipline still had a foot on the neck of the twentieth century". In one of her stories, when a child explains that Satan approached her—"furry dark skin, claws, red eyes, the lot"—and made her cross the street in front of a car, she realizes suddenly that her parents don't believe in Satan, or in most of what she's being taught at school. The writing instinct may begin in such jolts to apprehension, the registering of deep dissonance between two cultural systems—unbolting the door, as she puts it, "between perception and imagination". Two contradictory ways of seeing can coexist in the same world; best to test everything you're told.

Gallant's adored, glamorous father, a thwarted painter, died of kidney disease when she was just ten; they told her he'd gone to England, and she waited for him to return until, aged thirteen, she began to doubt, and set about uncovering the truth. Her mother remarried and Gallant was packed off to one school after another in Canada and America, where she didn't thrive. She returned eventually to Montreal: in actuality first, to work as a reporter on the *Montreal Standard*, and then forever afterwards, in some of her best stories. Aged twenty-seven, she writes, she was "becoming exactly what I did not want to be: a journalist who wrote fiction along some margin of spare time". She also dreaded finding she had "a vocation without the competence to sustain it"; her father had not lived long enough to discover whether or not he could actually paint well, and had made his living in a firm selling furniture. That anxiety never left her, it fuelled her: she was one of those writers driven by doubt to be good, to be better. Certain superstitions accompany that fear of being merely shoddy or ordinary: don't let the scaffolding show, allow the story to stand by itself. Don't waste space, don't state the obvious, don't say anything twice.

She'd had a couple of stories in a Canadian literary review, but now she set herself a test, and decided to send three to the *New Yorker*, one after another: one acceptance would be good enough. If she couldn't live on writing she would "destroy every scrap, every trace, every notebook, and live some other way". The second story was taken, the third she sent from Paris, where she would eventually settle for life: a youthful wartime marriage in Canada didn't last long, and she never had children. Her vocation, and the need to write anonymously, where no one knew who she was and she didn't know anyone, sent her to Europe. "I still do not know," she wrote, "what impels anyone sound of mind to leave dry land and spend a lifetime describing people who do not exist." In her diaries she recorded months of semi-starvation in Madrid in 1952, while she waited to see whether the *New Yorker* would take any more stories. In fact they already had, and a crooked literary agent had pocketed the money; she found this out eventually by a lucky chance. "The sensation of disgust was curious, as if a colony of flies were stuck to me... The first thing I bought was good white bread." Her relationship with the *New Yorker*, and with its fiction editor William Maxwell, would be fundamental. One hundred and sixteen stories, the lion's share of her work, appeared in the magazine.

Gallant did publish two novels—*Green Water, Green Sky* in 1959, and *A Fairly Good Time* in 1970—and for years she toiled on a book about Dreyfus which she eventually shelved, but it's for her short stories that she will be remembered. A certain density of reference, perfectly in proportion in a short story, can feel overfreighted and mannered across a longer distance. Her imagination works in pieces of broken-off intensity; life reveals itself to her in signs, snatches of speech, fragments of memory. "The first flash of fiction arrives without words. It consists of a fixed image, like a slide or (closer still) a freeze frame..." Sometimes she runs together "suites of connected stories", as Brandon Taylor calls them, which suit her vision exactly; these don't pretend to join the pieces of a life into a single shape, but place them side by side like discontinuous phases of experience, each with its own centre, its own sharp point—rather like an actual life, in fact. The invisible woman is an archaeologist assembling small shards of material evidence into partial shapes, and an anthropologist hungry with curiosity—setting one way of seeing alongside another, making both strange. Her stories compose a meticulous record of Europe in the aftermath of war, and then in the Cold War, as well as the lost world of the Canadian past. Each of the tribes she describes—French Canadians and English Canadians, German ex-prisoners-of-war, Jewish survivors, French bureaucrats, French novelists, French tax inspectors, Swiss moralists, intellectual exiles from behind the Iron Curtain—has its own tokens of exchange, its own ideology, its sacred images, its taboos, its secret dreams, its obscure shames. Each tribe gives the others very little thought; Gallant writes at the intersection of their worlds. She took note of everything that seemed of little importance.

Everyone is interesting in her fiction. Gallant's protagonists may not be particularly sympathetic, they may be dense or narrow or just feeble, yet they're all felt and conveyed with the same even-handedness, the same keen appetite. Stella, in the story "In Italy"—a foolish nice girl, a "compound of middle-class virtues" and married to a cynical sophisticate more than twice her age—tries to keep warm over the stove in their rented Italian villa, reading copies of *Woman's Own* and *The Lady* which her mother sends from England. "I thought it would be fun," she says mournfully about her marriage. Lightweight snob Peter Frazier in "The Ice Wagon Going Down the Street", trying and failing to profiteer in post-war Europe, is demoralized by his new colleague and Canadian compatriot Agnes—she's from such a different background to his, so solemn and so striving. He feels "as you feel the approach of a storm, the charge of moral certainty round her, the belief in work, the faith in undertakings... ashes in the mouth". The French-Canadian doctor who makes such a fuss of Linnet Muir, presenting her with a sentimental picture, won't help her when she runs away from school; to the child's disappointment he sides with her parents' adult authority.

But the stories strike surprises out of these individuals: for a moment they can see more than they know, become more than themselves. Peter Frazier can't forget what Agnes told him about watching the ice wagon in the mornings when she was a child; the doctor turns out to be a poet in his private life. Poor Madame Carette in "1933", a stickler for perfect manners, widowed at twenty-seven and forced to move to a smaller flat, weeps for her own wicked thoughts with her elbows on the table, to the dismay of her little daughters. Selfish Lena, in her eponymous story, ruined another woman's life but is magnificent in her extreme old age. These moments, when her protagonists are momentarily lifted out of their frames, aren't redemptive or anything so grandiose. Nor are they moments of love, exactly, although there may be true closeness and comradeship in the stories—between Peter Frazier and his wife, for example, or between the Carette sisters and their mother, or between the widowed grandmother in "Irina" and her new man-friend. Irina's tenderness toward her grandson is exquisite too. The most piercing apprehensions, however, can't be shared. Gallant's characters don't live all alone, but their perception is necessarily solitary: except that everything's noted and kept on their behalf by her narrator, with her compendious interest and her art.

Her interest, but not her identification—not even when Gallant is clearly telling something like her own story. She reports on Linnet Muir's childhood and youth in Canada in the first person, but as coolly as if they had happened to somebody else. The quirks and oddity of her history are for adding to the oddity of all those others. Gallant doesn't belong to any obvious tradition of women's writing: her protagonists are as likely as not to be men, and we're not much invited to identify with them—we are to watch them, rather. Her narrative approach and writing temperament feel almost opposite to those of her compatriot Alice Munro, who was ten years younger, and from such a different Canada. In a Munro story we're often submerged in the reality of one moment after another; in a Gallant story we seem to be told about events after the fact, across some distance of time. Both writers can, of course, do the other thing as well.

Munro builds out her stories warily, doubtfully, from a subjective root—and that hesitant awareness is usually, though not always, a woman's. Gallant's positioning in her stories is authoritative, as if she offered objective information; her writing loves to know things, she relishes the most arcane fragments. We're informed in "The Moslem Wife", for instance, that the "most trustworthy shipping agents in 1860 are the Montale brothers, converts to the Anglican Church, possessors of a British *laissez-passer* to Malta and Egypt". But what is a British *laissez-passer* to Malta and Egypt, and why does it matter? We don't need to know, we can half-guess: we only need Gallant to know on our behalf—she builds our trust out of her expertise. Forain the publisher is familiar, from attending the funerals of Central and Eastern European writers, with "all the Polish churches of Paris, the Hungarian mission, the synagogues on the Rue Copernic and the Rue de la Victoire, and the mock chapel of the crematorium at Père Lachaise cemetery"; we believe in his familiarity, and it becomes ours.

There's a great tradition, in fiction in English, of this kind of narration, staking its claim through an insider's dense information and know-how: Kipling is master of it, and so are Ford Madox Ford and Penelope Fitzgerald. It's not that Munro wouldn't be interested in those details: both writers were interested in everything. But Munro's women are sceptical of their men's worldly know-how even as they're attracted to it; they read the world out of some other centre. In the opaque compression of Gallant's prose, in her eschewing of lyrical flow, and in her shapes so elegantly knotted, she seems to assert the knowing authority Munro disclaims. Gallant's self-doubt is antecedent to the achievement of her stories, and doesn't show up on their surface. It's a nice twist of cultural fate that these fellow Canadians, two of the last century's greatest short-story writers in English, should read as so marvellously unlike.

Gallant's stories map out in forensic detail her worlds, and her considerable stretch of history: mid-century Canada, then post-war

Europe, then Europe post 1968. Her diaries of the *évènements*, published as *Paris Notebooks*, are a nuanced and complex record of heady days. She is an instinctively political writer, not partisan but a moralist, charting the shadowy black comedy of the intricacies of allegiance, ideology, history, action. "Even the name he had given his daughter was a sign of his sensitivity to the times. Nobody wanted to hear the pagan, Old Germanic names anymore—Sigrun and Brunhilde and Sieglinde." Reality is replayed and reinvented as farce in the collective imagination; her stories unpick with irony the political faux-narratives which override the mystery and subtlety of actual experience. In one story, not included here, a boy whose German-Jewish family was murdered in the camps finds work after the war playing victims in French films about the Nazis.

"The Latehomecomer" is especially poignant, painful: Thomas returns to Berlin having spent years after the war as a prisoner in France, through a series of bureaucratic errors. His mother meets him at the station and turns out to be remarried now to a boor, in a flat whose previous tenants left in a hurry; she has a new gesture, too, of hiding her mouth with her hand, ashamed of having lost her front teeth. When she tells Thomas to wish on the new moon, he wishes he were "a few hours younger, in the corridor of a packed train, clutching the top of the open window, my heart hammering as I strained to find the one beloved face". If Gallant isn't lyrical exactly, her flights of language can be breathtaking. But this story's fine emotional positioning couldn't work if its tone was merely outrage, or denunciation. That would be too sentimental in the face of what has happened to Thomas, the huge deception—not really his poor helpless mother's, but the brutal impersonal state's, and the world's—and his loss of everything. Gallant is a great comic writer, though, and finds absurdity in the darkest places. His mother's neighbour asks him what he was paid as a prisoner. "I had often wondered what the first question would be once I was home. Now I had it."

She's good, too, at skewering ponderous public conscientiousness. "Irina" is the elderly widow of a great man, a Swiss writer, Nobel prize winner—the last "of a Tolstoyan line of moral lightning rods... prophet, dissuader, despairingly opposed to evil, crack-voiced after having made so many pronouncements". Perhaps, if we could imagine a Swiss Solzhenitsyn, that might help? The comedy isn't broad, the man wasn't a fraud, but Gallant makes us feel the chilly shadow he's cast; there's an egotism in such austere probity and certainty. A cracked-voice puritan righteousness is thin nourishment finally, can't encompass life's joy or its uncertainty: Irina writes wistfully in a letter to her grown-up son about her childhood, when "mistakes were allowed". Even now, she confesses, "whatever she saw and thought and attempted was still fluid and vague. The shape of a table against afternoon light still held a mystery, awaited a final explanation". Gallant isn't obviously a feminist writer, and yet how eloquent Irina's account is, to her little grandson, of how women have been short-changed in their relationships, from generation to generation. "You see, in those days women had nothing of their own. They were like brown paper parcels tied with string. They were handed like parcels from their fathers to their husbands. To make the parcel look attractive it was decked with curls and piano lessons, and rings and gold coins and banknotes and shares. After appraising all the decoration, the new owner would undo the knots."

On every page of all Gallant's collections there are such sumptuous sentences: the intelligence so forceful and distinctively hers, the perception so original, the phrasing so economical and elegant, the words gorgeous in their solidity, comedy and tragedy tangled inseparably together. It was very difficult to make a selection from so many stories; she's not a writer who repeats herself. Some with very particular contemporary reference—to 1980s French politics, say—have become more difficult to decipher over time; and Gallant is so wary of being obvious that just occasionally her point can seem too obscure, too hard-won. I've tried to choose a representative mix of European and Canadian material, and also to cover a good stretch of her forty-four-year writing life; her first *New Yorker* story was published in 1951 and her last in 1995. She died in 2014: she had "lived in writing", she said, "like a spoonful of water in a river". I have broken up two of the suites of stories, only because of lack of space: there are two more about the Carette sisters, three more about Linnet Muir—and perhaps "The Wedding Ring" belongs with those too. I put in the whole of "Édouard, Juliette, Lena" because its ambition and achievement seem to me enormous, expressed through the detail of these three private lives. Taking note of the small things that seem of no importance, Gallant traces in them the large shapes of our history.

TESSA HADLEY

IN ITALY

"The joke of it is," Henry kept saying, "the joke is that there's nothing to leave, nothing at all. No money. Not in any direction. I used up most of the capital years ago. What's left will nicely do my lifetime."

Beaming, expectant, he waited for his wife to share the joke. Stella didn't think it as funny as all that. It was a fine thing to be told, at this stage, that there was no money, that your innocent little child sleeping upstairs had nothing to look forward to but a lifetime of work. She had just been bathing the innocent child. Usually, her evening task consisted only of kissing it good night, for the Mannings were fortunate in their Italian servants, who were efficient, loyal, and cheap.

"They don't let Stella lift a finger," Henry always told visitors. "Where can you get that kind of loyalty nowadays, and at such little cost? Not in England, I can tell you."

There had been two babies in the bath. The boy was Stella's; in the midst of less cheerful thoughts, it was still a matter of comfort that she had produced the only boy in the Manning family, the heir. The other baby, a girl, was, Stella supposed, her grandchild. That is, she was Henry's grandchild. It was too much, really, to be expected to consider oneself a grandmother at twenty-six. Stella pulled down her cardigan sleeves, brushing at the wet spots where the babies had splashed. In the presence of Henry's grown daughter, she had been grave and devoted, had knelt on the cold bathroom floor, as if no one, not even the most cheap and loyal of Italian servants, could take a mother's place.

Peggy, the daughter, had lounged in the doorway, not offering to help. She looked amused. "Doesn't Max Beerbohm live near here?" she said. "I expect everyone asks that."

"We know no one of that name," said Stella, soberly. "Henry says he came to Italy to meet Italians."

"I see," said Peggy. She shifted from one bony leg to the other, started to say something, changed her mind. She turned the talk to Henry. "How like the poor old boy to think he can go native," she said. "Actually, he chose this part of the coast because it was full of English. They must be doddering, most of them. It must be ghastly for you, at your age."

All Stella retained from this was the feeling that Henry had been criticized. She no more liked having him referred to as "the old boy" than she enjoyed Peggy's repeated references to Stella's youth. She was only ten months younger than her stepdaughter, but Peggy made it sound years. Of course, Peggy looked older, always would. She said of herself, as if the idea pleased her, that she had been born old. The features that were attractive in Henry had been dismayingly caricatured in his child. Peggy was too tall, too thin, her teeth were too large and white. Slumped in the doorway, she looked like a cynical horse.

There were so many things one could retort to Peggy, replies at once cutting and polite; the trouble was, Stella never thought of them in time. Now, embroiled in an unaccustomed labor (dressing her son for the night), she could not give her mind to anything else. She held the baby on her lap, struggling with him and with garments that seemed to have no openings or fastenings.

"Why don't you put it down on something, the infant, I mean," said Peggy. "You'll never manage that way. He's too lively and fat. And mine should be out of the bath. She'll catch pneumonia in this room." She beckoned to Stella's nurse, who, hovering in the passage, had been waiting to pounce.

"My little boy doesn't feel the cold," said Stella, unable to make this sound convincing. She dreaded her own baths here. The bathroom had been converted from something—a ballroom, she often thought. A chandelier in the form of glass roses dropped from the ceiling. The upper half of the walls was brown, except where paint had flaked away to reveal an undercoat of muddy blue. The bathroom grieved Stella more than any other part of the house. She knew that a proper bathroom should be small, steamy, draftless, and pale green, but try to convince Henry! The villa was only a rental, and even if they lived in it the rest of their lives, nothing would induce him to put a penny into repairs.

"Be sure that the nursery is warm," said Stella, surrendering the baby to its nurse with exaggerated care, as if it were an egg. "Mrs. Burleigh is worried about the cold."

But it was hopeless. No room could be kept warm. The rest of the house was of a piece with the bathroom, in style and in temperature. The ceilings were blistered and stained with damp; the furnishings ran to beaded lampshades and oil paintings of Calabrian maidens holding baskets of fruit. The marble staircase—a showpiece, Henry said—was a funnel of icy air. There was no heating, other than a fireplace in the dining room and a tiny open stove in the library. Over this stove, much of the year, Stella sat, crouched, reading *Lady* and *Woman's Own*, which her mother sent regularly from England.

Henry never seemed to notice the cold. He spent the mornings in bed writing letters, slept after lunch until five, drank until dinner, and then played bridge with the tattered remnants of the English colony, relics of the golden period called "before the war." "Why don't you do something—knit, for instance," he would tell Stella. "Sitting still slows the blood. That's why you're always shivering and complaining."

"Knitting isn't exercise," she would say, but after delivering an order or an opinion Henry always stopped paying attention.

Stella might have found some reason to move around if Henry hadn't had such definite ideas about getting value for money. She would have enjoyed housework, might even have done a little cooking, but they had inherited a family of servants along with the house. Their wages seemed so low, by English standards, that Henry felt offended and out-of-pocket if his wife so much as emptied an ashtray. Patient, he repeated that this was Italy. Italy explained their whole way of life: it explained the absence of heating and of something to do. It explained the wisteria trellis outside, placed so that no sun could enter the ground-floor rooms. During the summer, when the sudden heat rendered the trellis useful, it was Henry's custom to sublet the house, complete with staff, and move his family to a small flat in London. The flat was borrowed. Henry always managed that.

Although she spent much of the year abroad pining for England and reading English recipes, Stella was a country girl, alarmed and depressed by London. Her summers were nearly as lonely as her long Italian winters, for Henry, having settled her in London with a kindly injunction to go and look at shops, spent his holiday running around England visiting old cronies. He and Stella always returned to Italy after a stay of exactly three months less one day, so that Henry would not be subject to income tax.

"I've organized life for a delightful old age," Henry often said, with a gesture that included his young wife.

At times, a disconcerting thought crept into Stella's waking dreams: Henry was thirty years older than she, and might, presumably, die thirty years sooner. She would be free then, but perhaps too old to enjoy it. He might die a little earlier. He took frightfully good care of himself, with all that rest and those mornings in bed; but then he drank a lot. Did drink prolong or diminish life? Doctors were against it, but Stella knew of several old parties, particularly down here, who flourished on a bottle of brandy a day. A compound of middle-class virtues, she was thoroughly ashamed of this thought. Questioned about her life abroad, she was enthusiastic, praising servants she could neither understand nor direct, food that made her bilious, and a race of people ("so charming and childlike") who seemed to her dangerous and dishonest. Many people in England envied her; it was agreeable to be envied, even for a form of life that didn't exist. Peggy, she knew, envied her more than anyone in the world.

"It's wasted," Peggy had said at Stella's wedding, and Stella had overheard her. "That poor little thing in Italy? She'll be bored and lonely and miserable. It's like giving a fragile and costly toy to a child who would rather have a hammer and bricks." Stella had been too rushed and excited that day to pay much attention, but she had recorded for future scrutiny that Peggy was a mean, jealous girl.

"We adore Italy," said Stella now, playing her sad, tattered card. What were some of the arguments Henry used? "Servants are so loyal," she said. "Where can you get that loyalty nowadays?"

"I don't know what you mean by loyalty now," said Peggy. "You are much too young to remember loyalty then."

Stella looked depressed. No one ever answered Henry that way. She began, "I only meant—" But if you had to make excuses, where was the triumph?

"I know what you meant," said Peggy, softer. "Only don't catch that awful servant thing from Henry. He's gone sour and grasping, I think. He used to be quite different, when he still believed the world was made for people of his sort. But don't you get that way. There's no reason for it, and you're much too young. It will make you unfit for life anywhere but here, a foreigner in a foreign country with just a shade more money than the natives."

Peggy spoke with a downward drop at the end of each sentence, as if there could be no possible challenge. She was so sure of herself, and yet so plain. That was class, Stella thought, unhappy. She remembered something else she had heard Peggy say: "She's a nice little creature, but so bloody genteel." In Stella's milieu, one did not say "bloody," and one spoke of one's parents with respect. Stella had thought: They're worse than we are. It was the first acknowledgment she had made to the difference between Henry and herself (other than a secret surprise that he had chosen her) and it was also her first criticism. Since then, she had acknowledged it more and more, and, each time, felt a little stronger. She permitted Henry to correct some of the expressions she used—"Christ, Stella," was his usual educative remark—but, inwardly, she had developed a comforting phrase. We may be common, she would think, but we're really much nicer. She felt, in a confused way, that she was morally right where Henry was wrong in any number of instances, and that her being right was solidly based on being, as Peggy had said, so bloody genteel. But it was slow going, and, at this moment, standing in the untidy bathroom with a wet towel in her hand, she looked so downcast, so uncertain, that Peggy said, as nicely as she could, "Hadn't you better go down and cope with Henry? He's out on the terrace having far too many drinks. Besides, Nigel bores him. It's better if one of us is there."

Nigel was Peggy's husband, a plump young man in a blazer.

It was offensive, being ordered about in one's own home this way, having Henry referred to as a grasping old man, almost a drunk. Once again, she failed to think of the correct crushing remark. Nor was there time to worry about it. Stella was anxious to get Henry alone, to place him on her side, if she could, in the tug of war with his daughter. She didn't want to turn him against his own flesh and blood; in Stella's world, that kind of action was said not to bring happiness. She simply wanted him to acknowledge her, in front of the others, mistress of the house and mother of the heir. It seemed simple enough; a casual word would do it, she thought—even a look of pride.

*

She sped down the stairs and found Henry alone on the dining-room terrace. He was drinking the whiskey Nigel had brought from England and looking with admiration at the giant cacti in the garden. Stella wondered how he could bear to so much as glance in their direction. The garden was another of her grievances. Instead of grass, it grew gravel, raked into geometric patterns by the cook's son, who appeared to have no other occupation. There were the big cactus plants—on which tradesmen scratched their initials to while away the moments between the delivering of bread and the receiving of change—a few irises, and the inevitable geraniums. The first year of her marriage, Stella had rushed at the garden with enthusiasm. Part of her vision of herself as a bride, and a lady, had been in a floppy hat with cutting scissors and dewy, long-stemmed roses. She had planted seeds from England, and bedded out dozens of tender little plants, and buried dozens of bulbs. Nothing had come of it. The seeds rotted in the ground, the bulbs were devoured by rats, the little plants shrivelled and died. She bought *Gardening in Happy Lands* and discovered that the palm trees were taking all the good from the soil. Cut the palms, she had ordered. She had not been married to Henry long enough then to be out of the notion of herself as a spoiled young thing, cherished and capricious. The cook's son, to whom she had given the order, went straight to Henry. Henry lost his temper. It appeared that the cutting down of a palm was such a complicated undertaking that only a half-wit would have considered it. The trunks would neither burn nor sink. It was illegal to throw them into the sea, because they floated among the fishing nets. They had to be sliced down into bits, hauled away, and dumped on a mountainside somewhere in the back country. It was all very expensive, too; that was the part that seemed to bother Henry most.

"I wanted to make a garden," Stella had said, too numb from his shouting to mention palms again. "Other people have gardens here." She had never been shouted at in her life. Her family, self-made, and with self-made rules of gentility, considered it impolite to call from room to room.

"Other people have gardeners," Henry had said, dropping his tone. "Or, they spend all their time and all of their income trying to create a bit of England on the Mediterranean. You must try to adapt, Stella dear."

She had adapted. *Gardening in Happy Lands* had been donated to the British Library, and nearly forgotten; but she still could not look at the gravel, or the palms, or the hideous cacti, without regret.

Nigel had gone to change, Henry said, but changing was only an excuse to go away and restore his shattered composure.

"I told him I'd made my will entirely in favor of the boy," he told Stella, chuckling. "Only there won't be anything to leave. They can worry and stew until I'm dead. Then they'll see the joke."

Henry had begun hinting at this, his latest piece of humor, a fortnight before, with the arrival of Peggy's letter announcing her visit. Relations between Henry and his daughter had been cool since his marriage. It was no secret that Peggy had never expected him to marry again. She had wanted to keep house for her father and live in Italy. Three months after Stella's wedding, Peggy had married Nigel. (No one ever said that Nigel had married her.) Henry had not been in the least sentimental about Peggy's letter, which Stella considered a proper gesture of reconciliation. Nigel and Peggy were coming about money, he said, cheerful. They wanted to find out about his will, and were hoping he would make over some of his capital to them now. Nigel was fed up with the English climate and with English taxation. However, if they were counting on him to settle their future, they had better forget it. Henry still had a few surprises up his sleeve.

"Thank God for my sense of humor," he said now.

"Henry," said Stella bravely, "I don't think this is funny, and I must know if it's really true."

"It's enormously true and enormously funny." He was tight and looked quite devilish, with his long face, and the thinning hair plastered flat on his skull.

"Not to me," said Stella. She tried again: "You might think of your own innocent child."

"She's quite old enough to think for herself," Henry said.

"Not that child—*my* child," Stella almost screamed.

"By the time he grows up, the State will be taking care of everyone," Henry said. "I intend to enjoy my old age. Those who come after me can bloody well cope. And stop shrieking. They'll hear."

"What does it matter if they hear?" said Stella. "They think I'm common, anyway. Peggy called me that at our very own wedding. My mother heard her. A common little baggage, my mother heard Peggy say."

Henry's answer was scarcely consoling. He said, "Peggy was drunk. She didn't draw a sober breath from the time I announced my intentions. She read the engagement notice in the *Times*, poor girl."

"Oh, why did you marry me?" Stella wailed.

Henry took her in his arms. That was why he had married her. It was all very well, but Stella hadn't married in order to be buried in an Italian seaside town. And now, having had a son, having put all their noses out of joint by producing an heir, to be told there was no money!

It had not been Stella's ambition to marry money. She had cherished a great reverence for family and background, and she believed, deeply, in happiness, comfort, and endless romance. In Henry she thought she had found all these things; middle-aged, father of a daughter Stella's age, he was still a catch. She hadn't married money; the trouble was that during their courtship Henry had seduced her with talk of money. He talked stocks, shares, and Rhodesian Electric. He talked South Africa, and how it was the only sound place left for investment in the world. He spoke of the family trust and of how he had broken it years before, and what a good life this had given him. Stella had turned to him her round kitten face, with the faintly stupid kitten eyes, and had listened entranced, picturing Henry with the trust in his hands, breaking it in two.

"I don't believe in all this living on tiny incomes, keeping things intact for the sake of grown children who can earn their own way," he had said. "The next generation won't have anything in any event, the way the world is heading. There won't be anything but drudgery and dreariness. I intend to enjoy myself now. I *have* enjoyed myself. I can seriously say that I do not regret one moment of my life."

Stella had found his predictions about the future only mildly alarming. He was clever and experienced, and such people often frighten one without meaning to. She was glad he intended to enjoy life, and she intended to enjoy it with him. She hadn't dreamed that it would come down to living in an unheated villa in the damp Italian winter. When he continued to speak contemptuously of the next generation and its wretched lot, she had taken it for granted that he meant Peggy, and Peggy's child—never her own.

Nigel and Peggy came onto the terrace, ostentatiously letting the dining-room door slam in order to announce their presence.

"How noisy you are," Henry said to Peggy. "But you always were. I remember—" He poured himself a drink, frowning, presumably remembering. "Stella, I fancy, was a quiet little girl." Something had put her frighteningly out of temper. She paced about the terrace pulling dead leaves off the potted geraniums.

"Oh, damn," she said suddenly, for no reason.

They dined on the terrace, under a light buried in moths.

"How delicious," Peggy said. "Look at the lights on the sea. Those are the fishing boats, Nigel. It's the first sign of good weather."

"I think it's much more comfortable to eat indoors, even if you don't see the boats," Stella said sadly. "Sometimes we sit out here bundled in our overcoats. Henry thinks we must eat out just because it's Italy. So we do it all winter. Then, when it gets warm, there are ants in the bread."

"I suppose there is some stage between too cold and too warm when you enjoy it," Peggy said.

Stella looked at the gravy congealing on her plate and said, "We adore Italy, of course. It's just the question of eating in or out."

"One dreams of it in England," said Nigel. It was the first time he had opened his mouth except to eat or drink. "We think of how lucky you are to be here."

"My people never went in for it at home," said Stella, suddenly broken under Henry's jokes, and homesickness. "Although we had a lovely garden. We had lovely things—grass. You can't grow grass here. I tried it. I tried primroses and things."

"This extraordinary habit the English have of taking bits of England everywhere they go," said Peggy, jabbing at her plate. Nigel started to say something—something nice, one felt by his expression—and Peggy said, "Shut up, Nigel."

Soon after dinner Stella disappeared. It was some time before any of them noticed, and then it was Peggy who went to look. Stella was in the garden, sitting on a bench between two tree-sized cacti.

"You're not crying, are you?"

"Yes, I am. At least, I was. I'm all right now. I wish I were going home instead of you," Stella said. "I'd give anything. Do you know that there are rats in the palms? Big ones. They jump from tree to tree. Sometimes at night I can even hear them on the roof."

Peggy sat down on a stone. The moon had risen and was so bright it threw their shadows. "They've gone indoors," she said. "Henry's quite tight. I suppose that's one of the problems."

Stella sniffled, hiccuping. "It isn't just that. It's that you don't like me."

"Don't be silly," Peggy said. "Anyway, why should you care?

You've got what you wanted." Stella was silent. "I'm not angry with you," Peggy went on. "But I'm so angry with Henry that I can hardly speak to him. As for Nigel, he came upstairs in such a state that I thought we should have to take the next train home. We're furious with Henry and with his cheap, stupid little games. Henry's spent all his money. He spent his father's, my mother's, and mine. No one has complained and no one has minded. But why should he talk to Nigel of wills and of inheritance when we all know that he has nothing in the world but you?"

"Me?" said Stella. Astonishment dried her tears. She peered, puffy-eyed, through the moonlight. "I haven't anything."

"Then that was Henry's mistake," said Peggy calmly. "Or, perhaps it was your youth he wanted. As for you, what did you want, Stella? Did you think he was rich? Hadn't anyone else proposed to you—someone your own age?"

"There was a nice man in chemicals," said Stella. "We would have lived in Japan. There was another one, a boy in my father's business, a boy my father had trained."

"Why in the name of God didn't you choose one of them?"

Stella looked at her sodden handkerchief. "When Henry asked me to marry him, my mother said, 'It's better to be an old man's darling than a young man's slave.' And then, it seemed different. I thought it would be fun."

"Oh, Stella."

The lights of the fishing boats blinked and bobbed out at sea. They could hear the fishermen thumping the sides of the boats and shouting in order to wake up the fish.

"I should have been you, and you should have been me," Peggy said. "I love Italy, and I can cope with Henry. He was a good parent, before he went sour. You should have married Nigel—or *a* Nigel."

The crushing immorality of this blanked out Stella's power of speech. It had been suggested that she ought to marry her stepdaughter's husband—something like that. There was something good about being shocked. It placed her. It reaffirmed her sense of being morally right where Henry and his kind were morally wrong. She thought: I am Henry's wife, and I am the mistress of this house.

"I mean," said Peggy, "that sometimes people get dropped in the wrong pockets by mistake."

"Well," said Stella, "that is life. That's the way things are. You don't get dropped, you choose. And then you have to stick to it, that's all. At least, that's what I think."

"Poor little Stella," Peggy said.

THE ICE WAGON GOING DOWN THE STREET

NOW THAT THEY ARE out of world affairs and back where they started, Peter Frazier's wife says, "Everybody else did well in the international thing except us."

"You have to be crooked," he tells her.

"Or smart. Pity we weren't."

It is Sunday morning. They sit in the kitchen, drinking their coffee, slowly, remembering the past. They say the names of people as if they were magic. Peter thinks, Agnes Brusen, but there are hundreds of other names. As a private married joke, Peter and Sheilah wear the silk dressing gowns they bought in Hong Kong. Each thinks the other a peacock, rather splendid, but they pretend the dressing gowns are silly and worn in fun.

Peter and Sheilah and their two daughters, Sandra and Jennifer, are visiting Peter's unmarried sister, Lucille. They have been Lucille's guests seventeen weeks, ever since they returned to Toronto from the Far East. Their big old steamer trunk blocks a corner of the kitchen, making a problem of the refrigerator door; but even Lucille says the trunk may as well stay where it is, for the present. The Fraziers' future is so unsettled; everything is still in the air.

Lucille has given her bedroom to her two nieces, and sleeps on a camp cot in the hall. The parents have the living-room divan. They have no privileges here; they sleep after Lucille has seen the last television show that interests her. In the hall closet their clothes are crushed by winter overcoats. They know they are being judged for the first time. Sandra and Jennifer are waiting for Sheilah and Peter to decide. They are waiting to learn where these exotic parents will fly to next. What sort of climate will Sheilah consider? What job will Peter consent to accept? When the parents are ready, the children will make a decision of their own. It is just possible that Sandra and Jennifer will choose to stay with their aunt.

The peacock parents are watched by wrens. Lucille and her nieces are much the same—sandy-colored, proudly plain. Neither of the girls has the father's insouciance or the mother's appearance—her height, her carriage, her thick hair and sky-blue eyes. The children are more cautious than their parents; more Canadian. When they saw their aunt's apartment they had been away from Canada nine years, ever since they were two and four; and Jennifer, the elder, said, "Well, now we're home." Her voice is nasal and flat. Where did she learn that voice? And why should this be home? Peter's answer to anything about his mystifying children is, "It must be in the blood."

On Sunday morning Lucille takes her nieces to church. It seems to be the only condition she imposes on her relations: The children must be decent. The girls go willingly, with their new hats and purses and gloves and coral bracelets and strings of pearls. The parents, ramshackle, sleepy, dim in the brain because it is Sunday, sit down to their coffee and privacy and talk of the past.

"We weren't crooked," says Peter. "We weren't even smart."

Sheilah's head bobs up; she is no drowner. It is wrong to say they have nothing to show for time. Sheilah has the Balenciaga. It is a black afternoon dress, stiff and boned at the waist, long for the fashions of now, but neither Sheilah nor Peter would change a thread. The Balenciaga is their talisman, their treasure; and after they remember it they touch hands and think that the years are not behind them but hazy and marvelous and still to be lived.

The first place they went to was Paris. In the early fifties the pick of the international jobs was there. Peter had inherited the last scrap of money he knew he was ever likely to see, and it was enough to get them over: Sheilah and Peter and the babies and the steamer trunk. To their joy and astonishment they had money in the bank. They said to each other, "It should last a year." Peter was fastidious about the new job; he hadn't come all this distance to accept just anything. In Paris he met Hugh Taylor, who was earning enough smuggling gasoline to keep his wife in Paris and a girl in Rome. That impressed Peter, because he remembered Taylor as a sour scholarship student without the slightest talent for life. Taylor had a job, of course. He hadn't said to himself, I'll go over to Europe and smuggle gasoline. It gave Peter an idea; he saw the shape of things. First you catch your fish. Later, at an international party, he met Johnny Hertzberg, who told him Germany was the place. Hertzberg said that anyone who came out of Germany broke now was too stupid to be here, and deserved to be back home at a desk. Peter nodded, as if he had already thought of that. He began to think about Germany. Paris was fine for a holiday, but it had been picked clean. Yes, Germany. His money was running low. He thought about Germany quite a lot.

That winter was moist and delicate; so fragile that they daren't speak of it now. There seemed to be plenty of everything and plenty of time. They were living the dream of a marriage, the fabric uncut, nothing slashed or spoiled. All winter they spent their money, and went to parties, and talked about Peter's future job. It lasted four months. They spent their money, lived in the future, and were never as happy again.

After four months they were suddenly moved away from Paris, but not to Germany—to Geneva. Peter thinks it was because of the incident at the Trudeau wedding at the Ritz. Paul Trudeau was a French Canadian Peter had known at school and in the Navy.

Trudeau had turned into a snob, proud of his career and his Paris connections. He tried to make the difference felt, but Peter thought the difference was only for strangers. At the wedding reception Peter lay down on the floor and said he was dead. He held a white azalea in a brass pot on his chest, and sang, "Oh, hear us when we cry to Thee for those in peril on the sea." Sheilah bent over him and said, "Peter, darling, get up. Pete, listen, every single person who can do something for you is in this room. If you love me, you'll get up."

"I do love you," he said, ready to engage in a serious conversation. "She's so beautiful," he told a second face. "She's nearly as tall as I am. She was a model in London. I met her over in London in the war. I met her there in the war." He lay on his back with the azalea on his chest, explaining their history. A waiter took the brass pot away, and after Peter had been hauled to his feet he knocked the waiter down. Trudeau's bride, who was freshly out of an Ursuline convent, became hysterical; and even though Paul Trudeau and Peter were old acquaintances, Trudeau never spoke to him again. Peter says now that French Canadians always have that bit of spite. He says Trudeau asked the embassy to interfere. Luckily, back home there were still a few people to whom the name "Frazier" meant something, and it was to these people that Peter appealed. He wrote letters saying that a French-Canadian combine was preventing his getting a decent job, and could anything be done? No one answered directly, but it was clear that what they settled for was exile to Geneva: a season of meditation and remorse, as he explained to Sheilah, and it was managed tactfully, through Lucille. Lucille wrote that a friend of hers, May Fergus, now a secretary in Geneva, had heard about a job. The job was filing pictures in the information service of an international agency in the Palais des Nations. The pay was so-so, but Lucille thought Peter must be getting fed up doing nothing.

Peter often asks his sister now who put her up to it—what important person told her to write that letter suggesting Peter go to Geneva?

"Nobody," says Lucille. "I mean, nobody in the way *you* mean. I really did have this girl friend working there, and I knew you must be running through your money pretty fast in Paris."

"It must have been somebody pretty high up," Peter says. He looks at his sister admiringly, as he has often looked at his wife.

Peter's wife had loved him in Paris. Whatever she wanted in marriage she found that winter, there. In Geneva, where Peter was a file clerk and they lived in a furnished flat, she pretended they were in Paris and life was still the same. Often, when the children were at supper, she changed as though she and Peter were dining out. She wore the Balenciaga, and put candles on the card table where she and Peter ate their meal. The neckline of the dress was soiled with makeup. Peter remembers her dabbing on the makeup with a wet sponge. He remembers her in the kitchen, in the soiled Balenciaga, patting on the makeup with a filthy sponge. Behind her, at the kitchen table, Sandra and Jennifer, in buttonless pajamas and bunny slippers, ate their supper of marmalade sandwiches and milk. When the children were asleep, the parents dined solemnly, ritually, Sheilah sitting straight as a queen.

It was a mysterious period of exile, and he had to wait for signs, or signals, to know when he was free to leave. He never saw the job any other way. He forgot he had applied for it. He thought he had been sent to Geneva because of a misdemeanor and had to wait to be released. Nobody pressed him at work. His immediate boss had resigned, and he was alone for months in a room with two desks. He read the *Herald Tribune*, and tried to discover how things were here—how the others ran their lives on the pay they were officially getting. But it was a closed conspiracy. He was not dealing with adventurers now but civil servants waiting for pension day. No one ever answered his questions. They pretended to think his questions were a form of wit. His only solace in exile was the few happy weekends he had in the late spring and early summer. He had met another old acquaintance, Mike Burleigh. Mike was a serious liberal who had married a serious heiress. The Burleighs had two guest lists. The first was composed of stuffy people they felt obliged to entertain, while the second was made up of their real friends, the friends they wanted. The real friends strove hard to become stuffy and dull and thus achieve the first guest list, but few succeeded. Peter went on the first list straightaway. Possibly Mike didn't understand, at the beginning, why Peter was pretending to be a file clerk. Peter had such an air—he might have been sent by a universal inspector to see how things in Geneva were being run.

Every Friday in May and June and part of July, the Fraziers rented a sky-blue Fiat and drove forty miles east of Geneva to the Burleighs' summer house. They brought the children, a suitcase, the children's tattered picture books, and a token bottle of gin. This, in memory, is a period of water and water birds; swans, roses, and singing birds. The children were small and still belonged to them. If they remember too much, their mouths water, their stomachs hurt. Peter says, "It was fine while it lasted." Enough. While it lasted Sheilah and Madge Burleigh were close. They abandoned their husbands and spent long summer afternoons comparing their mothers and praising each other's skin and hair. To Madge, and not to Peter, Sheilah opened her Liverpool childhood with the words "rat poor." Peter heard about it later, from Mike. The women's friendship seemed to Peter a bad beginning. He trusted women but not with each other. It lasted ten weeks. One Sunday, Madge said she needed the two bedrooms the Fraziers usually occupied for a party of sociologists from Pakistan, and that was the end. In November, the Fraziers heard that the summer house had been closed, and that the Burleighs were in Geneva, in their winter flat; they gave no sign. There was no help for it, and no appeal.

Now Peter began firing letters to anyone who had ever known his late father. He was living in a mild yellow autumn. Why does he remember the streets of the city dark, and the windows everywhere black with rain? He remembers being with Sheilah and the children as if they clung together while just outside their small shelter it rained and rained. The children slept in the bedroom of the flat because the window gave on the street and they could breathe air. Peter and Sheilah had the living-room couch. Their window was not a real window but a square on a well of cement. The flat seemed damp as a cave. Peter remembers steam in the kitchen, pools under the sink, sweat on the pipes. Water streamed on him from the children's clothes, washed and dripping overhead. The trunk, upended in the children's room, was not quite unpacked. Sheilah had not signed her name to this life; she had not given in. Once Peter heard her drop her aitches. "You kids are lucky," she said to the girls. "I never 'ad so much as a sit-down meal. I ate chips out of a paper or I 'ad a butty out on the stairs." He never asked her what a butty was. He thinks it means bread and cheese.

The day he heard "You kids are lucky" he understood they were becoming in fact something they had only *appeared* to be until now—the shabby civil servant and his brood. If he had been European he would have ridden to work on a bicycle, in the uniform of his class and condition. He would have worn a tight coat, a turned collar, and a dirty tie. He wondered then if coming here had been a mistake, and if he should not, after all, still be in a place where his name meant something. Surely Peter Frazier should live where "Frazier" counts? In Ontario even now when he says "Frazier" an absent look comes over his hearer's face, as if its owner were consulting an interior guide. What is Frazier? What does it mean? Oil? Power? Politics? Wheat? Real estate? The creditors had the house sealed when Peter's father died. His aunt collapsed with a heart attack in somebody's bachelor apartment, leaving three sons and a widower to surmise they had never known her. Her will was a disappointment. None of that generation left enough. One made it:

the granite Presbyterian immigrants from Scotland. Their children, a generation of daunted women and maiden men, held still. Peter's father's crowd spent: They were not afraid of their fathers, and their grandfathers were old. Peter and his sister and his cousins lived on the remains. They were left the rinds of income, of notions, and the memories of ideas rather than ideas intact. If Peter can choose his reincarnation, let him be the oppressed son of a Scottish parson. Let Peter grow up on cuffs and iron principles. Let him make the fortune! Let him flee the manse! When he was small his patrimony was squandered under his nose. He remembers people dancing in his father's house. He remembers seeing and nearly understanding adultery in a guest room, among a pile of wraps. He thought he had seen a murder; he never told. He remembers licking glasses wherever he found them—on windowsills, on stairs, in the pantry. In his room he listened while Lucille read Beatrix Potter. The bad rabbit stole the carrot from the good rabbit without saying please, and downstairs was the noise of the party—the roar of the crouched lion. When his father died he saw the chairs upside down and the bailiff's chalk marks. Then the doors were sealed.

He has often tried to tell Sheilah why he cannot be defeated. He remembers his father saying, "Nothing can touch us," and Peter believed it and still does. It has prevented his taking his troubles too seriously. Nothing can be as bad as this, he will tell himself. It is happening to me. Even in Geneva, where his status was file clerk, where he sank and stopped on the level of the men who never emigrated, the men on the bicycles—even there he had a manner of strolling to work as if his office were a pastime, and his real life a secret so splendid he could share it with no one except himself.

In Geneva Peter worked for a woman—a girl. She was a Norwegian from a small town in Saskatchewan. He supposed they had been put together because they were Canadians; but they were as strange to each other as if "Canadian" meant any number of things, or had no real meaning. Soon after Agnes Brusen came to the office she hung her framed university degree on the wall. It was one of the gritty, prideful gestures that stand for push, toil, and family sacrifice. He thought, then, that she must be one of a family of immigrants for whom education is everything. Hugh Taylor had told him that in some families the older children never marry until the youngest have finished school. Sometimes every second child is sacrificed and made to work for the education of the next-born. Those who finish college spend years paying back. They are white-hot Protestants, and they live with a load of work and debt and obligation. Peter placed his new colleague on scraps of information. He had never been in the West.

She came to the office on a Monday morning in October. The office was overheated and painted cream. It contained two desks, the filing cabinets, a map of the world as it had been in 1945, and the Charter of the United Nations left behind by Agnes Brusen's predecessor. (She took down the Charter without asking Peter if he minded, with the impudence of gesture you find in women who wouldn't say boo to a goose; and then she hung her college degree on the nail where the Charter had been.) Three people brought her in—a whole committee. One of them said, "Agnes, this is Pete Frazier. Pete, Agnes Brusen. Pete's Canadian, too, Agnes. He knows all about the office, so ask him anything."

Of course he knew all about the office: He knew the exact spot where the cord of the venetian blind was frayed, obliging one to give an extra tug to the right.

The girl might have been twenty-three: no more. She wore a brown tweed suit with bone buttons, and a new silk scarf and new shoes. She clutched an unscratched brown purse. She seemed dressed in going-away presents. She said, "Oh, I never smoke," with a convulsive movement of her hand, when Peter offered his case. He was courteous, hiding his disappointment. The people he worked with had told him a Scandinavian girl was arriving, and he had expected a stunner. Agnes was a mole: She was small and brown, and round-shouldered as if she had always carried parcels or younger children in her arms. A mole's profile was turned when she said good-bye to her committee. If she had been foreign, ill-favored though she was, he might have flirted a little, just to show that he was friendly; but their being Canadian, and suddenly left together, was a sexual damper. He sat down and lit his own cigarette. She smiled at him, questionably, he thought, and sat as if she had never seen a chair before. He wondered if his smoking was annoying her. He wondered if she was fidgety about drafts, or allergic to anything, and whether she would want the blind up or down. His social compass was out of order because the others couldn't tell Peter and Agnes apart. There was a world of difference between them, yet it was she who had been brought in to sit at the larger of the two desks.

While he was thinking this she got up and walked around the office, almost on tiptoe, opening the doors of closets and pulling out the filing trays. She looked inside everything except the drawers of Peter's desk. (In any case, Peter's desk was locked. His desk is locked wherever he works. In Geneva he went into Personnel one morning, early, and pinched his application form. He had stated on the form that he had seven years' experience in public relations and could speak French, German, Spanish, and Italian. He has always collected anything important about himself—anything useful. But he can never get on with the final act, which is getting rid of the information. He has kept papers about for years, a constant source of worry.)

"I know this looks funny, Mr. Ferris," said the girl. "I'm not really snooping or anything. I just can't feel easy in a new place unless I know where everything is. In a new place everything seems so hidden."

If she had called him "Ferris" and pretended not to know he was Frazier, it could only be because they had sent her here to spy on him and see if he had repented and was fit for a better place in life. "You'll be all right here," he said. "Nothing's hidden. Most of us haven't got brains enough to have secrets. This is Rainbow Valley." Depressed by the thought that they were having him watched now, he passed his hand over his hair and looked outside to the lawn and the parking lot and the peacocks someone gave the Palais des Nations years ago. The peacocks love no one. They wander about the parked cars looking elderly, bad-tempered, mournful, and lost.

Agnes had settled down again. She folded her silk scarf and placed it just so, with her gloves beside it. She opened her new purse and took out a notebook and a shiny gold pencil. She may have written

> Duster for desk
> Kleenex
> Glass jar for flowers
> Air-Wick because he smokes
> Paper for lining drawers

because the next day she brought each of these articles to work. She also brought a large black Bible, which she unwrapped lovingly and placed on the left-hand corner of her desk. The flower vase—empty—stood in the middle, and the Kleenex made a counterpoise for the Bible on the right.

When he saw the Bible he knew she had not been sent to spy on his work. The conspiracy was deeper. She might have been dispatched by ghosts. He knew everything about her, all in a moment: He saw the ambition, the terror, the dry pride. She was the true heir of the men from Scotland; she was at the start. She had been sent to tell him, "You can begin, but not begin again." She never opened the Bible, but she dusted it as she dusted her desk, her chair, and any surface the cleaning staff had overlooked. And Peter, the first days, watching her timid movements, her insignificant little face, felt, as you feel the approach of a storm, the charge of moral certainty round her, the belief in work, the faith in undertakings, the bread of the Black Sunday. He recognized and tasted all of it: ashes in the mouth.

After five days their working relations were settled. Of course, there was the Bible and all that went with it, but his tongue had never held the taste of ashes long. She was an inferior girl of poor quality. She had nothing in her favor except the degree on the wall. In the real world, he would not have invited her to his house except to mind the children. That was what he said to Sheilah. He said that Agnes was a mole, and a virgin, and that her tics and mannerisms were sending him round the bend. She had an infuriating habit of covering her mouth when she talked. Even at the telephone she put up her hand as if afraid of losing anything, even a word. Her voice was nasal and flat. She had two working costumes, both dull as the wall. One was the brown suit, the other a navy-blue dress with changeable collars. She dressed for no one; she dressed for her desk, her jar of flowers, her Bible, and her box of Kleenex. One day she crossed the space between the two desks and stood over Peter, who was reading a newspaper. She could have spoken to him from her desk, but she may have felt that being on her feet gave her authority. She had plenty of courage, but authority was something else.

"I thought—I mean, they told me you were the person ..." She got on with it bravely: "If you don't want to do the filing or any work, all right, Mr. Frazier. I'm not saying anything about that. You might have poor health or your personal reasons. But it's got to be done, so if you'll kindly show me about the filing I'll do it. I've worked in Information before, but it was a different office, and every office is different."

"My dear girl," said Peter. He pushed back his chair and looked at her, astonished. "You've been sitting there fretting, worrying. How insensitive of me. How trying for you. Usually I file on the last

Wednesday of the month, so you see, you just haven't been around long enough to see a last Wednesday. Not another word, please. And let us not waste another minute." He emptied the heaped baskets of photographs so swiftly, pushing "Iran—Smallpox Control" into "Irish Red Cross" (close enough), that the girl looked frightened, as if she had raised a whirlwind. She said slowly, "If you'll only show me, Mr. Frazier, instead of doing it so fast, I'll gladly look after it, because you might want to be doing other things, and I feel the filing should be done every day." But Peter was too busy to answer, and so she sat down, holding the edge of her desk.

"There," he said, beaming. "All done." His smile, his sunburst, was wasted, for the girl was staring round the room as if she feared she had not inspected everything the first day after all; some drawer, some cupboard, hid a monster. That evening Peter unlocked one of the drawers of his desk and took away the application form he had stolen from Personnel. The girl had not finished her search.

"How could you *not* know?" wailed Sheilah. "You sit looking at her every day. You must talk about *something*. She must have told you."

"She did tell me," said Peter, "and I've just told you."

It was this: Agnes Brusen was on the Burleighs' guest list. How had the Burleighs met her? What did they see in her? Peter could not reply. He knew that Agnes lived in a bed-sitting room with a Swiss family and had her meals with them. She had been in Geneva three months, but no one had ever seen her outside the office. "You *should* know," said Sheilah. "She must have something, more than you can see. Is she pretty? Is she brilliant? What is it?"

"We don't really talk," Peter said. They talked in a way: Peter teased her and she took no notice. Agnes was not a sulker. She had taken her defeat like a sport. She did her work and a good deal of his. She sat behind her Bible, her flowers, and her Kleenex, and answered when Peter spoke. That was how he learned about the

Burleighs—just by teasing and being bored. It was a January afternoon. He said, "*Miss* Brusen. Talk to me. Tell me everything. Pretend we have perfect rapport. Do you like Geneva?"

"It's a nice clean town," she said. He can see to this day the red and blue anemones in the glass jar, and her bent head, and her small untended hands.

"Are you learning beautiful French with your Swiss family?"

"They speak English."

"Why don't you take an apartment of your own?" he said. Peter was not usually impertinent. He was bored. "You'd be independent then."

"I am independent," she said. "I earn my living. I don't think it proves anything if you live by yourself. Mrs. Burleigh wants me to live alone, too. She's looking for something for me. It mustn't be dear. I send money home."

Here was the extraordinary thing about Agnes Brusen: She refused the use of Christian names and never spoke to Peter unless he spoke first, but she would tell anything, as if to say, "Don't waste time fishing. Here it is."

He learned all in one minute that she sent her salary home, and that she was a friend of the Burleighs. The first he had expected; the second knocked him flat.

"She's got to come to dinner," Sheilah said. "We should have had her right from the beginning. If only I'd known! But *you* were the one. You said she looked like—oh, I don't even remember. A Norwegian mole."

She came to dinner one Saturday night in January, in her navyblue dress, to which she had pinned an organdy gardenia. She sat upright on the edge of the sofa. Sheilah had ordered the meal from a restaurant. There was lobster, good wine, and a *pièce-montée* full of kirsch and cream. Agnes refused the lobster; she had never eaten anything from the sea unless it had been sterilized and tinned, and said so. She was afraid of skin poisoning. Someone in her family had skin poisoning after having eaten oysters. She touched her cheeks and neck to show where the poisoning had erupted. She sniffed her wine and put the glass down without tasting it. She could not eat the cake because of the alcohol it contained. She ate an egg, bread and butter, a sliced tomato, and drank a glass of ginger ale. She seemed unaware she was creating disaster and pain. She did not help clear away the dinner plates. She sat, adequately nourished, decently dressed, and waited to learn why she had been invited here—that was the feeling Peter had. He folded the card table on which they had dined, and opened the window to air the room.

"It's not the same cold as Canada, but you feel it more," he said, for something to say.

"Your blood has gotten thin," said Agnes.

Sheilah returned from the kitchen and let herself fall into an armchair. With her eyes closed she held out her hand for a cigarette. She was performing the haughty-lady act that was a family joke. She flung her head back and looked at Agnes through half-closed lids; then she suddenly brought her head forward, widening her eyes.

"Are you skiing madly?" she said.

"Well, in the first place there hasn't been any snow," said Agnes. "So nobody's doing any skiing so far as I know. All I hear is people complaining because there's no snow. Personally, I don't ski. There isn't much skiing in the part of Canada I come from. Besides, my family never had that kind of leisure."

"Heavens," said Sheilah, as if her family had every kind.

I'll bet they had, thought Peter. On the dole.

Sheilah was wasting her act. He had a suspicion that Agnes knew it was an act but did not know it was also a joke. If so, it made Sheilah seem a fool, and he loved Sheilah too much to enjoy it.

"The Burleighs have been wonderful to me," said Agnes. She seemed to have divined why she was here, and decided to give them all the information they wanted, so that she could put on her coat and go home to bed. "They had me out to their place on the lake every weekend until the weather got cold and they moved back to town. They've rented a chalet for the winter, and they want me to come there, too. But I don't know if I will or not. I don't ski, and, oh, I don't know—I don't drink, either, and I don't always see the point. Their friends are too rich and I'm too Canadian."

She had delivered everything Sheilah wanted and more: Agnes was on the first guest list and didn't care. No, Peter corrected: doesn't know. Doesn't care and doesn't know.

"I thought with you Norwegians it was in the blood, skiing. And drinking," Sheilah murmured.

"Drinking, maybe," said Agnes. She covered her mouth and said behind her spread fingers, "In our family we were religious. We didn't drink or smoke. My brother was in Norway in the war. He saw some cousins. Oh," she said, unexpectedly loud, "Harry said it was just terrible. They were so poor. They had flies in their kitchen. They gave him something to eat a fly had been on. They didn't have a real toilet, and they'd been in the same house about two hundred years. We've only recently built our own home, and we have a bathroom and two toilets. I'm from Saskatchewan," she said. "I'm not from any other place."

Surely one winter here had been punishment enough? In the spring they would remember him and free him. He wrote Lucille, who said he was lucky to have a job at all. The Burleighs had sent the Fraziers a second-guest-list Christmas card. It showed a Moslem refugee child weeping outside a tent. They treasured the card and left it standing long after the others had been given the children to cut up. Peter had discovered by now what had gone wrong in the friendship—Sheilah had charged a skirt at a dressmaker to Madge's account. Madge had told her she might, and then changed her mind. Poor Sheilah! She was new to this part of it—to the changing humors of independent friends. Paris was already a year in the past. At Mardi Gras, the Burleighs gave their annual party. They invited everyone, the damned and the dropped, with the prodigality of a child at prayers. The invitation said "in costume," but the Fraziers were too happy to wear a disguise. They might not be recognized. Like many of the guests they expected to meet at the party, they had been disgraced, forgotten, and rehabilitated. They would be anxious to see one another as they were.

On the night of the party, the Fraziers rented a car they had never seen before and drove through the first snowstorm of the year. Peter had not driven since last summer's blissful trips in the Fiat. He could not find the switch for the windshield wiper in this car. He leaned over the wheel. "Can you see on your side?" he asked. "Can I make a left turn here? Does it look like a one-way?"

"I can't imagine why you took a car with a right-hand drive," said Sheilah.

He had trouble finding a place to park; they crawled up and down unknown streets whose curbs were packed with snow-covered cars. When they stood at last on the pavement, safe and sound, Peter said, "This is the first snow."

"I can see that," said Sheilah. "Hurry, darling. My hair."

"It's the first snow."

"You're repeating yourself," she said. "Please hurry, darling. Think of my poor shoes. My *hair*."

She was born in an ugly city, and so was Peter, but they have this difference: She does not know the importance of the first snow—the first clean thing in a dirty year. He would have told her then that this storm, which was wetting her feet and destroying her hair, was like the first day of the English spring, but she made a frightened gesture, trying to shield her head. The gesture told him he did not understand her beauty.

"Let me," she said. He was fumbling with the key, trying to lock the car. She took the key without impatience and locked the door on the driver's side; and then, to show Peter she treasured him and was not afraid of wasting her life or her beauty, she took his arm and they walked in the snow down a street and around a corner to the apartment house where the Burleighs lived. They were, and are, a united couple. They were afraid of the party, and each of them knew it. When they walk together, holding arms, they give each other whatever each can spare.

Only six people had arrived in costume. Madge Burleigh was disguised as Manet's "Lola de Valence," which everyone mistook for Carmen. Mike was an Impressionist painter, with a straw hat and a glued-on beard. "I am all of them," he said. He would rather have dressed as a dentist, he said, welcoming the Fraziers as if he had parted from them the day before, but Madge wanted him to look as if he had created her. "You know?" he said.

"Perfectly," said Sheilah. Her shoes were stained and the snow had softened her lacquered hair. She was not wasted: She was the most beautiful woman there.

About an hour after their arrival, Peter found himself with no one to talk to. He had told about the Trudeau wedding in Paris and the pot of azaleas, and after he mislaid his audience he began to look round for Sheilah. She was on a window seat, partly concealed by a green velvet curtain. Facing her, so that their profiles were neat and perfect against the night, was a man. Their conversation was private and enclosed, as if they had in minutes covered leagues of time and arrived at the place where everything was implied, understood. Peter began working his way across the room, toward his wife, when he saw Agnes. He was granted the sight of her drowning face. She had dressed with comic intention, obviously with care, and now she was a ragged hobo, half tramp, half clown. Her hair was tucked up under a bowler hat. The six costumed guests who had made the same mistake—the ghost, the gypsy, the Athenian maiden, the geisha, the Martian, and the apache—were delighted to find a seventh; but Agnes was not amused; she was gasping for life. When a waiter passed with a crowded tray, she took a glass without seeing it; then a wave of the party took her away.

Sheilah's new friend was named Simpson. After Simpson said he thought perhaps he'd better circulate, Peter sat down where he had been. "Now look, Sheilah," he began. Their most intimate conversations have taken place at parties. Once at a party she told him she was leaving him; she didn't, of course. Smiling, blue-eyed, she gazed lovingly at Peter and said rapidly, "Pete, shut up and listen. That man. The man you scared away. He's a big wheel in a company out in India or someplace like that. It's gorgeous out there. Pete, the *servants*. And it's warm. It never never snows. He says there's heaps of jobs. You pick them off the trees like ... orchids. He says it's even easier now than when we owned all those places, because now the poor pets can't run anything and they'll pay *fortunes*. Pete, he says it's warm, it's heaven, and Pete, they pay."

A few minutes later, Peter was alone again and Sheilah part of a closed, laughing group. Holding her elbow was the man from the place where jobs grew like orchids. Peter edged into the group and laughed at a story he hadn't heard. He heard only the last line, which was "Here comes another tunnel." Looking out from the tight laughing ring, he saw Agnes again, and he thought, I'd be like Agnes if I didn't have Sheilah. Agnes put her glass down on a table and lurched toward the doorway, head forward. Madge Burleigh, who never stopped moving around the room and smiling, was still smiling when she paused and said in Peter's ear, "Go with Agnes, Pete. See that she gets home. People will notice if Mike leaves."

"She probably just wants to walk around the block," said Peter. "She'll be back."

"Oh, stop thinking about yourself, for once, and see that that poor girl gets home," said Madge. "You've still got your Fiat, haven't you?"

He turned away as if he had been pushed. Any command is a release, in a way. He may not want to go in that particular direction, but at least he is going somewhere. And now Sheilah, who had moved inches nearer to hear what Madge and Peter were murmuring, said, "Yes, go, darling," as if he were leaving the gates of Troy.

Peter was to find Agnes and see that she reached home: This he repeated to himself as he stood on the landing, outside the Burleighs' flat, ringing for the elevator. Bored with waiting for it, he ran down the stairs, four flights, and saw that Agnes had stalled the lift by leaving the door open. She was crouched on the floor, propped on her fingertips. Her eyes were closed.

"Agnes," said Peter. "*Miss* Brusen, I mean. That's no way to leave a party. Don't you know you're supposed to curtsy and say thanks? My God, Agnes, anybody going by here just now might have seen you! Come on, be a good girl. Time to go home."

She got up without his help and, moving between invisible crevasses, shut the elevator door. Then she left the building and Peter followed, remembering he was to see that she got home. They walked along the snowy pavement, Peter a few steps behind her. When she turned right for no reason, he turned, too. He had no clear idea where they were going. Perhaps she lived close by. He had forgotten where the hired car was parked, or what it looked like; he could not remember its make or its color. In any case, Sheilah had the key. Agnes walked on steadily, as if she knew their destination, and he thought, Agnes Brusen is drunk in the street in Geneva and dressed like a tramp. He wanted to say, "This is the best thing that ever happened to you, Agnes; it will help you understand how things are for some of the rest of us." But she stopped and turned and, leaning over a low hedge, retched on a frozen lawn. He held her clammy forehead and rested his hand on her arched back, on muscles as tight as a fist. She straightened up and drew a breath but the cold air made her cough. "Don't breathe too deeply," he said. "It's the worst thing you can do. Have you got a handkerchief?" He passed his own handkerchief over her wet weeping face, upturned like the face of one of his little girls. "I'm out without a coat," he said, noticing it. "We're a pair."

"I never drink," said Agnes. "I'm just not used to it." Her voice was sweet and quiet. He had never seen her so peaceful, so composed. He thought she must surely be all right, now, and perhaps he might leave her here. The trust in her tilted face had perplexed him. He wanted to get back to Sheilah and have her explain something. He had forgotten what it was, but Sheilah would know. "Do you live around here?" he said. As he spoke, she let herself fall. He had wiped her face and now she trusted him to pick her up, set her on her feet, take her wherever she ought to be. He pulled her up and she stood, wordless, humble, as he brushed the snow from her tramp's clothes. Snow horizontally crossed the lamplight. The street was silent. Agnes had lost her hat. Snow, which he tasted, melted on her hands. His gesture of licking snow from her hands was formal as a handshake. He tasted snow on her hands and then they walked on.

"I never drink," she said. They stood on the edge of a broad avenue. The wrong turning now could lead them anywhere; it was the changeable avenue at the edge of towns that loses its houses and becomes a highway. She held his arm and spoke in a gentle voice. She said, "In our house we didn't smoke or drink. My mother was ambitious for me, more than for Harry and the others." She said, "I've never been alone before. When I was a kid I would get up in the summer before the others, and I'd see the ice wagon going down the street. I'm alone now. Mrs. Burleigh's found me an apartment. It's only one room. She likes it because it's in the old part of town. I don't like old houses. Old houses are dirty. You don't know who was there before."

"I should have a car somewhere," Peter said. "I'm not sure where we are."

He remembers that on this avenue they climbed into a taxi, but nothing about the drive. Perhaps he fell asleep. He does remember that when he paid the driver Agnes clutched his arm, trying to stop him. She pressed extra coins into the driver's palm. The driver was paid twice.

"I'll tell you one thing about us," said Peter. "We pay everything twice." This was part of a much longer theory concerning North American behavior, and it was not Peter's own. Mike Burleigh had held forth about it on summer afternoons.

Agnes pushed open a door between a stationer's shop and a grocery, and led the way up a narrow inside stair. They climbed one flight, frightening beetles. She had to search every pocket for the latchkey. She was shaking with cold. Her apartment seemed little warmer than the street. Without speaking to Peter she turned on all the lights. She looked inside the kitchen and the bathroom and then got down on her hands and knees and looked under the sofa. The room was neat and belonged to no one. She left him standing in this unclaimed room—she had forgotten him—and closed a door behind her. He looked for something to do—some useful action he could repeat to Madge. He turned on the electric radiator in the fireplace. Perhaps Agnes wouldn't thank him for it; perhaps she would rather undress in the cold. "I'll be on my way," he called to the bathroom door.

She had taken off the tramp's clothes and put on a dressing gown of orphanage wool. She came out of the bathroom and straight toward him. She pressed her face and rubbed her cheek on his shoulder as if hoping the contact would leave a scar. He saw her back and her profile and his own face in the mirror over the fireplace. He thought, This is how disasters happen. He saw floods of seawater moving with perfect punitive justice over reclaimed land; he saw lava covering vineyards and overtaking dogs and stragglers. A bridge over an abyss snapped in two and the long express train, suddenly V-shaped, floated like snow. He thought amiably of every kind of disaster and thought, This is how they occur.

Her eyes were closed. She said, "I shouldn't be over here. In my family we didn't drink or smoke. My mother wanted a lot from me, more than from Harry and the others." But he knew all that; he had known from the day of the Bible, and because once, at the beginning, she had made him afraid. He was not afraid of her now.

She said, "It's no use staying here, is it?"

"If you mean what I think, no."

"It wouldn't be better anywhere."

She let him see full on her blotched face. He was not expected to do anything. He was not required to pick her up when she fell or wipe her tears. She was poor quality, really—he remembered having thought that once. She left him and went quietly into the bathroom and locked the door. He heard taps running and supposed it was a hot bath. He was pretty certain there would be no more tears. He looked at his watch: Sheilah must be home, now, wondering what had become of him. He descended the beetles' staircase and for forty minutes crossed the city under a windless fall of snow.

The neighbor's child who had stayed with Peter's children was asleep on the living-room sofa. Peter woke her and sent her, sleepwalking, to her own door. He sat down, wet to the bone, thinking, I'll call the Burleighs. In half an hour I'll call the police. He heard a car stop and the engine running and a confusion of two voices laughing and calling good night. Presently Sheilah let herself in, rosy-faced, smiling. She carried his trench coat over her arm. She said, "How's Agnes?"

"Where were you?" he said. "Whose car was that?"

Sheilah had gone into the children's room. He heard her shutting their window. She returned, undoing her dress, and said, "Was Agnes all right?"

"Agnes is all right. Sheilah, this is about the worst ..."

She stepped out of the Balenciaga and threw it over a chair. She stopped and looked at him and said, "Poor old Pete, are you in love with Agnes?" And then, as if the answer were of so little importance she hadn't time for it, she locked her arms around him and said, "My love, we're going to Ceylon."

Two days later, when Peter strolled into his office, Agnes was at her desk. She wore the blue dress, with a spotless collar. White and yellow freesias were symmetrically arranged in the glass jar. The room was hot, and the spring snow, glued for a second when it touched the window, blurred the view of parked cars.

"Quite a party," Peter said.

She did not look up. He sighed, sat down, and thought if the snow held he would be skiing at the Burleighs' very soon. Impressed by his kindness to Agnes, Madge had invited the family for the first possible weekend.

Presently Agnes said, "I'll never drink again or go to a house where people are drinking. And I'll never bother anyone the way I bothered you."

"You didn't bother me," he said. "I took you home. You were alone and it was late. It's normal."

"Normal for you, maybe, but I'm used to getting home by myself. Please never tell what happened."

He stared at her. He can still remember the freesias and the Bible and the heat in the room. She looked as if the elements had no power. She felt neither heat nor cold. "Nothing happened," he said.

"I behaved in a silly way. I had no right to. I led you to think I might do something wrong."

"*I* might have tried something," he said gallantly. "But that would be my fault and not yours."

She put her knuckle to her mouth and he could scarcely hear.

"It was because of you. I was afraid you might be blamed, or else you'd blame yourself."

"There's no question of any blame," he said. "Nothing happened. We'd both had a lot to drink. Forget about it. Nothing *happened*. You'd remember if it had."

She put down her hand. There was an expression on her face. Now she sees me, he thought. She had never looked at him after the first day. (He has since tried to put a name to the look on her face; but how can he, now, after so many voyages, after Ceylon, and Hong Kong, and Sheilah's nearly leaving him, and all their difficulties—the money owed, the rows with hotel managers, the lost and found steamer trunk, the children throwing up the foreign food?) She sees me now, he thought. What does she see?

She said, "I'm from a big family. I'm not used to being alone. I'm not a suicidal person, but I could have done something after that party, just not to see anymore, or think or listen or expect anything. What can I think when I see these people? All my life I heard, Educated people don't do this, educated people don't do that. And now I'm here, and you're all educated people, and you're nothing but pigs. You're educated and you drink and do everything wrong and you know what you're doing, and that makes you worse than pigs. My family worked to make me an educated person, but they didn't know you. But what if I didn't see and hear and expect anything anymore? It wouldn't change anything. You'd all be still the same. Only *you* might have thought it was your fault. You might have thought you were to blame. It could worry you all your life. It would have been wrong for me to worry you."

He remembered that the rented car was still along a snowy curb somewhere in Geneva. He wondered if Sheilah had the key in her purse and if she remembered where they'd parked.

"I told you about the ice wagon," Agnes said. "I don't remember everything, so you're wrong about remembering. But I remember telling you that. That was the best. It's the best you can hope to have.

In a big family, if you want to be alone, you have to get up before the rest of them. You get up early in the morning in the summer and it's you, you, once in your life alone in the universe. You think you know everything that can happen.... Nothing is ever like that again."

He looked at the smeared window and wondered if this day could end without disaster. In his mind he saw her falling in the snow wearing a tramp's costume, and he saw her coming to him in the orphanage dressing gown. He saw her drowning face at the party. He was afraid for himself. The story was still unfinished. It had to come to a climax, something threatening to him. But there was no climax. They talked that day, and afterward nothing else was said. They went on in the same office for a short time, until Peter left for Ceylon; until somebody read the right letter, passed it on for the right initials, and the Fraziers began the Oriental tour that should have made their fortune. Agnes and Peter were too tired to speak after that morning. They were like a married couple in danger, taking care.

But what were they talking about that day, so quietly, such old friends? They talked about dying, about being ambitious, about being religious, about different kinds of love. What did she see when she looked at him—taking her knuckle slowly away from her mouth, bringing her hand down to the desk, letting it rest there? They were both Canadians, so they had this much together—the knowledge of the little you dare admit. Death, near death, the best thing, the wrong thing—God knows what they were telling each other. Anyway, nothing happened.

When, on Sunday mornings, Sheilah and Peter talk about those times, they take on the glamour of something still to come. It is then he remembers Agnes Brusen. He never says her name. Sheilah wouldn't remember Agnes. Agnes is the only secret Peter has from his wife, the only puzzle he pieces together without her help. He thinks about families in the West as they were fifteen, twenty years ago—the iron-cold ambition, and every member pushing the next one on. He thinks of his father's parties. When he thinks of his father he imagines him with Sheilah, in a crowd. Actually, Sheilah and Peter's father never met, but they might have liked each other. His father admired good-looking women. Peter wonders what they were doing over there in Geneva—not Sheilah and Peter, *Agnes* and Peter. It is almost as if they had once run away together, silly as children, irresponsible as lovers. Peter and Sheilah are back where they started. While they were out in world affairs picking up microbes and debts, always on the fringe of disaster, the fringe of a fortune, Agnes went on and did—what? They lost each other. He thinks of the ice wagon going down the street. He sees something he has never seen in his life—a Western town that belongs to Agnes. Here is Agnes—small, mole-faced, round-shouldered because she has always carried a younger child. She watches the ice wagon and the trail of ice water in a morning invented for her: hers. He sees the weak prairie trees and the shadows on the sidewalk. Nothing moves except the shadows and the ice wagon and the changing amber of the child's eyes. The child is Peter. He has seen the grain of the cement sidewalk and the grass in the cracks, and the dust, and the dandelions at the edge of the road. He is there. He has taken the morning that belongs to Agnes, he is up before the others, and he knows everything. There is nothing he doesn't know. He could keep the morning, if he wanted to, but what can Peter do with the start of a summer day? Sheilah is here, it is a true Sunday morning, with its dimness and headache and remorse and regrets, and this is life. He says, "We have the Balenciaga." He touches Sheilah's hand. The children have their aunt now, and he and Sheilah have each other. Everything works out, somehow or other. Let Agnes have the start of the day. Let Agnes think it was invented for her. Who wants to be alone in the universe? No, begin at the beginning: Peter lost Agnes. Agnes says to herself somewhere, Peter is lost.

PAOLA AND RENATA

During the weeks that preceded the engagement, Paola and Renata discovered new ways of combing their hair. Paola's was short and brushed forward in a style Renata's mother called "Charleston." Over the Charleston locks she tugged a bathing cap made up of yellow daisies. Renata's mother said that the sun and the lake water would turn Paola's lovely head to rust if she didn't take care now, while she was young. The older woman caressed Paola's hair—the dry crown and the silk wet fringe that had touched water—and said she wished her own daughter had thick curls and blackberry eyes; but that was polite hypocrisy and accepted as such. Renata was the one who was almost engaged. Her father was a corporation lawyer in Milan, and her mother could have provided Renata's dowry out of her own jewel box, if she had chosen to. Paola was the child of a widow. The father had died not quite two years ago, and there was a faint new difference between the girls, delicately felt, invisible still, like the turning of summer.

Renata could swim without wearing a cap—indeed, she was urged to do so, so that the sun and the water would bleach her hair to the washed-sand color for which her mother had another name: "Scandinavian." Renata idly swam on her back with her hair spread and floating, but she was not mad, not drowning, not Ophelia. She was making herself very beautiful for her engagement. Coming out of the water she was to Paola's sun-struck eyes a mythical girl. She raised her thin arms as if unconscious of them and pulled her

Scandinavian hair back and held it taut with a curving tortoise-shell comb. Unknown bathers peered through the bamboo fence that hedged their private beach, but Renata was calm and scornful. The hair-style, like the disdainful look on her face, was copied from a magazine; but it was also true she did not yet know other people existed. She had still to learn the hard darting glance her mother and Paola's mother could send other women: the measuring regard that ascertained clothes, hands, and weight in carats. Renata was aware of herself. Floating on her back with her eyes shut to the sky, wishing herself alone on the lake in the circle of mountains, she saw the reflection of a girl, Renata, long, brown, her thin arms outspread, her hands and her feet like marine plants. She saw with her eyes shut her shadow on the bottom of the lake, a cloud transversed with small quick fish. Hers was the exquisite shadow of summer, the most memorable, the most precisely cast.

Paola and Renata and Paola's little sister Anna and the two mothers lived that holiday, their last together, in Paola's mother's house. It was the last of anything; the house was sold to a Swiss couple from Zurich, and in the autumn the furniture would be sold at auction or stored in Milan. If Paola's father had put the deed to the house in his wife's name, it would have been a kind and practical gesture, and saved on income tax; but he died with the house his, and taxes owing, and only his mistress provided for. A block of flats in San Remo was in her name. Everything was going, now, and the family done for, and the father had struck at them within his lifetime, secretly, perhaps thinking he would never die; but he must have expected to die. Otherwise, would he have thought of his mistress, and provided for her? Of all this Paola said nothing as she brushed her Charleston hair forward or threaded ribbon through the lace of Renata's peignoirs. She thought, but said nothing. Everything was going, done, except Paola's mother's dowry, which her father had always said was never quite enough. Paola heard her mother crying, but it was difficult to tell if she was grieving for her dead husband, or mourning his infidelity—exposed and dissected by lawsuits—or simply lamenting the disorder of his memory. It was almost as though he had wanted to be assured of survival, no matter how. "Dead and gone, and jealous of the living," cried Paola's mother, in a fit of hate for which she immediately begged forgiveness. Paola forgave. The father's photograph, kept so that Anna would know what he looked like, gave way to the specter of a stoutish man with a rather large head and a mistress on the Mediterranean coast.

It was the last of everything; this house was, it had been, the last Italian villa. Everything else was German, Austrian, and German-Swiss. The campsites and hotels bore signs saying "German Spoken," and "German Management," the only Italians to be found were in the hotel kitchens, and one could walk miles without hearing a word in Italian: this the two mothers said with passion and spite. From their scrap of pebbly private beach, Paola and Renata watched with indifference shoals of floating inflated mattresses, each holding a Swiss, an Austrian, or a Bavarian, usually blistered red, but singing. The songs were melancholy and stirring, and although the words were in a foreign tongue the tunes were familiar. The girls could sing French and American songs, without understanding all the words. They were bored by the mothers' passions. They were as bored with them as with patriotism or tales of war. These were the only matters that bored them. No summer had ever been as distracting as this last summer on the lake with Renata about to become engaged.

The obstacle to the engagement was Renata's parents. The parents found nothing to criticize in Guilio's fortunes or his person, but they began as if it were a game with the premise that he was unfit and must be proved desirable. He was twenty-eight, eleven years older than Renata, and still had not passed his examinations. He was studying law. At the rate he failed his examinations he would be studying law at the age of forty. Renata's father—a lawyer—declared there were too many lawyers in Milan. Renata raged, Paola consoled. Up in Paola's room, which the girls shared, Renata lay prone on the marble floor, limp with tantrums, and cried, "They want me to be an old maid." "They don't, of course," said Paola sadly. Bereaved and mourning, undone by her father and the unknown San Remo whore, she wanted Renata to be engaged because that was the thing Renata wanted. Paola would always see a stout man with a large head signing papers, conspiring, casting his family on an ash-heap. Consoling her friend, she sat on the floor beside her and stroked her hair. Her hand was firm, and her voice warm and low and wise. "They don't want you to be an old maid. You know that." Renata knew that Paola was right.

Guilio had studied in Italy and Geneva and Heidelberg and now he wanted to go to the United States and study there for a time. Guilio's parents said that if Renata married him, and took over the moral responsibility for Guilio's life, they would send him to the United States or anywhere he liked; but Renata's father wanted Guilio to go away alone and come back for Renata when he had passed his examinations. The responsibility for Guilio was too great for a girl of seventeen. That was the story they told Renata. It might or might not be the truth.

That went on in July. In August Renata stopped raging and began to weep. She had to wear sunglasses at the dinner table to hide her bloated eyes. She scraped her increasingly Scandinavian-looking hair away from her innocent forehead, and sat as though rebuffed, contemplating an untouched dinner, while the others talked at once. Paola tried to feel, We shall be somewhere else this time next year, but only this summer counted as a faithful season. A father died without warning. Without warning Renata would say, "I am engaged."

The two mothers were thin and hard. The new difference between them was physical. Paola's mother had stopped tinting her hair, as a sign of sorrow or of desperation. It was half mahogany, half dull gray. Renata's mother was blonded white, and her head sleek and neat as a boy's. Paola admired her large glossy red earrings and her brown shoulders and her quick tongue. She admired her rings and her sweet hypocrisy and her temper and her car. None of those attributes had come with marriage. She was born with some and inherited the means to have the rest. Renata's mother was kind to Paola—so obviously not a threat—and took no notice of her own grieving girl, except when the sunglasses and the accusation they concealed seemed a reproach too great to ignore. Then she lost her temper. Once she lost her temper seriously and knocked the bowl of water in which grapes were cooling, half silver coated, half submerged, on to Renata's lap. Renata jumped up, screaming, with her dress ice cold and pasted against her thighs. Her mother tried to hit her across the face with her napkin, but missed.

"There will be no engagement," her mother cried. "You impertinent monster! *There will be no engagement.*"

Paola was laughing so that she could scarcely understand Renata's hysterical answer (probably a suicide threat) from the stairs. Presently Renata returned in a starched peignoir, with a white ribbon around her hair, and they had their coffee in peace on the terrace, beneath the trellis of green grapes and black wisteria branches and white roses that suddenly dropped petals like secret letters. The two mothers played gin rummy under a light surrounded by moths, and the girls listened to records of Anthony Perkins singing in French. The songs did not disturb the mothers; no one cared about the people sleeping in hotels on either side of the house, and little Anna could slumber through earthquakes.

The only person distressed by the tears, the lamentations, and Anthony Perkins's voice was the frightened young Austrian girl who had been employed as Anna's nurse for the summer. She was spending the most miserable summer of her life. Not only did she hear Austrians insulted in this house from morning till night, but she was bitten and spat upon by little Anna. When Anna spat the girl asked, "Are you doing it on purpose?" and Anna said, "Yes." Anna's hair had to be brushed and fastened with an elastic in the morning before they went down to swim. Just when the nurse had the hair brushed and ready, and the elastic stretched on her outspread fingers, Anna would shake her head and send the pony-tail flying. The nurse would then have to roll the elastic back on her wrist, clutch Anna, and begin again. She needed several hands: one for Anna, one to hold the brush, one to grasp the pony-tail, and one for the elastic band. When Anna's mother came to see what was keeping them, Anna clasped her mother's knees and bent her head meekly, so that her mother could slide the band on without trouble.

The Austrian girl had tears in her eyes. "Anna has bitten me again," she said, and held out her hand with the small crescent.

"If I had known you did not like children I would never have brought you here," Anna's mother said.

"How I hate children," said Renata, lying on Paola's bed. It was a hot day and neither of them had dressed.

"Oh, so do I," said Paola, with something in her voice that resembled Renata's in a rage.

"That cow expression people have when they look at Anna. It makes me vomit."

"You will have children if you get married," Paola said.

"I know. I've thought about it. Guilio hates children too."

"There are things you can do so as not to have them."

"I know. But I don't know what they are."

Paola would have said, "Guilio knows," but that was going far, even between Paola and Renata.

Renata sighed, with her chin on her hands, and contemplated the pictures on the wall above the bed: Anthony Perkins, Evtushenko, and Mrs. Kennedy. The fourth and most important picture lay beside her. It was a photograph of smiling Guilio, glassed over, surrounded by an imposing silver and leather frame. His name was signed obliquely across one corner. He lay smiling between the two girls. Renata had tried sleeping with the picture, but was afraid of rolling on it and smothering Guilio. Also, she shared Paola's bed, and Paola had not been hospitable. She did not object to Guilio, but to the heavy silver corners of the picture frame. She was not frightened of stifling Guilio, who was not a newly born kitten, but of hurting herself. Renata's engagement to Guilio had to do with the picture in its frame, with her red eyes and sunglasses, her scenes at dinner, and her remote hair drifting on the lake. There were also Guilio's letters.

Renata was permitted to write one letter to Guilio every week. This letter was read by her mother, who then took it to the post office and sent it by ordinary mail. Guilio was in Switzerland for the summer, quite close by, but a letter despatched by ordinary mail took as long as four days to reach him.

Renata wrote to Guilio every morning. Paola carried the daily letter downstairs to Spirella, the cook, who gave it to the groom in one of the hotels next door. The letter went out with the hotel post, marked "Most Urgent," and was in Guilio's hands a morning later.

"Where are you going?" Paola's mother asked her.

"To the kitchen, to get lemonade." Renata's letter was in the pocket of her shorts.

"Don't keep running to the kitchen. Don't bother Spirella. Tell Spirella to bring lemonade out for all of us." These were the contradictory orders of a widow in distress. Paola's disobedience was of little importance. She had no dowry and no prospects and was not even nearly engaged.

Renata was watched more closely than Paola that summer because the talk of her engagement, even the assurance that it would never come to pass, made her important, tricky, and furtive. She was more important than she had ever been. She might be up to anything.

Renata's mother looked as if she were trying to smuggle a forbidden object over a frontier. All summer she said, "Renata, where are you?" and "Where are you going?" and "Who was that on the telephone?" and "Wait for Paola," and "Wait for us."

Renata lay on the bed and looked at Guilio while Paola slipped down to the kitchen and gave the "Very Urgent" letter to the cook. Guilio's letters were sent to Spirella in care of the hotel next door, and came up in the morning with Renata's breakfast, under a napkin. "There is no law against posting letters," Spirella told Paola. Paola knew it was the cook's weapon against two mothers. What could the mothers do confronted with the smooth and guileless faces of Paola, Renata, Spirella, and the groom next door?

About once a week, a letter arrived for Renata, correctly addressed, in care of Paola's mother. Paola's mother gave it to Renata's mother, who read it in her room. In these official letters, Guilio doubted Renata's love, asked if she were reticent or simply pure, and insisted that he would marry her if she were penniless and in rags. Renata's mother sat on the edge of her bed with her legs crossed and the letter spread on one knee, and she bit the side of her thumb as she read. She kept the letter until evening so that she could read it over the telephone to her husband in Milan, who called every evening at eight o'clock. Renata was given the letter the next day. Weekends, when Renata's father arrived from Milan, he asked to see the letters and read them as if he had not understood his wife on the telephone. "There are no others?" he would ask. Renata looked at her hands, her mother shrugged.

The official letters, intended for parents, Renata read aloud to Paola in an affected voice. Paola, racked with laughter as if in pain, pressed her pillow to her face. Renata kissed the teeth on Guilio's smiling picture and put the picture away with the unofficial letters. His real, his clandestine letters, which she did not read aloud, were tied and hidden in Paola's old toy cupboard. There were perhaps twenty of them, less than half the number she had written him. They were ranged and marked in such a way that Renata would know instantly if anyone had touched them. Knowing that the packet of letters was full of snares, Paola let them be. Renata's mother, determined as the police, but less thorough and calm, ransacked the room but missed the cupboard of toys. Renata knew, or felt she knew, when her mother was up to a search, and it was her private pleasure to leave the cupboard door ajar, revealing stuffed animals and a wicker sewing basket. She imagined her mother, impatient and tough, banging the door shut, missing the treasure in her impatience to find it. The official letters were tied with ribbon and in a drawer. The mother untied the ribbon and counted the letters and flung them back between nightgowns. She said aloud, alone, that she wished God had never given her a daughter. Blessed was a mother with an only son!

Towards the end of August, Renata's father went to Geneva on business, and called casually on Guilio's family in their Swiss summer home. A few mornings later Renata was summoned to her mother's room.

"I have a letter here from Guilio," her mother said. "How many letters have you had from him?"

"You should know."

"One came this morning, and not in the usual way." She kept the letter face down, with her hand over it. Renata's eyes met her mother's and held the gaze. Neither stared the other down, but each moved, slightly, to break the deadlock.

Renata had saved face. "May I have my letter?" she said.

"I haven't decided. You know what it will mean if you have had a secret correspondence."

Renata did not know, but a threat was a threat. "Guilio is honorable," she said. "So am I. You make me wonder what you were like when you were young."

She was braced for a slap, but her mother said only, "I promise not to tell your father if you give me the others."

"What others?"

"The letters, you impudent monkey. The other letters. There is no question of an engagement now. A man who would lie to his mother-in-law would lie to his wife. If you give me the letters I won't tell your father."

"I haven't had any letters except the letters you have seen," said Renata.

The mother was looking away, watching Renata in a mirror across the room. The girl sat quietly and emptied her expression of unhappiness or reproach. She was a novice supreme in her innocence and decision. From Paola's mother's sitting room came the sound of half a conversation: "A good girl, but without imagination, and too severe. My Anna has been a martyr to discipline all summer. Apart from that—yes, honest enough."

"Is the nurse leaving?" said Renata.

"How should I know?" said Renata's mother. "Who cares about her?"

Renata suddenly smiled. "I shall marry Guilio when I'm twenty-one. It's only four years."

"Four years ago you were a monster of thirteen," her mother screamed. "A horror! Skinny, tall! Why couldn't I have had a son? Why couldn't I have had a daughter like Paola? I'm glad to be rid of you. There will be an engagement. Do you hear? There will be a wedding September twenty-seventh and Guilio is taking you with him to the United States. God help you, with a husband who tells lies and rushes the wedding. We have barely five weeks to get ready. We are leaving for Milan tomorrow. Now you know."

She crept into Paola's room and sat stiffly on the edge of the bed.

"I'm being married September twenty-seventh."

"You wanted to be engaged."

"Yes, but I'm not being engaged. I'm being married. There isn't a real engagement."

When she began to pack she said, "You can keep the letters."

"What do I want with Guilio's letters?" They were not friends as before.

After Renata and her mother had departed, distraught and waving scarves from the sky-blue Guilietta Sprint, Paola looked in the toy cupboard and found Guilio's picture and the secret letters. Renata had taken the official letters and would probably keep them and reread them all her life.

Paola unfolded one of the letters, but it was not a message of secret love; at least not as she had imagined it. It was about Guilio and water-skiing. She picked out another at random but it was about Guilio too. She tore the others up without reading them and got rid of them by swimming quite far out in the lake with scraps of paper in the top of her bikini. It was not as exciting as smuggling letters to the kitchen had been, but she relived the feeling of summer and secrecy, and the unrevealed act. She put the picture aside in case Renata should ask for the frame.

Paola and her mother were alone on the beach with Anna. The Austrian girl had left without regret, and it required both of them, Paola and her mother, to look after Anna. The mother said nothing about going back to the city, and there seemed to be nothing waiting there, except Renata's wedding. By the time all the letters had been torn up and dispersed, it was almost too cold for swimming. Paola shuddered and rubbed her arms and legs with a rough towel as soon as she came out of the water. In less than a week the climate changed. They dragged their towels and cushions away from the shade of the bamboo fence and followed the sun. When they sat on the beach—Paola, and her mother, and little Anna—Paola was conscious of them as a family without men. She did not miss Renata.

"I wish something would happen," she said.

"You'll be engaged later," said her mother. "Seventeen is too young."

"Can't anything happen without an engagement?"

"Don't be meaningless and clever," said her mother. "Don't be clever at all. Men don't like women who are too clever." She did not scream, like Renata's mother. Her voice was quiet. The girl shivered in the breeze from the lake as her mother said, "Renata would never have caught Guilio by being clever. Do you think it was her brains he admired? Her face? He was waiting for the marriage settlement. That was all."

Anna had taken off her bathing suit and was dancing in shallow water.

"Come here instantly," her mother said, without the hope of being obeyed. Anna splashed them. "Very well," said the mother. "Don't come. Break my heart. You'll regret it when I am dead." Anna took no notice, knowing perfectly well that nothing ever came of threats.

"I wish I were Anna," Paola said.

THE WEDDING RING

On my windowsill is a pack of cards, a bell, a dog's brush, a book about a girl named Jewel who is a Christian Scientist and won't let anyone take her temperature, and a white jug holding field flowers. The water in the jug has evaporated; the sand-and-amber flowers seem made of paper. The weather bulletin for the day can be one of several: No sun. A high arched yellow sky. Or, creamy clouds, stillness. Long motionless grass. The earth soaks up the sun. Or, the sky is higher than it ever will seem again, and the sun far away and small.

From the window, a field full of goldenrod, then woods; to the left as you stand at the front door of the cottage, the mountains of Vermont.

The screen door slams and shakes my bed. That was my cousin. The couch with the India print spread in the next room has been made up for him. He is the only boy cousin I have, and the only American relation my age. We expected him to be homesick for Boston. When he disappeared the first day, we thought we would find him crying with his head in the wild cucumber vine; but all he was doing was making the outhouse tidy, dragging out of it last year's magazines. He discovers a towel abandoned under his bed by another guest, and shows it to each of us. He has unpacked a trumpet, a hatchet, a pistol, and a water bottle. He is ready for anything except my mother, who scares him to death.

My mother is a vixen. Everyone who sees her that summer will remember, later, the gold of her eyes and the lovely movement of her head. Her hair is true russet. She has the bloom women have sometimes when they are pregnant or when they have fallen in love. She can be wild, bitter, complaining, and ugly as a witch, but that summer is her peak. She has fallen in love.

My father is—I suppose—in Montreal. The guest who seems to have replaced him except in authority over me (he is still careful, still courts my favor) drives us to a movie. It is a musical full of monstrously large people. My cousin sits intent, bites his nails, chews a slingshot during the love scenes. He suddenly dives down in the dark to look for lost, mysterious objects. He has seen so many movies that this one is nearly over before he can be certain he has seen it before. He always knows what is going to happen and what they are going to say next.

At night we hear the radio—disembodied voices in a competition, identifying tunes. My mother, in the living room, seen from my bed, plays solitaire and says from time to time, "That's an old song I like," and "When you play solitaire, do you turn out two cards or three?" My cousin is not asleep either; he stirs on his couch. He shares his room with the guest. Years later we will be astonished to realize how young the guest must have been—twenty-three, perhaps twenty-four. My cousin, in his memories, shared a room with a middle-aged man. My mother and I, for the first and last time, ever, sleep in the same bed. I see her turning out the cards, smoking, drinking cold coffee from a breakfast cup. The single light on the table throws the room against the black window. My cousin and I each have an extra blanket. We forget how the evening sun blinded us at suppertime—how we gasped for breath.

My mother remarks on my hair, my height, my teeth, my French, and what I like to eat, as if she had never seen me before. Together, we wash our hair in the stream. The stones at the bottom are the color of trout. There is a smell of fish and wildness as I kneel on a rock, as she does, and plunge my head in the water. Bubbles of soap dance in place, as if rooted, then the roots stretch and break. In a delirium of happiness I memorize ferns, moss, grass, seedpods. We sunbathe on camp cots dragged out in the long grass. The strands of wet hair on my neck are like melting icicles. Her "Never look straight at the sun" seems extravagantly concerned with my welfare. Through eyelashes I peep at the milky-blue sky. The sounds of this blissful moment are the radio from the house; my cousin opening a ginger-ale bottle; the stream, persistent as machinery. My mother, still taking extraordinary notice of me, says that while the sun bleaches her hair and makes it light and fine, dark hair (mine) turns ugly—"like a rusty old stove lid"—and should be covered up. I dart into the cottage and find a hat: a wide straw hat, belonging to an unknown summer. It is so large I have to hold it with a hand flat upon the crown. I may look funny with this hat on, but at least I shall never be like a rusty old stove lid. The cots are empty; my mother has gone. By mistake, she is walking away through the goldenrod with the guest, turned up from God knows where. They are walking as if they wish they were invisible, of course, but to me it is only a mistake, and I call and run and push my way between them. He would like to take my hand, or pretends he would like to, but I need my hand for the hat.

My mother is developing one of her favorite themes—her lack of roots. To give the story greater power, or because she really believes what she is saying at that moment, she gets rid of an extra parent: "I never felt I had any stake anywhere until my parents died and I had their graves. The graves were my only property. I felt I belonged somewhere."

Graves? What does she mean? My grandmother is still alive.

"That's so sad," he says.

"Don't you ever feel that way?"

He tries to match her tone. "Oh, I wouldn't care. I think everything was meant to be given away. Even a grave would be a tie. I'd pretend not to know where it was."

"My father and mother didn't get along, and that prevented me feeling close to any country," says my mother. This may be new to him, but, like my cousin at a musical comedy, I know it by heart, or something near it. "I was divorced from the landscape, as they were from each other. I was too taken up wondering what was going to happen next. The first country I loved was somewhere in the north of Germany. I went there with my mother. My father was dead and my mother was less tense and I was free of their troubles. That is the truth," she says, with some astonishment.

The sun drops, the surface of the leaves turns deep blue. My father lets a parcel fall on the kitchen table, for at the end of one of her long, shattering, analytical letters she has put "P.S. Please bring a four-pound roast and some sausages." Did the guest depart? He must have dissolved; he is no longer visible. To show that she is loyal, has no secrets, she will repeat every word that was said. But my father, now endlessly insomniac and vigilant, looks as if it were he who had secrets, who is keeping something back.

The children—hostages released—are no longer required. In any case, their beds are needed for Labor Day weekend. I am to spend six days with my cousin in Boston—a stay that will, in fact, be prolonged many months. My mother stands at the door of the cottage in nightgown and sweater, brown-faced, smiling. The tall field grass is gray with cold dew. The windows of the car are frosted with it. My father will put us on a train, in care of a conductor. Both my cousin and I are used to this.

"He and Jane are like sister and brother," she says—this of my cousin and me, who do not care for each other.

Uncut grass. I saw the ring fall into it, but I am told I did not—I was already in Boston. The weekend party, her chosen audience, watched her rise, without warning, from the wicker chair on the porch. An admirer of Russian novels, she would love to make an immediate,

Russian gesture, but cannot. The porch is screened, so, to throw her wedding ring away, she must have walked a few steps to the door and *then* made her speech, and flung the ring into the twilight, in a great spinning arc. The others looked for it next day, discreetly, but it had disappeared. First it slipped under one of those sharp bluish stones, then a beetle moved it. It left its print on a cushion of moss after the first winter. No one else could have worn it. My mother's hands were small, like mine.

THE LATEHOMECOMER

When I came back to Berlin out of captivity in the spring of 1950, I discovered I had a stepfather. My mother had never mentioned him. I had been writing from Brittany to "Grete Bestermann," but the "Toeppler" engraved on a brass plate next to the bellpull at her new address turned out to be her name, too. As she slipped the key in the lock, she said quietly, "Listen, Thomas. I'm Frau Toeppler now. I married a kind man with a pension. This is his key, his name, and his apartment. He wants to make you welcome." From the moment she met me at the railway station that day, she must have been wondering how to break it.

I put my hand over the name, leaving a perfect palm print. I said, "I suppose there are no razor blades and no civilian shirts in Berlin. But some ass is already engraving nameplates."

Martin Toeppler was an old man who had been a tram conductor. He was lame in one arm as the result of a working accident and carried that shoulder higher than the other. His eyes had the milky look of the elderly, lighter round the rim than at the center of the iris, and he had an old woman's habit of sighing, "Ah, yes, yes." The sigh seemed to be his way of pleading, "It can't be helped." He must have been forty-nine, at the most, but aged was what he seemed to me, and more than aged—useless, lost. His mouth hung open much of the time, as though he had trouble breathing through his nose, but it was only because he was a chronic talker, always ready to bite down on a word. He came from

Franconia, near the Czech border, close to where my grandparents had once lived.

"Grete and I can understand each other's dialects," he said—but we were not a dialect-speaking family. My brother and I had been made to say "bread" and "friend" and "tree" correctly. I turned my eyes to my mother, but she looked away.

Martin's one dream was to return to Franconia; it was almost the first thing he said to me. He had inherited two furnished apartments in a town close to an American military base. One of the two had been empty for years. The occupants had moved away, no one knew where—perhaps to Sweden. After their departure, which had taken place at five o'clock on a winter morning in 1943, the front door had been sealed with a government stamp depicting a swastika and an eagle. The vanished tenants must have died, perhaps in Sweden, and now no local person would live in the place, because a whole family of ghosts rattled about, opening and shutting drawers, banging on pipes, moving chairs and ladders. The ghosts were looking for a hoard of gold that had been left behind, Martin thought. The second apartment had been rented to a family who had disappeared during the confused migrations of the end of the war and were probably dead, too; at least they were dead officially, which was all that mattered. Martin intended to modernize the two flats, raise them up to American standards—he meant by this putting venetian blinds at the windows and gas-heated water tanks in the bathrooms—and let them to a good class of American officer, too foreign to care about a small-town story, too educated to be afraid of ghosts. But he would have to move quickly; otherwise his inheritance, his sole post-war capital, his only means of getting started again, might be snatched away from him for the sake of shiftless and illiterate refugees from the Soviet zone, or bombed-out families still huddled in barracks, or for latehomecomers. This last was a new category of persons, all one word. It was out of his mouth before he remembered that

I was one, too. He stopped talking, and then he sighed and said, "Ah, yes, yes."

He could not keep still for long: He drew out his wallet and showed me a picture of himself on horseback. He may have wanted to substitute this country image for any idea I had of him on the deck of a tram. He held the snapshot at arm's length and squinted at it. "That was Martin Toeppler once," he said. "It will be Martin Toeppler again." His youth, and a new right shoulder and arm, and the hot, leafy summers everyone his age said had existed before the war were waiting for him in Franconia. He sounded like a born winner instead of a physically broken tram conductor on the losing side. He put the picture away in a cracked celluloid case, pocketed his wallet, and called to my mother, "The boy will want a bath."

My mother, who had been preparing a bath for minutes now, had been receiving orders all her life. As a girl she had worked like a slave in her mother's village guesthouse, and after my father died she became a servant again, this time in Berlin, to my powerful Uncle Gerhard and his fat wife. My brother and I spent our winters with her, all three sleeping in one bed sometimes, in a cold attic room, sharing bread and apples smuggled from Uncle Gerhard's larder. In the summer we were sent to help our grandmother. We washed the chairs and tables, cleaned the toilets of vomit, and carried glasses stinking with beer back to the kitchen. We were still so small we had to stand on stools to reach the taps.

"It was lucky you had two sons," Uncle Gerhard said to my mother once. "There will never be a shortage of strong backs in the family."

"No one will exploit my children," she is supposed to have replied, though how she expected to prevent it only God knows, for we had no roof of our own and no money and we ate such food as we were given. Our uniforms saved us. Once we had joined the Hitler Jugend, even Uncle Gerhard never dared ask, "Where are you going?" or "Where have you been?" My brother was quicker than

I. By the time he was twelve he knew he had been trapped; I was sixteen and a prisoner before I understood. But from our mother's point of view we were free, delivered; we would not repeat her life. That was all she wanted.

In captivity I had longed for her and for the lost paradise of our poverty, where she had belonged entirely to my brother and to me and we had slept with her, one on each side. I had written letters to her full of remorse for past neglect and containing promises of future goodness: I would work hard and look after her forever. These letters, sent to blond, young, soft-voiced Grete Bestermann, had been read by Grete Toeppler, whose graying hair was pinned up in a sort of oval balloon, and who was anxious and thin, as afraid of things to come as she was of the past. I had not recognized her at the station, and when she said timidly, "Excuse me? Thomas?" I thought she was her own mother. I did not know then, or for another few minutes, that my grandmother had died or that my rich Uncle Gerhard, now officially de-Nazified by a court of law, was camped in two rooms carved out of a ruin, raising rabbits for a living and hoping that no one would notice him. She had last seen me when I was fifteen. We had been moving toward each other since early this morning, but I was exhausted and taciturn, and we were both shy, and we had not rushed into each other's arms, because we had each been afraid of embracing a stranger. I had one horrible memory of her, but it may have been only a dream. I was small, but I could speak and walk. I came into a room where she was nursing a baby. Two other women were with her. When they saw me they started to laugh, and one said to her, "Give some to Thomas." My mother leaned over and put her breast in my mouth. The taste was disgustingly sweet, and because of the two women I felt humiliated: I spat and backed off and began to cry. She said something to the women and they laughed harder than ever. It must have been a dream, for who could the baby have been? My brother was eleven months older than I.

She was cautious as an animal with me now, partly because of my reaction to the nameplate. She must have feared there was more to come. She had been raised to respect men, never to interrupt their conversation, to see that their plates were filled before hers—even, as a girl, to stand when they were sitting down. I was twenty-one, I had been twenty-one for three days, I had crossed over to the camp of the bullies and strangers. All the while Martin was talking and boasting and showing me himself on horseback, she crept in and out of the parlor, fetching wood and the briquettes they kept by the tile stove, carrying them down the passage to build a fire for me in the bathroom. She looked at me sidelong sometimes and smiled with her hand before her mouth—a new habit of hers—but she kept silent until it was time to say that the bath was ready.

My mother spread a towel for me to stand on and showed me a chair where, she said, Martin always sat to dry his feet. There was a shelf with a mirror and comb but no washbasin. I supposed that he shaved and they cleaned their teeth in the kitchen. My mother said the soap was of poor quality and would not lather, but she asked me, again from behind the screen of her hand, not to leave it underwater where it might melt and be wasted. A stone underwater might have melted as easily. "There is a hook for your clothes," she said, though of course I had seen it. She hesitated still, but when I began to unbutton my shirt she slipped out.

The bath, into which a family could have fitted, was as rough as lava rock. The water was boiling hot. I sat with my knees drawn up as if I were in the tin tub I had been lent sometimes in France. The starfish scar of a grenade wound was livid on one knee, and that leg was misshapen, as though it had been pressed the wrong way while the bones were soft. Long underwear I took to be my stepfather's hung over a line. I sat looking at it, and at a stiff thin towel hanging next to it, and at the water condensing on the cement walls, until the skin of my hands and feet became as ridged and soft as corduroy.

There is a term for people caught on a street crossing after the light has changed: "pedestrian-traffic residue." I had been in a prisoner-of-war camp at Rennes when an order arrived to repatriate everyone who was under eighteen. For some reason, my name was never called. Five years after that, when I was in Saint-Malo, where I had been assigned to a druggist and his wife as a "free worker"—which did not mean free but simply not in a camp—the police sent for me and asked what I was doing in France with a large "PG," for *"prisonnier de guerre,"* on my back. Was I a deserter from the Foreign Legion? A spy? Nearly every other prisoner in France had been released at least ten months before, but the file concerning me had been lost or mislaid in Rennes, and I could not leave until it was found—I had no existence. By that time the French were sick of me, because they were sick of the war and its reminders, and the scheme of using the prisoners the Americans had taken to rebuild the roads and bridges of France had not worked out. The idea had never been followed by a plan, and so some of the prisoners became farm help, some became domestic servants, some went into the Foreign Legion because the food was better, some sat and did nothing for three or four years, because no one could discover anything for them to do. The police hinted to me that if I were to run away no one would mind. It would have cleared up the matter of the missing file. But I was afraid of putting myself in the wrong, in which case they might have an excuse to keep me forever. Besides, how far could I have run with a large "PG" painted on my jacket and trousers? Here, where it would not be necessary to wear a label, because "latehomecomer" was written all over me, I sensed that I was an embarrassment, too; my appearance, my survival, my bleeding gums and loose teeth, my chronic dysentery and anemia, my craving for sweets, my reticence with strangers, the cast-off rags

I had worn on arrival, all said "war" when everyone wanted peace, "captivity" when the word was "freedom," and "dry bread" when everyone was thinking "jam and butter." I guessed that now, after five years of peace, most of the population must have elbowed onto the right step of the right staircase and that there was not much room left for pedestrian-traffic residue.

My mother came in to clean the tub after I was partly dressed. She used fine ash from the stove and a cloth so full of holes it had to be rolled into a ball. She said, "I called out to you but you didn't hear. I thought you had fallen asleep and drowned."

I was hard of hearing because of the anti-aircraft duty to which I'd been posted in Berlin while I was still in high school. After the boys were sent to the front, girls took our places. It was those girls, still in their adolescence, who defended the grown men in uniform down in the bunkers. I wondered if they had been deafened, too, and if we were a generation who would never hear anything under a shout. My mother knelt by the tub, and I sat on Martin's chair, like Martin, pulling on clean socks she had brought me. In a low voice, which I heard perfectly, she said that I had known Martin in my childhood. I said I had not. She said then that my father had known him. I stood up and waited until she rose from her knees, and I looked down at her face. I was afraid of touching her, in case we should both cry. She muttered that her family must surely have known him, for the Toepplers had a burial plot not far from the graveyard where my grandmother lay buried, and some thirty miles from where my father's father had a bakery once. She was looking for any kind of a link.

"I wanted you and Chris to have a place to stay when you came back," she said, but I believed she had not expected to see either of us again and that she had been afraid of being homeless and alone. My brother had vanished in Czechoslovakia with the Schörner army. All of that army had been given up for dead. My Uncle Gerhard, her only close relative, could not have helped her even if it had occurred to him; it had taken him four years to become officially and legally de-Nazified, and now, "as white as a white lilac," according to my mother, he had no opinions about anything and lived only for his rabbits.

"It is nice to have a companion at my age," my mother said. "Someone to talk to." Did the old need more than conversation? My mother must have been about forty-two then. I had heard the old men in prison camp comparing their wives and saying that no hen was ever too tough for boiling.

"Did you marry him before or after he had this apartment?"

"After." But she had hesitated, as if wondering what I wanted to hear.

The apartment was on the second floor of a large dark block—all that was left of a workers' housing project of the 1920s. Martin had once lived somewhere between the bathroom window and the street. Looking out, I could easily replace the back walls of the vanished houses, and the small balconies festooned with brooms and mops, and the moist oily courtyard. Winter twilight must have been the prevailing climate here until an air raid let the seasons in. Cinders and gravel had been raked evenly over the crushed masonry now; the broad concourse between the surviving house—ours—and the road beyond it that was edged with ruins looked solid and flat.

But no, it was all shaky and loose, my mother said. Someone ought to cause a cement walk to be laid down; the women were always twisting their ankles, and when it rained you walked in black mud, and there was a smell of burning. She had not lost her belief in an invisible but well-intentioned "someone." She then said, in a hushed and whispery voice, that Martin's first wife, Elke, was down there under the rubble and cinders. It had been impossible to get all the bodies out, and one day a bulldozer covered them over for all time. Martin had inherited those two apartments in a town in

Franconia from Elke. The Toepplers were probably just as poor as the Bestermanns, but Martin had made a good marriage.

"She had a dog, too," said my mother. "When Martin married her she had a white spitz. She gave it a bath in the bathtub every Sunday." I thought of Martin Toeppler crossing this new wide treacherous front court and saying, "Elke's grave. Ah, yes, yes." I said it, and my mother suddenly laughed loudly and dropped her hand, and I saw that some of her front teeth were missing.

"The house looks like an old tooth when you see it from the street," she said, as though deliberately calling attention to the very misfortune she wanted to hide. She knew nothing about the people who had lived in this apartment, except that they had left in a hurry, forgetting to pack a large store of black-market food, some pretty ornaments in a china cabinet, and five bottles of wine. "They left without paying the rent," she said, which didn't sound like her.

It turned out to be a joke of Martin Toeppler's. He repeated it when I came back to the parlor wearing a shirt that I supposed must be his, and with my hair dark and wet and combed flat. He pointed to a bright rectangle on the brown wallpaper. "That is where they took Adolf's picture down," he said. "When they left in a hurry without paying the rent."

My father had been stabbed to death one night when he was caught tearing an election poster off the schoolhouse wall. He left my mother with no money, two children under the age of five, and a political reputation. After that she swam with the current. I had worn a uniform of one kind or another most of my life until now. I remembered wearing civilian clothes once, when I was fourteen, for my confirmation. I had felt disguised, and wondered what to do with my hands; from the age of seven I had stuck my thumbs in a leather belt. I had impressions, not memories, of my father. Pictures were frozen things; they told me nothing. But I knew that when my hair was wet I looked something like him. A quick flash would come back out of a mirror, like a secret message, and I would think, There, that is how he was. I sat with Martin at the table, where my mother had spread a lace cloth (the vanished tenants') and over which the April sun through lace curtains laid still another design. I placed my hands flat under lace shadows and wondered if they were like my father's, too.

She had put out everything she could find to eat and drink—a few sweet biscuits, cheese cut almost as thin as paper, dark bread, small whole tomatoes, radishes, slices of salami arranged in a floral design on a dish to make them seem more. We had a bottle of fizzy wine that Martin called champagne. It had a brown tint, like watered iodine, and a taste of molasses. Through this murk bubbles climbed. We raised our glasses without saying what we drank to, other than my return. Perhaps Martin drank to his destiny in Franconia with the two apartments. I had a plan, but it was my own secret. By a common accord, there was no mutual past. Then my mother spoke from behind the cupped hand and said she would like us to drink to her missing elder son. She looked at Martin as she said this, in case the survival of Chris might be a burden, too.

Toward the end of that afternoon, a neighbor came in with a bottle of brandy—a stout man with three locks of slick gray hair across his skull. All the fat men of comic stories and of literature were to be Willy Wehler to me, in the future. But he could not have been all that plump in Berlin in 1950; his chin probably showed the beginnings of softness, and his hair must have been dark still, and there must have been plenty of it. I can see the start of his baldness, the two deep peninsulas of polished skin running from the corners of his forehead to just above his ears. Willy Wehler was another Franconian. He and Martin began speaking in dialect almost at once. Willy was at a remove, however—he mispronounced words as though to be funny, and he would grin and look at me. This was to say that he knew better, and he knew that I knew. Martin and Willy hated Berlin. They sounded as if they had been dragged to Berlin against their will, like displaced persons. In their eyes the deepest failure of a certain political authority was that it had enticed peace-loving persons with false promises of work, homes, pensions, lives afloat like little boats at anchor; now these innocent provincials saw they had been tricked, and they were going back where they had started from. It was as simple to them as that—the equivalent of an insurance company's no longer meeting its obligations. Willy even described the life he would lead now in a quiet town, where, in sight of a cobbled square with a fountain and an equestrian statue, he planned to open a perfume-and-cosmetics shop; people wanted beauty now. He would live above the shop—he was not too proud for that—and every morning he would look down on his blue store awnings, over window boxes stuffed with frilled petunias. My stepfather heard this with tears in his eyes, but perhaps he was thinking of his two apartments and of Elke and the spitz. Willy's future seemed so real, so close at hand, that it was almost as though he had dropped in to say good-bye. He sat with his daughter on his knees, a baby not yet three. This little girl, whose name was Gisela, became a part of my life from that afternoon, and so did fat Willy, though none of us knew it then. The secret to which I had drunk my silent toast was a girl in France, who would be a middle-aged woman, beyond my imagining now, if she had lived. She died by jumping or accidentally falling out of a fifth-floor window in Paris. Her parents had locked her in a room when they found out she was corresponding with me.

This was still an afternoon in April in Berlin, the first of my freedom. It was one day after old Adolf's birthday, but that was not mentioned, not even in dialect or in the form of a Berlin joke. I don't think they were avoiding it; they had simply forgotten. They would always be astonished when other people turned out to have more specific memories of time and events.

This was the afternoon about which I would always say to myself, "I should have known," and even "I knew"—knew that I would marry the baby whose movements were already so willful and quick that her father complained, "We can't take her anywhere," and sat holding both her small hands in his; otherwise she would have clutched at every glass within reach. Her winged brows reminded me of the girl I wanted to see again. Gisela's eyes were amber in color, and luminous, with the whites so pure they seemed blue. The girl in France had eyes that resembled dark petals, opaque and velvety, and slightly tilted. She had black hair from a Corsican grandmother, and long fine lashes. Gisela's lashes were stubby and thick. I found that I was staring at the child's small ears and her small perfect teeth, thinking all the while of the other girl, whose smile had been spoiled by the malnutrition and the poor dentistry of the Occupation. I should have realized then, as I looked at Willy and his daughter, that some people never go without milk and eggs and apples, whatever the landscape, and that the sparse feast on our table had more to do with my mother's long habit of poverty—a kind of fatalistic incompetence that came from never having had enough money—than with a real shortage of food. Willy had on a white nylon shirt, which was a luxury then. Later, Martin would say to me, "That Willy! Out of a black uniform and into the black market before you could say 'democracy,'" but I never knew whether it was a common Berlin joke or something Martin had made up or the truth about Willy.

Gisela, who was either slow to speak for her age or only lazy, looked at me and said, "Man"—all she had to declare. Her hair was so silky and fine that it reflected the day as a curve of mauve light. She was all light and sheen, and she was the first person—I can even say the first *thing*—I had ever seen that was unflawed, without shadow. She was as whole and as innocent as a drop of water, and she was without guilt.

Her hands, released when her father drank from his wineglass, patted the tablecloth, seized a radish, tried to stuff it in his mouth.

My mother sat with her chair pushed back a few respectful inches. "Do you like children, Thomas?" she said. She knew nothing about me now except that I was not a child.

The French girl was sixteen when she came to Brittany on a holiday with her father and mother. The next winter she sent me books so that I would not drop too far behind in my schooling, and the second summer she came to my room. The door to the room was in a bend of the staircase, halfway between the pharmacy on the ground floor and the flat where my employers lived. They were supposed to keep me locked in this room when I wasn't working, but the second summer they forgot or could not be bothered, and in any case I had made a key with a piece of wire by then. It was the first room I'd had to myself. I whitewashed the walls and boxed in the store of potatoes they kept on the floor in a corner. Bunches of wild plants and herbs the druggist used in prescriptions hung from hooks in the ceiling. One whole wall was taken up with shelves of drying leaves and roots—walnut leaves for treating anemia, chamomile for fainting spells, thyme and rosemary for muscular cramps, and nettles and mint, sage and dandelions. The fragrance in the room and the view of the port from the window could have given me almost enough happiness for a lifetime, except that I was too young to find any happiness in that.

How she escaped from her parents the first afternoon I never knew, but she was a brave, careless girl and had already escaped from them often. They must have known what could happen when they locked that wild spirit into a place where the only way out was a window. Perhaps they were trying to see how far they could go with a margin of safety. She left a message for them: "To teach you a lesson." She must have thought she would be there and not there, lost to them and yet able to see the result. There was no message for me, except that it is a terrible thing to be alone; but I had already learned it. She must have knelt on the windowsill. The autumn rain must have caught her lashes and hair. She was already alien on the windowsill, beyond recognition.

I had made my room as neat for her as though I were expecting a military inspection. I wondered if she knew how serious it would be for both of us if we were caught. She glanced at the view, but only to see if anyone could look in on us, and she laughed, starting to take off her pullover, arms crossed; then stopped and said, "What is it—are you made of ice?" How could she know that I was retarded? I had known nothing except imagination and solitude, and the preying of old soldiers; and I was too old for one and repelled by the other. I thought she was about to commit the sacrifice of her person—her physical self and her immortal soul. I had heard the old men talking about women as if women were dirt, but needed for "that." One man said he would cut off an ear for "that." Another said he would swim the Atlantic. I thought she would lie in some way convenient to me and that she would feel nothing but a kind of sorrow, which would have made it a pure gift. But there was nothing to ask; it was not a gift. It was her decision and not a gift but an adventure. She hadn't come here to look at the harbor, she told me, when I hesitated. I may even have said no, and it might have been then that she smiled at me over crossed arms, pulling off her sweater, and said, "Are you made of ice?" For all her jauntiness, she thought she was deciding her life, though she continued to use the word "adventure." I think it was the only other word she knew for "love." But all we were settling was her death, and my life was decided in Berlin when Willy Wehler came in with a bottle of brandy and Gisela, who refused to say more than "Man." I can still see the lace curtains, the mark on the wallpaper, the china ornaments left by the people who had gone in such a hurry—the chimney sweep with his matchstick broom, the girl with bobbed orange hair sitting on a crescent moon, the dog with the ruff around his neck—and when I remember this I say to myself, "I must have known."

We finished two bottles of Martin's champagne, and then my mother jumped to her feet to remove the glasses and bring others so that we could taste Willy Wehler's brandy.

"The dirty Belgian is still hanging around," he said to Martin, gently rocking the child, who now had her thumb in her mouth.

"What does he want?" said my stepfather. He repeated the question; he was slow and he thought that other people, unless they reacted at once and with a show of feeling, could not hear him.

"He was in the Waffen-S.S.—he says. He complains that the girls here won't go out with him, though only five or six years ago they were like flies."

"They are afraid of him," came my mother's timid voice. "He stands in the court and stares...."

"I don't like men who look at pure young girls," said Willy Wehler. "He said to me, 'Help me; you owe me help.' He says he fought for us and nobody thanked him."

"He did? No wonder we lost," said Martin. I had already seen that the survivors of the war were divided into those who said they had always known how it would all turn out and those who said they had been indifferent. There are also those who like wars and those who do not. Martin had never been committed to winning or to losing or to anything—that explained his jokes. He had gained two apartments and one requisitioned flat in Berlin. He had lost a wife, but he often said to me later that people were better off out of this world.

"In Belgium he was in jail," said Willy. "He says he fought for us and then he was in jail and now we won't help him and the girls won't speak to him."

"Why is he here?" my stepfather suddenly shouted. "Who let him in? All this is his own affair, not ours." He rocked in his chair in a peculiar way, perhaps only imitating the gentle motion Willy made to keep Gisela asleep and quiet. "Nobody owes him anything," cried my stepfather, striking the table so that the little girl started and shuddered. My mother touched his arm and made a sort of humming sound, with her lips pressed together, that I took to be a signal between them, for he at once switched to another topic. It was a theme of conversation I was to hear about for many years after that afternoon. It was what the old men had to say when they were not boasting about women or their own past, and it was this: What should the Schörner army have done in Czechoslovakia to avoid capture by the Russians, and why did General Eisenhower (the villain of the story) refuse to help?

Eisenhower was my stepfather's left hand, General Schörner was his right, and the Russians were a plate of radishes. I turned very slightly to look at my mother. She had that sad cast of feature women have when their eyes are fixed nowhere. Her hand still lay lightly on Martin Toeppler's sleeve. I supposed then that he really was her husband and that they slept in the same bed. I had seen one or two closed doors in the passage on my way to the bath. Of my first prison camp, where everyone had been under eighteen or over forty, I remembered the smell of the old men—how they stopped being clean when there were no women to make them wash—and I remembered their long boasting. And yet, that April afternoon, as the sunlight of my first hours of freedom moved over the table and up along the brown wall, I did my boasting, too. I told about a prisoner I had captured. It seemed to be the thing I had to say to two men I had never seen before.

"He landed in a field just outside my grandmother's village," I told them. "I was fourteen. Three of us saw him—three boys. We had French rifles captured in the 1870 war. He'd had time to fold his parachute and he was sitting on it. I knew only one thing in English; it was 'Hands up.'"

My stepfather's mouth was open, as it had been when I first walked into the flat that day. My mother stood just out of sight.

"We advanced, pointing our 1870 rifles," I went on, droning, just like the old prisoners of war. "We all now said, 'Hands up.' The prisoner just—" I made the gesture the American had made, of chasing a fly away, and I realized I was drunk. "He didn't stand up. He had put everything he had on the ground—a revolver, a wad of German money, a handkerchief with a map of Germany, and some smaller things we couldn't identify at once. He had on civilian shoes with thick soles. He very slowly undid his watch and handed it over, but we had no ruling about that, so we said no. He put the watch on the ground next to the revolver and the map. Then he slowly got up and strolled into the village, with his hands in his pockets. He was chewing gum. I saw he had kept his cigarettes, but I didn't know the rule about that, either. We kept our guns trained on him. The schoolmaster ran out of my grandmother's guesthouse—everyone ran to stare. He was excited and kept saying in English, 'How do you do? How do you do?' but then an officer came running, too, and he was screaming, 'Why are you interfering? You may ask only one thing: Is he English or American.' The teacher was glad to show off his English, and he asked, 'Are you English or American?' and the American seemed to move his tongue all round his mouth before he answered. He was the first foreigner any of us had ever seen, and they took him away from us. We never saw him again."

That seemed all there was to it, but Martin's mouth was still open. I tried to remember more. "There was hell because we had left the gun and the other things on the ground. By the time they got out to the field, someone had stolen the parachute—probably for the cloth. We were in trouble over that, and we never got credit for having taken a prisoner. I went back to the field alone later on. I wanted to cry, for some reason—because it was over. He was from an adventure story to me. The whole war was a Karl May adventure, when I was fourteen and running around in school holidays with a gun. I found some small things in the field that had been overlooked—pills for keeping awake, pills in transparent envelopes. I had never seen that before. One envelope was called 'motion sickness.' It was a crime to keep anything, but I kept it anyway. I still had it when the Americans captured me, and they took it away. I had kept it because it was from another world. I would look at it and wonder. I kept it because of *The Last of the Mohicans*, because, because."

This was the longest story I had ever told in my life. I added, "My grandmother is dead now." My stepfather had finally shut his mouth. He looked at my mother as if to say that she had brought him a rival in the only domain that mattered—the right to talk everyone's ear off. My mother edged close to Willy Wehler and urged him to eat bread and cheese. She was still in the habit of wondering what the other person thought and how important he might be and how safe it was to speak. But Willy had not heard more than a sentence or two. That was plain from the way the expression on his face came slowly awake. He opened his eyes wide, as if to get sleep out of them, and—evidently imagining I had been talking about my life in France—said, "What were you paid as a prisoner?"

I had often wondered what the first question would be once I was home. Now I had it.

"Ha!" said my stepfather, giving the impression that he expected me to be caught out in a monstrous lie.

"One franc forty centimes a month for working here and there on a farm," I said. "But when I became a free worker with a druggist the official pay was three thousand francs a month, and that was what he gave me." I paused. "And of course I was fed and housed and had no laundry bills."

"Did you have bedsheets?" said my mother.

"With the druggist's family, always. I had one sheet folded in half. It was just right for a small cot."

"Was it the same sheet as the kind the family had?" she said, in the hesitant way that was part of her person now.

"They didn't buy sheets especially for me," I said. "I was treated fairly by the druggist, but not by the administration."

"Aha," said the two older men, almost together.

"The administration refused to pay my fare home," I said, looking down into my glass the way I had seen the men in prison camp stare at a fixed point when they were recounting a grievance.

"A prisoner of war has the right to be repatriated at administration expense. The administration would not pay my fare because I had stayed too long in France—but that was their mistake. I bought a ticket as far as Paris on the pay I had saved. The druggist sold me some old shoes and trousers and a jacket of his. My own things were in rags. In Paris I went to the YMCA. The YMCA was supposed to be in charge of prisoners' rights. The man wouldn't listen to me. If I had been left behind, then I was not a prisoner, he said; I was a tourist. It was his duty to help me. Instead of that, he informed the police." For the first time my voice took on the coloration of resentment. I knew that this complaint about a niggling matter of train fare made my whole adventure seem small, but I had become an old soldier. I remembered the police commissioner, with his thin lips and dirty nails, who said, "You should have been repatriated years ago, when you were sixteen."

"It was a mistake," I told him.

"Your papers are full of strange mistakes," he said, bending over them. "There, one capital error. An omission, a grave omission. What is your mother's maiden name?"

"Wickler," I said.

I watched him writing "W-i-e-c-k-l-a-i-r," slowly, with the tip of his tongue sticking out of the corner of his mouth as he wrote. "You have been here for something like five years with an incomplete dossier. And what about this? Who crossed it out?"

"I did. My father was not a pastry cook."

"You could be fined or even jailed for this," he said.

"My father was not a pastry cook," I said. "He had tuberculosis. He was not allowed to handle food."

Willy Wehler did not say what he thought of my story. Perhaps not having any opinion about injustice, even the least important, had become a habit of his, like my mother's of speaking through her fingers. He was on the right step of that staircase I've spoken of. Even the name he had given his daughter was a sign of his sensitivity to the times. Nobody wanted to hear the pagan, Old Germanic names anymore—Sigrun and Brunhilde and Sieglinde. Willy had felt the change. He would have called any daughter something neutral and pretty—Gisela, Marianne, Elisabeth—anytime after the battle of Stalingrad. All Willy ever had to do was sniff the air.

He pushed back his chair (in later years he would be able to push a table away with his stomach) and got to his feet. He had to tip his head to look up into my eyes. He said he wanted to give me advice that would be useful to me as a latehomecomer. His advice was to forget. "Forget everything," he said. "Forget, forget. That was what I said to my good neighbor Herr Silber when I bought his wife's topaz brooch and earrings before he emigrated to Palestine. I said, 'Dear Herr Silber, look forward, never back, and forget, forget, forget.'"

The child in Willy's arms was in the deepest of sleeps. Martin Toeppler followed his friend to the door, they whispered together; then the door closed behind both men.

"They have gone to have a glass of something at Herr Wehler's," said my mother. I saw now that she was crying quietly. She dried her eyes on her apron and began clearing the table of the homecoming feast. "Willy Wehler has been kind to us," she said. "Don't repeat that thing."

"About forgetting?"

"No, about the topaz brooch. It was a crime to buy anything from Jews."

"It doesn't matter now."

She lowered the tray she held and looked pensively out at the wrecked houses across the street. "If only people knew beforehand what was allowed," she said.

"My father is probably a hero now," I said.

"Oh, Thomas, don't travel too fast. We haven't seen the last of the changes. Yes, a hero. But too late for me. I've suffered too much."

"What does Martin think that he died of?"

"A working accident. He can understand that."

"You could have said consumption. He did have it." She shook her head. Probably she had not wanted Martin to imagine he could ever be saddled with two sickly stepsons. "Where do you and Martin sleep?"

"In the room next to the bathroom. Didn't you see it? You'll be comfortable here in the parlor. The couch pulls out. You can stay as long as you like. This is your home. A home for you and Chris." She said this so stubbornly that I knew some argument must have taken place between her and Martin.

I intended this room to be my home. There was no question about it in my mind. I had not yet finished high school; I had been taken out for anti-aircraft duty, then sent to the front. The role of adolescents in uniform had been to try to prevent the civilian population from surrendering. We were expected to die in the ruins together. When the women ran pillowcases up flagpoles, we shinnied up to drag them down. We were prepared to hold the line with our 1870 rifles until we saw the American tanks. There had not been tanks in our Karl May adventure stories, and the Americans, finally, were not out of *The Last of the Mohicans*. I told my mother that I had to go back to high school and then I would apply for a scholarship and take a degree in French. I would become a schoolmaster. French was all I had from my captivity; I might as well use it. I would earn money doing translations.

That cheered her up. She would not have to ask the ex-tram conductor too many favors. "Translations" and "scholarship" were an exalted form of language, to her. As a schoolmaster, I would have the most respectable job in the family, now that Uncle Gerhard was raising rabbits. "As long as it doesn't cost *him* too much," she said, as if she had to say it and yet was hoping I wouldn't hear.

It was not strictly true that all I had got out of my captivity was the ability to speak French. I had also learned to cook, iron, make beds, wait on table, wash floors, polish furniture, plant a vegetable garden, paint shutters. I wanted to help my mother in the kitchen now, but that shocked her. "Rest," she said, but I did not know what "rest" meant. "I've never seen a man drying a glass," she said, in apology. I wanted to tell her that while the roads and bridges of France were still waiting for someone to rebuild them I had been taught how to make a tomato salad by the druggist's wife; but I could not guess what the word "France" conveyed to her imagination. I began walking about the apartment. I looked in on a store cupboard, a water closet smelling of carbolic, the bathroom again, then a room containing a high bed, a brown wardrobe, and a table covered with newspapers bearing half a dozen of the flowerless spiky dull green plants my mother had always tended with so much devotion. I shut the door as if on a dark past, and I said to myself, I am free. This is the beginning of life. It is also the start of the good half of a rotten century. Everything ugly and corrupt and vicious is behind us. My thoughts were not exactly in those words, but something like them. I said to myself, This apartment has a musty smell, an old and dirty smell that sinks into clothes. After a time I shall probably smell like the dark parlor. The smell must be in the cushions, in the bed that pulls out, in the lace curtains. It is a smell that creeps into nightclothes. The blankets will be permeated. I thought, I shall get used to the smell, and the smell of burning in the stone outside. The view of ruins will be my view. Every day on my way home from school I shall walk over Elke. I shall get used to the wood staircase, the bellpull, the polished nameplate, the white enamel fuses in the hall—my mother had said, "When you want light in the parlor you give the center fuse in the lower row a half turn." I looked at a framed drawing of cartoon people with puffy hair. A strong wind had blown their umbrella inside out. They would be part of my view, like the ruins. I took in the ancient gas bracket in the kitchen and the stone sink. My mother, washing glasses without soap, smiled at me, forgetting to hide her teeth. I reexamined the tiled stove in the parlor, the wood and the black briquettes that would be next to my head at night, and the glass-fronted cabinet full of the china ornaments God had selected to survive the Berlin air raids. These would be removed to make way for my books. For Martin Toeppler need not imagine he could count on my pride, or that I would prefer to starve rather than take his charity, or that I was too arrogant to sleep on his dusty sofa. I would wear out his soap, borrow his shirts, spread his butter on my bread. I would hang on Martin like an octopus. He had a dependent now—a ravenous, egocentric, latehomecoming high school adolescent of twenty-one. The old men owed this much to me—the old men in my prison camp who would have sold mother and father for an extra ounce of soup, who had already sold their children for it; the old men who had fouled my idea of women; the old men in the bunkers who had let the girls defend them in Berlin; the old men who had dared to survive.

The bed that pulled out was sure to be all lumps. I had slept on worse. Would it be wide enough for Chris, too?

People in the habit of asking themselves silent useless questions look for answers in mirrors. My hair was blond again now that it had dried. I looked less like my idea of my father. I tried to see the reflection of the man who had gone out in the middle of the night and who never came back. You don't go out alone to tear down election posters in a village where nobody thinks as you do—not unless you *want* to be stabbed in the back. So the family had said.

"You were well out of it," I said to the shadow that floated on the glass panel of the china cabinet, though it would not be my father's again unless I could catch it unaware.

I said to myself, It is quieter than France. They keep their radios low.

In captivity I had never suffered a pain except for the cramps of hunger the first years, which had been replaced by a scratching, morbid anxiety, and the pain of homesickness, which takes you in the stomach and the throat. Now I felt the first of the real pains that were to follow me like little dogs for the rest of my life, perhaps: The first compressed my knee, the second tangled the nerves at the back of my neck. I discovered that my eyes were sensitive and that it hurt to blink.

This was the hour when, in Brittany, I would begin peeling the potatoes for dinner. I had seen food my mother had never heard of— oysters, and artichokes. My mother had never seen a harbor or a sea.

My American prisoner had left his immediate life spread on an alien meadow—his parachute, his revolver, his German money. He had strolled into captivity with his hands in his pockets.

"I know what you are thinking," said my mother, who was standing behind me. "I know that you are judging me. If you could guess what my life has been—the whole story, not only the last few years—you wouldn't be hard on me."

I turned too slowly to meet her eyes. It was not what I had been thinking. I had forgotten about her, in that sense.

"No, no, nothing like that," I said. I still did not touch her. What I had been moving along to in my mind was: Why am I in this place? Who sent me here? Is it a form of justice or injustice? How long does it last?

"Now we can wait together for Chris," she said. She seemed young and happy all at once. "Look, Thomas. A new moon. Bow to it three times. Wait—you must have something silver in your hand." I saw that she was hurrying to finish with this piece of nonsense before Martin came back. She rummaged in the china cabinet and brought out a silver napkin ring—left behind by the vanished tenants, probably. The name on it was "Meta"—no one we knew. "Bow to the moon and hold it and make your wish," she said. "Quickly."

"You first."

She wished, I am sure, for my brother. As for me, I wished that I was a few hours younger, in the corridor of a packed train, clutching the top of the open window, my heart hammering as I strained to find the one beloved face.

IRINA

ONE OF IRINA'S GRANDSONS, nicknamed Riri, was sent to her at Christmas. His mother was going into hospital, but nobody told him that. The real cause of his visit was that since Irina had become a widow her children worried about her being alone. The children, as Irina would call them forever, were married and in their thirties and forties. They did not think they were like other people, because their father had been a powerful old man. He was a Swiss writer, Richard Notte. They carried his reputation and the memory of his puritan equity like an immense jar filled with water of which they had been told not to spill a drop. They loved their mother, but they had never needed to think about her until now. They had never fretted about which way her shadow might fall, and whether to stay in the shade or get out by being eccentric and bold. There were two sons and three daughters, with fourteen children among them. Only Riri was an only child. The girls had married an industrial designer, a Lutheran minister (perhaps an insolent move, after all, for the daughter of a militant atheist), and an art historian in Paris. One boy had become a banker and the other a lecturer on Germanic musical tradition. These were the crushed sons and loyal daughters to whom Irina had been faithful, whose pictures had traveled with her and lived beside her bed.

Few of Notte's obituaries had even mentioned a family. Some of his literary acquaintances were surprised to learn there had been any children at all, though everyone paid homage to the soft, quiet wife to whom he had dedicated his books, the subject of his first rapturous poems. These poems, conventional verse for the most part, seldom translated out of German except by unpoetical research scholars, were thought to be the work of his youth. Actually, Notte was forty when he finally married, and Irina barely nineteen. The obituaries called Notte the last of a breed, the end of a Tolstoyan line of moral lightning rods—an extinction which was probably hard on those writers who came after him, and still harder on his children. However, even to his family the old man had appeared to be the very archetype of a respected European novelist—prophet, dissuader, despairingly opposed to evil, crack-voiced after having made so many pronouncements. Otherwise, he was not all that typical as a Swiss or as a Western, liberal, Protestant European, for he neither saved, nor invested, nor hid, nor disguised his material returns.

"What good is money, except to give away?" he often said. He had a wife, five children, and an old secretary who had turned into a dependent. It was true that he claimed next to nothing for himself. He rented shabby, ramshackle houses impossible to heat or even to clean. Owning was against his convictions, and he did not want to be tied to a gate called home. His room was furnished with a cot, a lamp, a desk, two chairs, a map of the world, a small bookshelf—no more, not even carpets or curtains. Like his family, he wore thick sweaters indoors as out, and crouched over inadequate electric fires. He seldom ate meat—though he did not deprive his children—and drank water with his meals. He had married once—once and for all. He could on occasion enjoy wine and praise and restaurants and good-looking women, but these festive outbreaks were on the rim of his real life, as remote from his children—as strange and as distorted to them—as some other country's colonial wars. He grew old early, as if he expected old age to suit him. By sixty, his eyes were sunk in pockets of lizard skin. His hair became bleached and lustrous, like the scrap of wedding dress Irina kept in a jeweler's box. He was photographed wearing a dark suit and a woman's plaid shawl—he was always cold by then, even in summer—and with a rakish felt hat shading half his face. His wife still let a few photographers in, at the end—but not many. Her murmured "He is working" had for decades been a double lock. He was as strong as Rasputin, his enemies said; he went on writing and talking and traveling until he positively could not focus his eyes or be helped aboard a train. Nearly to the last, he and Irina swung off on their seasonal cycle of journeys to Venice, to Rome, to cities where their married children lived, to Liège and Oxford for awards and honors. His place in a hotel dining room was recognizable from the door because of the pills, drops, and powders lined up to the width of a dinner plate. Notte's hypochondria had been known and gently caricatured for years. His sons, between them, had now bought up most of the original drawings: Notte, in infant's clothing, downing his medicine like a man (he had missed the Nobel); Notte quarreling with Aragon and throwing up Surrealism; a grim female figure called "Existentialism" taking his pulse; Notte catching Asian flu on a cultural trip to Peking. During the final months of his life his children noticed that their mother had begun acquiring medicines of her own, as if hoping by means of mirror-magic to draw his ailments into herself.

If illness became him, it was only because he was fond of ritual, the children thought—even the hideous ceremonial of pain. But Irina had not been intended for sickness and suffering; she was meant to be burned dry and consumed by the ritual of him. The children believed that the end of his life would surely be the death of their mother. They did not really expect Irina to turn her face to the wall and die, but an exclusive, even a selfish, alliance with Notte had seemed her reason for being. As their father grew old, then truly old, then old in mind, and querulous, and unjust, they observed the patient tenderness with which she heeded his sulks and caprices, his almost insane commands. They supposed this ardent submission of hers had to do with love, but it was not a sort of love they had ever experienced or tried to provoke. One of his sons saw Notte crying because Irina had buttered toast for him when he wanted it dry. She stroked the old man's silky hair, smiling. The son hated this. Irina was diminishing a strong, proud man, making a senile child of him, just as Notte was enslaving and debasing her. At the same time the son felt a secret between the two, a mystery. He wondered then, but at no other time, if the secret might not be Irina's invention and property.

Notte left a careful will for such an unworldly person. His wife was to be secure in her lifetime. Upon her death the residue of income from his work would be shared among the sons and daughters. There were no gifts or bequests. The will was accompanied by a testament which the children had photocopied for the beauty of the handwriting and the charm of the text. Irina, it began, belonged to a generation of women shielded from decisions, allowed to grow in the sun and shade of male protection. This flower, his flower, he wrote, was to be cherished now as if she were her children's child.

"In plain words," said Irina, at the first reading, in a Zurich lawyer's office, "I am the heir." She was wearing dark glasses because her eyes were tired, and a tight hat. She looked tense and foreign.

Well, yes, that was it, although Notte had put it more gracefully. His favorite daughter was his literary executor, entrusted with the unfinished manuscripts and the journals he had kept for sixty-five years. But it soon became evident that Irina had no intention of giving these up. The children adored their mother, but even without love as a factor would not have made a case of it; Notte's lawyer had already told them about disputes ending in maze-like litigation, families sundered, contents of a desk sequestered, diaries rotting in bank vaults while the inheritors thrashed it out. Besides, editing Notte's papers would keep Irina busy and an occupation was essential now. In loving and unloving families alike, the same problem arises after a death: What to do about the widow?

Irina settled some of it by purchasing an apartment in a small Alpine town. She chose a tall, glassy, urban-looking building of the kind that made conservationist groups send round-robin letters, accompanied by incriminating photographs, to newspapers in Lausanne. The apartment had a hall, an up-to-date kitchen, a bedroom for Irina, a spare room with a narrow bed in it, one bathroom, and a living room containing a couch. There was a glassed-in cube of a balcony where in a pinch an extra cot might have fitted, but Irina used the space for a table and chairs. She ordered red lampshades and thick curtains and the pale furniture that is usually sold to young couples. She seemed to come into her own in that tight, neutral flat, the children thought. They read some of the interviews she gave, and approved: She said, in English and Italian, in German and French, that she would not be a literary widow, detested by critics, resented by Notte's readers. Her firm diffidence made the children smile, and they were proud to read about her dignified beauty. But as for her intelligence—well, they supposed that the interviewers had confused fluency with wit. Irina's views and her way of expressing them were all camouflage, simply part of a ladylike undereducation, long on languages and bearing, short on history and arithmetic. Her origins were Russian and Swiss and probably pious; the children had not been drawn to that side of the family. Their father's legendary peasant childhood, his isolated valley-village had filled their imaginations and their collective past. There was a sudden April lightness in her letters now that relieved and yet troubled them. They knew it was a sham happiness. Nature's way of protecting the survivor from immediate grief. The crisis would come later, when her most secret instincts had built a seawall. They took turns invading her at Easter and in the summer, one couple at a time, bringing a child apiece—there was no room for more. Winter was a problem, however, for the skiing was not good just there, and none of them liked to break up their families at Christmastime. Not only was Irina's apartment lacking in beds but there was absolutely no space for a tree. Finally, she offered to visit them, in regular order. That was how they settled it. She went to Bern, to Munich, to Zurich, and then came the inevitable Christmas when it was not that no one wanted her but just that they were all doing different things.

She had written in November of that year that a friend, whom she described, with some quaintness, as "a person," had come for a long stay. They liked that. A visit meant winter company, lamps on at four, China tea, conversation, the peppery smell of carnations (her favorite flower) in a warm room. For a week or two of the visit her letters were blithe, but presently they noticed that "the person" seemed to be having a depressing effect on their mother. She wrote that she had been working on Notte's journals for three years now. Who would want to read them except old men and women? His moral and political patterns were fossils of liberalism. He had seen the cracks in the Weimar Republic. He had understood from the beginning what Hitler meant. If at first he had been wrong about Mussolini, he had changed his mind even before Croce changed his, and had been safely back on the side of democracy in time to denounce Pirandello. He had given all he could, short of his life, to the Spanish Republicans. His measure of Stalin had been so wise and unshakably just that he had never been put on the Communist index—something rare for a Western Socialist. No one could say, ever, that Notte had hedged or retreated or kept silent when a voice was needed. Well, said Irina, what of it? He had written, pledged, warned, signed, declared. And what had he changed, diverted, or stopped? She suddenly sent the same letter to all five children: "This Christmas I don't want to go anywhere. I intend to stay here, in my own home."

They knew this was the crisis and that they must not leave her to face it alone, but that was the very winter when all their plans ran down, when one daughter was going into hospital, another moving to a different city, the third probably divorcing. The elder son was committed to a Christmas with his wife's parents, the younger lecturing in South Africa—a country where Irina, as Notte's constant reflection, would certainly not wish to set foot. They wrote and called and cabled one another: What shall we do? Can you? Will you? I can't.

Irina had no favorites among her children, except possibly one son who had been ill with rheumatic fever as a child and required long nursing. To him she now confided that she longed for her own childhood sometimes, in order to avoid having to judge herself. She was homesick for a time when nothing had crystallized and mistakes were allowed. Now, in old age, she had no excuse for errors. Every thought had a long meaning; every motive had angles and corners, and could be measured. And yet whatever she saw and thought and attempted was still fluid and vague. The shape of a table against afternoon light still held a mystery, awaited a final explanation. You looked for clarity, she wrote, and the answer you had was paleness, the flat white cast that a snowy sky throws across a room.

Part of this son knew about death and dying, but the rest of him was a banker and thoroughly active. He believed that, given an ideal situation, one should be able to walk through a table, which would save time and roundabout decisions. However, like all of Notte's children he had been raised with every awareness of solid matter too. His mother's youthful, yearning, and probably religious letter made him feel bland and old. He told his wife what he thought it contained, and she told a sister-in-law what she thought he had said. Irina was tired. Her eyesight was poor, perhaps as a result of prolonged work on those diaries. Irina did not need adult company, which might lead to morbid conversation; what she craved now was a symbol of innocent, continuing life. An animal might do it. Better still, a child.

Riri did not know that his mother would be in hospital the minute his back was turned. Balanced against a tame Christmas with a grandmother was a midterm holiday, later, of high-altitude skiing with his father. There was also some further blackmail involving his holiday homework, and then the vague state of behavior called "being reasonable"—that was all anyone asked. They celebrated a token Christmas on the twenty-third, and the next day he packed his presents (a watch and a tape recorder) and was put on a plane at Orly West. He flew from Paris to Geneva, where he spent the real Christmas Eve in a strange, bare apartment into which an aunt and a large family of cousins had just moved. In the morning he was wakened when it was dark and taken to a six o'clock train. He said good-bye to his aunt at the station, and added, "If you ask the conductor or anyone to look after me, I'll—" Whatever threat was in his mind he seemed ready to carry out. He wore an RAF badge on his jacket and carried a Waffen-S.S. emblem in his pocket. He knew better than to keep it in sight. At home they had already taken one away but he had acquired another at school. He had Astérix comic books for reading, chocolate-covered hazelnuts for support, and his personal belongings in a fairly large knapsack. He made a second train on his own and got down at the right station.

He had been told that he knew this place, but his memory, if it was a memory, had to do with fields and a picnic. No one met him. He shared a taxi through soft snow with two women, and paid his share—actually more than his share, which annoyed the women; they could not give less than a child in the way of a tip. The taxi let him off at a dark, shiny tower on stilts with granite steps. In the lobby a marble panel, looking like the list of names of war dead in his school, gave him his grandmother on the eighth floor. The lift, like the façade of the building, was made of dark mirrors into which he gazed seriously. A dense, thoughtful person looked back. He took off his glasses and the blurred face became even more remarkable. His grandmother had both a bell and a knocker at her door. He tried both. For quite a long time nothing happened. He knocked and rang again. It was not nervousness that he felt but a new sensation that had to do with a shut, foreign door.

His grandmother opened the door a crack. She had short white hair and a pale face and blue eyes. She held a dressing gown gripped at the collar. She flung the door back and cried, "Darling Richard, I thought you were arriving much later. Oh," she said, "I must look dreadful to you. Imagine finding me like this, in my dressing gown!" She tipped her head away and talked between her fingers, as he had been told never to do, because only liars cover their mouths. He saw a dark hall and a bright kitchen that was in some disorder, and a large, dark, curtained room opposite the kitchen. This room smelled stuffy, of old cigarettes and of adults. But then his grandmother pushed the draperies apart and wound up the slatted shutters, and what had been dark, moundlike objects turned into a couch and a bamboo screen and a round table and a number of chairs. On a bookshelf stood a painting of three tulips that must have fallen out of their vase. Behind them was a sky that was all black except for a rainbow. He unpacked a portion of the things in his knapsack—wrapped presents for his grandmother, his new tape recorder, two school textbooks, a notebook, a Bic pen. The start of this Christmas lay hours behind him and his breakfast had died long ago.

"Are you hungry?" said his grandmother. He heard a telephone ringing as she brought him a cup of hot milk with a little coffee in it and two fresh croissants on a plate. She was obviously someone who never rushed to answer any bell. "My friend, who is an early riser, even on Christmas Day, went out and got these croissants. Very bravely, I thought." He ate his new breakfast, dipping the croissants in the milk, and heard his grandmother saying, "Well, I must have misunderstood. But he managed.... He didn't bring his skis. Why not? ... I see." By the time she came back he had a book open. She watched him for a second and said, "Do you read at meals at home?"

"Sometimes."

"That's not the way I brought up your mother."

He put his nose nearer the page without replying. He read aloud from the page in a soft schoolroom plainchant: "'Go, went, gone. Stand, stood, stood. Take, took, taken.'"

"Richard," said his grandmother. When he did not look up at once, she said, "I know what they call you at home, but what are you called in school?"

"Riri."

"I have three Richard grandsons," she said, "and not one is called Richard exactly."

"I have an Uncle Richard," he said.

"Yes, well, he happens to be a son of mine. I never allowed nicknames. Have you finished your breakfast?"

"Yes."

"Yes who? Yes what? What is your best language, by the way?"

"I am French," he said, with a sharp, sudden, hard hostility, the first tense bud of it, that made her murmur, "So soon?" She was about to tell him that he was not French—at least, not really—when an old man came into the room. He was thin and walked with a cane.

"Alec, this is my grandson," she said. "Riri, say how do you do to Mr. Aiken, who was kind enough to go out in this morning's snow to buy croissants for us all."

"I knew he would be here early," said the old man, in a stiff French that sounded extremely comical to the boy. "Irina has an odd ear for times and trains." He sat down next to Riri and clasped his hands on his cane; his hands at once began to tremble violently. "What does that interesting-looking book tell you?" he asked.

"'The swallow flew away,'" answered Irina, reading over the child's head. "'The swallow flew away with my hopes.'"

"Good God, let me look at that!" said the old man in his funny French. Sure enough, those were the words, and there was a swallow of a very strange blue, or at least a sapphire-and-turquoise creature with a swallow's tail. Riri's grandmother took her spectacles out of her dressing-gown pocket and brought the book up close and said in a loud, solemn way, "'The swallows will have flown away.'" Then she picked up the tape recorder, which was the size of a glasses case, and after snapping the wrong button on and off, causing agonizing confusion and wastage, she said with her mouth against it, "'When shall the swallows have flown away?'"

"No," said Riri, reaching, snatching almost. As if she had always given in to men, even to male children, she put the book down and the recorder too, saying, "Mr. Aiken can help with your English. He has the best possible accent. When he says 'the girl' you will think he is saying 'de Gaulle.'"

"Irina has an odd ear for English," said the old man calmly. He got up slowly and went to the kitchen, and she did too, and Riri could hear them whispering and laughing at something. Mr. Aiken came back alone carrying a small glass of clear liquid. "The morning heart-starter," he said. "Try it." Riri took a sip. It lay in his stomach like a warm stone. "No more effect on you than a gulp of milk," said the old man, marveling, sitting down close to Riri again. "You could probably do with pints of this stuff. I can tell by looking at you you'll be a drinking man." His hands on the walking stick began to tremble anew. "I'm not the man I was," he said. "Not by any means." Because he did not speak English with a French or any foreign accent, Riri could not really understand him. He went on, "Fell down the staircase at the Trouville casino. Trouville, or that other place. Shock gave me amnesia. Hole in the stair carpet—must have been. I went there for years," he said. "Never saw a damned hole in anything. Now my hands shake."

"When you lift your glass to drink they don't shake," called Riri's grandmother from the kitchen. She repeated this in French, for good measure.

"She's got an ear like a radar unit," said Mr. Aiken.

Riri took up his tape recorder. In a measured chant, as if demonstrating to his grandmother how these things should be done, he said, "'The swallows would not fly away if the season is fine.'"

"Do you know what any of it means?" said Mr. Aiken.

"He doesn't need to know what it means," Riri's grandmother answered for him. "He just needs to know it by heart."

They were glassed in on the balcony. The only sound they could hear was of their own voices. The sun on them was so hot that Riri wanted to take off his sweater. Looking down, he saw a chalet crushed in the shadows of two white blocks, not so tall as their own. A large, spared spruce tree suddenly seemed to retract its branches and allow a great weight of snow to slip off. Cars went by, dogs barked, children called—all in total silence. His grandmother talked English to the old man. Riri, when he was not actually eating, read *Astérix in Brittany* without attracting her disapproval.

"If people can be given numbers, like marks in school," she said, "then children are zero." She was enveloped in a fur cloak, out of which her hands and arms emerged as if the fur had dissolved in certain places. She was pink with wine and sun. The old man's blue eyes were paler than hers. "Zero." She held up thumb and forefinger in an O. "I was there with my five darling zeros while he ... You are probably wondering if I was *ever* happy. At the beginning, in the first days, when I thought he would give me interesting books to read, books that would change all my life. Riri," she said, shading her eyes, "the cake and the ice cream were, I am afraid, the end of things for the moment. Could I ask you to clear the table for me?"

"I don't at home." Nevertheless he made a wobbly pile of dishes and took them away and did not come back. They heard him, indoors, starting all over: "'Go, went, gone.'"

"I have only half a memory for dates," she said. "I forget my children's birthdays until the last minute and have to send them telegrams. But I know *that* day...."

"The twenty-sixth of May," he said. "What I forget is the year."

"I know that I felt young."

"You were. You *are* young," he said.

"Except that I was forty if a day." She glanced at the hands and wrists emerging from her cloak as if pleased at their whiteness. "The river was so sluggish, I remember. And the willows trailed in the river."

"Actually, there was a swift current after the spring rains."

"But no wind. The clouds were heavy."

"It was late in the afternoon," he said. "We sat on the grass."

"On a raincoat. You had thought in the morning those clouds meant rain."

"A young man drowned," he said. "Fell out of a boat. Funny, he didn't try to swim. So people kept saying."

"We saw three firemen in gleaming metal helmets. They fished for him so languidly—the whole day was like that. They had a grappling hook. None of them knew what to do with it. They kept pulling it up and taking the rope from each other."

"They might have been after water lilies, from the look of them."

"One of them bailed out the boat with a blue saucepan. I remember that. They'd got that saucepan from the restaurant."

"Where we had lunch," he said. "Trout, and a coffee cream pudding. You left yours."

"It was soggy cake. But the trout was perfection. So was the wine. The bridge over the river filled up slowly with holiday people. The three firemen rowed to shore."

"Yes, and one of them went off on a shaky bicycle and came back with a coil of frayed rope on his shoulders."

"The railway station was just behind us. All those people on the bridge were waiting for a train. When the firemen's boat slipped off down the river, they moved without speaking from one side of the bridge to the other, just to watch the boat. The silence of it."

"Like the silence here."

"This is planned silence," she said.

Riri played back his own voice. A tinny, squeaky Riri said, "'Go, went, gone. Eat, ate, eaten. See, saw, sen.'"

"'Seen'!" called his grandmother from the balcony. "'Seen,' not 'sen.' His mother made exactly that mistake," she said to the old man. "Oh, stop that," she said. He was crying. "Please, please stop that. How could I have left five children?"

"Three were grown," he gasped, wiping his eyes.

"But they didn't know it. They didn't know they were grown. They still don't know it. And it made six children, counting him."

"The secretary mothered him," he said. "All he needed."

"I know, but you see she wasn't his wife, and he liked saying to strangers 'my wife,' 'my wife this,' 'my wife that.' What is it, Riri? Have you come to finish doing the thing I asked?"

He moved close to the table. His round glasses made him look desperate and stern. He said, "Which room is mine!" Darkness had gathered round him in spite of the sparkling sky and a row of icicles gleaming and melting in the most dazzling possible light. Outrage, a feeling that consideration had been wanting—that was how homesickness had overtaken him. She held his hand (he did not resist—another sign of his misery) and together they explored the apartment. He saw it all—every picture and cupboard and doorway—and in the end it was he who decided that Mr. Aiken must keep the spare room and he, Riri, would be happy on the living-room couch.

The old man passed them in the hall; he was obviously about to rest on the very bed he had just been within an inch of losing. He carried a plastic bottle of Evian. "Do you like the bland taste of water?" he said.

Riri looked boldly at his grandmother and said, "Yes," bursting into unexplained and endless-seeming laughter. He seemed to feel a relief at this substitute for impertinence. The old man laughed too, but broke off, coughing.

At half past four, when the windows were as black as the sky in the painting of tulips and began to reflect the lamps in a disturbing sort of way, they drew the curtains and had tea around the table. They pushed Riri's books and belongings to one side and spread a cross-stitched tablecloth. Riri had hot chocolate, a croissant left from breakfast and warmed in the oven, which made it deliciously greasy and soft, a slice of lemon sponge cake, and a banana. This time he helped clear away and even remained in the kitchen, talking, while his grandmother rinsed the cups and plates and stacked them in the machine.

The old man sat on a chair in the hall struggling with snow boots. He was going out alone in the dark to post some letters and to buy a newspaper and to bring back whatever provisions he thought were required for the evening meal.

"Riri, do you want to go with Mr. Aiken? Perhaps you should have a walk."

"At home I don't have to."

His grandmother looked cross; no, she looked worried. She was biting something back. The old man had finished the contention with his boots and now he put on a scarf, a fur-lined coat, a fur hat with earflaps, woolen gloves, and he took a list and a shopping bag and a different walking stick, which looked something like a ski pole. His grandmother stood still, as if dreaming, and then (addressing Riri) decided to wash all her amber necklaces. She fetched a wicker basket from her bedroom. It was lined with orange silk and filled with strings of beads. Riri followed her to the bathroom and sat on the end of the tub. She rolled up her soft sleeves and scrubbed the amber with laundry soap and a stiff brush. She scrubbed and rinsed and then began all over again.

"I am good at things like this," she said. "Now, unless you hate to discuss it, tell me something about your school."

At first he had nothing to say, but then he told her how stupid the younger boys were and what they were allowed to get away with.

"The younger boys would be seven, eight?" Yes, about that. "A hopeless generation?"

He wasn't sure; he knew that his class had been better.

She reached down and fetched a bottle of something from behind the bathtub and they went back to the sitting room together. They put a lamp between them, and Irina began to polish the amber with cotton soaked in turpentine. After a time the amber began to shine. The smell made him homesick, but not unpleasantly. He carefully selected a necklace when she told him he might take one for his mother, and he rubbed it with a soft cloth. She showed him how to make the beads magnetic by rolling them in his palms.

"You can do that even with plastic," he said.

"Can you? How very sad. It is dead matter."

"Amber is too," he said politely.

"What do you want to be later on? A scientist?"

"A ski instructor." He looked all round the room, at the shelves and curtains and at the bamboo folding screen, and said, "If you didn't live here, who would?"

She replied, "If you see anything that pleases you, you may keep it. I want you to choose your own present. If you don't see anything, we'll go out tomorrow and look in the shops. Does that suit you?" He did not reply. She held the necklace he had picked and said, "Your mother will remember seeing this as I bent down to kiss her good night. Do you like old coins? One of my sons was a collector." In the wicker basket was a lacquered box that contained his uncle's coin collection. He took a coin but it meant nothing to him; he let it fall. It clinked, and he said, "We have a dog now." The dog wore a metal tag that rang when the dog drank out of a china bowl. Through a sudden rainy blur of new homesickness he saw that she had something else, another lacquered box, full of old canceled stamps. She showed him a stamp with Hitler and one with an Italian king. "I've kept funny things," she said. "Like this beautiful Russian box. It belonged to my grandmother, but after I have died I expect it will be thrown out. I gave whatever jewelry I had left to my daughters. We never had furniture, so I became attached to strange little baskets and boxes of useless things. My poor daughters—I had precious little to give. But they won't be able to wear rings any more than I could. We all come into our inherited arthritis, these knotted-up hands. Our true heritage. When I was your age, about, my mother was dying of … I wasn't told. She took a ring from under her pillow and folded my hand on it. She said that I could always sell it if I had to, and no one need know. You see, in those days women had nothing of their own. They were like brown paper parcels tied with string. They were handed like parcels from their fathers to their husbands. To make the parcel look attractive it was decked with curls and piano lessons, and rings and gold coins and banknotes and shares. After appraising all the decoration, the new owner would undo the knots."

"Where is that ring?" he said. The blur of tears was forgotten.

"I tried to sell it when I needed money. The decoration on the brown paper parcel was disposed of by then. Everything thrown, given away. Not by me. My pearl necklace was sold for Spanish refugees. Victims, flotsam, the injured, the weak—they were important. I wasn't. The children weren't. I had my ring. I took it to a municipal pawnshop. It is a place where you take things and they give you money. I wore dark glasses and turned up my coat collar, like a spy." He looked as though he understood that. "The man behind the counter said that I was a married woman and I needed my husband's written consent. I said the ring was mine. He said nothing could be mine, or something to that effect. Then he said he might have given me something for the gold in the band of the ring but the stones were worthless. He said this happened in the finest of families. Someone had pried the real stones out of their setting."

"Who did that?"

"A husband. Who else would? Someone's husband—mine, or my mother's or my mother's mother's, when it comes to that."

"With a knife?" said Riri. He said, "The man might have been pretending. Maybe he took out the stones and put in glass."

"There wasn't time. And they were perfect imitations—the right shapes and sizes."

"He might have had glass stones all different sizes."

"The women in the family never wondered if men were lying," she said. "They never questioned being dispossessed. They were taught to think that lies were a joke on the liar. That was why they lost out. He gave me the price of the gold in the band, as a favor, and I left the ring there. I never went back."

He put the lid on the box of stamps, and it fitted; he removed it, put it back, and said, "What time do you turn on your TV?"

"Sometimes never. Why?"

"At home I have it from six o'clock."

The old man came in with a pink-and-white face, bearing about him a smell of cold and of snow. He put down his shopping bag and took things out—chocolate and bottles and newspapers. He said, "I had to go all the way to the station for the papers. There is only one shop open, and even then I had to go round to the back door."

"I warned you that today was Christmas," Irina said.

Mr. Aiken said to Riri, "When I was still a drinking man this was the best hour of the day. If I had a glass now, I could put ice in it. Then I might add water. Then if I had water I could add whiskey. I know it is all the wrong way around, but at least I've started with a glass."

"You had wine with your lunch and gin instead of tea and I believe you had straight gin before lunch," she said, gathering up the beads and coins and the turpentine and making the table Riri's domain again.

"Riri drank that," he said. It was so obviously a joke that she turned her head and put the basket down and covered her laugh with her fingers, as she had when she'd opened the door to him—oh, a long time ago now.

"I haven't a drop of anything left in the house," she said. That didn't matter, the old man said, for he had found what he needed. Riri watched and saw that when he lifted his glass his hand did not tremble at all. What his grandmother had said about that was true.

They had early supper and then Riri, after a courageous try at keeping awake, gave up even on television and let her make his bed of scented sheets, deep pillows, a feather quilt. The two others sat for a long time at the table, with just one lamp, talking in low voices. She had a pile of notebooks from which she read aloud and sometimes she showed Mr. Aiken things. He could see them through the chinks in the bamboo screen. He watched the lamp shadows for a while and then it was as if the lamp had gone out and he slept deeply.

The room was full of mound shapes, as it had been that morning when he arrived. He had not heard them leave the room. His Christmas watch had hands that glowed in the dark. He put on his glasses. It was half past ten. His grandmother was being just a bit loud at the telephone; that was what had woken him up. He rose, put on his slippers, and stumbled out to the bathroom.

"Just answer yes or no," she was saying. "No, he can't. He has been asleep for an hour, two hours, at least.... Don't lie to me—I am bound to find the truth out. Was it a tumor? An extrauterine pregnancy? ... Well, look.... Was she or was she not pregnant? What can you mean by 'not exactly'? If you don't know, who will?"

She happened to turn her head, and saw him and said without a change of tone, "Your son is here, in his pajamas; he wants to say good night to you."

She gave up the telephone and immediately went away so that the child could talk privately. She heard him say, "I drank some kind of alcohol."

So that was the important part of the day: not the journey, not the necklace, not even the strange old guest with the comic accent. She could tell from the sound of the child's voice that he was smiling. She picked up his bathrobe, went back to the hall, and put it over his shoulders. He scarcely saw her: He was concentrated on the distant voice. He said, in a matter-of-fact way, "All right, goodbye," and hung up.

"What a lot of things you have pulled out of that knapsack," she said.

"It's a large one. My father had it for military service."

Now, why should that make him suddenly homesick when his father's voice had not? "You are good at looking after yourself," she said. "Independent. No one has to tell you what to do. Of course, your mother had sound training. Once when I was looking for a nurse for your mother and her sisters, a great peasant woman came to see me, wearing a black apron and black buttoned boots. I said, 'What can you teach children?' And she said, 'To be clean and polite.' Your grandfather said, 'Hire her,' and stamped out of the room."

His mother interested, his grandfather bored him. He had the Christian name of a dead old man.

"You will sleep well," his grandmother promised, pulling the feather quilt over him. "You will dream short dreams at first, and by morning they will be longer and longer. The last one of all just before you wake up will be like a film. You will wake up wondering where you are, and then you will hear Mr. Aiken. First he will go round shutting all the windows, then you will hear his bath. He will start the coffee in an electric machine that makes a noise like a door rattling. He will pull on his snow boots with a lot of cursing and swearing and go out to fetch our croissants and the morning papers. Do you know what day it will be? The day after Christmas." He was almost asleep. Next to his watch and his glasses on a table close to the couch was an Astérix book and Irina's Russian box with old stamps in it. "Have you decided you want the stamps?"

"The box. Not the stamps."

He had taken, by instinct, the only object she wanted to keep. "For a special reason?" she said. "Of course, the box is yours. I am only wondering."

"The cover fits," he said.

She knew that the next morning he would have been here forever and that at parting time, four days later, she would have to remind him that leaving was the other half of arriving. She smiled, knowing how sorry he would be to go and how soon he would leave her behind. "This time yesterday …," he might say, but no more than once. He was asleep. His mouth opened slightly and the hair on his forehead became dark and damp. A doubled-up arm looked uncomfortable but Irina did not interfere; his sunken mind, his unconscious movements, had to be independent, of her or anyone, particularly of her. She did not love him more or less than any of her grandchildren. You see, it all worked out, she was telling him. You, and your mother, and the children being so worried, and my old friend. Anything can be settled for a few days at a time, though not for longer. She put out the light, for which his body was grateful. His mind, at that moment, in a sunny icicle brightness, was not only skiing but flying.

THE MOSLEM WIFE

IN THE SOUTH OF FRANCE, in the business room of a hotel quite near to the house where Katherine Mansfield (whom no one in this hotel had ever heard of) was writing "The Daughters of the Late Colonel," Netta Asher's father announced that there would never be a man-made catastrophe in Europe again. The dead of that recent war, the doomed nonsense of the Russian Bolsheviks had finally knocked sense into European heads. What people wanted now was to get on with life. When he said "life," he meant its commercial business.

Who would have contradicted Mr. Asher? Certainly not Netta. She did not understand what he meant quite so well as his French solicitor seemed to, but she did listen with interest and respect, and then watched him signing papers that, she knew, concerned her for life. He was renewing the long lease her family held on the Hotel Prince Albert and Albion. Netta was then eleven. One hundred years should at least see her through the prime of life, said Mr. Asher, only half jokingly, for of course he thought his seed was immortal.

Netta supposed she might easily live to be more than a hundred—at any rate, for years and years. She knew that her father did not want her to marry until she was twenty-six and that she was then supposed to have a pair of children, the elder a boy. Netta and her father and the French lawyer shook hands on the lease, and she was given her first glass of champagne. The date on the bottle was 1909, for the year of her birth. Netta bravely pronounced the wine delicious, but her father said she would know much better vintages before she was through.

Netta remembered the handshake but perhaps not the terms. When the lease had eighty-eight years to run, she married her first cousin, Jack Ross, which was not at all what her father had had in mind. Nor would there be the useful pair of children—Jack couldn't abide them. Like Netta he came from a hotelkeeping family where the young were like blight. Netta had up to now never shown a scrap of maternal feeling over anything, but Mr. Asher thought Jack might have made an amiable parent—a kind one, at least. She consoled Mr. Asher on one count, by taking the hotel over in his lifetime. The hotel was, to Netta, a natural life; and so when Mr. Asher, dying, said, "She behaves as I wanted her to," he was right as far as the drift of Netta's behavior was concerned but wrong about its course.

The Ashers' hotel was not down on the seafront, though boats and sea could be had from the south-facing rooms.

Across a road nearly empty of traffic were handsome villas, and behind and to either side stood healthy olive trees and a large lemon grove. The hotel was painted a deep ocher with white trim. It had white awnings and green shutters and black iron balconies as lacquered and shiny as Chinese boxes. It possessed two tennis courts, a lily pond, a sheltered winter garden, a formal rose garden, and trees full of nightingales. In the summer dark, *belles-de-nuit* glowed pink, lemon, white, and after their evening watering they gave off a perfume that varied from plant to plant and seemed to match the petals' coloration. In May the nights were dense with stars and fireflies. From the rose garden one might have seen the twin pulse of cigarettes on a balcony, where Jack and Netta sat drinking a last brandy-and-soda before turning in. Most of the rooms were shuttered by then, for no traveler would have dreamed of being south except in winter. Jack and Netta and a few servants had the whole place to themselves. Netta would hire workmen and have the rooms that needed it repainted—the blue cardroom, and the red-walled bar, and the white dining room, where Victorian mirrors gave back glossy walls and blown curtains and nineteenth-century views of the Ligurian coast, the work of an Asher great-uncle. Everything upstairs and down was soaked and wiped and polished, and even the pictures were relentlessly washed with soft cloths and ordinary laundry soap. Netta also had the boiler overhauled and the linen mended and new monograms embroidered and the looking glasses resilvered and the shutters taken off their hinges and scraped and made spruce green again for next year's sun to fade, while Jack talked about decorators and expert gardeners and even wrote to some, and banged tennis balls against the large new garage. He also read books and translated poetry for its own sake and practiced playing the clarinet. He had studied music once, and still thought that an important life, a musical life, was there in the middle distance. One summer, just to see if he could, he translated pages of Saint-John Perse, which were as blank as the garage wall to Netta, in any tongue.

Netta adored every minute of her life, and she thought Jack had a good life too, with nearly half the year for the pleasures that suited him. As soon as the grounds and rooms and cellar and roof had been put to rights, she and Jack packed and went traveling somewhere. Jack made the plans. He was never so cheerful as when buying Baedekers and dragging out their stickered trunks. But Netta was nothing of a traveler. She would have been glad to see the same sun rising out of the same sea from the window every day until she died. She loved Jack, and what she liked best after him was the hotel. It was a place where, once, people had come to die of tuberculosis, yet it held no trace or feeling of danger. When Netta walked with her workmen through sheeted summer rooms, hearing the cicadas and hearing Jack start, stop, start some deeply alien music (alien even when her memory automatically gave her a composer's name), she was reminded that here the dead had never been allowed to corrupt the living; the dead had been dressed for an outing and removed as soon as their first muscular stiffness relaxed. Some were wheeled out in chairs, sitting, and some reclined on portable cots, as if merely resting.

That is why there is no bad atmosphere here, she would say to herself. Death has been swept away, discarded. When the shutters are closed on a room, it is for sleep or for love. Netta could think this easily because neither she nor Jack was ever sick. They knew nothing about insomnia, and they made love every day of their lives—they had married in order to be able to.

Spring had been the season for dying in the old days. Invalids who had struggled through the dark comfort of winter took fright as the night receded. They felt without protection. Netta knew about this, and about the difference between darkness and brightness, but neither affected her. She was not afraid of death or of the dead—they were nothing but cold, heavy furniture. She could have tied jaws shut and weighted eyelids with native instinctiveness, as other women were born knowing the temperature for an infant's milk.

"There are no ghosts," she could say, entering the room where her mother, then her father had died. "If there were, I would know."

Netta took it for granted, now she was married, that Jack felt as she did about light, dark, death, and love. They were as alike in some ways (none of them physical) as a couple of twins, spoke much the same language in the same accents, had the same jokes—mostly about other people—and had been together as much as their families would let them for most of their lives. Other men seemed dull to Netta—slower, perhaps, lacking the spoken shorthand she had with Jack. She never mentioned this. For one thing, both of them had the idea that, being English, one must not say too much. Born abroad, they worked hard at an Englishness that was innocently inaccurate, rooted mostly in attitudes. Their families had been innkeepers along this coast for a century, even before Dr. James Henry Bennet had discovered "the Genoese Rivieras." In one of his guides to the region, a "Mr. Ross" is mentioned as a hotel owner who will accept English bank checks, and there is a "Mr. Asher," reliable purveyor of English groceries. The most trustworthy shipping agents in 1860 are the Montale brothers, converts to the Anglican Church, possessors of a British *laissez-passer* to Malta and Egypt. These families, by now plaited like hair, were connections of Netta's and Jack's and still in business from beyond Marseilles to Genoa. No wonder that other men bored her, and that each thought the other both familiar and unique. But of course they were unalike too. When once someone asked them, "Are you related to Montale, the poet?" Netta answered, "What poet?" and Jack said, "I wish we were."

There were no poets in the family. Apart from the great-uncle who had painted landscapes, the only person to try anything peculiar had been Jack, with his music. He had been allowed to study, up to a point; his father had been no good with hotels—had been a failure, in fact, bailed out four times by his cousins, and it had been thought, for a time, that Jack Ross might be a dunderhead too. Music might do him; he might not be fit for anything else.

Information of this kind about the meaning of failure had been gleaned by Netta years before, when she first became aware of her little cousin. Jack's father and mother—the commercial blunderers—had come to the Prince Albert and Albion to ride out a crisis. They were somewhere between undischarged bankruptcy and annihilation, but one was polite: Netta curtsied to her aunt and uncle. Her eyes were on Jack. She could not read yet, though she could sift and classify attitudes. She drew near him, sucking her lower lip, her hands behind her back. For the first time she was conscious of the beauty of another child. He was younger than Netta, imprisoned in a portable-fence arrangement in which he moved tirelessly, crabwise, hanging on a barrier he could easily have climbed. He was as fair as his Irish mother and sunburned a deep brown. His blue gaze was not a baby's—it was too challenging. He was naked except for shorts that were large and seemed about to fall down. The sunburn, the undress were because his mother was reckless and rather odd. Netta—whose mother was perfect—wore boots, stockings, a longsleeved frock, and a white sun hat. She heard the adults laugh and say that Jack looked like a prizefighter. She walked around his prison, staring, and the blue-eyed fighter stared back.

The Rosses stayed for a long time, while the family sent telegrams and tried to raise money for them. No one looked after Jack much. He would lie on a marble step of the staircase watching the hotel guests going into the cardroom or the dining room. One night, for a reason that remorse was to wipe out in a minute, Netta gave him such a savage kick (though he was not really in her way) that one of his legs remained paralyzed for a long time.

"*Why* did you do it?" her father asked her—this in the room where she was shut up on bread and water. Netta didn't know. She loved Jack, but who would believe it now? Jack learned to walk, then to run, and in time to ski and play tennis; but her lifelong gift to him was a loss of balance, a sudden lopsided bend of a knee. Jack's parents had meantime been given a small hotel to run at Bandol. Mr. Asher, responsible for a bank loan, kept an eye on the place. He went often, in a hotel car with a chauffeur, Netta perched beside him. When, years later, the families found out that the devoted young cousins had become lovers, they separated them without saying much. Netta was too independent to be dealt with. Besides, her father did not want a rift; his wife had died, and he needed Netta. Jack, whose claim on music had been the subject of teasing until now, was suddenly sent to study in England. Netta saw that he was secretly dismayed. He wanted to be almost anything as long as it was impossible, and then only as an act of grace. Netta's father did think it was his duty to tell her that marriage was, at its best, a parched arrangement, intolerable without a flow of golden guineas and fresh blood. As cousins, Jack and Netta could not bring each other anything except stale money.

Nothing stopped them: They were married four months after Jack became twenty-one. Netta heard someone remark at her wedding, "She doesn't need a husband," meaning perhaps the practical, matter-of-fact person she now seemed to be. She did have the dry, burned-out look of someone turned inward. Her dark eyes glowed out of a thin face. She had the shape of a girl of fourteen. Jack, who was large, and fair, and who might be stout at forty if he wasn't careful, looked exactly his age, and seemed quite ready to be married.

Netta could not understand why, loving Jack as she did, she did not look more like him. It had troubled her in the past when they did not think exactly the same thing at almost the same time. During the secret meetings of their long engagement she had noticed how even before a parting they were nearly apart—they had begun to "unmesh," as she called it. Drinking a last drink, usually in the buffet of a railway station, she would see that Jack was somewhere else, thinking about the next-best thing to Netta. The next-best thing might only be a book he wanted to finish reading, but it was enough to make her feel exiled. He often told Netta, "I'm not holding on to you. You're free," because he thought it needed saying, and of course he wanted freedom for himself. But to Netta "freedom" had a cold sound. Is that what I do want, she would wonder. Is that what I think he should offer? Their partings were often on the edge of parting forever, not just because Jack had said or done or thought the wrong thing but because between them they generated the high sexual tension that leads to quarrels. Barely ten minutes after agreeing that no one in the world could possibly know what they knew, one of them, either one, could curse the other out over something trivial. Yet they were, and remained, much in love, and when they were apart Netta sent him letters that were almost despairing with enchantment.

Jack answered, of course, but his letters were cautious. Her exploration of feeling was part of an unlimited capacity she seemed to have for passionate behavior, so at odds with her appearance, which had been dry and sardonic even in childhood. Save for an erotic sentence or two near the end (which Netta read first) Jack's messages might have been meant for any girl cousin he particularly liked. Love was memory, and he was no good at the memory game; he needed Netta there. The instant he saw her he knew all he had missed. But Netta, by then, felt forgotten, and she came to each new meeting aggressive and hurt, afflicted with the physical signs of her doubts and injuries—cold sores, rashes, erratic periods, mysterious temperatures. If she tried to discuss it he would say, "We aren't going over all that again, are we?" Where Netta was concerned he had settled for the established faith, but Netta, who had a wilder, more secret God, wanted a prayer a minute, not to speak of unending miracles and revelations.

When they finally married, both were relieved that the strain of partings and of tense disputes in railway stations would come to a stop. Each privately blamed the other for past violence, and both believed that once they could live openly, without interference, they would never have a disagreement again. Netta did not want Jack to regret the cold freedom he had vainly tried to offer her. He must have his liberty, and his music, and other people, and, oh, anything he wanted—whatever would stop him from saying he was ready to let her go free. The first thing Netta did was to make certain they had the best room in the hotel. She had never actually owned a room until now. The private apartments of her family had always been surrendered in a crisis: Everyone had packed up and moved as beds were required. She and Jack were hopelessly untidy, because both had spent their early years moving down hotel corridors, trailing belts and raincoats, with tennis shoes hanging from knotted strings over their shoulders, their arms around books and sweaters and gray flannel bundles. Both had done lessons in the corners of lounges, with cups and glasses rattling, and other children running, and English voices louder than anything. Jack, who had been vaguely educated, remembered his boarding schools as places where one had a permanent bed. Netta chose for her marriage a south-facing room with a large balcony and an awning of dazzling white. It was furnished with lemonwood that had been brought to the Riviera by Russians for their own villas long before. To the lemonwood Netta's mother had added English chintzes; the result, in Netta's eyes, was not bizarre but charming. The room was deeply mirrored; when the shutters were closed on hot afternoons a play of light became as green as a forest on the walls, and as blue as seawater in the glass. A quality of suspension, of disbelief in gravity, now belonged to Netta. She became tidy, silent, less introspective, as watchful and as reflective as her bedroom mirrors. Jack stayed as he was, luckily; any alteration would have worried her, just as a change in an often-read story will trouble a small child. She was intensely, almost unnaturally happy.

One day she overheard an English doctor, whose wife played bridge every afternoon at the hotel, refer to her, to Netta, as "the little Moslem wife." It was said affectionately, for the doctor liked her. She wondered if he had seen through walls and had watched her picking up the clothing and the wet towels Jack left strewn like clues to his presence. The phrase was collected and passed from mouth to mouth in the idle English colony. Netta, the last person in the world deliberately to eavesdrop (she lacked that sort of interest in other people), was sharp of hearing where her marriage was concerned. She had a special antenna for Jack, for his shades of meaning, secret intentions, for his innocent contradictions. Perhaps "Moslem wife" meant several things, and possibly it was plain to anyone with eyes that Jack, without meaning a bit of harm by it, had a way with women. Those he attracted were a puzzling lot, to Netta. She had already catalogued them—elegant elderly parties with tongues like carving knives; gentle, clever girls who flourished on the unattainable; untouchable-daughter types, canny about their virginity, wondering if Jack would be father enough to justify the sacrifice. There was still another kind—tough, sunburned, clad in dark colors—who made Netta think in the vocabulary of horoscopes: Her gem—diamonds. Her color—black. Her language—worse than Netta's. She noticed that even when Jack had no real use for a woman he never made it apparent; he adopted anyone who took a liking to him. He assumed—Netta thought—a tribal, paternal air that was curious in so young a man. The plot of attraction interested him, no matter how it turned out. He was like someone reading several novels at once, or like someone playing simultaneous chess.

Netta did not want her marriage to become a world of stone. She said nothing except, "Listen, Jack, I've been at this hotel business longer than you have. It's wiser not to be too pally with the guests." At Christmas the older women gave him boxes of expensive soap. "They must think someone around here wants a good wash," Netta remarked. Outside their fenced area of private jokes and private love was a landscape too open, too light-drenched, for serious talk. And then, when? Jack woke up quickly and early in the morning and smiled as naturally as children do. He knew where he was and the day of the week and the hour. The best moment of the day was the first cigarette. When something bloody happened, it was never before six in the evening. At night he had a dark look that went with a dark mood, sometimes. Netta would tell him that she could see a cruise ship floating on the black horizon like a piece of the Milky Way, and she would get that look for an answer. But it never lasted. His memory was too short to let him sulk, no matter what fragment of night had crossed his mind. She knew, having heard other couples all her life, that at least she and Jack never made the conjugal sounds that passed for conversation and that might as well have been bowwow and quack quack.

If, by chance, Jack found himself drawn to another woman, if the tide of attraction suddenly ran the other way, then he would discover in himself a great need to talk to his wife. They sat out on their balcony for much of one long night and he told her about his Irish mother. His mother's eccentricity—"Vera's dottiness," where the family was concerned—had kept Jack from taking anything seriously. He had been afraid of pulling her mad attention in his direction. Countless times she had faked tuberculosis and cancer and announced her own imminent death. A telephone call from a hospital had once declared her lost in a car crash. "It's a new life, a new life," her husband had babbled, coming away from the phone. Jack saw his father then as beautiful. Women are beautiful when they fall in love, said Jack; sometimes the glow will last a few hours, sometimes even a day or two.

"You know," said Jack, as if Netta knew, "the look of amazement on a girl's face …"

Well, that same incandescence had suffused Jack's father when he thought his wife had died, and it continued to shine until a taxi deposited dotty Vera with her cheerful announcement that she had certainly brought off a successful April Fool. After Jack's father died she became violent. "Getting away from her was a form of violence in me," Jack said. "But I did it." That was why he was secretive; that was why he was independent. He had never wanted any woman to get her hands on his life.

Netta heard this out calmly. Where his own feelings were concerned she thought he was making them up as he went along. The garden smelled coolly of jasmine and mimosa. She wondered who his new girl was, and if he was likely to blurt out a name. But all he had been working up to was that his mother—mad, spoiled, devilish, whatever she was—would need to live with Jack and Netta, unless Netta agreed to giving her an income. An income would let her remain where she was—at the moment, in a Rudolph Steiner community in Switzerland, devoted to medieval gardening and to getting the best out of Goethe. Netta's father's training prevented even the thought of spending the money in such a manner.

"You won't regret all you've told me, will you?" she asked. She saw that the new situation would be her burden, her chain, her mean little joke sometimes. Jack scarcely hesitated before saying that where Netta mattered he could never regret anything. But what really interested him now was his mother.

"Lifts give her claustrophobia," he said. "She mustn't be higher than the second floor." He sounded like a man bringing a legal concubine into his household, scrupulously anxious to give all his women equal rights. "And I hope she will make friends," he said. "It won't be easy, at her age. One can't live without them." He probably meant that he had none. Netta had been raised not to expect to have friends: You could not run a hotel and have scores of personal ties. She expected people to be polite and punctual and to mean what they said, and that was the end of it. Jack gave his friendship easily, but he expected considerable diversion in return.

Netta said dryly, "If she plays bridge, she can play with Mrs. Blackley." This was the wife of the doctor who had first said "Moslem wife." He had come down here to the Riviera for his wife's health; the two belonged to a subcolony of flat-dwelling expatriates. His medical practice was limited to hypochondriacs and rheumatic patients. He had time on his hands: Netta often saw him in the hotel reading room, standing, leafing—he took pleasure in handling books. Netta, no reader, did not like touching a book unless it was new. The doctor had a trick of speech Jack loved to imitate: He would break up his words with an extra syllable, some words only, and at that not every time. "It is all a matter of stu-hyle," he said, for "style," or, Jack's favorite, "Oh, well, in the end it all comes down to su-hex." "Uh-hebb and flo-ho of hormones" was the way he once described the behavior of saints—Netta had looked twice at him over that. He was a firm agnostic and the first person from whom Netta heard there existed a magical Dr. Freud. When Netta's father had died of pneumonia, the doctor's "I'm su-horry, Netta" had been so heartfelt she could not have wished it said another way.

His wife, Georgina, could lower her blood pressure or stop her heartbeat nearly at will. Netta sometimes wondered why Dr. Blackley had brought her to a soft climate rather than to the man at Vienna he so admired. Georgina was well enough to play fierce bridge, with Jack and anyone good enough. Her husband usually came to fetch her at the end of the afternoon when the players stopped for tea. Once, because he was obliged to return at once to a patient who needed him, she said, "Can't you be competent about anything?" Netta thought she understood, then, his resigned repetition of "It's all su-hex." "Oh, don't explain. You bore me," said his wife, turning her back.

Netta followed him out to his car. She wore an India shawl that had been her mother's. The wind blew her hair; she had to hold it back. She said, "Why don't you kill her?"

"I am not a desperate person," he said. He looked at Netta, she looking up at him because she had to look up to nearly everyone except children, and he said, "I've wondered why we haven't been to bed."

"Who?" said Netta. "You and your wife? Oh. You mean me." She was not offended; she just gave the shawl a brusque tug and said, "Not a hope. Never with a guest," though of course that was not the reason.

"You might have to, if the guest were a maharaja," he said, to make it all harmless. "I am told it is pu-hart of the courtesy they expect."

"We don't get their trade," said Netta. This had not stopped her liking the doctor. She pitied him, rather, because of his wife, and because he wasn't Jack and could not have Netta.

"I do love you," said the doctor, deciding finally to sit down in his car. "Ee-nee-ormously." She watched him drive away as if she loved him too, and might never see him again. It never crossed her mind to mention any of this conversation to Jack.

That very spring, perhaps because of the doctor's words, the hotel did get some maharaja trade—three little sisters with ebony curls, men's eyebrows, large heads, and delicate hands and feet. They had four rooms, one for their governess. A chauffeur on permanent call lodged elsewhere. The governess, who was Dutch, had a perfect triangle of a nose and said "whom" for "who," pronouncing it "whum." The girls were to learn French, tennis, and swimming. The chauffeur arrived with a hairdresser, who cut their long hair; it lay on the governess's carpet, enough to fill a large pillow. Their toe- and fingernails were filed to points and looked like a kitten's teeth. They came smiling down the marble staircase, carrying new tennis racquets, wearing blue linen skirts and navy blazers. Mrs. Blackley glanced up from the bridge game as they went by the cardroom. She had been one of those opposed to their having lessons at the English Lawn Tennis Club, for reasons that were, to her, perfectly evident.

She said, loudly, "They'll have to be in white."

"End whayt, pray?" cried the governess, pointing her triangle nose.

"They can't go on the courts except in white. It is a private club. Entirely white."

"Whum do they all think they are?" the governess asked, prepared to stalk on. But the girls, with their newly cropped heads, and their vulnerable necks showing, caught the drift and refused to go.

"Whom indeed," said Georgina Blackley, fiddling with her bridge hand and looking happy.

"My wife's seamstress could run up white frocks for them in a minute," said Jack. Perhaps he did not dislike children all that much.

"Whom could," muttered Georgina.

But it turned out that the governess was not allowed to choose their clothes, and so Jack gave the children lessons at the hotel. For six weeks they trotted around the courts looking angelic in blue, or hopelessly foreign, depending upon who saw them. Of course they fell in love with Jack, offering him a passionate loyalty they had nowhere else to place. Netta watched the transfer of this gentle, anxious gift. After they departed, Jack was bad-tempered for several evenings and then never spoke of them again; they, needless to say, had been dragged from him weeping.

When this happened the Rosses had been married nearly five years. Being childless but still very loving, they had trouble deciding which of the two would be the child. Netta overheard "He's a darling, but she's a sergeant major and no mistake. And so *mean*." She also heard "He's a lazy bastard. He bullies her. She's a fool." She searched her heart again about children. Was it Jack or had it been Netta who had first said no? The only child she had ever admired was Jack, and not as a child but as a fighter, defying her. She and Jack were not the sort to have animal children, and Jack's dotty mother would probably soon be child enough for any couple to handle. Jack still seemed to adopt, in a tribal sense of his, half the women who fell in love with him. The only woman who resisted adoption was Netta—still burned-out, still ardent, in a manner of speaking still fourteen. His mother had turned up meanwhile, getting down from a train wearing a sly air of enjoying her own jokes, just as she must have looked on the day of the April Fool. At first she was no great trouble, though she did complain about an ulcerated leg. After years of pretending, she at last had something real. Netta's policy of silence made Jack's mother confident. She began to make a mockery of his music: "All that money gone for nothing!" Or else, "The amount we wasted on schools! The hours he's thrown away with his nose in a book. All that reading—if at least it had got him somewhere." Netta noticed that he spent more time playing bridge and chatting to cronies in the bar now. She thought hard, and decided not to make it her business. His mother had once been pretty; perhaps he still saw her that way. She came of a ramshackle family with a usable past; she spoke of the Ashers and the Rosses as if she had known them when they were tinkers. English residents who had a low but solid barrier with Jack and Netta were fences-down with his mad mother: They seemed to take her at her own word when it was about herself. She began then to behave like a superior sort of guest, inviting large parties to her table for meals, ordering special wines and dishes at inconvenient hours, standing endless rounds of drinks in the bar.

Netta told herself, Jack wants it this way. It is his home too. She began to live a life apart, leaving Jack to his mother. She sat wearing her own mother's shawl, hunched over a new, modern adding machine, punching out accounts. "Funny couple," she heard now. She frowned, smiling in her mind; none of these people knew what bound them, or how tied they were. She had the habit of dodging out of her mother-in-law's parties by saying, "I've got such an awful lot to do." It made them laugh, because they thought this was Netta's term for slave-driving the servants. They thought the staff did the work, and that Netta counted the profits and was too busy with bookkeeping to keep an eye on Jack—who now, at twenty-six, was as attractive as he ever would be.

A woman named Iris Cordier was one of Jack's mother's new friends. Tall, loud, in winter dully pale, she reminded Netta of a blond penguin. Her voice moved between a squeak and a moo, and was a mark of the distinguished literary family to which her father belonged. Her mother, a Frenchwoman, had been in and out of nursing homes for years. The Cordiers haunted the Riviera, with Iris looking after her parents and watching their diets. Now she lived in a flat somewhere in Roquebrune with the survivor of the pair—the mother, Netta believed. Iris paused and glanced in the business room where Mr. Asher had signed the hundred-year lease. She was on her way to lunch—Jack's mother's guest, of course.

"I say, aren't you Miss Asher?"

"I was." Iris, like Dr. Blackley, was probably younger than she looked. Out of her own childhood Netta recalled a desperate adolescent Iris with middle-aged parents clamped like handcuffs on her life. "How is your mother?" Netta had been about to say "How is Mrs. Cordier?" but it sounded servile.

"I didn't know you knew her."

"I remember her well. Your father too. He was a nice person."

"And still is," said Iris, sharply. "He lives with me, and he always will. French daughters don't abandon their parents." No one had ever sounded more English to Netta. "And your father and mother?"

"Both dead now. I'm married to Jack Ross."

"Nobody told me," said Iris, in a way that made Netta think, Good Lord, Iris too? Jack could not possibly seem like a patriarchal figure where she was concerned; perhaps this time the game was reversed and Iris played at being tribal and maternal. The idea of Jack, or of any man, flinging himself on that iron bosom made Netta smile. As if startled, Iris covered her mouth. She seemed to be frightened of smiling back.

Oh, well, and what of it, Iris too, said Netta to herself, suddenly turning back to her accounts. As it happened, Netta was mistaken (as she never would have been with a bill). That day Jack was meeting Iris for the first time.

The upshot of these errors and encounters was an invitation to Roquebrune to visit Iris's father. Jack's mother was ruthlessly excluded, even though Iris probably owed her a return engagement because of the lunch. Netta supposed that Iris had decided one had to get past Netta to reach Jack—an inexactness if ever there was one. Or perhaps it was Netta Iris wanted. In that case the error became a farce. Netta had almost no knowledge of private houses. She looked around at something that did not much interest her, for she hated to leave her own home, and saw Iris's father, apparently too old and shaky to get out of his armchair. He smiled and he nodded, meanwhile stroking an aged cat. He said to Netta, "You resemble your mother. A sweet woman. Obliging and quiet. I used to tell her that I longed to live in her hotel and be looked after."

Not by me, thought Netta.

Iris's amber bracelets rattled as she pushed and pulled everyone through introductions. Jack and Netta had been asked to meet a young American Netta had often seen in her own bar, and a couple named Sandy and Sandra Braunsweg, who turned out to be Anglo-Swiss and twins. Iris's long arms were around them as she cried to Netta, "Don't you know these babies?" They were, like the Rosses, somewhere in their twenties. Jack looked on, blue-eyed, interested, smiling at everything new. Netta supposed that she was now seeing some of the rather hard-up snobbish—snobbish what? "Intelligumhen-sia," she imagined Dr. Blackley supplying. Having arrived at a word, Netta was ready to go home; but they had only just arrived. The American turned to Netta. He looked bored, and astonished by it. He needs the word for "bored," she decided. Then he can go home, too. The Riviera was no place for Americans. They could not sit all day waiting for mail and the daily papers and for the clock to show a respectable drinking time. They made the best of things when they were caught with a house they'd been rash enough to rent unseen. Netta often had them then *en pension* for meals: A hotel dining room was one way of meeting people. They paid a fee to use the tennis courts, and they liked the bar. Netta would notice then how Jack picked up any accent within hearing.

Jack was now being attentive to the old man, Iris's father. Though this was none of Mr. Cordier's business, Jack said, "My wife and I are first cousins, as well as second cousins twice over."

"You don't look it."

Everyone began to speak at once, and it was a minute or two before Netta heard Jack again. This time he said, "We are from a family of great ..." It was lost. What now? Great innkeepers?

Worriers? Skinflints? Whatever it was, old Mr. Cordier kept nodding to show he approved.

"We don't see nearly enough of young men like you," he said.

"True!" said Iris loudly. "We live in a dreary world of ill women down here." Netta thought this hard on the American, on Mr. Cordier, and on the male Braunsweg twin, but none of them looked offended. "I've got no time for women," said Iris. She slapped down a glass of whiskey so that it splashed, and rapped on a table with her knuckles. "Shall I tell you why? Because women don't tick over. They just simply don't tick over." No one disputed this. Iris went on: Women were underinformed. One could have virile conversations only with men. Women were attached to the past through fear, whereas men had a fearless sense of history. "Men tick," she said, glaring at Jack.

"I am not attached to a past," said Netta, slowly. "The past holds no attractions." She was not used to general conversation. She thought that every word called for consideration and for an answer. "Nothing could be worse than the way we children were dressed. And our mothers—the hard waves of their hair, the white lips. I think of those pale profiles and I wonder if those women were ever young."

Poor Netta, who saw herself as profoundly English, spread consternation by being suddenly foreign and gassy. She talked the English of expatriate children, as if reading aloud. The twins looked shocked. But she had appealed to the American. He sat beside her on a scuffed velvet sofa. He was so large that she slid an inch or so in his direction when he sat down. He was Sandra Braunsweg's special friend: They had been in London together. He was trying to write.

"What do you mean?" said Netta. "Write what?"

"Well—a novel, to start," he said. His father had staked him to one year, then another. He mentioned all that Sandra had borne with, how she had actually kicked and punched him to keep him from being too American. He had embarrassed her to death in London by asking a waitress, "Miss, where's the toilet?"

Netta said, "Didn't you mind being corrected?"

"Oh, no. It was just friendly."

Jack meanwhile was listening to Sandra telling about her English forebears and her English education. "I had many years of undeniably excellent schooling," she said. "Mitten Todd."

"What's that?" said Jack.

"It's near Bristol. I met excellent girls from Italy, Spain. I took *him* there to visit," she said, generously including the American. "I said, 'Get a yellow necktie.' He went straight out and bought one. I wore a little Schiaparelli. Bought in Geneva but still a real ... A yellow jacket over a gray ... Well, we arrived at my excellent old school, and even though the day was drizzly I said, 'Put the top of the car back.' He did so at once, and then he understood. The interior of the car harmonized perfectly with the yellow and gray." The twins were orphaned. Iris was like a mother.

"When Mummy died we didn't know where to put all the Chippendale," said Sandra. "Iris took a lot of it."

Netta thought, She is so silly. How can he respond? The girl's dimples and freckles and soft little hands were nothing Netta could have ever described: She had never in her life thought a word like "pretty." People were beautiful or they were not. Her happiness had always been great enough to allow for despair. She knew that some people thought Jack was happy and she was not.

"And what made you marry your young cousin?" the old man boomed at Netta. Perhaps his background allowed him to ask impertinent questions; he must have been doing so nearly forever. He stroked his cat; he was confident. He was spokesman for a roomful of wondering people.

"Jack was a moody child and I promised his mother I would look after him," said Netta. In her hopelessly un-English way she believed she had said something funny.

*

At eleven o'clock the hotel car expected to fetch the Rosses was nowhere. They trudged home by moonlight. For the last hour of the evening Jack had been skewered on virile conversations, first with Iris, then with Sandra, to whom Netta had already given "Chippendale" as a private name. It proved that Iris was right about concentrating on men and their ticking—Jack even thought Sandra rather pretty.

"Prettier than me?" said Netta, without the faintest idea what she meant, but aware she had said something stupid.

"Not so attractive," said Jack. His slight limp returned straight out of childhood. *She* had caused his accident.

"But she's not always clear," said Netta. "Mitten Todd, for example."

"Who're you talking about?"

"Who are *you*?"

"Iris, of course."

As if they had suddenly quarreled they fell silent. In silence they entered their room and prepared for bed. Jack poured a whiskey, walked on the clothes he had dropped, carried his drink to the bathroom. Through the half-shut door he called suddenly, "Why did you say that asinine thing about promising to look after me?"

"It seemed so unlikely, I thought they'd laugh." She had a glimpse of herself in the mirrors picking up his shed clothes.

He said, "Well, is it true?"

She was quiet for such a long time that he came to see if she was still in the room. She said, "No, your mother never said that or anything like it."

"We shouldn't have gone to Roquebrune," said Jack. "I think those bloody people are going to be a nuisance. Iris wants her father to stay here, with the cat, while she goes to England for a month. How do we get out of that?"

"By saying no."

"I'm rotten at no."

"I told you not to be too pally with women," she said, as a joke again, but jokes were her way of having floods of tears.

Before this had a chance to heal, Iris's father moved in, bringing his cat in a basket. He looked at his room and said, "Medium large." He looked at his bed and said, "Reasonably long." He was, in short, daft about measurements. When he took books out of the reading room, he was apt to return them with "This volume contains about 70,000 words" written inside the back cover.

Netta had not wanted Iris's father, but Jack had said yes to it. She had not wanted the sick cat, but Jack had said yes to that too. The old man, who was lost without Iris, lived for his meals. He would appear at the shut doors of the dining room an hour too early, waiting for the menu to be typed and posted. In a voice that matched Iris's for carrying power, he read aloud, alone: "Consommé. Good Lord, again? Is there a choice between the fish and the cutlet? I can't possibly eat all of that. A bit of salad and a boiled egg. That's all I could possibly want." That was rubbish, because Mr. Cordier ate the menu and more, and if there were two puddings, or a pudding and ice cream, he ate both and asked for pastry, fruit, and cheese to follow. One day, after Dr. Blackley had attended him for faintness, Netta passed a message on to Iris, who had been back from England for a fortnight now but seemed in no hurry to take her father away.

"Keith Blackley thinks your father should go on a diet."

"He can't," said Iris. "Our other doctor says dieting causes cancer."

"You can't have heard that properly," Netta said.

"It is like those silly people who smoke to keep their figures," said Iris. "Dieting."

"Blackley hasn't said he should smoke, just that he should eat less of everything."

"My father has never smoked in his life," Iris cried. "As for his diet, I weighed his food out for years. He's not here forever. I'll take him back as soon as he's had enough of hotels."

He stayed for a long time, and the cat did too, and a nuisance they both were to the servants. When the cat was too ailing to walk, the old man carried it to a path behind the tennis courts and put it down on the gravel to die. Netta came out with the old man's tea on a tray (not done for everyone, but having him out of the way was a relief) and she saw the cat lying on its side, eyes wide, as if profoundly thinking. She saw unlicked dirt on its coat and ants exploring its paws. The old man sat in a garden chair, wearing a panama hat, his hands clasped on a stick. He called, "Oh, Netta, take her away. I am too old to watch anything die. I know what she'll do," he said, indifferently, his voice falling as she came near. "Oh, I know that. Turn on her back and give a shriek. I've heard it often."

Netta disburdened her tray onto a garden table and pulled the tray cloth under the cat. She was angered at the haste and indecency of the ants. "It would be polite to leave her," she said. "She doesn't want to be watched."

"I always sit here," said the old man.

Jack, making for the courts with Chippendale, looked as if the sight of the two conversing amused him. Then he understood and scooped up the cat and tray cloth and went away with the cat over his shoulder. He laid it in the shade of a Judas tree, and within an hour it was dead. Iris's father said, "I've got no one to talk to here. That's my trouble. That shroud was too small for my poor Polly. Ask my daughter to fetch me."

Jack's mother said that night, "I'm sure you wish that I had a devoted daughter to take me away too." Because of the attention given the cat she seemed to feel she had not been nuisance enough. She had taken to saying, "My leg is dying before I am," and imploring

Jack to preserve her leg, should it be amputated, and make certain it was buried with her. She wanted Jack to be close by at nearly any hour now, so that she could lean on him. After sitting for hours at bridge she had trouble climbing two flights of stairs; nothing would induce her to use the lift.

"Nothing ever came of your music," she would say, leaning on him. "Of course, you have a wife to distract you now. I needed a daughter. Every woman does." Netta managed to trap her alone, and forced her to sit while she stood over her. Netta said, "Look, Aunt Vera, I forbid you, I absolutely forbid you, do you hear, to make a nurse of Jack, and I shall strangle you with my own hands if you go on saying nothing came of his music. You are not to say it in my hearing or out of it. Is that plain?"

Jack's mother got up to her room without assistance. About an hour later the gardener found her on a soft bed of wallflowers. "An inch to the left and she'd have landed on a rake," he said to Netta. She was still alive when Netta knelt down. In her fall she had crushed the plants, the yellow minted *giroflées de Nice*. Netta thought that she was now, at last, for the first time, inhaling one of the smells of death. Her aunt's arms and legs were turned and twisted; her skirt was pulled so that her swollen leg showed. It seemed that she had jumped carrying her walking stick—it lay across the path. She often slept in an armchair, afternoons, with one eye slightly open. She opened that eye now and, seeing she had Netta, said, "My son." Netta was thinking, I have never known her. And if I knew her, then it was Jack or myself I could not understand. Netta was afraid of giving orders, and of telling people not to touch her aunt before Dr. Blackley could be summoned, because she knew that she had always been mistaken. Now Jack was there, propping his mother up, brushing leaves and earth out of her hair. Her head dropped on his shoulder. Netta thought from the sudden heaviness that her aunt had died, but she sighed and opened that one eye again, saying this time, "Doctor?" Netta left everyone doing the wrong things to her dying—no, her murdered—aunt. She said quite calmly into a telephone, "I am afraid that my aunt must have jumped or fallen from the second floor."

Jack found a letter on his mother's night table that began, "Why blame Netta? I forgive." At dawn he and Netta sat at a card table with yesterday's cigarettes still not cleaned out of the ashtray, and he did not ask what Netta had said or done that called for forgiveness. They kept pushing the letter back and forth. He would read it and then Netta would. It seemed natural for them to be silent, Jack had sat beside his mother for much of the night. Each of them then went to sleep for an hour, apart, in one of the empty rooms, just as they had done in the old days when their parents were juggling beds and guests and double and single quarters. By the time the doctor returned for his second visit Jack was neatly dressed and seemed wide awake. He sat in the bar drinking black coffee and reading a travel book of Evelyn Waugh's called *Labels*. Netta, who looked far more untidy and underslept, wondered if Jack wished he might leave now, and sail from Monte Carlo on the *Stella Polaris*.

Dr. Blackley said, "Well, you are a dim pair. She is not in pu-hain, you know." Netta supposed this was the roundabout way doctors have of announcing death, very like "Her sufferings have ended." But Jack, looking hard at the doctor, had heard another meaning. "Jumped or fell," said Dr. Blackley. "She neither fell nor jumped. She is up there enjoying a damned good thu-hing."

Netta went out and through the lounge and up the marble steps. She sat down in the shaded room on the chair where Jack had spent most of the night. Her aunt did not look like anyone Netta knew, not even like Jack. She stared at the alien face and said, "Aunt Vera, Keith Blackley says there is nothing really the matter. You must have made a mistake. Perhaps you fainted on the path, overcome by the scent of wallflowers. What would you like me to tell Jack?"

Jack's mother turned on her side and slowly, tenderly, raised herself on an elbow. "Well, Netta," she said, "I daresay the fool is right. But as I've been given quite a lot of sleeping stuff, I'd as soon stay here for now."

Netta said, "Are you hungry?"

"I should very much like a ham sandwich on English bread, and about that much gin with a lump of ice."

She began coming down for meals a few days later. They knew she had crept down the stairs and flung her walking stick over the path and let herself fall hard on a bed of wallflowers—had even plucked her skirt up for a bit of accuracy; but she was also someone returned from beyond the limits, from the other side of the wall. Once she said, "It was like diving and suddenly realizing there was no water in the sea." Again, "It is not true that your life rushes before your eyes. You can see the flowers floating up to you. Even a short fall takes a long time."

Everyone was deeply changed by this incident. The effect on the victim herself was that she got religion hard.

"We are all hopeless nonbelievers!" shouted Iris, drinking in the bar one afternoon. "At least, I hope we are. But when I see you, Vera, I feel there might be something in religion. You look positively temperate."

"I am allowed to love God, I hope," said Jack's mother.

Jack never saw or heard his mother anymore. He leaned against the bar, reading. It was his favorite place. Even on the sunniest of afternoons he read by the red-shaded light. Netta was present only because she had supplies to check. Knowing she ought to keep out of this, she still said, "Religion is more than love. It is supposed to tell you why you exist and what you are expected to do about it."

"You have no religious feelings at all?" This was the only serious and almost the only friendly question Iris was ever to ask Netta.

"None," said Netta. "I'm running a business."

"I love God as Jack used to love music," said his mother. "At least he said he did when we were paying for lessons."

"Adam and Eve had God," said Netta. "They had nobody *but* God. A fat lot of good that did them." This was as far as their dialectic went. Jack had not moved once except to turn pages. He read steadily but cautiously now, as if every author had a design on him. That was one effect of his mother's incident. The other was that he gave up bridge and went back to playing the clarinet. Iris hammered out an accompaniment on the upright piano in the old music room, mostly used for listening to radio broadcasts. She was the only person Netta had ever heard who could make Mozart sound like an Irish jig. Presently Iris began to say that it was time Jack gave a concert. Before this could turn into a crisis Iris changed her mind and said what he wanted was a holiday. Netta thought he needed something: He seemed to be exhausted by love, friendship, by being a husband, someone's son, by trying to make a world out of reading and sense out of life. A visit to England to meet some stimulating people, said Iris. To help Iris with her tiresome father during the journey. To visit art galleries and bookshops and go to concerts. To meet people. To talk.

This was a hot, troubled season, and many persons were planning journeys—not to meet other people but for fear of a war. The hotel had emptied out by the end of March. Netta, whose father had known there would never be another catastrophe, had her workmen come in, as usual. She could hear the radiators being drained and got ready for painting as she packed Jack's clothes. They had never been separated before. They kept telling each other that it was only for a short holiday—for three or four weeks. She was surprised at how neat marriage was, at how many years and feelings could be folded and put under a lid. Once, she went to the window so that he would not see her tears and think she was trying to blackmail him.

Looking out, she noticed the American, Chippendale's lover, idly knocking a tennis ball against the garage, as Jack had done in the early summers of their life; he had come round to the hotel looking for a partner, but that season there were none. She suddenly knew to a certainty that if Jack were to die she would search the crowd of mourners for a man she could live with. She would not return from the funeral alone.

Grief and memory, yes, she said to herself, but what about three o'clock in the morning?

By June nearly everyone Netta knew had vanished, or, like the Blackleys, had started to pack. Netta had new tablecloths made, and ordered new white awnings, and two dozen rosebushes from the nursery at Cap Ferrat. The American came over every day and followed her from room to room, talking. He had nothing better to do. The Swiss twins were in England. His father, who had been backing his writing career until now, had suddenly changed his mind about it—now, when he needed money to get out of Europe. He had projects for living on his own, but they required a dose of funds. He wanted to open a restaurant on the Riviera where nothing but chicken pie would be served. Or else a vast and expensive café where people would pay to make their own sandwiches. He said that he was seeing the food of the future, but all that Netta could see was customers asking for their money back. He trapped her behind the bar and said he loved her; Netta made other women look like stuffed dolls. He could still remember the shock of meeting her, the attraction, the brilliant answer she had made to Iris about attachments to the past.

Netta let him rave until he asked for a loan. She laughed and wondered if it was for the chicken-pie restaurant. No—he wanted to get on a boat sailing from Cannes. She said, quite cheerfully, "I can't be Venus and Barclays Bank. You have to choose."

He said, "Can't Venus ever turn up with a letter of credit?"

She shook her head. "Not a hope."

But when it was July and Jack hadn't come back, he cornered her again. Money wasn't in it now: His father had not only relented but had virtually ordered him home. He was about twenty-two, she guessed. He could still plead successfully for parental help and for indulgence from women. She said, no more than affectionately, "I'm going to show you a very pretty room."

A few days later Dr. Blackley came alone to say good-bye.

"Are you really staying?" he asked.

"I am responsible for the last eighty-one years of this lease," said Netta. "I'm going to be thirty. It's a long tenure. Besides, I've got Jack's mother and she won't leave. Jack has a chance now to visit America. It doesn't sound sensible to me, but she writes encouraging him. She imagines him suddenly very rich and sending for her. I've discovered the limit of what you can feel about people. I've discovered something else," she said abruptly. "It is that sex and love have nothing in common. Only a coincidence, sometimes. You think the coincidence will go on and so you get married. I suppose that is what men are born knowing and women learn by accident."

"I'm su-horry."

"For God's sake, don't be. It's a relief."

She had no feeling of guilt, only of amazement. Jack, as a memory, was in a restricted area—the tennis courts, the cardroom, the bar. She saw him at bridge with Mrs. Blackley and pouring drinks for temporary friends. He crossed the lounge jauntily with a cluster of little dark-haired girls wearing blue. In the mirrored bedroom there was only Netta. Her dreams were cleansed of him. The looking glasses still held their blue-and-silver-water shadows, but they lost the habit of giving back the moods and gestures of a Moslem wife.

About five years after this, Netta wrote to Jack. The war had caught him in America, during the voyage his mother had so wanted him to have. His limp had kept him out of the Army. As his mother (now dead) might have put it, all that reading had finally got him somewhere: He had spent the last years putting out a two-pager on aspects of European culture—part of a scrupulous effort Britain was making for the West. That was nearly all Netta knew. A Belgian Red Cross official had arrived, apparently in Jack's name, to see if she was still alive. She sat in her father's business room, wearing a coat and a shawl because there was no way of heating any part of the hotel now, and she tried to get on with the letter she had been writing in her head, on and off, for many years.

"In June, 1940, we were evacuated," she started, for the tenth or eleventh time. "I was back by October. Italians had taken over the hotel. They used the mirror behind the bar for target practice. Oddly enough it was not smashed. It is covered with spiderwebs, and the bullet hole is the spider. I had great trouble over Aunt Vera, who disappeared and was found finally in one of the attic rooms.

"The Italians made a pet of her. Took her picture. She enjoyed that. Everyone who became thin had a desire to be photographed, as if knowing they would use this intimidating evidence against those loved ones who had missed being starved. Guilt for life. After an initial period of hardship, during which she often had her picture taken at her request, the Italians brought food and looked after her, more than anyone. She was their mama. We were annexed territory and in time we had the same food as the Italians. The thin pictures of your mother are here on my desk.

"She buried her British passport and would never say where. Perhaps under the Judas tree with Mr. Cordier's cat, Polly. She remained just as mad and just as spoiled, and that became dangerous when life stopped being ordinary. She complained about me to the Italians. At that time a complaint was a matter of prison and of death if it was made to the wrong person. Luckily for me, there was also the right person to take the message.

"A couple of years after that, the Germans and certain French took over and the Italians were shut up in another hotel without food or water, and some people risked their well-being to take water to them (for not everyone preferred the new situation, you can believe me). When she was dying I asked her if she had a message for one Italian officer who had made such a pet of her and she said, 'No, why?' She died without a word for anybody. She was buried as 'Rossini,' because the Italians had changed people's names. She had said she was French, a Frenchwoman named Ross, and so some peculiar civil status was created for us—the two Mrs. Rossinis.

"The records were topsy-turvy; it would have meant going to the Germans and explaining my dead aunt was British, and of course I thought I would not. The death certificate and permission to bury are for a Vera Rossini. I have them here on my desk for you with her pictures.

"You are probably wondering where I have found all this writing paper. The Germans left it behind. When we were being shelled I took what few books were left in the reading room down to what used to be the wine cellar and read by candlelight. You are probably wondering where the candles came from. A long story. I even have paint for the radiators, large buckets that have never been opened.

"I live in one room, my mother's old sitting room. The business room can be used but the files have gone. When the Italians were here your mother was their mother, but I was not their Moslem wife, although I still had respect for men. One yelled '*Luce, luce,*' because your mother was showing a light. She said, 'Bugger you, you little toad.' He said, 'Granny, I said "*luce,*" not "*Duce.*"'"

"Not long ago we crept out of our shelled homes, looking like cave dwellers. When you see the hotel again, it will be functioning. I shall have painted the radiators. Long shoots of bramble come in through the cardroom windows. There are drifts of leaves in the old music room and I saw scorpions and heard their rustling like the rustle of death. Everything that could have been looted has gone. Sheets, bedding, mattresses. The neighbors did quite a lot of that. At the risk of their lives. When the Italians were here we had rice and oil. Your mother, who was crazy, used to put out grains to feed the mice.

"When the Germans came we had to live under Vichy law, which meant each region lived on what it could produce. As ours produces nothing, we got quite thin again. Aunt Vera died plump. Do you know what it means when I say she used to complain about me?

"Send me some books. As long as they are in English. I am quite sick of the three other languages in which I've heard so many threats, such boasting, such a lot of lying.

"For a time I thought people would like to know how the Italians left and the Germans came in. It was like this: They came in with the first car moving slowly, flying the French flag. The highest-ranking French official in the region. Not a German. No, just a chap getting his job back. The Belgian Red Cross people were completely uninterested and warned me that no one would ever want to hear.

"I suppose that you already have the fiction of all this. The fiction must be different, oh very different, from Italians sobbing with homesickness in the night. The Germans were not real, they were specially got up for the events of the time. Sat in the white dining room, eating with whatever plates and spoons were not broken or looted, ate soups that were mostly water, were forbidden to complain. Only in retreat did they develop faces and I noticed then that some were terrified and many were old. A radio broadcast from some untouched area advised the local population not to attack them as they retreated, it would make wild animals of them. But they were attacked by some young boys shooting out of a window and eight hostages were taken, including the son of the man who cut the maharaja's daughters' black hair, and they were shot and left along the wall of a café on the more or less Italian side of the border. And the man who owned the café was killed too, but later, by civilians—he had given names to the Gestapo once, or perhaps it was something else. He got on the wrong side of the right side at the wrong time, and he was thrown down the deep gorge between the two frontiers.

"Up in one of the hill villages Germans stayed till no one was alive. I was at that time in the former wine cellar, reading books by candlelight.

"The Belgian Red Cross team found the skeleton of a German deserter in a cave and took back the helmet and skull to Knokke-le-Zoute as souvenirs.

"My war has ended. Our family held together almost from the Napoleonic adventures. It is shattered now. Sentiment does not keep families whole—only mutual pride and mutual money."

This true story sounded so implausible that she decided never to send it. She wrote a sensible letter asking for sugar and rice and for new books; nothing must be older than 1940.

Jack answered at once: There were no new authors (he had been asking people). Sugar was unobtainable, and there were queues for rice. Shoes had been rationed. There were no women's stockings but lisle, and the famous American legs looked terrible. You could not find butter or meat or tinned pineapple. In restaurants, instead of butter you were given miniature golf balls of cream cheese. He supposed that all this must sound like small beer to Netta.

A notice arrived that a CARE package awaited her at the post office. It meant that Jack had added his name and his money to a mailing list. She refused to sign for it; then she changed her mind and discovered it was not from Jack but from the American she had once taken to such a pretty room. Jack did send rice and sugar and delicious coffee but he forgot about books. His letters followed; sometimes three arrived in a morning. She left them sealed for days. When she sat down to answer, all she could remember were implausible things.

Iris came back. She was the first. She had grown puffy in England—the result of drinking whatever alcohol she could get her hands on and grimly eating her sweets allowance: There would be that much less gin and chocolate for the Germans if ever they landed. She put her now wide bottom on a comfortable armchair—one of the few chairs the first wave of Italians had not burned with cigarettes or idly hacked at with daggers—and said Jack had been living with a woman in America and to spare the gossip had let her be known as his wife. Another Mrs. Ross? When Netta discovered it was dimpled Chippendale, she laughed aloud.

"I've seen them," said Iris. "I mean I saw them together. King Charles and a spaniel. Jack wiped his feet on her."

Netta's feelings were of lightness, relief. She would not have to tell Jack about the partisans hanging by the neck in the arches of the Place Masséna at Nice. When Iris had finished talking, Netta said, "What about his music?"

"I don't know."

"How can you not know something so important?"

"Jack had a good chance at things, but he made a mess of everything," said Iris. "My father is still living. Life really is too incredible for some of us."

A dark girl of about twenty turned up soon after. Her costume, a gray dress buttoned to the neck, gave her the appearance of being in uniform. She unzipped a military-looking bag and cried, in an unplaceable accent, "*Ha*llo, *ha*llo, Mrs. Ross? A few small gifts for you," and unpacked a bottle of Haig, four tins of corned beef, a jar of honey, and six pairs of American nylon stockings, which Netta had never seen before, and were as good to have under a mattress as gold. Netta looked up at the tall girl.

"Remember? I was the middle sister. With," she said gravely, "the typical middle-sister problems." She scarcely recalled Jack, her beloved. The memory of Netta had grown up with her. "I remember you laughing," she said, without loving that memory. She was a severe, tragic girl. "You were the first adult I ever heard laughing. At night in bed I could hear it from your balcony. You sat smoking with, I suppose, your handsome husband. I used to laugh just to hear you."

She had married an Iranian journalist. He had discovered that political prisoners in the United States were working under lamentable conditions in tin mines. President Truman had sent them there. People from all over the world planned to unite to get them out. The girl said she had been to Germany and to Austria, she had visited camps, they were all alike, and that was already the past, and the future was the prisoners in the tin mines.

Netta said, "In what part of the country are these mines?"

The middle sister looked at her sadly and said, "Is there more than one part?"

For the first time in years, Netta could see Jack clearly. They were silently sharing a joke; he had caught it too. She and the girl lunched in a corner of the battered dining room. The tables were scarred with initials. There were no tablecloths. One of the great-uncle's paintings still hung on a wall. It showed the Quai Laurenti, a country road alongside the sea. Netta, who had no use for the past, was discovering a past she could regret. Out of a dark, gentle silence—silence imposed by the impossibility of telling anything real—she counted the cracks in the walls. When silence failed she heard power saws ripping into olive trees and a lemon grove. With a sense of deliverance she understood that soon there would be nothing left to spoil. Her great-uncle's picture, which ought to have changed out of sympathetic magic, remained faithful. She regretted everything now, even the three anxious little girls in blue linen. Every calamitous season between then and now seemed to descend directly from Georgina Blackley's having said "white" just to keep three children in their place. Clad in buttoned-up gray, the middle sister now picked at corned beef and said she had hated her father, her mother, her sisters, and most of all the Dutch governess.

"Where is she now?" said Netta.

"Dead, I hope." This was from someone who had visited camps. Netta sat listening, her cheek on her hand. Death made death casual: she had always known. Neither the vanquished in their flight nor the victors returning to pick over rubble seemed half so vindictive as a tragic girl who had disliked her governess.

Dr. Blackley came back looking positively cheerful. In those days men still liked soldiering. It made them feel young, if they needed to feel it, and it got them away from home. War made the break few men could make on their own. The doctor looked years younger, too, and very fit. His wife was not with him. She had survived everything, and the hardships she had undergone had completely restored her to health—which had made it easy for her husband to leave her. Actually, he had never gone back, except to wind up the matter.

"There are things about Georgina I respect and admire," he said, as husbands will say from a distance. His war had been in Malta. He had come here, as soon as he could, to the shelled, gnawed, tarnished coast (as if he had not seen enough at Malta) to ask Netta to divorce Jack and to marry him, or live with him—anything she wanted, on any terms.

But she wanted nothing—at least, not from him.

"Well, one can't defeat a memory," he said. "I always thought it was mostly su-hex between the two of you."

"So it was," said Netta. "So far as I remember."

"Everyone noticed. You would vanish at odd hours. Dis-huppear."

"Yes, we did."

"You can't live on memories," he objected. "Though I respect you for being faithful, of course."

"What you are talking about is something of which one has no specific memory," said Netta. "Only of seasons. Places. Rooms. It is as abstract to remember as to read about. That is why it is boring in talk except as a joke, and boring in books except for poetry."

"You never read poetry."

"I do now."

"I guessed that," he said.

"That lack of memory is why people are unfaithful, as it is so curiously called. When I see closed shutters I know there are lovers behind them. That is how the memory works. The rest is just convention and small talk."

"Why lovers? Why not someone sleeping off the wine he had for lunch?"

"No. Lovers."

"A middle-aged man cutting his toenails in the bathtub," he said with unexpected feeling. "Wearing bifocal lenses so that he can see his own feet."

"No, lovers. Always."

He said, "Have you missed him?"

"Missed who?"

"Who the bloody hell are we talking about?"

"The Italian commander billeted here. He was not a guest. He was here by force. I was not breaking a rule. Without him I'd have perished in every way. He may be home with his wife now. Or in that fortress near Turin where he sent other men. Or dead." She looked at the doctor and said, "Well, what would you like me to do? Sit here and cry?"

"I can't imagine you with a brute."

"I never said that."

"Do you miss him still?"

"The absence of Jack was like a cancer which I am sure has taken root, and of which I am bound to die," said Netta.

"You'll bu-hury us all," he said, as doctors tell the condemned.

"I haven't said I won't." She rose suddenly and straightened her skirt, as she used to do when hotel guests became pally. "Conversation over," it meant.

"Don't be too hard on Jack," he said.

"I am hard on myself," she replied.

After he had gone he sent her a parcel of books, printed on grayish paper, in warped wartime covers. All of the titles were, to Netta, unknown. There was *Fireman Flower* and *The Horse's Mouth* and *Four Quartets* and *The Stuff to Give the Troops* and *Better Than a Kick in the Pants* and *Put Out More Flags*. A note added that the next package would contain Henry Green and Dylan Thomas. She guessed he would not want to be thanked, but she did so anyway. At the end of her letter was "Please remember, if you mind too much, that I said no to you once before." Leaning on the bar, exactly as Jack used to, with a glass of the middle sister's drink at hand, she opened *Better Than a Kick in the Pants* and read, "... two Fascists came in, one of them tall and thin and tough looking; the other smaller, with only one arm and an empty sleeve pinned up to his shoulder. Both of them were quite young and wore black shirts."

Oh, thought Netta, I am the only one who knows all this. No one will ever realize how much I know of the truth, the truth, the truth, and she put her head on her hands, her elbows on the scarred bar, and let the first tears of her after-war run down her wrists.

The last to return was the one who should have been first. Jack wrote that he was coming down from the north as far as Nice by bus. It was a common way of traveling and much cheaper than by train. Netta guessed that he was mildly hard up and that he had saved nothing from his war job. The bus came in at six, at the foot of the Place Masséna. There was a deep blue late-afternoon sky and pale sunlight. She could hear birds from the public gardens nearby. The

Place was as she had always seen it, like an elegant drawing room with a blue ceiling. It was nearly empty. Jack looked out on this sunlighted, handsome space and said, "Well, I'll just leave my stuff at the bus office, for the moment"—perhaps noticing that Netta had not invited him anywhere. He placed his ticket on the counter, and she saw that he had not come from far away: he must have been moving south by stages. He carried an aura of London pub life; he had been in London for weeks.

A frowning man hurrying to wind things up so he could have his first drink of the evening said, "The office is closing and we don't keep baggage here."

"People used to be nice," Jack said.

"Bus people?"

"Just people."

She was hit by the sharp change in his accent. As for the way of speaking, which is something else again, he was like the heir to great estates back home after a Grand Tour. Perhaps the estates had run down in his absence. She slipped the frowning man a thousand francs, a new pastel-tinted bill, on which the face of a calm girl glowed like an opal. She said, "We shan't be long."

She set off over the Place, walking diagonally—Jack beside her, of course. He did not ask where they were headed, though he did make her smile by saying, "Did you bring a car?" expecting one of the hotel cars to be parked nearby, perhaps with a driver to open the door; perhaps with cold chicken and wine in a hamper, too. He said, "I'd forgotten about having to tip for every little thing." He did not question his destination, which was no farther than a café at the far end of the square. What she felt at that instant was intense revulsion. She thought, I don't want him, and pushed away some invisible flying thing—a bat or a blown paper. He looked at her with surprise. He must have been wondering if hardship had taught Netta to talk in her mind.

This is it, the freedom he was always offering me, she said to herself, smiling up at the beautiful sky.

They moved slowly along the nearly empty square, pausing only when some worn-out Peugeot or an old bicycle, finding no other target, made a swing in their direction. Safely on the pavement, they walked under the arches where partisans had been hanged. It seemed to Netta the bodies had been taken down only a day or so before. Jack, who knew about this way of dying from hearsay, chose a café table nearly under a poor lad's bound, dangling feet.

"I had a woman next to me on the bus who kept a hedgehog all winter in a basketful of shavings," he said. "He can drink milk out of a wineglass." He hesitated. "I'm sorry about the books you asked for. I was sick of books by then. I was sick of rhetoric and culture and patriotic crap."

"I suppose it is all very different over there," said Netta.

"God, yes."

He seemed to expect her to ask questions, so she said, "What kind of clothes do they wear?"

"They wear quite a lot of plaids and tartans. They eat at peculiar hours. You'll see them eating strawberries and cream just when you're thinking of having a drink."

She said, "Did you visit the tin mines, where Truman sends his political prisoners?"

"*Tin* mines?" said Jack. "No."

"Remember the three little girls from the maharaja trade?"

Neither could quite hear what the other had to say. They were partially deaf to each other.

Netta continued softly, "Now, as I understand it, she first brought an American to London, and then she took an Englishman to America."

He had too much the habit of women, he was playing too close a game, to waste points saying, "Who? What?"

"It was over as fast as it started," he said. "But then the war came and we were stuck. She became a friend," he said. "I'm quite fond of her"—which Netta translated as, "It is a subterranean river that may yet come to light." "You wouldn't know her," he said. "She's very different now. I talked so much about the south, down here, she finally found some land going dirt cheap at Bandol. The mayor arranged for her to have an orchard next to her property, so she won't have neighbors. It hardly cost her anything. He said to her, 'You're very pretty.'"

"No one ever had a bargain in property because of a pretty face," said Netta.

"Wasn't it lucky," said Jack. He could no longer hear himself, let alone Netta. "The war was unsettling, being in America. She minded not being active. Actually she was using the Swiss passport, which made it worse. Her brother was killed over Bremen. She needs security now. In a way it was sorcerer and apprentice between us, and she suddenly grew up. She'll be better off with a roof over her head. She writes a little now. Her poetry isn't bad," he said, as if Netta had challenged its quality.

"Is she at Bandol now, writing poetry?"

"Well, no." He laughed suddenly. "There isn't a roof yet. And, you know, people don't sit writing that way. They just think they're going to."

"Who has replaced you?" said Netta. "Another sorcerer?"

"Oh, *he* ... he looks like George the Second in a strong light. Or like Queen Anne. Queen Anne and Lady Mary, somebody called them." Iris, that must have been. Queen Anne and Lady Mary wasn't bad—better than King Charles and his spaniel. She was beginning to enjoy his story. He saw it, and said lightly, "I was too preoccupied with you to manage another life. I couldn't see myself going on and on away from you. I didn't want to grow middle-aged at odds with myself."

But he had lost her; she was enjoying a reverie about Jack now, wearing one of those purple sunburns people acquire at golf. She saw him driving an open car, with large soft freckles on his purple skull. She saw his mistress's dog on the front seat and the dog's ears flying like pennants. The revulsion she felt did not lend distance but brought a dreamy reality closer still. He must be thirty-four now, she said to herself. A terrible age for a man who has never imagined thirty-four.

"Well, perhaps you have made a mess of it," she said, quoting Iris.

"What mess? I'm here. *He*—"

"Queen Anne?"

"Yes, well, actually Gerald is his name; he wears nothing but brown. Brown suit, brown tie, brown shoes. I said, '*He* can't go to Mitten Todd. He won't match.'"

"Harmonize," she said.

"That's it. Harmonize with the—"

"What about Gerald's wife? I'm sure he has one."

"Lucretia."

"No, really?"

"On my honor. When I last saw them they were all together, talking."

Netta was remembering what the middle sister had said about laughter on the balcony. She couldn't look at him. The merest crossing of glances made her start laughing rather wildly into her hands. The hysterical quality of her own laughter caught her in midair. What were they talking about? He hitched his chair nearer and dared to take her wrist.

"Tell me, now," he said, as if they were to be two old confidence men getting their stories straight. "What about you? Was there ever ..." The glaze of laughter had not left his face and voice. She saw that he would make her his business, if she let him. Pulling back, she felt another clasp, through a wall of fog. She groped for this other, invisible hand, but it dissolved. It was a lost, indifferent hand; it no longer recognized her warmth. She understood: He is dead ... Jack, closed to ghosts, deaf to their voices, was spared this. He would be spared everything, she saw. She envied him his imperviousness, his true unhysterical laughter.

Perhaps that's why I kicked him, she said. I was always jealous. Not of women. Of his short memory, his comfortable imagination. And I am going to be thirty-seven and I have a dark, an accurate, a deadly memory.

He still held her wrist and turned it another way, saying, "Look, there's paint on it."

"Oh, God, where is the waiter?" she cried, as if that were the one important thing. Jack looked his age, exactly. She looked like a burned-out child who had been told a ghost story. Desperately seeking the waiter, she turned to the café behind them and saw the last light of the long afternoon strike the mirror above the bar—a flash in a tunnel; hands juggling with fire. That unexpected play, at a remove, borne indoors, displayed to anyone who could stare without blinking, was a complete story. It was the brightness on the looking glass, the only part of a life, or a love, or a promise, that could never be concealed, changed, or corrupted.

Not a hope, she was trying to tell him. He could read her face now. She reminded herself, If I say it, I am free. I can finish painting the radiators in peace. I can read every book in the world. If I had relied on my memory for guidance, I would never have crept out of the wine cellar. Memory is what ought to prevent you from buying a dog after the first dog dies, but it never does. It should at least keep you from saying yes twice to the same person.

"I've always loved you," he chose to announce—it really was an announcement, in a new voice that stated nothing except facts.

The dark, the ghosts, the candlelight, her tears on the scarred bar—*they* were real. And still, whether she wanted to see it or not, the light of imagination danced all over the square. She did not dare to turn again to the mirror, lest she confuse the two and forget which light was real. A pure white awning on a cross street seemed to her to be of indestructible beauty. The window it sheltered was hollowed with sadness and shadow. She said with the same deep sadness, "I believe you." The wave of revulsion receded, sucked back under another wave—a powerful adolescent craving for something simple, such as true love.

Her face did not show this. It was set in adolescent stubbornness, and this was one of their old, secret meetings when, sullen and hurt, she had to be coaxed into life as Jack wanted it lived. It was the same voyage, at the same rate of speed. The Place seemed to her to be full of invisible traffic—first a whisper of tires, then a faint, high screeching, then a steady roar. If Jack heard anything, it could be only the blood in the veins and his loud, happy thought. To a practical romantic like Jack, dying to get Netta to bed right away, what she was hearing was only the uh-hebb and flo-ho of hormones, as Dr. Blackley said. She caught a look of amazement on his face: *Now* he knew what he had been deprived of. *Now* he remembered. It had been Netta, all along.

Their evening shadows accompanied them over the long square. "I still have a car," she remarked. "But no petrol. There's a train." She did keep on hearing a noise, as of heavy traffic rushing near and tearing away. Her own quiet voice carried across it, saying, "Not a hope." He must have heard that. Why, it was as loud as a shout. He held her arm lightly. He was as buoyant as morning. This *was* his morning—the first light on the mirror, the first cigarette. He pulled her into an archway where no one could see. What could I do, she asked her ghosts, but let my arm be held, my steps be guided?

Later, Jack said that the walk with Netta back across the Place Masséna was the happiest event of his life. Having no reliable counter-event to put in its place, she let the memory stand.

THE DOCTOR

(from "Linnet Muir")

WHO CAN REMEMBER now a picture called *The Doctor*? From 1891, when the original was painted, to the middle of the Depression, when it finally went out of style, reproductions of this work flowed into every crevice and corner of North America and the British Empire, swamping continents. Not even *The Angelus* supplied as rich a mixture of art and lesson. The two people in *The Angelus* are there to tell us clearly that the meek inherit nothing but seem not to mind; in *The Doctor* a cast of four enacts a more complex statement of Christian submission or Christian pessimism, depending on the beholder: God's Will is manifest in a dying child, Helpless Materialism in a baffled physician, and Afflicted Humanity in the stricken parents. The parable is set in a spotless cottage; the child's bed, composed of three chairs, is out of a doll's house. In much of the world—the world as it was, so much smaller than now—two full generations were raised with the monochrome promise that existence is insoluble, tragedy static, poverty endearing, and heavenly justice a total mystery.

It must have come as a shock to overseas visitors when they discovered *The Doctor* incarnated as an oil painting in the Tate Gallery in London, in the company of other Victorian miseries entitled *Hopeless Dawn* and *The Last Day in the Old Home*. *The Doctor* had not been divinely inspired and distributed to chasten us after all, but was the work of someone called Sir Luke Fildes—nineteenth-century rationalist and atheist, for all anyone knew. Perhaps it was simply a scene from a three-decker novel, even a joke. In museum surroundings—classified, ticketed—*The Doctor* conveyed a new instruction: Death is sentimental, art is pretense.

Some people had always hated *The Doctor*. My father, for one. He said, "You surely don't want *that* thing in your room."

The argument (it became one) took place in Montreal, in a house that died long ago without leaving even a ghost. He was in his twenties, to match the century. I had been around about the length of your average major war. I had my way but do not remember how; neither tears nor temper ever worked. What probably won out was his wish to be agreeable to Dr. Chauchard, the pediatrician who had given me the engraving. My father seemed to like Chauchard, as he did most people—just well enough—while my mother, who carried an uncritical allegiance from person to person, belief to belief, had recently declared Chauchard to be mentally, morally, and spiritually without fault.

Dr. Chauchard must have been in his thirties then, but he seemed to me timeless, like God the Father. When he took the engraving down from the wall of his office, I understood him to be offering me a portrait of himself. My mother at first refused it, thinking I had asked; he assured her I had not, that he had merely been struck by my expression when I looked at the ailing child. "*C'est une sensible*," he said—an appraisal my mother dismissed by saying I was as tough as a boot, which I truly believe to have been her opinion.

What I was sensitive to is nearly too plain to be signaled: The dying child, a girl, is the heart of the composition. The parents are in the shadow, where they belong. Their function is to be sorry. The doctor has only one patient; light from a tipped lampshade falls on her and her alone.

The street where Dr. Chauchard lived began to decline around the same time as the popularity of *The Doctor* and is now a slum.

No citizens' committee can restore the natural elegance of those gray stone houses, the swept steps, the glittering windows, because, short of a miracle, it cannot resurrect the kind of upper-bourgeois French Canadians who used to live there. They have not migrated or moved westward in the city—they have ceased to exist. The handful of dust they sprang from, with its powerful components of religion and history, is part of another clay. They were families who did not resent what were inaccurately called "The English" in Montreal; they had never acknowledged them. The men read a newspaper sometimes, the women never. The women had a dark version of faith for private drama, a family tree to memorize for intellectual exercise, intense family affection for the needs of the heart. Their houses, like Dr. Chauchard's, smelled of cleanness as if cleanness were a commodity, a brand of floor wax. Convents used to have that smell; the girls raised in them brought to married life an ideal of housekeeping that was a memory of the polished convent corridor, with strict squares of sunlight falling where and as they should. Two sons and five daughters was the average for children; Simone, Pauline, Jeanne, Yvonne, and Louise the feminine names of the decade. The girls when young wore religious medals like golden flower petals on thin chains, had positive torrents of curls down to their shoulder blades, and came to children's parties dressed in rose velvet and white stockings, too shy to speak. Chauchard, a bachelor, came out of this world, which I can describe best only through its girls and women.

His front door, painted the gloomy shade my father called Montreal green, is seen from below, at an angle—a bell too high for me during the first visits, a letter box through which I called, "Open the door; *c'est moi*," believing still that "*moi*" would take me anywhere. But no one could hear in any language, because two vestibules, one behind the other, stood in the way. In the first one overshoes dripped on a mat, then came a warmer place for coats. Each vestibule had its door, varnished to imitate the rings of a tree trunk, enhanced by a nature scene made of frosted glass; you unbuckled galoshes under herons and palm trees and shed layers of damp wool under swans floating in a landscape closer to home.

Just over the letter box of the green door a large, beautifully polished brass plate carried, in sloped writing:

> Docteur Raoul Chauchard
> Spécialiste en Médecine Infantile
> Ancien Externe et Interne
> des Hôpitaux de Paris
> Sur Rendez-vous

On the bottom half of the plate this information was repeated in English, though the only English I recall in the waiting room was my mother's addressed to me.

He was not Parisian but native to the city, perhaps to the street, even to the house, if I think of how the glass-shaded lamps and branched chandeliers must have followed an evolution from oil to kerosene to gas to electricity without changing shape or place. Rooms and passages were papered deep blue fading to green (the brighter oblong left by the removal of *The Doctor* was about the color of a teal), so that the time of day indoors was winter dusk, with pools of light like uncurtained windows. An assemblage of gilt-framed pictures began between the heron and swan doors with brisk scenes of biblical injustice—the casting-out of Hagar, the swindling of Esau—and moved along the hall with European history: Vercingetorix surrendering to the Romans, the earthquake at Lisbon, Queen Victoria looking exactly like a potato pancake receiving some dark and humble envoy; then, with a light over him to mark his importance, Napoléon III reviewing a regiment from a white horse. (The popularity of "Napoléon" as a Christian name did not connect with the first Bonaparte, as English Canadians supposed—when any thought was given to any matter concerning French Canadians at all—but with his nephew, the lesser Bonaparte, who had never divorced or insulted the Pope, and who had established clerical influence in the saddle as firmly as it now sat upon Quebec.) The sitting-room-converted-to-waiting-room had on display landmarks of Paris, identified in two languages:

> Le Petit Palais—The Petit Palais
> Place Vendôme—Place Vendôme
> Rue de la Paix—Rue de la Paix

as if the engraver had known they would find their way to a wall in Montreal.

Although he had trained in Paris, where, as our English doctor told my mother, leeches were still sold in pharmacies and babies died like flies, Chauchard was thought modern and forward-looking. He used the most advanced methods imported from the United States, or, as one would have said then, "from Boston," which meant both stylish and impeccably right. Ultraviolet irradiation was one, recommended for building up delicate children. I recall the black mask tied on, and the danger of blindness should one pull it off before being told. I owe him irradiation to the marrow and other sources of confusion: It was he who gave my mother the name of a convent where Jansenist discipline still had a foot on the neck of the twentieth century and where, as an added enchantment, I was certain not to hear a word of English. He never dreamed, I am sure, that I would be packed off there as a boarder from the age of four. Out of goodness and affection he gave me books to read—children's stories from nineteenth-century France which I hated and still detest. In these oppressive stories children were punished and punished hard for behavior that seemed in another century, above all on another continent, natural and right. I could never see the right-and-wrong over which they kept stumbling and only much later recognized it in European social fiddle-faddle—the trivial yardsticks that measure a man's character by the way he eats a boiled egg. The prose was stiff, a bit shrill, probably pitched too high for a North American ear. Even the bindings, a particularly ugly red, were repellent to me, while their gilt titles lent them the ceremonial quality of school prizes. I had plenty of English Victorian books, but the scolding could be got over, because there was no unfairness. Where there was, it was done away with as part of the plot. The authors were on the side of morality but also of the child. For a long time I imagined that most of my English books had been written by other children, but I never made that mistake with French; I saw these authors as large, scowling creatures with faces as flushed with crossness as the books' covers. Still, the books were presents, therefore important, offered without a word or a look Dr. Chauchard would not have bestowed on an adult. They had been his mother's; she lived in rooms at the top of the house, receiving her own friends, not often mingling with his. She must have let him have these treasures for a favored patient who did not understand the courtesy, even the sacrifice, until it was too late to say "Thank you." Another child's name—his mother's—was on the flyleaf; I seldom looked at it, concentrated as I was on my own. It is not simply rhetoric to say that I see him still—Fildes profile, white cuff, dark sleeve, writing the new dedication with a pen dipped in a blue inkwell, hand and book within the circle cast by the lamp on his desk. At home I would paste inside the front cover the plate my father had designed for me, which had "Linnet: Her Book" as ex libris, and the drawing of a stream flowing between grassy banks—his memory of the unhurried movement of England, no reflection of anything known to me in Quebec—bearing a single autumn leaf. Under the stream came the lines

> Time, Time, which none can bind
> While flowing fast leaves love behind.

The only child will usually give and lend its possessions easily, having missed the sturdy training in rivalry and forced sharing afforded by sisters and brothers, yet nothing would have made me part willingly with any of the grim red books. Grouped on a special shelf, seldom opened after the first reading, they were not reminders but a true fragment of his twilit house, his swan and heron doors, Napoléon III so cunningly lighted, "Le Petit Palais—The Petit Palais," and, finally, Dr. Chauchard himself at the desk of his shadowy room writing "*Pour ma chère petite Linnet*" in a book that had once belonged to another girl.

Now, how to account for the changed, stern, disapproving Chauchard who in that same office gave me not a book but a lecture beginning "Think of your unfortunate parents" and ending "You owe them everything; it is your duty to love them." He had just telephoned for my father to come and fetch me. "How miserable they would be if anything ever happened to you," he said. He spoke of my *petit Papa* and my *petite Maman* with that fake diminution of authority characteristic of the Latin tongues which never works in English. I sat on a chair still wearing outdoor clothes—navy reefer over my convent uniform, HMS *Nelson* sailor hat held on by a black elastic—neither his patient nor his guest at this dreadful crisis, wondering, What does he mean? For a long time now my surprise visits to friends had been called, incorrectly, "running away." Running away was one of the reasons my parents gave when anyone asked why I had been walled up in such a severe school at an early age. Dr. Chauchard, honored by one of my visits, at once asked his office nurse, "Do her parents know she's here?" Women are supposed to make dangerous patients for bachelor doctors; besotted little girls must seem even worse. But I was not besotted; I believed we were equals. It was he who had set up the equality, and for that reason I still think he should have invited me to remove my coat.

The only thing worth remarking about his dull little sermon is that it was in French. French was his language for medicine; I never heard him give an opinion in English. It was evidently the language to which he retreated if one became a nuisance, his back to a wall of white marble syntax. And when it came to filial devotion he was one with the red-covered books. Calling on my parents, not as my doctor but as their friend, he spoke another language. It was not merely English instead of French but the private dialect of a younger person who was playful, charming, who smoked cigarettes in a black-and-silver holder, looking round to see the effect of his puns and jokes. You could notice then, only then, that his black-currant eyes were never still.

The house he came to remained for a long time enormous in memory, though the few like it still standing—"still living," I nearly say—are narrow, with thin, steep staircases and close, high-ceilinged rooms. They were the work of Edinburgh architects and dated from when Montreal was a Scottish city; it had never been really English. A Saturday-evening gathering of several adults, one child, and a couple of dogs created a sort of tangle in the middle of the room—an entwining that was surely not of people's feet: In those days everyone sat straight. The women had to, because their girdles had hooks and stays. Men sat up out of habit, probably the habit of prosperity; the Depression created the physical slump, a change in posture to match the times. Perhaps desires and secrets and second thoughts threading from person to person, from bachelor to married woman, from mother of none to somebody's father, formed a cat's cradle—matted, invisible, and quite dangerous. Why else would Ruby, the latest homesick underpaid Newfoundland import, have kept tripping up as she lurched across the room with cups and glasses on a tray?

Transformed into jolly Uncle Raoul (his request), Dr. Chauchard would arrive with a good friend of his, divorced Mrs. Erskine, and a younger friend of both, named Paul-Armand. Paul-Armand was temporary, one of a sequence of young men who attended Mrs. Erskine as her bard, her personal laureate. His role did not outlive a certain stage of artless admiration; at the first sign of falling away, the first mouse squeak of disenchantment from him, a replacement was found. All of these young men were good-looking, well brought up, longing to be unconventional, and entirely innocent. Flanked by her pair of males, Mrs. Erskine would sway into the room, as graceful as a woman can be when she is boned from waist to thigh. She would keep on her long moleskin coat, even though like all Canadian rooms this one was vastly overheated, explaining that she was chilly. This may have been an attempt to reduce the impression she gave of general largeness by suggesting an inner fragility. Presently the coat would come off, revealing a handwoven tea-cozy sort of garment—this at a time when every other woman was showing her knees. My mother sat with her legs crossed and one sandal dangling. Her hair had recently been shingled; she seemed to be groping for its lost comfortable warmth. Other persons, my father apart, are a dim choir muttering, "Isn't it past your bedtime?" My father sat back in a deep, chintz-covered chair and said hardly anything except for an occasional "Down" to his dogs.

In another season, in the country, my parents had other friends, summer friends, who drank old-fashioneds and danced to gramophone records out on the lawn. Winter friends were mostly coffee drinkers, who did what people do between wars and revolutions—sat in a circle and talked about revolutions and wars. The language was usually English, though not everyone was native to English. Mrs. Erskine commanded what she called "*good* French" and rather liked displaying it, but after a few sentences, which made those who could not understand French very fidgety and which annoyed the French Canadians present exactly in the way an affected accent will grate on Irish nerves, she would pick her way back to English. In mixed society, such little of it as existed, English seemed to be the social rule. It did not enter the mind of any English speaker that the French were at a constant disadvantage, like a team obliged to play all their matches away from home. Dr. Chauchard never addressed me in French here, not even when he would ask me to recite a French poem learned at my convent school. It began, "If I were a fly, Maman, I would steal a kiss from your lips." The nun in charge of memory work was fiddly about liaison, which produced an accidentally appropriate "*Si j'étaiszzzzzzzune mouche, Maman.*" Dr. Chauchard never seemed to tire of this and may have thought it a reasonable declaration to make to one's mother.

It was a tactless rhyme, if you think of all the buzzing and stealing that went on in at least part of the winter circle, but I could not have known that. At least not consciously. Unconsciously, everyone under the age of ten knows everything. Under-ten can come into a room and sense at once everything felt, kept silent, held back in the way of love, hate, and desire, though he may not have the right words for such sentiments. It is part of the clairvoyant immunity to hypocrisy we are born with and that vanishes just before puberty. I knew, though no one had told me, that my mother was a bit foolish about Dr. Chauchard; that Mrs. Erskine would have turned cartwheels to get my father's attention but that even cartwheels would have failed; that Dr. Chauchard and Mrs. Erskine were somehow together but never went out alone. Paul-Armand was harder to place; too young to be a parent, he was a pest, a tease to someone smaller. His goading was never noticed, though my reaction to it, creeping behind his chair until I was in a position to punch him, brought an immediate response from the police: "Linnet, if you don't sit down I'm afraid you will have to go to your room." "If" and "I'm afraid" meant there was plenty of margin. Later: "Wouldn't you be happier if you just went to bed? No? Then get a book and sit down and read it." Presently, "Down, I said, sit down; did you hear what I've just said to you? I said, sit down, *down*." There came a point like convergent lines finally meeting where orders to dogs and instructions to children were given in the same voice. The only difference was that a dog got "Down, damn it," and, of course, no one ever swore at me.

This overlapping in one room of French and English, of Catholic and Protestant—my parents' way of being, and so to me life itself— was as unlikely, as unnatural to the Montreal climate as a school of tropical fish. Only later would I discover that most other people simply floated in mossy little ponds labeled "French and Catholic" or "English and Protestant," never wondering what it might be like to step ashore; or wondering, perhaps, but weighing up the danger. To be out of a pond is to be in unmapped territory. The earth might be flat; you could fall over the edge quite easily. My parents and their friends were, in their way, explorers. They had in common a fear of being bored, which is a fear one can afford to nourish in times of prosperity and peace. It makes for the most ruthless kind of exclusiveness, based as it is on the belief that anyone can be the richest of this or cleverest of that and still be the dullest dog that ever barked. I wince even now remembering those wretched once-only guests who were put on trial for a Saturday night and unanimously condemned. This heartlessness apart, the winter circle shared an outlook, a kind of humor, a certain vocabulary of the mind. No one made any of the standard Montreal statements, such as "What a lot of books you've got! Don't tell me you've read them," or "I hear you're some kind of artist. What do you really *do*?" Explorers like Dr. Chauchard and Mrs. Erskine and my mother and the rest recognized each other on sight; the recognition cut through disguisements of class, profession, religion, language, and even what poll takers call "other interests."

Once you have jumped out of a social enclosure, your eye is bound to be on a real, a geographical elsewhere; theirs seemed to consist of a few cities of Europe with agreeable-sounding names like Vienna and Venice. The United States consisted only of Boston and Florida then. Adults went to Florida for therapeutic reasons—for chronic bronchitis, to recover from operations, for the sake of mysterious maladies that had no names and were called in obituaries "a long illness bravely borne." Boston seemed to be an elegant little republic with its own parliament and flag. To English Montreal, cocooned in that other language nobody bothered to learn, the rest of the continent, Canada included, barely existed; travelers would disembark after long, sooty train trips expressing relief to be in the only city where there were decent restaurants and well-dressed women and where proper English could be heard. Elsewhere, then, became other people, and little groups would form where friends, to the tune of vast mutual admiration, could find a pleasing remoteness in each other. They resembled, in their yearnings, in their clinging together as a substitute for motion, in their craving for "someone to talk to," the kind of marginal social clans you find today in the capitals of Eastern Europe.

I was in the dining room cutting up magazines. My mother brought her coffee cup in, sat down, and said, "Promise me you will never be caught in a situation where you have to compete with a younger woman."

She must have been twenty-six at the very most; Mrs. Erskine was well over thirty. I suppose she was appraising the amount of pickle Mrs. Erskine was in. They had become rivals. With her pale braids, her stately figure, her eyes the color of a stoneware teapot, Mrs. Erskine seemed to me like a white statue with features painted on. I had heard my mother praising her beauty, but for a child she was too large, too still. "Age has its points," my mother went on. "The longer your life goes on, the more chance it has to be interesting. Promise me that when you're thirty you'll have a lot to look back on."

My mother had on her side her comparative youth, her quickness, her somewhat giddy intelligence. She had been married, as she said, "for ever and ever" and was afraid nothing would ever happen to her again. Mrs. Erskine's chief advantage over my mother—being unmarried and available—was matched by an enviable biography. "Ah, don't ask me for my life's story now," she would cry, settling back to tell it. When the others broke into that sighing, singing recital of cities they went in for, repeating strings of names that sounded like sleigh bells (Venice, London, Paris, Rome), Mrs. Erskine would narrow her stoneware eyes and annihilate my mother with "But Charlotte, I've *been* to all those places, I've *seen* all those people." What, indeed, hadn't she seen—crown princes dragged out of Rolls-Royces by cursing mobs, duchesses clutching their tiaras while being raped by anarchists, strikers in England kicking innocent little Border terriers.

"... And as for the Hunga*r*ians and that Béla *Kun*, let me tell you ... tore the uniforms right off the Red Cross *nurses* ... made them dance the Charleston naked on top of *street*cars ..."

"Linnet, wouldn't you be better off in your room?"

The fear of the horde was in all of them; it haunted even their jokes. "Bolshevik" was now "bolshie," to make it harmless. Petrograd had been their early youth; the Red years just after the war were still within earshot. They dreaded yet seemed drawn to tales of conspiracy and enormous might. The English among them were the first generation to have been raised on *The Wind in the Willows*. Their own Wild Wood was a dark political mystery; its rude inhabitants were still to be tamed. What was needed was a leader, a Badger. But when a Badger occurred they mistrusted him, too; my mother had impressed on me early that Mussolini was a "bad, wicked man." Fortunate Mrs. Erskine had seen "those people" from legation windows; she had, in another defeat for my mother, been married twice, each time to a diplomat. The word "diplomat" had greater cachet then than it has now. Earlier in the century a diplomat was believed to have attended universities in more than one country, to have two or three languages at his disposal and some slender notion of geography and history. He could read and write quite easily, had probably been born in wedlock, possessed tact and discretion, and led an exemplary private life. Obviously there were no more of these paragons then than there might be now, but fewer were needed, because there were only half as many capitals. Those who did exist spun round and round the world, used for all they were worth, until they became like those coats that outlast their buttons, linings, and pockets: Your diplomat, recalled from Bulgaria, by now a mere warp and woof, would be given a new silk lining, bone buttons, have his collar turned, and, after a quick reading of Norse myths, would be shipped to Scandinavia. Mrs. Erskine, twice wedded to examples of these freshened garments, had been everywhere—everywhere my mother longed to be.

"My *life*," said Mrs. Erskine. "Ah, Charlotte, don't ask me to tell you everything—you'd never believe it!" My mother asked, and believed, and died in her heart along with Mrs. Erskine's first husband, a Mr. Sparrow, shot to death in Berlin by a lunatic Russian refugee. (Out of the decency of his nature Mr. Sparrow had helped the refugee's husband emigrate accompanied by a woman Mr. Sparrow had taken to be the Russian man's wife.) In the hours that preceded his "going," as Mrs. Erskine termed his death, Mr. Sparrow had turned into a totally other person, quite common and gross. She had seen exactly how he would rise from the dead for his next incarnation. She had said, "Now then, Alfred, I think it has been a blissful marriage but perhaps not blissful enough. As I am the best part of your karma, we are going to start all over again in another existence." Mr. Sparrow, in his new coarse, uneducated voice, replied, "Believe you me, Bimbo, if I see you in another world, this time I'm making a detour." His last words—not what every woman hopes to hear, probably, but nothing in my mother's experience could come ankle-high to having a husband assassinated in Berlin by a crazy Russian. Mr. Erskine, the second husband, was not quite so interesting, for he merely "drank and drank and *drank*," and finally, unwittingly, provided grounds for divorce. Since in those days adultery was the only acceptable grounds, the divorce ended his ambitions and transformed Mrs. Erskine into someone déclassée; it was not done for a woman to spoil a man's career, and it was taken for granted that no man ever ruined his own. I am certain my mother did not see Mr. Sparrow as an ass and Mr. Erskine as a soak. They were men out of novels—half diplomat, half secret agent. The natural progress of such men was needed to drag women out of the dullness that seemed to be woman's fate.

There was also the matter of Mrs. Erskine's French: My mother could read and speak it but had nothing of her friend's intolerable fluency. Nor could my mother compete with her special status as the only English and Protestant girl of her generation to have attended French and Catholic schools. She had spent ten years with the Ursulines in Quebec City (languages took longer to learn in those days, when you were obliged to start by memorizing all the verbs) and had emerged with the chic little Ursuline lisp.

"Tell me again," my entranced mother would ask. "How do you say 'squab stuffed with sage dressing'?"

"Charlotte, I've told you and told you. '*Pouthin farthi au thauge.*'"

"Thankth," said my mother. Such was the humor of that period.

For a long time I would turn over like samples of dress material the reasons why I was sent off to a school where by all the rules of the world we lived in I did not belong. A sample that nearly matches is my mother's desire to tease Mrs. Erskine, perhaps to overtake her through me: If she had been unique in her generation, then I would be in mine. Unlikely as it sounds today, I believe that I was. At least I have never met another, just as no French-Canadian woman of my period can recall having sat in a classroom with any other English-speaking Protestant disguised in convent uniform. Mrs. Erskine, rising to the tease, warned that convents had gone downhill since the war and that the appalling French I spoke would be a handicap in Venice, London, Paris, Rome; if the Ursuline French of Quebec City was the best in the world after Tours, Montreal French was just barely a language.

How could my mother, so quick and sharp usually, have been drawn in by this? For a day or two my parents actually weighed the advantages of sending their very young daughter miles away, for no good reason. Why not even to France? "You know perfectly well why not. Because we can't afford it. Not that or anything like it."

Leaning forward in her chair as if words alone could not convince her listener, more like my mother than herself at this moment, Mrs. Erskine with her fingertips to her cheek, the other hand held palm outward, cried, "Ah, Angus, don't ask me for my life's story now!" This to my father, who barely knew other people had lives.

My father made this mysterious answer: "Yes, Frances, I do see what you mean, but I have a family, and once you've got children you're never quite so free."

There was only one child, of course, and not often there, but in my parents' minds and by some miracle of fertility they had produced a whole tribe. At any second this tribe might rampage through the house, scribbling on the wallpaper, tearing up books, scratching gramophone records with a stolen diamond brooch. They dreaded mischief so much that I can only suppose them to have been quite disgraceful children.

"What's Linnet up to? She's awfully quiet."

"Sounds suspicious. Better go and look."

I would be found reading or painting or "building," which meant the elaboration of a foreign city called Marigold that spread and spread until it took up a third of my room and had to be cleared away when my back was turned, upon which, as relentless as a colony of beavers, I would start building again. To a visitor Marigold was a slum of empty boxes, serving trays, bottles, silver paper, overturned chairs, but these were streets and houses, churches and convents, restaurants and railway stations. The citizens of Marigold were cut out of magazines: Gloria Swanson was the Mother Superior, Herbert Hoover a convent gardener. Entirely villainous, they did their plotting and planning in an empty cigar box.

Whatever I was doing, I would be told to do something else immediately: I think they had both been brought up that way. "Go out and play in the snow" was a frequent interruption. Parents in bitter climates have a fixed idea about driving children out to be frozen. There was one sunken hour on January afternoons, just before the street lamps were lighted, that was the gray of true wretchedness, as if one's heart and stomach had turned into the same dull, cottony stuff as the sky; it was attached to a feeling of loss, of helpless sadness, unknown to children in other latitudes.

I was home weekends but by no means every weekend. Friday night was given to spoiling and rejoicing, but on Saturday I would hear, "When does she go back?"

"Not till tomorrow night."

Ruby, the homesick offshore import, sometimes sat in my room, just for company. She turned the radiator on so that you saw a wisp of steam from the overflow tap. A wicker basket of mending was on her lap; she wiped her eyes on my father's socks. I was not allowed to say to anyone "Go away," or anything like it. I heard her sniffles, her low, muttered grievances. Then she emerged from her impenetrable cloud of Newfoundland gloom to take an interest in the life of Marigold. She did not get down on the floor or in the way, but from her chair suggested some pretty good plots. Ruby was the inspirer of "The Insane Stepmother," "The Rich, Selfish Cousins," "The Death from Croup of Baby Sister" ("Is her face blue yet?" "No; in a minute"), and "The Broken Engagement," with its cast of three—rejected maiden, fickle lover, and chaperon. Paper dolls did the acting, the voices were ours. Ruby played the cast-off fiancée from the heart: "Don't chew men ever know what chew want?" Chaperon was a fine bossy part: "That's enough, now. Sit down; I said, *down.*"

My parents said, "What does she see in Ruby?" They were cross and jealous. The jealousness was real. They did not drop their voices to say "When does she go back?" but were alert to signs of disaffection, and offended because I did not crave their company every minute. Once, when Mrs. Erskine, a bit of a fool probably, asked, "Who do you love best, your father or your mother?" and I apparently (I have no memory of it) answered, "Oh, I'm not really dying about anybody," it was recalled to me for a long time, as if I had set fire to the curtains or spat on the Union Jack.

"Think of your unfortunate parents," Dr. Chauchard had said in the sort of language that had no meaning to me, though I am sure it was authentic to him.

When he died and I read his obituary, I saw there had been still another voice. I was twenty and had not seen him since the age of nine. *The Doctor* and the red-covered books had been lost even before that, when during a major move from Montreal to a house in the country a number of things that belonged to me and that my parents were tired of seeing disappeared.

There were three separate death notices, as if to affirm that Chauchard had been three men. All three were in a French newspaper; he neither lived nor died in English. The first was a jumble of family names and syntax: "After a serene and happy life it has pleased our Lord to send for the soul of his faithful servant Raoul Étienne Chauchard, piously deceased in his native city in his fifty-first year after a short illness comforted by the sacraments of the Church." There followed a few particulars—the date and place of the funeral, and the names and addresses of the relatives making the announcement. The exact kinship of each was mentioned: sister, brother-in-law, uncle, nephew, cousin, second cousin.

The second obituary, somewhat longer, had been published by the medical association he belonged to; it described all the steps and stages of his career. There were strings of initials denoting awards and honors, ending with: "Dr. Chauchard had also been granted the Medal of Epidemics (Belgium)." Beneath this came the third notice: "The Arts and Letters Society of Quebec announces the irreparable loss of one of its founder members, the poet R. É. Chauchard." R. É. had published six volumes of verse, a book of critical essays, and a work referred to as "the immortal 'Progress,'" which did not seem to fall into a category or, perhaps, was too well known to readers to need identification.

That third notice was an earthquake, the collapse of the cities we build over the past to cover seams and cracks we cannot account for. He must have been writing when my parents knew him. Why they neglected to speak of it is something too shameful to dwell on; he probably never mentioned it, knowing they would believe it impossible. French books were from France; English books from England or the United States. It would not have entered their minds that the languages they heard spoken around them could be written, too.

I met by accident years after Dr. Chauchard's death one of Mrs. Erskine's ex-minnesingers, now an elderly bachelor. His name was Louis. He had never heard of Paul-Armand, not even by rumor. He had not known my parents and was certain he had never accompanied Dr. Chauchard and Mrs. Erskine to our house. He said that when he met these two he had been fresh from a seminary, aged about nineteen, determined to live a life of ease and pleasure but not sure how to begin. Mrs. Erskine had by then bought and converted a farmhouse south of Montreal, where she wove carpets, hooked rugs, scraped and waxed old tables, kept bees, and bottled tons of pickled beets, preparing for some dark proletarian future should the mob—the horde, "those people"—take over after all. Louis knew the doctor only as the poet R. É. of the third notice. He had no knowledge of the Medal of Epidemics (Belgium) and could not explain it to me. I had found "Progress" by then, which turned out to be R.É.'s diary. I could not put faces to the X, Y, and Z that covered real names, nor could I discover any trace of my parents, let alone of *ma chère petite Linnet*. There were long thoughts about Mozart—people like that.

Louis told me of walking with Mrs. Erskine along a snowy road close to her farmhouse, she in a fur cape that came down to her boot tops and a fur bonnet that hid her braided hair. She talked about her unusual life and her two husbands and about what she now called "the predicament." She told him how she had never been asked to meet Madame Chauchard *mère* and how she had slowly come to realize that R.É. would never marry. She spoke of people who had drifted through the predicament, my mother among them, not singling her out as someone important, just as a wisp of cloud on the edge of the sky. "Poor Charlotte" was how Mrs. Erskine described the thin little target on which she had once trained her biggest guns. Yet "poor Charlotte"—not even an X in the diary, finally—had once been the heart of the play. The plot must have taken a full turning after she left the stage. Louis became a new young satellite, content to circle the powerful stars, to keep an eye on the predicament, which seemed to him flaming, sulfurous. Nobody ever told him what had taken place in the first and second acts.

Walking, he and Mrs. Erskine came to a railway track quite far from houses, and she turned to Louis and opened the fur cloak and said, smiling, "*Viens voir Mrs. Erskine*." (Owing to the Ursuline lisp this must have been "Mitheth Erthkine.") Without coyness or any more conversation she lay down—he said "on the track," but he must have meant near it, if you think of the ties. Folded into the cloak, Louis at last became part of a predicament. He decided that further experience could only fall short of it, and so he never married.

In this story about the cloak Mrs. Erskine is transmuted from the pale, affected statue I remember and takes on a polychrome life. She seems cheerful and careless, and I like her for that. Carelessness might explain her unreliable memory about Charlotte. And yet not all that careless: "She even knew the train times," said Louis. "She must have done it before." Still, on a sharp blue day, when some people were still in a dark classroom writing "*abyssus abyssum invocat*" all over their immortal souls, she, who had been through this and escaped with nothing worse than a lisp, had the sun, the snow, the wrap of fur, the bright sky, the risk. There is a raffish kind of nerve to her, the only nerve that matters.

For that one conversation Louis and I wondered what our appearance on stage several scenes apart might make us to each other: If A was the daughter of B, and B rattled the foundations of C, and C, though cautious and lazy where women were concerned, was committed in a way to D, and D was forever trying to tell her life's story to E, the husband of B, and E had enough on his hands with B without taking on D, too, and if D decided to lie down on or near a railway track with F, then what are A and F? Nothing. Minor satellites floating out of orbit and out of order after the stars burned out. Mrs. Erskine reclaimed Dr. Chauchard but he never married anyone. Angus reclaimed Charlotte but he died soon after. Louis, another old bachelor, had that one good anecdote about the fur cloak. I lost even the engraving of *The Doctor*, spirited away quite shabbily, and I never saw Dr. Chauchard again or even tried to. What if I had turned up one day, aged eighteen or so, only to have him say to his nurse, "Does anyone know she's here?"

When I read the three obituaries it was the brass plate on the door I saw and "*Sur Rendez-vous.*" That means "No dropping in." After the warning came the shut heron door and the shut swan door and, at another remove, the desk with the circle of lamplight and R. É. himself, writing about X, Y, Z, and Mozart. A bit humdrum perhaps, a bit prosy, not nearly as good as his old winter Saturday self, but I am sure that it was his real voice, the voice that transcends this or that language. His French-speaking friends did not hear it for a long time (his first book of verse was not sold to anyone outside his immediate family), while his English-speaking friends never heard it at all. But I should have heard it then, at the start, standing on tiptoe to reach the doorbell, calling through the letter box every way I could think of, "I, me." I ought to have heard it when I was still under ten and had all my wits about me.

VOICES LOST IN SNOW

(from "Linnet Muir")

HALFWAY BETWEEN our two great wars, parents whose own early years had been shaped with Edwardian firmness were apt to lend a tone of finality to quite simple remarks: "Because I say so" was the answer to "Why?" and a child's response to "What did I just tell you?" could seldom be anything but "Not to"—not to say, do, touch, remove, go out, argue, reject, eat, pick up, open, shout, appear to sulk, appear to be cross. Dark riddles filled the corners of life because no enlightenment was thought required. Asking questions was "being tiresome," while persistent curiosity got one nowhere, at least nowhere of interest. How much has changed? Observe the drift of words descending from adult to child—the fall of personal questions, observations, unnecessary instructions. Before long the listener seems blanketed. He must hear the voice as authority muffled, a hum through snow. The tone has changed—it may be coaxing, even plaintive—but the words have barely altered. They still claim the ancient right-of-way through a young life.

"Well, old cock," said my father's friend Archie McEwen, meeting him one Saturday in Montreal. "How's Charlotte taking life in the country?" Apparently no one had expected my mother to accept the country in winter.

"Well, old cock," I repeated to a country neighbor, Mr. Bainwood. "How's life?" What do you suppose it meant to me, other than a kind of weather vane? Mr. Bainwood thought it over, then came round to our house and complained to my mother.

"It isn't blasphemy," she said, not letting him have much satisfaction from the complaint. Still, I had to apologize. "I'm sorry" was a ritual habit with even less meaning than "old cock." "Never say that again," my mother said after he had gone.

"Why not?"

"Because I've just told you not to."

"What does it mean?"

"Nothing."

It must have been after yet another "Nothing" that one summer's day I ran screaming around a garden, tore the heads off tulips, and—no, let another voice finish it; the only authentic voices I have belong to the dead: "... then she *ate* them."

It was my father's custom if he took me with him to visit a friend on Saturdays not to say where we were going. He was more taciturn than any man I have known since, but that wasn't all of it; being young, I was the last person to whom anyone owed an explanation. These Saturdays have turned into one whitish afternoon, a windless snowfall, a steep street. Two persons descend the street, stepping carefully. The child, reminded every day to keep her hands still, gesticulates wildly—there is the flash of a red mitten. I will never overtake this pair. Their voices are lost in snow.

We were living in what used to be called the country and is now a suburb of Montreal. On Saturdays my father and I came in together by train. I went to the doctor, the dentist, to my German lesson. After that I had to get back to Windsor station by myself and on time. My father gave me a boy's watch so that the dial would be good and large. I remember the No. 83 streetcar trundling downhill and myself, wondering if the watch was slow, asking strangers to tell me the hour. Inevitably—how could it have been otherwise?—after his death, which would not be long in coming, I would dream that someone important had taken a train without me. My route to the meeting place—deviated, betrayed by stopped clocks—was always downhill. As soon as I was old enough to understand from my reading of myths and legends that this journey was a pursuit of darkness, its terminal point a sunless underworld, the dream vanished.

Sometimes I would be taken along to lunch with one or another of my father's friends. He would meet the friend at Pauzé's for oysters or at Drury's or the Windsor Grill. The friend would more often than not be Scottish- or English-sounding, and they would talk as if I were invisible, as Archie McEwen had done, and eat what I thought of as English food—grilled kidneys, sweetbreads—which I was too finicky to touch. Both my parents had been made wretched as children by having food forced on them and so that particular torture was never inflicted on me. However, the manner in which I ate was subject to precise attention. My father disapproved of the North American custom that he called "spearing" (knife laid on the plate, fork in the right hand). My mother's eye was out for a straight back, invisible chewing, small mouthfuls, immobile silence during the interminable adult loafing over dessert. My mother did not care for food. If we were alone together, she would sit smoking and reading, sipping black coffee, her elbows used as props—a posture that would have called for instant banishment had I so much as tried it. Being constantly observed and corrected was like having a fly buzzing around one's plate. At Pauzé's, the only child, perhaps the only female, I sat up to an oak counter and ate oysters quite neatly, not knowing exactly what they were and certainly not that they were alive. They were served as in "The Walrus and the Carpenter," with bread and butter, pepper and vinegar. Dessert was a chocolate biscuit—plates of them stood at intervals along the counter. When my father and I ate alone, I was not required to say much, nor could I expect a great deal in the way of response. After I had been addressing him for minutes, sometimes he would suddenly come to life and I would know he had been elsewhere. "Of course I've been listening," he would protest, and he would repeat by way of proof the last few words of whatever it was I'd been saying. He was seldom present. I don't know where my father spent his waking life: just elsewhere.

What was he doing alone with a child? Where was his wife? In the country, reading. She read one book after another without looking up, without scraping away the frost on the windows. "The Russians, you know, the Russians," she said to her mother and me, glancing around in the drugged way adolescent readers have. "They put salt on the windowsills in winter." Yes, so they did, in the nineteenth century, in the boyhood of Turgenev, of Tolstoy. The salt absorbed the moisture between two sets of windows sealed shut for half the year. She must have been in a Russian country house at that moment, surrounded by a large Russian family, living out vast Russian complications. The flat white fields beyond her imaginary windows were like the flat white fields she would have observed if only she had looked out. She was myopic; the pupil when she had been reading seemed to be the whole of the eye. What age was she then? Twenty-seven, twenty-eight. Her husband had removed her to the country; now that they were there he seldom spoke. How young she seems to me now—half twenty-eight in perception and feeling, but with a husband, a child, a house, a life, an illiterate maid from the village whose life she confidently interfered with and mismanaged, a small zoo of animals she alternately cherished and forgot; and she was the daughter of such a sensible, truthful, pessimistic woman—pessimistic in the way women become when they settle for what actually exists.

Our rooms were not Russian—they were aired every day and the salt became a great nuisance, blowing in on the floor.

"There, Charlotte, what did I tell you?" my grandmother said. This grandmother did not care for dreams or for children. If I sensed the first, I had no hint of the latter. Out of decency she kept it quiet, at least in a child's presence. She had the reputation, shared with a long-vanished nurse named Olivia, of being able to "do anything" with me, which merely meant an ability to provoke from a child behavior convenient for adults. It was she who taught me to eat in the Continental way, with both hands in sight at all times upon the table, and who made me sit at meals with books under my arms so I would learn not to stick out my elbows. I remember having accepted this nonsense from her without a trace of resentment. Like Olivia, she could make the most pointless sort of training seem a natural way of life. (I think that as discipline goes this must be the most dangerous form of all.) She was one of three godparents I had—the important one. It is impossible for me to enter the mind of this agnostic who taught me prayers, who had already shed every remnant of belief when she committed me at the font. I know that she married late and reluctantly; she would have preferred a life of solitude and independence, next to impossible for a woman in her time. She had the positive voice of the born teacher, sharp manners, quick blue eyes, and the square, massive figure common to both lines of her ancestry—the west of France, the north of Germany. When she said "There, Charlotte, what did I tell you?" without obtaining an answer, it summed up mother and daughter both.

My father's friend Malcolm Whitmore was the second godparent. He quarreled with my mother when she said something flippant about Mussolini, disappeared, died in Europe some years later, though perhaps not fighting for Franco, as my mother had it. She often rewrote other people's lives, providing them with suitable and harmonious endings. In her version of events you were supposed to die as you'd lived. He would write sometimes, asking me, "Have you been confirmed yet?" He had never really held a place and could not by dying leave a gap. The third godparent was a young woman named Georgie Henderson. She was my mother's choice, for a long time her confidante, partisan, and close sympathizer. Something happened, and they stopped seeing each other. Georgie was not her real name—it was Edna May. One of the reasons she had fallen out with my mother was that I had not been called Edna May too. Apparently, this had been promised.

Without saying where we were going, my father took me along to visit Georgie one Saturday afternoon.

"You didn't say you were bringing Linnet" was how she greeted him. We stood in the passage of a long, hot, high-ceilinged apartment, treading snow water into the rug.

He said, "Well, she is your godchild, and she has been ill."

My godmother shut the front door and leaned her back against it. It is in this surprisingly dramatic pose that I recall her. It would be unfair to repeat what I think I saw then, for she and I were to meet again once, only once, many years after this, and I might substitute a lined face for a smooth one and tough, large-knuckled hands for fingers that may have been delicate. One has to allow elbowroom in the account of a rival: "She must have had something" is how it generally goes, long after the initial "What can he see in her? He must be deaf and blind." Georgie, explained by my mother as being the natural daughter of Sarah Bernhardt and a stork, is only a shadow, a tracing, with long arms and legs and one of those slightly puggy faces with pulled-up eyes.

Her voice remains—the husky Virginia-tobacco whisper I associate with so many women of that generation, my parents' friends; it must have come of age in English Montreal around 1920, when girls began to cut their hair and to smoke. In middle life the voice would slide from low to harsh, and develop a chronic cough. For the moment it was fascinating to me—opposite in pitch and speed from my mother's, which was slightly too high and apt to break off, like that of a singer unable to sustain a long note.

It was true that I had been ill, but I don't think my godmother made much of it that afternoon, other than saying, "It's all very well to talk about that now, but I was certainly never told much, and as for that doctor, you ought to just hear what Ward thinks." Out of this whispered jumble my mother stood accused—of many transgressions, certainly, but chiefly of having discarded Dr. Ward Mackey, everyone's doctor and a family friend. At the time of my birth my mother had all at once decided she liked Ward Mackey better than anyone else and had asked him to choose a name for me. He could not think of one, or, rather, thought of too many, and finally consulted his own mother. She had always longed for a daughter, so that she could call her after the heroine of a novel by, I believe, Marie Corelli. The legend so often repeated to me goes on to tell that when I was seven weeks old my father suddenly asked, "What did you say her name was?"

"*Votre fille a frôlé la phtisie*," the new doctor had said, the one who had now replaced Dr. Mackey. The new doctor was known to me as Uncle Raoul, though we were not related. This manner of declaring my brush with consumption was worlds away from Ward Mackey's "subject to bilious attacks." Mackey's objections to Uncle Raoul were neither envious nor personal, for Mackey was the sort of bachelor who could console himself with golf. The Protestant in him truly believed those other doctors to be poorly trained and superstitious, capable of recommending the pulling of teeth to cure tonsillitis, and of letting their patients cough to death or perish from septicemia just through Catholic fatalism.

What parent could fail to gasp and marvel at Uncle Raoul's announcement? Any but either of mine. My mother could invent and produce better dramas any day; as for my father, his French wasn't all that good and he had to have it explained. Once he understood that I had grazed the edge of tuberculosis, he made his decision to remove us all to the country, which he had been wanting a reason to do for some time. He was, I think, attempting to isolate his wife, but by taking her out of the city he exposed her to a danger that, being English, he had never dreamed of: This was the heart-stopping cry of the steam train at night, sweeping across a frozen river, clattering on the ties of a wooden bridge. From our separate rooms my mother and I heard the unrivaled summons, the long, urgent, uniquely North American beckoning. She would follow and so would I, but separately, years and desires and destinations apart. I think that women once pledged in such a manner are more steadfast than men.

"*Frôler*" was the charmed word in that winter's story; it was a hand brushing the edge of folded silk, a leaf escaping a spiderweb. Being caught in the web would have meant staying in bed day and night in a place even worse than a convent school. Charlotte and Angus, whose lives had once seemed so enchanted, so fortunate and free that I could not imagine lesser persons so much as eating the same kind of toast for breakfast, had to share their lives with me, whether they wanted to or not—thanks to Uncle Raoul, who always supposed me to be their principal delight. I had been standing on one foot for months now, midway between "*frôler*" and "falling into," propped up by a psychosomatic guardian angel. Of course I could not stand that way forever; inevitably my health improved and before long I was declared out of danger and then restored—to the relief and pleasure of all except the patient.

"I'd like to see more of you than eyes and nose," said my godmother. "Take off your things." I offer this as an example of unnecessary instruction. Would anyone over the age of three prepare to spend the afternoon in a stifling room wrapped like a mummy in outdoor clothes? "She's smaller than she looks," Georgie remarked, as I began to emerge. This authentic godmother observation drives me to my only refuge, the insistence that she must have had something—he could not have been completely deaf and blind. Divested of hat, scarf, coat, overshoes, and leggings, grasping the handkerchief pressed in my hand so I would not interrupt later by asking for one, responding to my father's muttered "Fix your hair," struck by the command because it was he who had told me not to use "fix" in that sense, I was finally able to sit down next to him on a white sofa. My godmother occupied its twin. A low table stood between, bearing a decanter and glasses and a pile of magazines and, of course, Georgie's ashtrays; I think she smoked even more than my mother did.

On one of these sofas, during an earlier visit with my mother and father, the backs of my dangling feet had left a smudge of shoe polish. It may have been the last occasion when my mother and Georgie were ever together. Directed to stop humming and kicking, and perhaps bored with the conversation in which I was not expected to join, I had soon started up again.

"It doesn't matter," my godmother said, though you could tell she minded.

"Sit up," my father said to me.

"I am sitting up. What do you think I'm doing?" This was not answering but answering back; it is not an expression I ever heard from my father, but I am certain it stood like a stalled truck in Georgie's mind. She wore the look people put on when they are thinking, Now what are you spineless parents going to do about that?

"Oh, for God's sake, she's only a child," said my mother, as though that had ever been an excuse for anything.

Soon after the sofa-kicking incident she and Georgie moved into the hibernation known as "not speaking." This, the lingering condition of half my mother's friendships, usually followed her having said the very thing no one wanted to hear, such as "Who wants to be called Edna May, anyway?"

Once more in the hot pale room where there was nothing to do and nothing for children, I offended my godmother again, by pretending I had never seen her before. The spot I had kicked was pointed out to me, though, owing to new slipcovers, real evidence was missing. My father was proud of my quite surprising memory, of its long backward reach and the minutiae of detail I could describe. My failure now to shine in a domain where I was naturally gifted, that did not require lessons or create litter and noise, must have annoyed him. I also see that my guileless-seeming needling of my godmother was a close adaptation of how my mother could be, and I attribute it to a child's instinctive loyalty to the absent one. Giving me up, my godmother placed a silver dish of mint wafers where I could reach them—white, pink, and green, overlapping—and suggested I look at a magazine. Whatever the magazine was, I had probably seen it, for my mother subscribed to everything then. I may have turned the pages anyway, in case at home something had been censored for children. I felt and am certain I have not invented Georgie's disappointment at not seeing Angus alone. She disliked Charlotte now, and so I supposed he came to call by himself, having no quarrel of his own; he was still close to the slighted Ward Mackey.

My father and Georgie talked for a while—she using people's initials instead of their names, which my mother would not have done—and they drank what must have been sherry, if I think of the shape of the decanter. Then we left and went down to the street in a wood-paneled elevator that had sconce lights, as in a room. The end of the afternoon had a particular shade of color then, which is not tinted by distance or enhancement but has to do with how streets were lighted. Lamps were still gas, and their soft gradual blooming at dusk made the sky turn a peacock blue that slowly deepened to marine, then indigo. This uneven light falling in blurred pools gave the snow it touched a quality of phosphorescence, beyond which were night shadows in which no one lurked. There were few cars, little sound. A fresh snowfall would lie in the streets in a way that seemed natural. Sidewalks were dangerous, casually sanded; even on busy streets you found traces of the icy slides children's feet had made. The reddish brown of the stone houses, the curve and slope of the streets, the constantly changing sky were satisfactory in a way that I now realize must have been aesthetically comfortable. This is what I saw when I read "city" in a book; I had no means of knowing that "city" one day would also mean drab, filthy, flat, or that city blocks could turn into dull squares without mystery.

We crossed Sherbrooke Street, starting down to catch our train. My father walked everywhere in all weathers. Already mined, colonized by an enemy prepared to destroy what it fed on, fighting it with every wrong weapon, squandering strength he should have been storing, stifling pain in silence rather than speaking up while there might have been time, he gave an impression of sternness that was a shield against suffering. One day we heard a mob roaring four syllables over and over, and we turned and went down a different street. That sound was starkly terrifying, something a child might liken to the baying of wolves.

"What is it?"

"Howie Morenz."

"Who is it? Are they chasing him?"

"No, they like him," he said of the hockey player admired to the point of dementia. He seemed to stretch, as if trying to keep every bone in his body from touching a nerve; a look of helplessness such as I had never seen on a grown person gripped his face and he said this strange thing: "Crowds eat me. Noise eats me." The kind of physical pain that makes one seem rat's prey is summed up in my memory of this.

When we came abreast of the Ritz-Carlton after leaving Georgie's apartment, my father paused. The lights within at that time of day were golden and warm. If I barely knew what "hotel" meant, never having stayed in one, I connected the lights with other snowy afternoons, with stupefying adult conversation (Oh, those shut-in velvet-draped unaired low-voice problems!) compensated for by creamy bitter hot chocolate poured out of a pink-and-white china pot.

"You missed your gootay," he suddenly remembered. Established by my grandmother, "*goûter*" was the family word for tea. He often transformed French words, like putty, into shapes he could grasp. No, Georgie had not provided a *goûter*, other than the mint wafers, but it was not her fault—I had not been announced. Perhaps if I had not been so disagreeable with her, he might have proposed hot chocolate now, though I knew better than to ask. He merely pulled my scarf up over my nose and mouth, as if recalling something Uncle Raoul had advised. Breathing inside knitted wool was delicious—warm, moist, pungent when one had been sucking on mint candies, as now. He said, "You didn't enjoy your visit much."

"Not very," through red wool.

"No matter," he said. "You needn't see Georgie again unless you want to," and we walked on. He must have been smarting, for he liked me to be admired. When I was not being admired I was supposed to keep quiet. "You needn't see Georgie again" was also a private decision about himself. He was barely thirty-one and had a full winter to live after this one—little more. Why? "Because I say so." The answer seems to speak out of the lights, the stones, the snow; out of the crucial second when inner and outer forces join, and the environment becomes part of the enemy too.

Ward Mackey used to mention me as "Angus's precocious pain in the neck," which is better than nothing. Long after that afternoon, when I was about twenty, Mackey said to me, "Georgie didn't play her cards well where he was concerned. There was a point where if she had just made one smart move she could have had him. Not for long, of course, but none of us knew that."

What cards, I wonder. The cards have another meaning for me—they mean a trip, a death, a letter, tomorrow, next year. I saw only one move that Saturday: My father placed a card faceup on the table and watched to see what Georgie made of it. She shrugged, let it rest. There she sits, looking puggy but capable, Angus waiting, the precocious pain in the neck turning pages, hoping to find something in the *National Geographic* harmful for children. I brush in memory against the spiderweb: What if she had picked it up, remarking in her smoky voice, "Yes, I can use that"? It was a low card, the kind that only a born gambler would risk as part of a long-term strategy. She would never have weakened a hand that way; she was not gambling but building. He took the card back and dropped his hand, and their long intermittent game came to an end. The card must have been the eight of clubs—"a female child."

A RECOLLECTION

("Édouard, Juliette, Lena")

I MARRIED MAGDALENA HERE, in Paris, more than forty years ago. It was at the time when anti-Jewish thoughts and feelings had suddenly hardened into laws, and she had to be protected. She was a devout, lighthearted, probably wayward Catholic convert, of the sort Dominicans like to have tea with, but she was also Jewish and foreign—to be precise, born in Budapest, in 1904. A Frenchman who had grown rich manufacturing and exporting fine china brought her to Paris—oh, a long time ago, even before the Popular Front. He gave her up for the daughter of a count, and for his new career in right-wing politics, preaching moral austerity and the restoration of Christian values. Whenever Magdalena opened *Le Temps* and saw his name, she would burst out laughing. (I never noticed Magdalena actually *reading* a newspaper. She subscribed to a great many, but I think it was just to see what her friends and former friends were up to.) He let her keep the apartment on Quai Voltaire and the van Dongen portraits he'd bought because they looked like her—the same pert face and slender throat.

I never lived with Magdalena. After our wedding we spent part of a week together (to calm my parents down, I went home to sleep) and a night sitting up in a train. I never imagined sharing an address, my name over the doorbell, friends calling me at Magdalena's number, myself any more than a guest in the black-red-and-white-lacquered apartment on Quai Voltaire. The whole place smelled of gardenias. Along the hall hung stills from films she had worked in, in Vienna, Berlin—silent, minor, forgotten pictures, probably all destroyed. (The apartment was looted during the Occupation. When Magdalena came back, she had to sleep on the floor.) Her two pug dogs yapped and wore little chimes. The constant jangling drove them crazy. She washed them with scented soap and fed them at table, sitting on her lap. They had rashes all over their bodies, and were always throwing up.

I was twenty-two, still a student. My parents, both teachers in the lower grades, had made great sacrifices so that I could sit reading books into early manhood. The only home I could have offered Magdalena was a corner of their flat, in the Rue des Solitaires, up in the Nineteenth Arrondissement. Arabs and Africans live there now. In those days, it was the kind of district Jean Renoir and René Clair liked to use for those films that show chimney pots, and people walking around with loaves of bread, and gentle young couples that find and lose a winning lottery ticket. Until she met me, Magdalena had never heard of the Rue des Solitaires, or of my Métro stop, Place des Fêtes. The names sounded so charming that she thought I'd made them up. I begged her to believe that I never invented anything.

She was fair and slight, like all the women in Paris. In my view of the past, the streets are filled with blond-haired women, wearing absurd little hats, walking miniature dogs. (Wait, my memory tells me; not all women—not my mother.) Why had she given up acting? "Because I wasn't much good," she told me once. "And I was so lazy. I could work, really work, for a man in love with me—to do him a favor. That was all." From her sitting room, everything in it white, you saw across the Seine to the Place du Carrousel and part of the Tuileries. Between five and eight, men used to drop in, stand about with their backs to the view, lean down to scratch the ears of the pugs. Raymonde, the maid, knew everyone by name. They treated me kindly, though nobody ever went so far as to scratch my ears.

My parents were anticlerical and republican. In their conversation, Church and Republic locked horns like a couple of battling rams. I was never baptized. It broke their hearts that my marriage to Magdalena had to be blessed, at her insistence. The blessing was given in the church of Saint-Thomas-d'Aquin, in deep shadow, somewhere behind the altar. I had never been in a church before, except to admire windows or paintings; art belonged to the people, whatever the Vatican claimed. The ceremony was quick, almost furtive, but not because of Magdalena: *I* was the outsider, the pagan, unbaptized, unsaved.

My father and mother stayed home that day, eating the most solid lunch they could scrape together, to steady their nerves. They would have saved Magdalena, if only someone had asked—gladly, bravely, and without ruining my life. (That was how they saw it.) I suppose they could have locked her up in the broom closet. She could have stood in the dark, for years and years—as many as she needed. They could only hope, since they never prayed, that there would be no children.

I had already signed our children over to Rome a few days before the wedding, one afternoon just after lunch. Bargaining for their souls, uncreated, most certainly unwished for (I did not separate soul from body, since the first did not exist), went on in the white sitting room. Magdalena, as ever blithe and lighthearted, repeated whatever she'd been told to tell me, and I said yes, and signed. I can still hear the sound of her voice, though not the words she used; it was lower in pitch than a Frenchwoman's, alien to the ear because of its rhythm. It was a voice that sang a foreign song. Did she really expect to have children? She must have been thirty-six, and we were about to be separated for as long as the war might last. My signature was part of an elaborate ritual, in which she seemed to take immense delight. She had never been married before.

She had on a soft navy-blue dress, which had only that morning been brought to the door. This in war, in defeat. There were dressmakers and deliverymen. There was Chanel's Gardenia. There was coffee and sugar, there were polished silver trays and thin coffee cups. There was Raymonde, in black with white organdy, and Magdalena, with her sunny hair, her deep red nails, to pour.

I looked over at the far side of the Place du Carrousel, to some of the windows of the Ministry of Finance. Until just a few months ago, Magdalena had been invited to private ministry apartments to lunch. The tables were set with the beautiful glass and china that belonged to the people. Steadfast, uncomplaining men and women like my father and mother had paid their taxes so that Magdalena could lunch off plates they would never see—unless some further revolution took place, after which they might be able to view the plates in a museum.

I felt no anger thinking this. It was Magdalena I intended to save. As my wife, she would have an identity card with a French name. She would never have to baste a yellow star on her coat. She would line up for potatoes at a decent hour once France had run out of everything else.

Actually, Magdalena never lined up for anything. On the day when the Jews of Paris stood in long queues outside police stations, without pushing and shoving, and spelled their names and addresses clearly, so that the men coming to arrest them later on would not make a mistake, Magdalena went back to bed and read magazines. Nobody ever offered her a yellow star, but she found one for herself. It was lying on the ground, in front of the entrance to the Hôtel Meurice—so she said.

Walking the pugs in the rain, Magdalena had looked back to wave at Raymonde, polishing a window. (A publisher of comic books has the place now.) She crossed the Tuileries, then the Rue de Rivoli, and, stepping under the arcades, furled her silk umbrella. Rain had driven in; she skirted puddles in her thin shoes. Just level with the Meurice, where there were so many German officers that some people were afraid to walk there, or scorned to, she stopped to examine a star—soiled, trodden on. She moved it like a wet leaf with the point of her umbrella, bent, picked it up, dropped it in her purse.

"Why?" I had good reason to ask, soon after.

"To keep as a souvenir, a curiosity. To show my friends in Cannes, so that they can see what things are like in Paris."

I didn't like that. I had wanted to pull her across to my side, not to be dragged over to hers.

A day later we set off by train for the South, which was still a free zone. The only Nazis she would be likely to encounter there would be French; I gave Magdalena a lecture on how to recognize and avoid them. We sat side by side in a second-class compartment, in the near dark. (Much greater suspicion attended passengers in first; besides that, I could not afford it.) Magdalena, unfortunately, was dressed for tea at the Ritz. She would have retorted that nothing could be plainer than a Molyneux suit and a diamond pin. The other passengers, three generations of a single family, seemed to be asleep. On the new, unnatural frontier dividing France North from South, the train came to a halt. We heard German soldiers coming on board, to examine our papers. Trying not to glance at Magdalena, I fixed my eyes on the small overnight case she had just got down from the rack and sat holding on her lap. When the train stopped, all the lights suddenly blazed—seemed to blaze; they were dull and brown. Magdalena at once stood up, got her case down without help, removed a novel (it was *Bella*, by Jean Giraudoux), and began to read.

I thought that she had done the very thing bound to make her seem suspect. Her past, intricate and inscrutable, was summed up by the rich leather of the case and the gold initials on the lid and the tiny gold padlock and key, in itself a piece of jewelry. That woman could not possibly be the wife of that young man, with his rolled-up canvas holdall with the cracked leather straps. The bag was not even mine; it had belonged to my mother, or an aunt. I reached over and turned her case around, so that I could open it, as if I were anxious to cooperate, to get things ready for inspection. The truth was, I did not want the German peasants in uniform to read her initials, to ask what her maiden name was, or to have cause for envy; the shut case might have been offered for sale in a window along the Rue du Faubourg-Saint-Honoré, at extortionate cost. I thought that if those peasants, now approaching our compartment, had not been armed, booted, temporarily privileged, they might have served a different apprenticeship—learned to man mirror-walled elevators, carry trays at shoulder level, show an underling's gratitude for Magdalena's escort's tip. I flung the lid back, against her jacket of thin wool; and there, inside, on top of some folded silk things the color of the palest edge of sunrise, lay a harsh star. I smoothed the silken stuff and palmed the star and got it up my sleeve.

In my terrible fright my mind caught on something incidental—that Magdalena had never owned anything else so coarse to the touch. She had never been a child, had never played with sand and mud. She had been set down in a large European city, smart hat tilted, rings swiveled so that she could pull her gloves on, knowing all there is about gold padlocks and keys. "Cosmopolitan," an incendiary word now, flared in my mind. In the quiet train (no train is so still as one under search), its light seemed to seek out crude editorials, offensive cartoons, repulsive graffiti.

The peasants in uniform—they were two—slid open the compartment door. They asked no more than any frontier inspector, but the reply came under the heading of life and death. "Cosmopolitan" had flared like a star; it dissolved into a dirty little puddle. Its new, political meaning seeped into my brain and ran past my beliefs and convictions, and everything my parents stood for. I felt it inside my skull, and I wondered if it would ever evaporate.

One of the peasants spoke, and Magdalena smiled. She told me later that he had the accent said to have been Wagner's. Seeing the open case, he plunged his hand under the silks and struck a hairbrush. He shut the lid and stared dumbly at the initials. The other one in the meanwhile frowned at our papers. Then the pair of them stumbled out.

Our fellow passengers looked away, as people do when someone with the wrong ticket is caught in first class. I put the case back on the rack and muttered an order. Magdalena obediently followed me out to the corridor. It may have looked as if we were just standing, smoking, but I was trying to find out how she, who had never owned anything ugly, had come into possession of this thing. She told me about the Rue de Rivoli, and that she had thought the star would interest her friends in Cannes: They would be able to see how things were now up in Paris. If she had buried it next to her hairbrush, it would have seemed as though she had something to hide. She said she had nothing to hide; absolutely nothing.

I had been running with sweat; now I felt cold. I asked her if she was crazy. She took this for the anxious inquiry of a young man deeply in love. Her nature was sunny, and as good as gold. She laughed and told me she had been called different things but never crazy. She started to repeat some of them, and I kissed her to shut her up. The corridor was jammed with people lying sprawled or sitting on their luggage, and she sounded demented and foreign.

I wondered what she meant by "friends in Cannes." To women of her sort, "friend" is often used as a vague substitute for "lover." (Notice how soon after thinking "cosmopolitan" I thought "of her sort.") She had mentioned the name of the people who were offering her shelter in Cannes; it was a French name but perhaps an alias.

I had a right to know more. She was my wife. For the first and the last time I considered things in that particular way: After all, she *is* my wife. I was leaving the train at Marseilles, though my ticket read Cannes. From Marseilles, I would try to get to North Africa, then to England. Magdalena would sit the war out in an airy villa—the kind aliens can afford.

When I next said something—about getting back to our seats—my voice was too high. It still rises and thins when I feel under strain. (In the 1950s, when I was often heard over the radio, interviewing celebrated men about their early struggles and further ambitions, I would get about two letters a year from women saying they envied my mother.)

It was probably just as well that we were spending our last night among strangers. After our wedding we had almost ceased to be lovers. I had to keep the peace at home, and Magdalena to prepare to leave without showing haste. I thought she was tense and tired; but I appreciate now that Magdalena was never fatigued or wrought-up, and I can only guess she had to say good-bye to someone else. She sent the dogs away to Raymonde's native town in Normandy, mentioning to the concierge that it was for the sake of their health and for a few days only. At the first sign of fright, of hurry, or of furniture removed to storage, the concierge might have been halfway to the police station to report on the tenant who had so many good friends, and whose voice sang a foreign tune.

In the compartment, I tried to finish the thoughts begun in the corridor. I had married her to do the right thing; that was established. Other men have behaved well in the past, and will continue to do so. It comforted me to know I was not the only one with a safe conscience. Thinking this in the darkened, swaying compartment meant that I was lucid and generous, and also something of a louse. I whispered to Magdalena, "What is bad behavior? What is the worst?" The question did not seem to astonish her. Our union was blessed, and she was my wife forevermore, and she could fall back on considerable jurisprudence from the ledgers of Heaven to prove it; but I was still the student who had brought his books to Quai Voltaire, who had looked up to make sure she was still in the room, and asked some question from beyond his experience. She took my hand and said the worst *she* remembered was the Viennese novelist who had taken some of her jewelry (she meant "stolen") and pawned it and kept all the money.

We said good-bye in Marseilles, on the station platform. In the southern morning light her eyes were pale blue. There were armed men in uniform everywhere. She wore a white suit and a thin blouse and a white hat I had never seen before. She had taken a suitcase into the filthy toilet and emerged immaculate. I had the feeling that she could hardly wait to get back on the train and roll on to new adventures.

"And now I am down here, away from all my friends in Paris," she had the gall to say, shading her eyes. It was a way of showing spirit, but I had never known anyone remotely like her, and I probably thought she should be tight-lipped. By "all my friends" she must have meant men who had said, "If you ever need help," knowing she would never ask; who might have said, "Wasn't it awful, tragic, about Magdalena?" if she had never been seen again.

She had left her luggage and jewelry untended in the compartment. I was glad to see she wore just her wedding ring; otherwise, she might have looked too actressy, and drawn attention. (I had no idea how actresses were supposed to look.) Sometimes she used an amber cigarette holder with a swirl of diamond dust like the tail of a comet. She must have sold it during the war; or perhaps lost it, or given it away.

"You look like a youth leader," she said. I was Paris-pale, but healthy. My hair was clipped short. I might have been about to lead police and passengers in patriotic singsong. I was patriotic, but not as the new regime expected its young to be; I was on my way to be useful to General de Gaulle, if he would have me. I saw myself floating over the map of France, harnessed to a dazzling parachute, with a gun under my arm.

We had agreed not to stare at each other once we'd said goodbye. Magdalena kissed me and turned and pulled herself up the high steps of the train. I got a soft, bent book out of my canvas holdall and began to read something that spoke only to me. So the young think, and I was still that young: Poetry is meant for one reader only. Magdalena, gazing tenderly down from the compartment window, must have seen just the shape of the poem on the page. I turned away from the slant of morning sunlight—not away from her. When the train started to move, she reached down to me, but I was too far to touch. A small crucifix on a chain slipped free of her blouse. I stuck to our promise and never once raised my eyes. At the same time, I saw everything—the shade of her white hat brim aslant on her face, her hand with the wedding ring.

I put the star in my book, to mark the place: I figured that if I was caught I was done for anyway. When my adventures were over, I would show it to my children; I did not for a second see Magdalena as their mother. They were real children, not souls to be bargained. So it seems to me now. It shows how far into the future I thought you could safely carry a piece of the past. Long after the war, I found the star, still in the same book, and I offered to give it back to Magdalena, but she said she knew what it was like.

THE COLONEL'S CHILD

("Édouard, Juliette, Lena")

I GOT TO LONDON by way of Marseilles and North Africa, having left Paris more than a year before. My aim was to join the Free French and General de Gaulle. I believed the weight of my presence could tip the scales of war, like one vote in a close election. There was no vanity in this. London was the peak of my hopes and desires. I could look back and see a tamed landscape. My past life dwindled and vanished in that long perspective. I was twenty-three.

In my canvas holdall I carried a tobacco pouch someone had given me, filled with thin reddish soil from Algeria. In those days earth from France and earth from Algeria meant the same thing. Only years later was I able to think, I must have been crazy. When you are young, your patriotism is like metaphysical frenzy. Later, it becomes one more aspect of personal crankiness.

Instead of a hero's welcome I was given forms to fill out. These questionnaires left no room for postscripts, and so only a skeleton of myself could be drawn. I was Édouard B., born in Paris, father a schoolteacher (so was my mother, but I wasn't asked), student of literature and philosophy, single, no dependents.

Some definitions seemed incomplete. For instance, I was not entirely single: Before leaving Paris I had married a Jewish-born actress, so as to give her the security of my name. As far as I knew, she was now safe and in Cannes. At the same time, I was not a married man. The marriage was an incident, gradually being rubbed out in the long perspective I've described. So I saw it; so I would insist. You have to remember the period, and France occupied, to imagine how one could think, and behave. We always say this—"Think of the times we had to live in"—when the past is dragged forward, all the life gone out of it, and left unbreathing at our feet.

Instead of sending me off to freeze on a parade ground, the Free French kept me in London. I took it to mean they wanted to school me in sabotage work and drop me into France. I did not know special parachute training might be needed. I thought you held your breath and jumped.

Two months later I lay in a hospital ward with a broken nose, broken left arm, and fractures in both legs. They had been trying to teach me to ride a motorbike, and on my first time out I skidded into a wall. The instructor came and sat by my bedside. He was about twice my age, a former policeman from Rouen. He said the Free French weren't quite casting me off, but some of them wondered if I was meant for a fighting force in exile. I was a cerebral type, who needed the peace of an office job, with no equipment to smash—not even a typewriter. I asked if General de Gaulle had been informed about my accident.

"Is he a friend of yours?" said the instructor.

"I've seen him," I said. "I saw him in Carlton Gardens. He came out the door and down some steps, and got into his car. I was carrying a lot of parcels, so I couldn't salute. I don't think he noticed. I hope not."

There was a silence, during which the instructor stared at his watch. Presently, he inquired what I wanted to do with my life.

"I think I am a poet," I said. "I can't be sure."

After that they sent me a regular hospital visitor, a volunteer. Juliette was her name. She was seventeen, from Bordeaux, the daughter of a colonel who had followed de Gaulle to London.

She had a precise, particular way of speaking, with every syllable given full value and the consonants treated like little stones. It was not the native accent of Bordeaux, which anyone can imitate, or the everyday French of Paris I'd grown up with, but the tone, almost undefinable, of the French Protestant upper class. I had not heard it before, not consciously, and for the moment had no means of placing it. I thought she had picked up an affectation of some sort while learning English and had carried it over to French. She had, besides, the habit of thrusting into French conversation brief, joyous, and usually irrelevant remarks in English: "You don't say!" "Oh, what a shame!" "How glad I am for you!" "How gorgeous!"

From behind a mask of splints and bandages I appraised her face, which was still childlike, rounded as if over a layer of cream. A beret kept slipping and sliding off her dark hair. "Oh, what a pity!" she remarked, pulling it back on. She was dressed in the least becoming clothes I had ever seen on a young woman—a worn and drooping tunic, thick black stockings, and a navy sweater frayed at the cuffs. She had spent five months in an English girls' school, she told me, and this was the remains of a uniform. She had nothing else to wear, nothing that fitted. Her mother was too busy to shop.

"Can't you shop for yourself?"

"It's not done," she said. "I mean, we don't do things that way."

"Who is we?"—for she still puzzled me.

"Besides, I've got no money." This seemed a sensible explanation. I wondered why she had bothered to make another. "My mother teaches English to French recruits. Actually, she doesn't know much, but she can make them read traffic signs."

"You mean, 'Stop'?"

"Well, there are other things—'No Entry.'" She looked troubled, as if she were not succeeding in the tranquil, sleepy conversation that is supposed to keep a victim's mind off his wounds.

I had lost six front teeth in the accident. Through the gap, Juliette fed me the mess the English call custard. My right arm was fine, but I let her do it. She was grave, intent—a little girl playing. She might have been poking a spoon into a doll's porcelain face. When I refused to swallow any more, she got a bottle of eau de cologne and a facecloth out of a satchel and carefully wiped my hands and wrists and around my neck—whatever was bare and visible. I wondered if she would offer to comb my hair and cut my nails, but the nursing part of the game was over. She sat with her ankles crossed and her hands clasped, a good girl on a visit, and told me that her father, the colonel, was an outcast with a price on his head. From the care she took not to say where he was, I understood they had sent him to France, on a mission. Forgetting about secrets, she suddenly said she yearned to be smuggled into France, too, so that she could join him and they might blow up bridges together.

"I wanted to do that," I said. "That's why I came here. But I'm useless. I may come out of this with a scarred face, or a limp. I'd be at risk."

"Oh, I know," said Juliette. "The Germans would catch you and shoot you. They'd look for a secret agent all covered with scars. Oh, what a nuisance!"

Sweet Juliette. Her dark eyes held all the astonished eagerness of a child of twelve. I often think I should want to be back there, with a Juliette still virginal, untouched, saying encouraging things such as "all covered with scars," but at the age I am now it would bore me.

She came to the hospital twice a week, then every day. Her mother was at work, and I felt the girl had time on her hands and was often lonely. She was with me when they took the last of the mask off. "Well?" I said. "Tell me the worst."

"I can't," she said. "I don't know how you were before." She held up a pocket mirror. My nose was broken, all right, and I had thick, bruised cheekbones, like a Cossack. For someone who had never been to war, I was amazingly the image of an old soldier.

I left the hospital on crutches. There was no such thing as therapy—you got going or you did not. The organization found me a room on Baker Street, not far from where Juliette lived with her mother, as it turned out, and they gave me low-grade and harmless work to do. As my instructor had predicted, I was let nowhere near a typewriter, and once, I remember, someone even snatched a pencil sharpener away. Juliette used to come to the office, though she wasn't supposed to, and sit by my desk as if it were a bed. She had got rid of the uniform, but her new clothes, chosen by her mother, were English and baggy, in the grays and mustards Englishwomen favored. They seemed picked deliberately to make her creamy skin sallow, her slenderness gaunt. The mother was keeping her plain, I thought, perhaps to keep her out of trouble. Why didn't Juliette rebel? She was eighteen by now, but forty years ago eighteen was young. I wondered why she hung around me, what she wanted. I thought I guessed, but I decided not to know. I didn't want it said I had destroyed two items of French property—a motorcycle and a colonel's child. It was here, in London, that I was starting to get the hang of French society. In our reduced world, everyone in it a symbol of native, inborn rank, Juliette stood higher than some random young man who had merely laid his life on the line. She had connections, simply by the nature of how things were ordered.

I asked her once if there was a way of getting a message to my mother, in Paris—just a word to say I was safe. She pretended not to hear but about a month later said, "No, it's too dangerous. Besides, they don't trust you."

"Don't trust me? Why not?"

"I'm not sure."

"Do you?" I said.

"That's different."

Her mother was out most evenings. When Juliette was alone, I brought my rations around, and she cooked our supper. We drank— only because everybody did—replacing the whiskey in her mother's precious Haig bottle with London tap water. Once, Juliette tried restoring the color with cold tea, and there was hell to pay. When the news came from France that her father had been arrested and identified, she came straight to me.

"I'll never see him again," she said. "I haven't even got a decent snapshot of him. My mother has them all. She's got them in a suitcase. I feel sick. Feel my forehead. Feel my cheeks." She took my hand. "Feel the back of my neck. Feel my throat," she said, dragging my hand. We left the office and went to her flat and pulled the blackout curtain. The sun was shining on the other side of the street, where everything was bombed, but she didn't want to see it.

"How do you know your mother's not going to walk in?" I said. "She may want to be alone with you. She may want a quiet place to cry."

Juliette shook her head. "We're not like that. We don't do those things."

I think of the love and despair she sent out to me, the young shoots wild and blind, trusting me for support. She asked me to tell my most important secret, so that we would be bound. The most intimate thing I could say was that I was writing less poetry and had started a merciless novel about the French in London.

"I could tell you a lot," said Juliette. "Heroes' wives sleeping with other men."

"It's not that sort of novel," I said. "In my novel, they're all dead, but they don't know it. Every character is in a special Hell, made to measure."

"That's not how it is," she said. "We're not dead or in Hell. We're just here, waiting. We don't know what Hell will be like. Nobody knows. And some of us are going to be together in Heaven." She put her face against mine, saying this. It never occurred to me that she meant it, literally. I thought her Calvinism was just an organized form of disbelief. "Haven't you got some better secret?" she said. I supposed that schoolgirls talked this way, pledging friendship, and I wondered what she was taking me for. "Well," she said presently, "will you marry me anyway, even without a secret?"

Nobody coerced me into a life with Juliette. There were no tears, no threats, and I was not afraid of her mother. All I had to say was "I don't know yet" or "We'll see." I think I wanted to get her out of her loneliness. When for all her shyness she asked if I loved her, I said I would never leave her, and I am sure we both thought it meant the same thing. A few days later she told her mother that we were engaged and that nothing would keep her from marrying me after the war, and, for the first time since she could remember, she saw her mother cry.

Instead of a ring I gave Juliette some of the Algerian soil. She thanked me but confessed she had no idea what to do with it. Should it be displayed in a saucer, on a low table? Should she seal it up in a labeled, dated envelope? Tactful from infancy, she offered the gift to her mother, her rival in grief.

Now that we were "engaged," I began to see what the word covered for Juliette, and I had no qualms about smuggling her into my room—though never, of course, late at night. We took the mattress off the sagging daybed and put it on the floor, in front of the gas fire. Juliette would take her clothes off and tell me about her early years, though I didn't always listen. Sometimes she talked about the life waiting for us in Paris, and the number of children we would have, and the names we would give them. I remember a Thomas and a Claire.

"How many children should we have?" she said. "I'd say about ten. Well, seven. At least five."

Her clothes were scattered all over the floor, and the room was cold, in spite of the fire, but she didn't seem to feel it. "I hate children," I said. I was amazed that I could say something so definite and so cruel, and that sounded so true. When had I stopped liking them? Perhaps when I adopted the colonel's child, believing she would never grow up. I could have said, "I don't like *other* children," but nothing about this conversation was thought out.

"You will love them," she said happily. "You'll see." She held her spread fingers against the gas flame, counting off their names. Each finger stood for a greedy, willful personality, as tough as a fist. An only child, she invented playmates and named them, and I was supposed to bring them to life.

"I know it sounds stupid," she said, "but I kept my dolls until I was fifteen. My mother finally gave them away."

"Brothers and sisters," I said.

"No, just dolls. But they did have names."

"Is that one of your secrets?" "Secrets" had become charged with erotic meaning, when we were alone.

"You've got a special secret," she said.

"Yes. I've torn up my novel."

"Oh, how lovely for you! Or is that sad?"

"I'm just giving it up. I'll never start another."

"You've got another secret," she said. "You're married to someone." As she said this, she seemed to become aware that the room was cold. She shivered and reached for her dress, and drew it around her like a shawl. "A person went to see your mother. She—your mother—said to tell you your wife was all right. Your *wife*," said Juliette, trying to control her voice, "is in the south of France. She has managed to send your mother a pound of onions. To eat," said Juliette, as I went on staring. "Onions, to eat."

"I did get married," I said. "But she's not my wife. I did it to save her. I've got her yellow star somewhere."

"I'd like to see it," said Juliette, politely.

"It is made of cheap, ugly material," I said, as if that were the only thing wrong.

"I think you should put some clothes on," said Juliette. "If you're going to tell about your wife."

"She isn't my wife," I said. "The marriage was just something legal. Apart from being legal, it doesn't count."

"She may not be your wife," said Juliette, "but she is your mother's daughter-in-law." She drew up her knees and bent her head on them, as if it were disgraceful to watch me dressing. "You mean," she said, after a time, "that it doesn't count as a secret?" I gathered up the rest of her clothes and put them beside her on the mattress. "Does it count as anything?"

"I'll walk you home," I said.

"You don't need to."

"It's late. I can't have you wandering around in the blackout."

She dressed, slowly, sitting and kneeling. "I am glad she is safe and well," she said. "It would be too bad if you had done all that for nothing. She must be very grateful to you."

I had never thought about gratitude. It seemed to me that, yes, she was probably grateful. I suddenly felt impatient for the war to end, so that I could approach her, hand in hand with Juliette, and ask for a divorce and a blessing.

Juliette, kneeling, fastened the buttons of the latest flour sack her mother had chosen. "Why did you tear up your novel?" she said.

Because I can't wrench life around to make it fit some fantasy. Because I don't know how to make life sound worse or better, or how to make it sound true. Instead of saying this, I said, "How do you expect me to support ten children?" The colonel's wife didn't like me much, but she had said that after the war there were a few people she could introduce me to. She had mentioned something about radio broadcasting, and I liked the idea. Juliette was still kneeling, with only part of the hideous dress buttoned up. I looked down at her bent head. She must have been thinking that she had tied herself to a man with no money, no prospects, and no connections. Who wasn't entirely single. Who might be put on a charge for making a false declaration. Who had a broken nose and a permanent limp. Who, so far, had never finished anything he'd started. Perhaps she was forgetting one thing: I had got to London.

"I could stay all night," she said. "If you want me to."

"Your mother would have the police out," I said.

"She'd never dare," said Juliette. "I've never called the police because *she* didn't come home."

"It would be …" I tried to think of what it could be for us. "It would be radical."

Her hands began to move again, the other way, unbuttoning. She was the colonel's child, she had already held her breath and jumped, and that was the start and the end of it.

"We may be in big trouble over this," I said.

"Oh, what a pity," she said. "We'll always be together. We will always be happy. How lovely! What a shame!"

I think she still trusted me at that moment; I hope so.

RUE DE LILLE

("Édouard, Juliette, Lena")

MY SECOND WIFE, Juliette, died in the apartment on Rue de Lille, where she had lived—at first alone, more or less, then with me—since the end of the war. All the rooms gave onto the ivy-hung well of a court, and were for that reason dark. We often talked about looking for a brighter flat, on a top floor with southern exposure and a wide terrace, but Parisians seldom move until they're driven to. "We know the worst of what we've got," we told each other. "It's better than a bad surprise."

"And what about your books?" Juliette would add. "It would take you months to get them packed, and in the new place you'd never get them sorted." I would see myself as Juliette saw me, crouched over a slanting, shaking stack of volumes piled on a strange floor, cursing and swearing as I tried to pry out a dictionary. "Just the same, I don't intend to die here," she also said.

I once knew someone who believed drowning might be easy, even pleasant, until he almost drowned by accident. Juliette's father was a colonel who expected to die in battle or to be shot by a German firing squad, but he died of typhus in a concentration camp. I had once, long ago, imagined for myself a clandestine burial with full honors after some Resistance feat, but all I got out of the war was a few fractures and a broken nose in a motorcycle accident.

Juliette had thirty-seven years of blacked-out winter mornings in Rue de Lille. She was a few days short of her sixtieth birthday when I found her stretched out on the floor of our bedroom, a hand slackened on a flashlight. She had been trying to see under a chest of drawers, and her heart stopped. (Later, I pulled the chest away from the wall and discovered a five-franc coin.) Her gray-and-dark hair, which had grown soft and wayward with age, was tied back with a narrow satin ribbon. She looked more girlish than at any time since I'd first met her. (She fell in love with me young.) She wore a pleated flannel skirt, a tailored blouse, and one of the thick cardigans with gilt buttons she used to knit while watching television. She had been trained to believe that to look or to listen quietly is to do nothing; she would hum along with music, to show she wasn't idle. She was discreet, she was generous to a sensible degree, she was anything but contentious. I often heard her remark, a trifle worriedly, that she was never bored. She was faithful, if "faithful" means avoiding the acknowledged forms of trouble. She was patient. I know she was good. Any devoted male friend, any lover, any husband would have shown up beside her as selfish, irritable, even cruel. She displayed so little of the ordinary kinds of jealousy, the plain marital do-you-often-have-lunch-with-her? sort, that I once asked her if she had a piece missing.

"Whoever takes this place over," she said, when we spoke of moving, "will be staggered by the size of the electricity bills." (Juliette paid them; I looked after a number of other things.) We had to keep the lights turned on all day in winter. The apartment was L-shaped, bent round two sides of a court, like a train making a sharp turn. From our studies, at opposite ends of the train, we could look out and see the comforting glow of each other's working life, a lamp behind a window. Juliette would be giving some American novel a staunch, steady translation; I might be getting into shape my five-hour television series, *Stendhal and the Italian Experience*, which was to win an award in Japan.

We were together for a duration of time I daren't measure against the expanse of Juliette's life; it would give me the feeling that I had decamped to a height of land, a survivor's eminence, so as to survey the point at which our lives crossed and mingled and began to move in the same direction: a long, narrow reach of time in the Rue de Lille. It must be the washy, indefinite colorations of blue that carpeted, papered, and covered floors, walls, and furniture and shaded our lamps which cast over that reach the tone of a short season. I am thinking of the patches of distant, neutral blue that appear over Paris in late spring, when it is still wet and cold in the street and tourists have come too early. The tourists shelter in doorways, trying to read their soaked maps, perennially unprepared in their jeans and thin jackets. Overhead, there are scrapings of a color that carries no threat and promises all.

That choice, Juliette's preference, I sometimes put down to her Calvinist sobriety—call it a temperament—and sometimes to a refinement of her Huguenot taste. When I was feeling tired or impatient, I complained that I had been consigned to a Protestant Heaven by an arbitrary traffic cop, and that I was better suited to a pagan Hell. Again, as I looked round our dining-room table at the calm, clever faces of old friends of Juliette's family, at their competent and unassuming wives, I saw what folly it might be to set such people against a background of buttercup yellow or apple green. The soft clicking of their upper-class Protestant consonants made conversation distant and neutral, too. It was a voice that had puzzled me the first time I'd heard it from Juliette. I had supposed, mistakenly, that she was trying it on for effect; but she was wholly natural.

The sixteenth-century map of Paris I bought for her birthday is still at the framer's; I sent a check but never picked it up. I destroyed her private correspondence without reading it, and gave armfuls of clothes away to a Protestant charity. To the personal notice of her death in *Le Monde* was attached a brief mention of her father, a hero of the Resistance for whom suburban streets are named; and of her career as a respected translator, responsible for having introduced post-war American literature to French readers; and of her husband, the well-known radio and television interviewer and writer, who survived her.

Another person to survive her was my first wife. One night when Juliette and I were drinking coffee in the little sitting room where she received her women friends, and where we watched television, Juliette said, again, "But how much of what she says does she believe? About her Catholicism, and all those fantasies running round in her head—that she is your true and only wife, that your marriage is registered in Heaven, that you and she will be together in another world?"

"Those are things people put in letters," I said. "They sit down alone and pour it out. It's sincere at that moment. I don't know why she would suddenly be *in*sincere."

"After all the trouble she's made," said Juliette. She meant that for many years my wife would not let me divorce.

"She couldn't help that," I said.

"How do you know?"

"I don't know. It's what I think. I hardly knew her."

"You must have known *something*."

"I haven't seen her more than three or four times in the last thirty-odd years, since I started living with you."

"What do you mean?" said Juliette. "You saw her just once, with me. We had lunch. You backed off asking for the divorce."

"You can't ask for a divorce at lunch. It had to be done by mail."

"And since then she hasn't stopped writing," said Juliette. "Do you mean three or four times, or do you mean once?"

I said, "Once, probably. Probably just that once."

Viewing me at close range, as if I were a novel she had to translate, Juliette replied that one ought to be spared unexpected visions. Just now, it was as if three walls of the court outside had been bombed flat. Through a bright new gap she saw straight through to my first marriage. We—my first wife and I—postured in the distance, like characters in fiction.

I had recently taken part in a panel discussion, taped for television, on the theme "What Literature, for Which Readers, at Whose Price?" I turned away from Juliette and switched on the set, about ten minutes too early. Juliette put the empty cups and the coffeepot on a tray she had picked up in Milan, the summer I was researching the Stendhal, and carried the tray down the dim passage to the kitchen. I watched the tag end of the late news. It must have been during the spring of 1976. Because of the energy crisis, daylight saving had been established. Like any novelty, it was deeply upsetting. People said they could no longer digest their food or be nice to their children, and that they needed sedation to help them through the altered day. A doctor was interviewed; he advised a light diet and early bed until mind and body adjusted to the change.

I turned, smiling, to where Juliette should have been. My program came on then, and I watched myself making a few points before I got up and went to find her. She was in the kitchen, standing in the dark, clutching the edge of the sink. She did not move when I turned the light on. I put my arms around her, and we came back to her sitting room and watched the rest of the program together. She was knitting squares of wool to be sewn together to make a blanket; there was always, somewhere, a flood or an earthquake or a flow of refugees, and those who outlasted jeopardy had to be covered.

LENA

("Édouard, Juliette, Lena")

IN HER PRIME, by which I mean in her beauty, my first wife, Magdalena, had no use for other women. She did not depend upon women for anything that mattered, such as charm and enjoyment and getting her bills paid; and as for exchanging Paris gossip and intimate chitchat, since she never confided anything personal and never complained, a man's ear was good enough. Magdalena saw women as accessories, to be treated kindly—maids, seamstresses, manicurists—or as comic minor figures, the wives and official fiancées of her admirers. It was not in her nature to care what anyone said, and she never could see the shape of a threat even when it rolled over her, but I suspect that she was called some of the senseless things she was called, such as "Central European whore" and "Jewish adventuress," by women.

Now that she is nearly eighty and bedridden, she receives visits from women—the residue of an early wave of Hungarian emigration. They have small pink noses, wear knitted caps pulled down to their eyebrows, and can see on dark street corners the terrible ghost of Béla Kun. They have forgotten that Magdalena once seemed, perhaps, disreputable. She is a devout Catholic, and she says cultivated, moral-sounding things, sweet to the ears of half a dozen widows of generals and bereft sisters of bachelor diplomats. They crowd her bedside table with bottles of cough mixture, lemons, embroidered table napkins, jars of honey, and covered bowls of stewed plums, the juice from which always spills. They call Magdalena "Lena."

She occupies a bed in the only place that would have her—a hospital on the northern rim of Paris, the color of jails, daubed with graffiti. The glass-and-marble lobby commemorates the flashy prosperity of the 1960s. It contains, as well as a vandalized coffee machine and a plaque bearing the name of a forgotten minister of health, a monumental example of the art of twenty years ago: a white foot with each toenail painted a different color. In order to admire this marvel, and to bring Magdalena the small comforts I think she requires, I need to travel a tiring distance by the underground suburban train. On these expeditions I carry a furled umbrella: The flat, shadeless light of this line is said to attract violent crime. In my wallet I have a card attesting to my right to sit down, because of an accident suffered in wartime. I never dare show the card. I prefer to stand. Anything to do with the Second World War, particularly its elderly survivors, arouses derision and ribaldry and even hostility in the young.

Magdalena is on the fourth floor (no elevator) of a wing reserved for elderly patients too frail to be diverted to nursing homes—assuming that a room for her in any such place could be found. The old people have had it drummed into them that they are lucky to have a bed, that the waiting list for their mattress and pillow lengthens by the hour. They must not seem too capricious, or dissatisfied, or quarrelsome, or give the nurses extra trouble. If they persist in doing so, their belongings are packed and their relatives sent for. A law obliges close relatives to take them in. Law isn't love, and Magdalena has seen enough distress and confusion to make her feel thoughtful.

"Families are worse than total war," she says. I am not sure what her own war amounted to. As far as I can tell, she endured all its rigors in Cannes, taking a daily walk to a black-market restaurant, her legs greatly admired by famous collaborators and German officers along the way. Her memory, when she wants to be bothered with it, is like a brief, blurry, self-centered dream.

"But what were you *doing* during those years?" I have asked her. (My mother chalked Gaullist slogans on walls in Paris. The father of my second wife died deported. I joined the Free French in London.)

"I was holding my breath," she answers, smiling.

She shares a room with a woman who suffers from a burning rash across her shoulders. Medicine that relieves the burning seems to affect her mind, and she will wander the corridors, wondering where she is, weeping. The hospital then threatens to send her home, and her children, in a panic, beg that the treatment be stopped. After a few days the rash returns, and the woman keeps Magdalena awake describing the pain she feels—it is like being flogged with blazing nettles, she says. Magdalena pilfers tranquilizers and gets her to take them, but once she hit the woman with a pillow. The hospital became nasty, and I had to step in. Fortunately, the supervisor of the aged-and-chronic department had seen me on television, taking part in a literary game ("Which saint might Jean-Paul Sartre have wanted most to meet?"), and that helped our case.

Actually, Magdalena cannot be evicted—not just like that. She has no family, and nowhere to go. Her continued existence is seen by the hospital as a bit of a swindle. They accepted her in the first place only because she was expected to die quite soon, releasing the bed.

"Your broken nose is a mistake," she said to me the other day.

My face was damaged in the same wartime accident that is supposed to give me priority seating rights in public transport. "It lends you an air of desperate nerve, as if a Malraux hero had wandered into a modern novel and been tossed out on his face."

Now, this was hard on a man who had got up earlier than usual and bought a selection of magazines for Magdalena before descending to the suburban line, with its flat, worrying light. A man who had just turned sixty-five. Whose new bridge made him lisp. She talks the way she talked in the old days, in her apartment with the big windows and the sweeping view across the Seine. She used to wear white, and sit on a white sofa. There were patches of red in the room—her long fingernails and her lipstick, and the Legion of Honor on some admirer's lapel. She had two small, funny dogs whose eyes glowed red in the dusk.

"I heard you speaking just the other day," she went on. "You were most interesting about the way Gide always made the rounds of the bookstores to see how his work was selling. Actually, I think I told you that story."

"It couldn't have been just the other day," I said. "It sounds like a radio program I had in the 1950s."

"It couldn't have been you, come to think of it," she said. "The man lisped. I said to myself, It *might* be Édouard."

Her foreign way of speaking enchanted me when I was young. Now it sharpens my temper. Fifty years in France and she still cannot pronounce my name, Édouard, without putting the stress on the wrong syllable and rolling the r. "When you come to an r," I have told her, "keep your tongue behind your lower front teeth."

"It won't stay," she says. "It curls up. I am sorry." As if she cared. She will accept any amount of petulance shown by me, because she thinks she owes me tolerance: She sees me as youthful, boyish, to be teased and humored. She believes we have a long, unhampered life before us, and she expects to occupy it as my wife and widow-to-be. To that end, she has managed to outlive my second wife, and she may well survive me, even though I am fourteen years younger than she is and still on my feet.

Magdalena's Catholic legend is that she was converted after hearing Jacques Maritain explain neo-Thomism at a tea party. Since then, she has never stopped heaping metaphysical rules about virtue on top of atavistic arguments concerning right and wrong. The result is a moral rock pile, ready to slide. Only God himself could stand up to the avalanche, but in her private arrangements he is behind her, egging her on. I had to wait until a law was passed that allowed divorce on the ground of separation before I was free to marry again. I waited a long time. In the meantime, Magdalena was writing letters to the Pope, cheering his stand on marriage and urging him to hold firm. She can choose among three or four different languages, her choice depending on where her dreams may have taken her during the night. She used to travel by train to Budapest and Prague wearing white linen. She had sleek, fair hair, and wore a diamond hair clip behind one ear. Now no one goes to those places, and the slim linen suits are crumpled in trunks. Her mind is clear, but she says absurd things. "I never saw her," she said about Juliette, my second wife. "Was she anything like me?"

"You did see her. We had lunch, the three of us."

"Show me her picture. It might bring back the occasion."

"No."

They met, once, on the first Sunday of September, 1954—a hot day of quivering horizons and wasps hitting the windshield. I had a new Renault—a model with a reputation for rolling over and lying with its wheels in the air. I drove, I think, grimly. Magdalena was beside me, in a nimbus of some scent—jasmine, or gardenia—that made me think of the opulent, profiteering side of wars. Juliette sat behind, a road map on her knee, her finger on the western outskirts of Fontainebleau. Her dark hair was pulled back tight and tied at the nape of her neck with a dark blue grosgrain ribbon. It is safe to say that she smelled of soap and lemons.

We were taking Magdalena out to lunch. It was Juliette's idea. Somewhere between raspberries-and-cream and coffee, I was supposed to ask for a divorce—worse, to coax from Magdalena the promise of collusion in obtaining one. So far, she had resisted any mention of the subject and for ten years had refused to see me. Juliette and

I had been living together since the end of the war. She was thirty now, and tired of waiting. We were turning into one of those uneasy, shadowy couples, perpetually waiting for a third person to die or divorce. I was afraid of losing her. That summer, she had traveled without me to America (so much farther from Europe then than it is today), and she had come back with a different coloration to her manner, a glaze of independence, as though she had been exposed to a new kind of sun.

I remember how she stared at Magdalena with gentle astonishment, as if Magdalena were a glossy illustration that could not look back. Magdalena had on a pale dress of some soft, floating stuff, and a pillbox hat tied on with a white veil, and long white gloves. I saw her through Juliette's eyes, and I thought what Juliette must be thinking: Where does Magdalena think we're taking her? To a wedding? Handing her into the front seat, I had shut the door on her skirt. I wondered if she had turned into one of the limp, pliant women whose clothes forever catch.

It was Juliette's custom to furnish social emptiness with some rattling anecdote about her own activities. Guests were often grateful. Without having to cast far, they could bring up a narrative of their own, and the result was close to real conversation. Juliette spoke of her recent trip. She said she was wearing an American dress made of a material called cotton seersucker. It washed like a duster and needed next to no ironing.

For answer, she received a side view of Magdalena's hat and a blue eye shadowed with paler blue. Magdalena was not looking but listening, savoring at close quarters the inflections of the French Protestant gentry. She knew she was privileged. As a rule, they speak only to one another. Clamped to gearshift and wheel, I was absolved of the need to comment. My broken profile had foxed Magdalena at first. She had even taken me for an impostor. But then the remembered face of a younger man slid over the fraud and possessed him.

Juliette had combed through the *Guide Michelin* and selected a restaurant with a wide terrace and white umbrellas, set among trees. At some of the tables there were American officers, in uniform, with their families—this is to show how long ago it was. Juliette adjusted our umbrella so that every inch of Magdalena was in shade. She took it for granted that my wife belonged to a generation sworn to paleness. From where I was sitting, I could see the interior of the restaurant. It looked cool and dim, I thought, and might have been better suited to the soft-footed conversation to come.

I adjusted my reading glasses, which Magdalena had never seen, and stared at a long handwritten menu. Magdalena made no move to examine hers. She had all her life let men decide. Finally, Juliette wondered if our guest might not like to start with asparagus. I was afraid the asparagus would be canned. Well, then, said Juliette, what about melon. On a hot day, something cool followed by cold salmon. She broke off. I started to remove my glasses, but Juliette reminded me about wine.

Magdalena was engaged in a ritual that Juliette may not have seen before and that I had forgotten: pulling off her tight, long gloves finger by finger and turning her rings right side up. Squeezed against a great sparkler of some kind was a wedding ring. Rallying, Juliette gave a little twitch to the collar of the washable seersucker and went on about America. In Philadelphia, a celebrated Pentecostal preacher had persuaded the Holy Spirit to settle upon a member of the congregation, a woman whose hearing had been damaged when she was brained by a flying shoe at a stock-car race. The deaf woman rose and said she could hear sparrows chirping in High German, on which the congregation prayed jubilant thanks.

Juliette did not stoop to explain that she was no Pentecostalist. She mentioned the Holy Spirit as an old acquaintance of her own class and background, a cultivated European with an open mind.

We were no longer young lovers, and I had heard this story several times. I said that the Holy Spirit might find something more useful to attend to than a ruptured eardrum. We were barely ten years out of a disastrous war. All over the world, there were people sick, afraid, despairing. Only a few days before, the President of Brazil had shot himself to death.

Juliette replied that there were needs beyond our understanding. "God knows what he wants," she said. I am sure she believed it.

"God wanted Auschwitz?" I said.

I felt a touch on my arm, and I looked down and saw a middle-aged hand and a wedding ring.

With her trained inclination to move back from rising waters, Juliette made the excuse of a telephone call. I knew that her brief departure was meant to be an intermission. When she came back, we would speak about other things. Magdalena and I sat quietly, she with her hand still on my arm, as if she had finally completed a gesture begun a long time before. Juliette, returning, her eyes splashed with cold water, her dark hair freshly combed, saw that I was missing a good chance to bring up the divorce. She sat down, smiled, picked up her melon spoon. She was working hard these days, she said. She was translating an American novel that should never have been written. (Juliette revealed nothing more about this novel.) From there, she slid along to the subject of drastic separations—not so much mine from Magdalena as divorcement in general. Surely, she said, a clean parting was a way of keeping life pleasant and neat? This time, it was Magdalena's hearing that seemed impaired, and the Holy Spirit was nowhere. The two women must have been thinking the same thing at that moment, though for entirely different reasons: that I had forfeited any chance of divine aid by questioning God's intentions.

It was shortly before her removal to the hospital that Magdalena learned about Juliette's death. One of her doddering friends may have seen the notice in a newspaper. She at once resumed her place as my only spouse and widow-to-be. In fact, she had never relinquished it, but now the way back to me shone clear. The divorce, that wall of pagan darkness, had been torn down and dispersed with the concubine's ashes. She saw me delivered from an adulterous and heretical alliance. It takes a convert to think "heretical" with a straight face. She could have seen Juliette burned at the stake without losing any sleep. It is another fact about converts that they make casual executioners.

She imagined that I would come to her at once, but I went nowhere. Juliette had asked to be cremated, thinking of the purification of the flame, but the rite was accomplished by clanking, hidden, high-powered machinery that kept starting and stopping, on cycle. At its loudest, it covered the voice of the clergyman, who affirmed that Juliette was eyeing us with great goodwill from above, and it prevailed over Juliette's favorite recordings of Mozart and Bach. Her ashes were placed in a numbered niche that I never saw, for at some point in the funeral service I lost consciousness and had to be carried out. This nightmare was dreamed in the crematorium chapel of Père Lachaise cemetery. I have not been back. It is far from where I live, and I think Juliette is not there, or anywhere. From the moment when her heart stopped, there has been nothing but silence.

Last winter, I had bronchitis and seldom went out. I managed to send Magdalena a clock, a radio, an azalea, and enough stamps and stationery to furnish a nineteenth-century literary correspondence. Nevertheless, the letters that reached my sickbed from hers were scrawled in the margins of newspapers, torn off crookedly. Sometimes she said her roommate had lent her the money for a stamp. The message was always the same: I must not allow my wife to die in a public institution. Her pink-nosed woman friends wrote me, too, signing their alien names, announcing their titles—there was a princess.

It was no good replying that everybody dies in hospital now. The very idea made them sick, of a sickness beyond any wasting last-ditch illusion. Then came from Magdalena "On Saturday at nine o'clock, I shall be dressed and packed, and waiting for you to come and take me away."

Away from the hospital bed? It took weeks of wangling and soft-soaping and even some mild bribery to obtain it. Public funds, to which she is not entitled, and a voluntary contribution from me keep her in it. She has not once asked where the money comes from. When she was young, she decided never to worry, and she has kept the habit.

I let several Saturdays go by, until the folly had quit her mind. Late in April I turned up carrying a bottle of Krug I had kept on ice until the last minute and some glasses in a paper bag. The woman who shares her room gave a great groan when she saw me, and showed the whites of her eyes. I took this to mean that Magdalena had died. The other bed was clean and empty. The clock and the radio on the table had the look of objects left behind. I felt shock, guilt, remorse, and relief, and I wondered what to do with the wine. I turned, and there in the doorway stood Magdalena, in dressing gown and slippers, with short white hair. She shuffled past me and lay on the bed with her mouth open, struggling for breath.

"Shouldn't I ring for a nurse?" I said, unwrapping the bottle.

"No one will come. Open the champagne."

"I'd better fetch a nurse." Instead, I made room on the table for the glasses. I'd brought three, because of the roommate.

Magdalena gasped, "Today is my birthday." She sat up, apparently recovered, and got her spectacles out from under the pillow. Leaning toward me, she said, "What's that red speck on your lapel? It looks like the Legion of Honor."

"I imagine that's what it is."

"Why?" she said. "Was there a reason?"

"They probably had a lot to give away. Somebody did say something about 'cultural enrichment of the media.'"

"I am glad about the enrichment," she said. "I am also very happy for you. Will you wear it all the time, change it from suit to suit?"

"It's new," I said. "There was a ceremony this morning." I sat down on the shaky chair kept for visitors, and with a steadiness that silenced us both I poured the wine. "What about your neighbor?" I said, the bottle poised.

"Let her sleep. This is a good birthday surprise."

I felt as if warm ashes were banked round my heart, like a residue of good intentions. I remembered that when Magdalena came back to Paris after the war, she found her apartment looted, laid waste. One of the first letters to arrive in the mail was from me, to say that I was in love with a much younger woman. "If it means anything at all to you," I said, the coals glowing brighter, "if it can help you to understand me in any way—well, no one ever fascinated me as much as you." This after only one glass.

"But, perhaps, you never loved me," she said.

"Probably not," I said. "Although I must have."

"You mean, in a way?" she said.

"I suppose so."

The room became so quiet that I could hear the afternoon movie on television in the next room. I recognized the voice of the actor who dubs Robert Redford.

Magdalena said, "Even a few months ago this would have been my death sentence. Now I am simply thankful I have so little time left to wander between 'perhaps' and 'probably not' and 'in a way.' A crazy old woman, wringing my hands."

I remembered Juliette's face when she learned that her menopause was irreversible. I remember her shock, her fright, her gradual understanding, her storm of grief. She had hoped for children, then finally a child, a son she would have called "Thomas." "Your death sentence," I said. "Your death sentence. What about Juliette's life sentence? She never had children. By the time I was able to marry her, it was too late."

"She could have had fifteen children without being married," said Magdalena.

I wanted to roar at her, but my voice went high and thin. "Women like Juliette, people like Juliette, don't do that sort of thing. It was a wonder she consented to live with me for all those years. What about her son, her Thomas? I couldn't even have claimed him—not legally, as long as I was married to you. Imagine him, think of him, applying for a passport, finding out he had no father. Nothing on his birth certificate. Only a mother."

"You could have adopted Thomas," said Magdalena. "That way, he'd have been called by your name."

"I couldn't—not without your consent. *You* were my wife. Besides, why should I have to adopt my own son?" I think this was a shout; that is how it comes back to me. "And the inheritance laws, as they were in those days. Have you ever thought about that? I couldn't even make a will in his favor."

Cheek on hand, blue eyes shadowed, my poor, mad, true, and only wife said, "Ah, Édouard, you shouldn't have worried. You know I'd have left him all that I had."

It wasn't the last time I saw Magdalena, but after that day she sent no more urgent messages, made no more awkward demands. Twice since then, she has died and come round. Each time, just when the doctor said, "I think that's it," she has squeezed the nurse's hand. She loves rituals, and she probably wants the last Sacraments, but hospitals hate that. Word that there is a priest in the place gets about, and it frightens the other patients. There are afternoons when she can't speak and lies with her eyes shut, the lids quivering. I hold her hand, and feel the wedding ring. Like the staunch little widows, I call her "Lena," and she turns her head and opens her eyes.

I glance away then, anywhere—at the clock, out the window. I have put up with everything, but I intend to refuse her last imposition, the encounter with her blue, enduring look of pure love.

1933

(from "The Carette Sisters")

About a year after the death of M. Carette, his three survivors—Berthe and her little sister, Marie, and their mother—had to leave the comfortable flat over the furniture store in Rue Saint-Denis and move to a smaller place. They were not destitute: There was the insurance and the money from the sale of the store, but the man who had bought the store from the estate had not yet paid and they had to be careful.

Some of the lamps and end tables and upholstered chairs were sent to relatives, to be returned when the little girls grew up and got married. The rest of their things were carried by two small, bent men to the second floor of a stone house in Rue Cherrier near the Institute for the Deaf and Dumb. The men used an old horse and an open cart for the removal. They told Mme. Carette that they had never worked outside that quarter; they knew only some forty streets of Montreal but knew them thoroughly. On moving day, soft snow, like graying lace, fell. A patched tarpaulin protected the Carettes' wine-red sofa with its border of silk fringe, the children's brass bedstead, their mother's walnut bed with the carved scallop shells, and the round oak table, smaller than the old one, at which they would now eat their meals. Mme. Carette told Berthe that her days of entertaining and cooking for guests were over. She was just twenty-seven.

They waited for the moving men in their new home, in scrubbed, empty rooms. They had already spread sheets of *La Presse* over the floors, in case the men tracked in snow. The curtains were hung, the cream-colored blinds pulled halfway down the sash windows. Coal had been delivered and was piled in the lean-to shed behind the kitchen. The range and the squat, round heater in the dining room issued tidal waves of dense metallic warmth.

The old place was at no distance. Parc Lafontaine, where the children had often been taken to play, was just along the street. By walking an extra few minutes, Mme. Carette could patronize the same butcher and grocer as before. The same horse-drawn sleighs would bring bread, milk, and coal to the door. Still, the quiet stone houses, the absence of heavy traffic and shops made Rue Cherrier seem like a foreign country.

Change, death, absence—the adult mysteries—kept the children awake. From their new bedroom they heard the clang of the first streetcar at dawn—a thrilling chord, metal on metal, that faded slowly. They would have jumped up and dressed at once, but to their mother this was still the middle of the night. Presently, a new, continuous sound moved in the waking streets, like a murmur of leaves. From the confused rustle broke distinct impressions: an alarm clock, a man speaking, someone's radio. Marie wanted to talk and sing. Berthe had to invent stories to keep her quiet. Once she had placed her hand over Marie's mouth and been cruelly bitten.

They slept on a horsehair mattress, which had a summer and a winter side, and was turned twice a year. The beautiful stitching at the edge of the sheets and pillows was their mother's work. She had begun to sew her trousseau at the age of eleven; her early life was spent in preparation for a wedding. Above the girls' bed hung a gilt crucifix with a withered spray of box hedge that passed for the Easter palms of Jerusalem.

Marie was afraid to go to the bathroom alone after dark. Berthe asked if she expected to see their father's ghost, but Marie could not say: She did not yet know whether a ghost and the dark meant the same thing. Berthe was obliged to get up at night and accompany her along the passage. The hall light shone out of a blue glass tulip set upon a column painted to look like marble. Berthe could just reach it on tiptoe; Marie not at all.

Marie would have left the bathroom door open for company, but Berthe knew that such intimacy was improper. Although her First Communion was being delayed because Mme. Carette wanted the two sisters to come to the altar together, she had been to practice confession. Unfortunately, she had soon run out of invented sins. Her confessor seemed to think there should be more: He asked if she and her little sister had ever been in a bathroom with the door shut, and warned her of grievous fault.

On their way back to bed, Berthe unhooked a calendar on which was a picture of a family of rabbits riding a toboggan. She pretended to read stories about the rabbits and presently both she and Marie fell asleep.

They never saw their mother wearing a bathrobe. As soon as Mme. Carette got up she dressed herself in clothes that were in the colors of half mourning—mauve, dove gray. Her fair hair was brushed straight and subdued under a net. She took a brush to everything—hair, floors, the children's elbows, the kitchen chairs. Her scent was of Baby's Own soap and Florida Water. When she bent to kiss the children, a cameo dangled from a chain. She trained the girls not to lie, or point, or gobble their food, or show their legs above the knee, or leave fingerprints on windowpanes, or handle the parlor curtains—the slightest touch could crease the lace, she said. They learned to say in English, "I don't understand" and "I don't know" and "No, thank you." That was all the English anyone needed between Rue Saint-Denis and Parc Lafontaine.

In the dining room, where she kept her sewing machine, Mme. Carette held the treadle still, rested a hand on the stopped wheel. "What are you doing in the parlor?" she called. "Are you touching the curtains?" Marie had been spitting on the window and drawing her finger through the spit. Berthe, trying to clean the mess with her flannelette petticoat, said, "Marie's just been standing here saying 'Saint Marguerite, pray for us.'"

Downstairs lived M. Grosjean, the landlord, with his Irish wife and an Airedale named Arno. Arno understood English and French; Mme. Grosjean could only speak English. She loved Arno and was afraid he would run away: He was a restless dog who liked to be doing something all the time. Sometimes M. Grosjean took him to Parc Lafontaine and they played at retrieving a collapsed and bitten tennis ball. Arno was trained to obey both "*Cherchez!*" and "Go fetch it!" but he paid attention to neither. He ran with the ball and Mme. Grosjean had to chase him.

Mme. Grosjean stood outside the house on the back step, just under the Carettes' kitchen window, holding Arno's supper. She wailed, "Arno, where have you got to?" M. Grosjean had probably taken Arno for a walk. He made it a point never to say where he was going: He did not think it a good thing to let women know much.

Mme. Grosjean and Mme. Carette were the same age, but they never became friends. Mme. Carette would say no more than a few negative things in English ("No, thank you" and "I don't know" and "I don't understand") and Mme. Grosjean could not work up the conversation. Mme. Carette had a word with Berthe about Irish marriages: An Irish marriage, while not to be sought, need not be scorned. The Irish were not English. God had sent them to Canada to keep people from marrying Protestants.

That winter the girls wore white leggings and mittens, knitted by their mother, and coats and hats of white rabbit fur. Each of them carried a rabbit muff. Marie cried when Berthe had to go to school. On Sunday afternoons they played with Arno and M. Grosjean. He tried to take their picture but it wasn't easy. The girls stood on the front steps, hand in hand, mitten to mitten, while Arno was harnessed to a sled with curved runners. The red harness had once been worn by another Airedale, Ruby, who was smarter even than Arno.

M. Grosjean wanted Marie to sit down on the sled, hold the reins, and look sideways at the camera. Marie clung to Berthe's coat. She was afraid that Arno would bolt into the Rue Saint-Denis, where there were streetcars. M. Grosjean lifted her off the sled and tried the picture a different way, with Berthe pretending to drive and Marie standing face-to-face with Arno. As soon as he set Marie on her feet, she began to scream. Her feet were cold. She wanted to be carried. Her nose ran; she felt humiliated. He got out his handkerchief, checked green and white, and wiped her whole face rather hard.

Just then his wife came to the front door with a dish of macaroni and cut-up sausages for Arno. She had thrown a sweater over her cotton housecoat; she was someone who never felt the cold. A gust of wind lifted her loose hair. M. Grosjean told her that the kid was no picnic. Berthe, picking up English fast, could not have repeated his exact words, but she knew what they meant.

Mme. Carette was still waiting for the money from the sale of the store. A brother-in-law helped with the rent, sending every month a generous postal order from Fall River. It was Mme. Carette's belief that God would work a miracle, allowing her to pay it all back. In the meantime, she did fine sewing. Once she was hired to sew a trousseau, working all day in the home of the bride-to-be. As the date of the wedding drew near she had to stay overnight.

Mme. Grosjean looked after the children. They sat in her front parlor, eating fried-egg sandwiches and drinking cream soda (it did not matter if they dropped crumbs) while she played a record of a man singing, "Dear one, the world is waiting for the sunrise."

Berthe asked, in French, "What is he saying?" Mme. Grosjean answered in English, "A well-known Irish tenor."

When Mme. Carette came home the next day, she gave the girls a hot bath, in case Mme. Grosjean had neglected their elbows and heels. She took Berthe in her arms and said she must never tell anyone their mother had left the house to sew for strangers. When she grew up, she must not refer to her mother as a seamstress, but say instead, "My mother was clever with her hands."

That night, when they were all three having supper in the kitchen, she looked at Berthe and said, "You have beautiful hair." She sounded so tired and stern that Marie, eating mashed potatoes and gravy, with a napkin under her chin, thought Berthe must be getting a scolding. She opened her mouth wide and started to howl. Mme. Carette just said, "Marie, don't cry with your mouth full."

Downstairs, Mme. Grosjean set up her evening chant, calling for Arno. "Oh, where have you got to?" she wailed to the empty backyard.

"The dog is the only thing keeping those two together," said Mme. Carette. "But a dog isn't the same as a child. A dog doesn't look after its masters in their old age. We shall see what happens to the marriage after Arno dies." No sooner had she said this than she covered her mouth and spoke through her fingers: "God forgive my unkind thoughts." She propped her arms on each side of her plate, as the girls were forbidden to do, and let her face slide into her hands.

Berthe took this to mean that Arno was doomed. Only a calamity about to engulf them all could explain her mother's elbows on the table. She got down from her chair and tried to pull her mother's hands apart, and kiss her face. Her own tears ran into her long hair, down onto her starched piqué collar. She felt tears along her nose and inside her ears. Even while she sobbed out words of hope and comfort (Arno would never die) and promises of reassuring behavior (she and Marie would always be good) she wondered how tears could flow in so many directions at once.

Of course, M. Grosjean did not know that all the female creatures in his house were frightened and lonely, calling and weeping. He was in Parc Lafontaine with Arno, trying to play go-fetch-it in the dark.

THE CHOSEN HUSBAND

(from "The Carette Sisters")

IN 1949, a year that contained no other news of value, Mme. Carette came into a legacy of eighteen thousand dollars from a brother-in-law who had done well in Fall River. She had suspected him of being a Freemason, as well as of other offenses, none of them trifling, and so she did not make a show of bringing out his photograph; instead, she asked her daughters, Berthe and Marie, to mention him in their prayers. They may have, for a while. The girls were twenty-two and twenty, and Berthe, the elder, hardly prayed at all.

The first thing that Mme. Carette did was to acquire a better address. Until now she had kept the Montreal habit of changing her rented quarters every few seasons, a conversation with a landlord serving as warranty, rent paid in cash. This time she was summoned by appointment to a rental agency to sign a two-year lease. She had taken the first floor of a stone house around the corner from the church of Saint Louis de France. This was her old parish (she held to the network of streets near Parc Lafontaine) but a glorious strand of it, Rue Saint-Hubert.

Before her inheritance Mme. Carette had crept to church, eyes lowered; had sat where she was unlikely to disturb anyone whose life seemed more fortunate, therefore more deserving, than her own. She had not so much prayed as petitioned. Now she ran a glove along the pew to see if it was dusted, straightened the unread pamphlets that called for more vocations for missionary service in Africa, told a confessor that, like all the prosperous, she was probably without fault. When the holy-water font looked mossy, she called the parish priest and had words with his housekeeper, even though scrubbing the church was not her job. She still prayed every day for the repose of her late husband, and the unlikelier rest of his Freemason brother, but a tone of briskness caused her own words to rattle in her head. Church was a hushed annex to home. She prayed to insist upon the refinement of some request, and instead of giving thanks simply acknowledged that matters used to be worse.

Her daughter Berthe had been quick to point out that Rue Saint-Hubert was in decline. Otherwise, how could the Carettes afford to live here? (Berthe worked in an office and was able to pay half the rent.) A family of foreigners were installed across the road. A seamstress had placed a sign in a ground-floor window—a sure symptom of decay. True, but Mme. Carette had as near neighbors a retired opera singer and the first cousins of a city councillor—calm, courteous people who had never been on relief. A few blocks north stood the mayor's private dwelling, with a lamppost on each side of his front door. (During the recent war the mayor had been interned, like an enemy alien. No one quite remembered why. Mme. Carette believed that he had refused an invitation to Buckingham Palace, and that the English had it in for him. Berthe had been told that he had tried to annex Montreal to the state of New York and that someone had minded. Marie, who spoke to strangers on the bus, once came home with a story about Fascist views; but as she could not spell "Fascist," and did not know if it was a kind of landscape or something to eat, no one took her seriously. The mayor had eventually been released, was promptly reelected, and continued to add luster to Rue Saint-Hubert.)

Mme. Carette looked out upon long façades of whitish stone, windowpanes with beveled edges that threw rainbows. In her childhood this was how notaries and pharmacists had lived, before they began to copy the English taste for freestanding houses, blank lawns, ornamental willows, leashed dogs. She recalled a moneyed aunt and uncle, a family of well-dressed, soft-spoken children, heard the echo of a French more accurately expressed than her own. She had tried to imitate the peculiarity of every syllable, sounded like a plucked string, had tried to make her little girls speak that way. But they had rebelled, refused, said it made them laughed at.

When she had nothing to request, or was tired of repeating the same reminders, she shut her eyes and imagined her funeral. She was barely forty-five, but a long widowhood strictly observed had kept her childish, not youthful. She saw the rosary twined round her hands, the vigil, the candles perfectly still, the hillock of wreaths. Until the stunning message from Fall River, death had been her small talk. She had never left the subject, once entered, without asking, "And what will happen then to my poor little Marie?" Nobody had ever taken the question seriously except her Uncle Gildas. This was during their first Christmas dinner on Rue Saint-Hubert. He said that Marie should pray for guidance, the sooner the better. God had no patience with last-minute appeals. (Uncle Gildas was an elderly priest with limited social opportunities, though his niece believed him to have wide and worldly connections.)

"Prayer can fail," said Berthe, testing him.

Instead of berating her he said calmly, "In that case, Berthe can look after her little sister."

She considered him, old and eating slowly. His cassock exhaled some strong cleaning fluid—tetrachloride; he lived in a rest home, and nuns took care of him.

Marie was dressed in one of Berthe's cast-offs—marine-blue velvet with a lace collar. Mme. Carette wore a gray-white dress Berthe thought she had seen all her life. In her first year of employment Berthe had saved enough for a dyed rabbit coat. She also had an electric seal, and was on her way to sheared raccoon. "Marie had better get married," she said.

Mme. Carette still felt cruelly the want of a husband, someone—not a daughter—to help her up the step of a streetcar, read *La Presse* and tell her what was in it, lay down the law to Berthe. When Berthe was in adolescence, laughing and whispering and not telling her mother the joke, Mme. Carette had asked Uncle Gildas to speak as a father. He sat in the parlor, in a plush chair, all boots and cassock, knees apart and a hand on each knee, and questioned Berthe about her dreams. She said she had never in her life dreamed anything. Uncle Gildas replied that anyone with a good conscience could dream events pleasing to God; he himself had been doing it for years. God kept the dreams of every living person on record, like great rolls of film. He could have them projected whenever he wanted. Montreal girls, notoriously virtuous, had his favor, but only up to a point. He forgave, but never forgot. He was the embodiment of endless time—though one should not take "embodiment" literally. Eternal remorse in a pit of flames was the same to him as a rap on the fingers with the sharp edge of a ruler. Marie, hearing this, had fainted dead away. That was the power of Uncle Gildas.

Nowadays, shrunken and always hungry, he lived in retirement, had waxed linoleum on his floor, no carpet, ate tapioca soup two or three times a week. He would have stayed in bed all day, but the nuns who ran the place looked upon illness as fatigue, fatigue as shirking. He was not tired or lazy; he had nothing to get up for. The view from his window was a screen of trees. When Mme. Carette came to visit—a long streetcar ride, then a bus—she had just the trees to look at: She could not stare at her uncle the whole time. The trees put out of sight a busy commercial garage. It might have distracted him to watch trucks backing out, perhaps to witness a bloodless accident. In the morning he went downstairs to the chapel, ate breakfast, sat on his bed after it was made. Or crossed the gleaming floor to a small table, folded back the oilcloth cover, read the first sentence of a memoir he was writing for his great-nieces: "I was born in Montreal, on the 22nd of May, 1869, of pious Christian parents, connected to Montreal families for whom streets and bridges have been named." Or shuffled out to the varnished corridor, where there was a pay phone. He liked dialing, but out of long discipline never did without a reason.

Soon after Christmas Mme. Carette came to see him, wearing Berthe's velvet boots with tassels, Berthe's dyed rabbit coat, and a feather turban of her own. Instead of praying for guidance Marie had fallen in love with one of the Greeks who were starting to move into their part of Montreal. There had never been a foreigner in the family, let alone a pagan. Her uncle interrupted to remark that Greeks were usually Christians, though of the wrong kind for Marie. Mme. Carette implored him to find someone, not a Greek, of the right kind: sober, established, Catholic, French-speaking, natively Canadian. "Not Canadian from New England," she said, showing a brief ingratitude to Fall River. She left a store of nickels, so that he could ring her whenever he liked.

Louis Driscoll, French in all but name, called on Marie for the first time on the twelfth of April, 1950. Patches of dirty snow still lay against the curb. The trees on Rue Saint-Hubert looked dark and brittle, as though winter had killed them at last. From behind the parlor curtain, unseen from the street, the Carette women watched him coming along from the bus stop. To meet Marie he had put on a beige tweed overcoat, loosely belted, a beige scarf, a bottle-green snap-brim fedora, crêpe-soled shoes, pigskin gloves. His trousers were sharply pressed, a shade darker than the hat. Under his left arm he held close a parcel in white paper, the size and shape of a two-pound box of Laura Secord chocolates. He stopped frequently to consult the house numbers (blue and white, set rather high,

Montreal style), which he compared with a slip of paper brought close to his eyes.

It was too bad that he had to wear glasses; the Carettes were not prepared for that, or for the fringe of ginger hair below his hat. Uncle Gildas had said he was of distinguished appearance. He came from Moncton, New Brunswick, and was employed at the head office of a pulp-and-paper concern. His age was twenty-six. Berthe thought that he must be a failed seminarist; they were the only Catholic bachelors Uncle Gildas knew.

Peering at their front door, he walked into a puddle of slush. Mme. Carette wondered if Marie's children were going to be nearsighted. "How can we be sure he's the right man?" she said.

"Who else could he be?" Berthe replied. What did he want with Marie? Uncle Gildas could not have promised much in her name, apart from a pliant nature. There could never be a meeting in a notary's office to discuss a dowry, unless you counted some plates and furniture. The old man may have frightened Louis, reminded him that prolonged celibacy—except among the clergy—is displeasing to God. Marie is poor, he must have said, though honorably connected. She will feel grateful to you all her life.

Their front steps were painted pearl gray, to match the building stone. Louis's face, upturned, was the color of wood ash. Climbing the stair, ringing the front doorbell could change his life in a way he did not wholly desire. Probably he wanted a woman without sin or risk or coaxing or remorse; but did he want her enough to warrant setting up a household? A man with a memory as transient as his, who could read an address thirty times and still let it drift, might forget to come to the wedding. He crumpled the slip of paper, pushed it inside a tweed pocket, withdrew a large handkerchief, blew his nose.

Mme. Carette swayed back from the curtain as though a stone had been flung. She concluded some private thought by addressing

Marie: "... although I will feel better on my deathbed if I know you are in your own home." Louis meanwhile kicked the bottom step, getting rid of snow stuck to his shoes. (Rustics kicked and stamped. Marie's Greek had wiped his feet.) Still he hesitated, sliding a last pale look in the direction of buses and streetcars. Then, as he might have turned a gun on himself, he climbed five steps and pressed his finger to the bell.

"Somebody has to let him in," said Mme. Carette.

"Marie," said Berthe.

"It wouldn't seem right. She's never met him."

He stood quite near, where the top step broadened to a small platform level with the window. They could have leaned out, introduced him to Marie. Marie at this moment seemed to think he would do; at least, she showed no sign of distaste, such as pushing out her lower lip or crumpling her chin. Perhaps she had been getting ready to drop her Greek: Mme. Carette had warned her that she would have to be a servant to his mother, and eat peculiar food. "He's never asked me to," said Marie, and that was part of the trouble. He hadn't asked anything. For her twenty-first birthday he had given her a locket on a chain and a box from Maitland's, the West End confectioner, containing twenty-one chocolate mice. "He loves me," said Marie. She kept counting the mice and would not let anyone eat them.

In the end it was Berthe who admitted Louis, accepted the gift of chocolates on behalf of Marie, showed him where to leave his hat and coat. She approved of the clean white shirt, the jacket of a tweed similar to the coat but lighter in weight, the tie with a pattern of storm-tossed sailboats. Before shaking hands he removed his glasses, which had misted over, and wiped them dry. His eyes meeting the bright evening at the window (Marie was still there, but with her back to the street) flashed ultramarine. Mme. Carette hoped Marie's children would inherit that color.

He took Marie's yielding hand and let it drop. Freed of the introduction, she pried open the lid of the candy box and said, distinctly, "No mice." He seemed not to hear, or may have thought she was pleased to see he had not played a practical joke. Berthe showed him to the plush armchair, directly underneath a chandelier studded with lightbulbs. From this chair Uncle Gildas had explained the whims of God; against its linen antimacassar the Greek had recently rested his head.

Around Louis's crêpe soles pools of snow water formed. Berthe glanced at her mother, meaning that she was not to mind; but Mme. Carette was trying to remember where Berthe had said that she and Marie were to sit. (On the sofa, facing Louis.) Berthe chose a gilt upright chair, from which she could rise easily to pass refreshments. These were laid out on a marble-topped console: vanilla wafers, iced sultana cake, maple fudge, marshmallow biscuits, soft drinks. Behind the sofa a large pier glass reflected Louis in the armchair and the top of Mme. Carette's head. Berthe could tell from her mother's posture, head tilted, hands clasped, that she was silently asking Louis to trust her. She leaned forward and asked him if he was an only child. Berthe closed her eyes. When she opened them, nothing had changed except that Marie was eating chocolates. Louis seemed to be reflecting on his status.

He was the oldest of seven, he finally said. The others were Joseph, Raymond, Vincent, Francis, Rose, and Claire. French was their first language, in a way. But, then, so was English. A certain Louis Joseph Raymond Driscoll, Irish, veteran of Waterloo on the decent side, proscribed in England and Ireland as a result, had come out to Canada and grafted on pure French stock a number of noble traits: bright, wavy hair, a talent for public speaking, another for social aplomb. In every generation of Driscolls, there had to be a Louis, a Joseph, a Raymond. (Berthe and her mother exchanged a look. He wanted three sons.)

His French was slow and muffled, as though strained through wool. He used English words, or French words in an English way. Mme. Carette lifted her shoulders and parted her clasped hands as if to say, "Never mind, English is better than Greek." At least, they could be certain that the Driscolls were Catholic. In August his father and mother were making the Holy Year pilgrimage to Rome.

Rome was beyond their imagining, though all three Carettes had been to Maine and Old Orchard Beach. Louis hoped to spend a vacation in Old Orchard (in response to an ardent question from Mme. Carette), but he had more feeling for Quebec City. His father's people had entered Canada by way of Quebec.

"The French part of the family?" said Mme. Carette.

"Yes, yes," said Berthe, touching her mother's arm.

Berthe had been to Quebec City, said Mme. Carette. She was brilliant, reliable, fully bilingual. Her office promoted her every January. They were always sending her away on company business. She knew Plattsburgh, Saranac Lake. In Quebec City, at lunch at the Château Frontenac, she had seen well-known politicians stuffing down oysters and fresh lobster, at taxpayers' expense.

Louis's glance tried to cross Berthe's, as he might have sought out and welcomed a second man in the room. Berthe reached past Mme. Carette to take the candy box away from Marie. She nudged her mother with her elbow.

"The first time I ever saw Old Orchard," Mme. Carette resumed, smoothing the bodice of her dress, "I was sorry I had not gone there on my honeymoon." She paused, watching Louis accept a chocolate. "My husband and I went to Fall River. He had a brother in the lumber business."

At the mention of lumber, Louis took on a set, bulldog look. Berthe wondered if the pulp-and-paper firm had gone bankrupt. Her thoughts rushed to Uncle Gildas—how she would have it out with him, not leave it to her mother, if he had failed to examine Louis's prospects. But then Louis began to cough and had to cover his mouth. He was in trouble with a caramel. The Carettes looked away, so that he could strangle unobserved. "How dark it is," said Berthe, to let him think he could not be seen. Marie got up, with a hiss and rustle of taffeta skirt, and switched on the twin floor lamps with their cerise silk shades.

"There," she seemed to be saying to Berthe. "Have I done the right thing? Is this what you wanted?"

Louis still coughed, but weakly. He moved his fingers, like a child made to wave good-bye. Mme. Carette wondered how many contagious children's diseases he had survived; in a large family everything made the rounds. His eyes, perhaps seeking shade, moved across the brown wallpaper flecked with gold and stopped at the only familiar sight in the room—his reflection in the pier glass. He sat up straighter and quite definitely swallowed. He took a long drink of ginger ale. "When Irish eyes are smiling," he said, in English, as if to himself. "When Irish eyes are smiling. There's a lot to be said for that. A lot to be said."

Of course he was at a loss, astray in an armchair, with the Carettes watching like friendly judges. When he reached for another chocolate, they looked to see if his nails were clean. When he crossed his legs, they examined his socks. They were fixing their first impression of the stranger who might take Marie away, give her a modern kitchen, children to bring up, a muskrat coat, a charge account at Dupuis Frères department store, a holiday in Maine. Louis continued to examine his bright Driscoll hair, the small nose along which his glasses slid. Holding the glasses in place with a finger, he answered Mme. Carette: His father was a dental surgeon, with a degree from Pennsylvania. It was the only degree worth mentioning. Before settling into a dentist's chair the patient should always read the writing on the wall. His mother was born Lucarne, a big name in

Moncton. She could still get into her wedding dress. Everything was so conveniently arranged at home—cavernous washing machine, giant vacuum cleaner—that she seldom went out. When she did, she wore a two-strand cultured-pearl necklace and a coat and hat of Persian lamb.

The Carettes could not match this, though they were related to families for whom bridges were named. Mme. Carette sat on the edge of the sofa, ankles together. Gentility was the brace that kept her upright. She had once been a young widow, hard pressed, had needed to sew for money. Berthe recalled a stricter, an unsmiling mother, straining over pleats and tucks for clients who reneged on pennies. She wore the neutral shades of half mourning, the whitish grays of Rue Saint-Hubert, as though everything had to be used up—even remnants of grief.

Mme. Carette tried to imagine Louis's mother. She might one day have to sell the pearls; even a dentist trained in Pennsylvania could leave behind disorder and debts. Whatever happened, she said to Louis, she would remain in this flat. Even after the girls were married. She would rather beg on the steps of the parish church than intrude upon a young marriage. When her last, dreadful illness made itself known, she would creep away to the Hôtel Dieu and die without a murmur. On the other hand, the street seemed to be filling up with foreigners. She might have to move.

Berthe and Marie were dressed alike, as if to confound Louis, force him to choose the true princess. Leaving the sight of his face in the mirror, puzzled by death and old age, he took notice of the two moiré skirts, organdy blouses, patent-leather belts. "I can't get over those twins of yours," he said to Mme. Carette. "I just can't get over them."

Once, Berthe had tried Marie in her own office—easy work, taking messages when the switchboard was closed. She knew just enough English for that. After two weeks the office manager, Mr.

Macfarlane, had said to Berthe, "Your sister is an angel, but angels aren't in demand at Prestige Central Burners."

It was the combination of fair hair and dark eyes, the enchanting misalliance, that gave Marie the look of an angel. She played with the locket the Greek had given her, twisting and unwinding the chain. What did she owe her Greek? Fidelity? An explanation? He was punctual and polite, had never laid a hand on her, in temper or eagerness, had traveled a long way by streetcar to bring back the mice. True, said Berthe, reviewing his good points, while Louis ate the last of the fudge. It was true about the mice, but he should have become more than "Marie's Greek." In the life of a penniless unmarried young woman, there was no room for a man merely in love. He ought to have presented himself as *something*: Marie's future.

In May true spring came, moist and hot. Berthe brought home new dress patterns and yards of flowered rayon and piqué. Louis called three evenings a week, at seven o'clock, after the supper dishes were cleared away. They played hearts in the dining room, drank Salada tea, brewed black, with plenty of sugar and cream, ate éclairs and mille-feuilles from Celentano, the bakery on Avenue Mont Royal. (Celentano had been called something else for years now, but Mme. Carette did not take notice of change of that kind, and did not care to have it pointed out.) Louis, eating coffee éclairs one after another, told stories set in Moncton that showed off his family. Marie wore a blue dress with a red collar, once Berthe's, and a red barrette in her hair. Berthe, a master player, held back to let Louis win. Mme. Carette listened to Louis, kept some of his stories, discarded others, garnering information useful to Marie. Marie picked up cards at random, disrupting the game. Louis's French was not as woolly as before, but he had somewhere acquired a common Montreal accent. Mme. Carette wondered who his friends were and how Marie's children would sound.

They began to invite him to meals. He arrived at half past five, straight from work, and was served at once. Mme. Carette told Berthe that she hoped he washed his hands at the office, because he never did here. They used the blue-willow-pattern china that would go to Marie. One evening, when the tablecloth had been folded and put away, and the teacups and cards distributed, he mentioned marriage—not his own, or to anyone in particular, but as a way of life. Mme. Carette broke in to say that she had been widowed at Louis's age. She recalled what it had been like to have a husband she could consult and admire. "Marriage means children," she said, looking fondly at her own. She would not be alone during her long, final illness. The girls would take her in. She would not be a burden; a couch would do for a bed.

Louis said he was tired of the game. He dropped his hand and spread the cards in an arc.

"So many hearts," said Mme. Carette, admiringly.

"Let me see." Marie had to stand: there was a large teapot in the way. "Ace, queen, ten, eight, five ... a wedding." Before Berthe's foot reached her ankle, she managed to ask, sincerely, if anyone close to him was getting married this year.

Mme. Carette considered Marie as good as engaged. She bought a quantity of embroidery floss and began the ornamentation of guest towels and tea towels, place mats and pillow slips. Marie ran her finger over the pretty monogram with its intricate frill of vine leaves. Her mind, which had sunk into hibernation when she accepted Louis and forgot her Greek, awoke and plagued her with a nightmare. "I became a nun" was all she told her mother. Mme. Carette wished it were true. Actually, the dream had stopped short of vows. Barefoot, naked under a robe of coarse brown wool, she moved along an aisle in and out of squares of sunlight. At the altar they were waiting to shear her hair. A strange man—not Uncle Gildas, not Louis, not the Greek—got up out of a pew and stood barring her way. The rough gown turned out to be frail protection. All that kept the dream from sliding into blasphemy and abomination was Marie's entire unacquaintance, awake or asleep, with what could happen next.

Because Marie did not like to be alone in the dark, she and Berthe still shared a room. Their childhood bed had been taken away and supplanted by twin beds with quilted satin headboards. Berthe had to sleep on three pillows, because the aluminum hair curlers she wore ground into her scalp. First thing every morning, she clipped on her pearl earrings, sat up, and unwound the curlers, which she handed one by one to Marie. Marie put her own hair up and kept it that way until suppertime.

In the dark, her face turned to the heap of pillows dimly seen, Marie told Berthe about the incident in the chapel. If dreams are life's opposite, what did it mean? Berthe saw that there was more to it than Marie was able to say. Speaking softly, so that their mother would not hear, she tried to tell Marie about men—what they were like and what they wanted. Marie suggested that she and Berthe enter a cloistered convent together, now, while there was still time. Berthe supposed that she had in mind the famous Martin sisters of Lisieux, in France, most of them Carmelites and one a saint. She touched her own temple, meaning that Marie had gone soft in the brain. Marie did not see; if she had, she would have thought that Berthe was easing a curler. Berthe reminded Marie that she was marked out not for sainthood in France but for marriage in Montreal. Berthe had a salary and occasional travel. Mme. Carette had her Fall River bounty. Marie, if she put her mind to it, could have a lifetime of love.

"Is Louis love?" said Marie.

There were girls ready to line up in the rain for Louis, said Berthe.

"What girls?" said Marie, perplexed rather than disbelieving.

"Montreal girls," said Berthe. "The girls who cry with envy when you and Louis walk down the street."

"We have never walked down a street," said Marie.

*

The third of June was Louis's birthday. He arrived wearing a new seersucker suit. The Carettes offered three monogrammed hemstitched handkerchiefs—he was always polishing his glasses or mopping his face. Mme. Carette had prepared a meal he particularly favored—roast pork and coconut layer cake. The sun was still high. His birthday unwound in a steady, blazing afternoon. He suddenly put his knife and fork down and said that if he ever decided to get married he would need more than his annual bonus to pay for the honeymoon. He would have to buy carpets, lamps, a refrigerator. People talked lightly of marriage without considering the cost for the groom. Priests urged the married condition on bachelors—priests, who did not know the price of eight ounces of tea.

"Some brides bring lamps and lampshades," said Mme. Carette. "A glass-front bookcase. Even the books to put in it." Her husband had owned a furniture shop on Rue Saint-Denis. Household goods earmarked for Berthe and Marie had been stored with relatives for some twenty years, waxed and polished and free of dust. "An oak table that seats fourteen," she said, and stopped with that. Berthe had forbidden her to draw up an inventory. They were not bartering Marie.

"Some girls have money," said Marie. Her savings—eighteen dollars—were in a drawer of her mother's old treadle sewing machine.

A spasm crossed Louis's face; he often choked on his food. Berthe knew more about men than Marie—more than her mother, who knew only how children come about. Mr. Ryder, of Berthe's office, would stand in the corridor, letting elevators go by, waiting for a chance to squeeze in next to Berthe. Mr. Sexton had offered her money, a regular allowance, if she would go out with him every Friday, the night of his Legion meeting. Mr. Macfarlane had left a lewd poem on her desk, then a note of apology, then a poem even worse than the first. Mr. Wright-Ashburton had offered to leave his wife—for, of course, they had wives, Mr. Ryder, Mr. Sexton, Mr. Macfarlane, none of whom she had ever encouraged, and Mr. Wright-Ashburton, with whom she had been to Plattsburgh and Saranac Lake, and whose private behavior she had described, kneeling, in remote parishes, where the confessor could not have known her by voice.

When Berthe accepted Mr. Wright-Ashburton's raving proposal to leave his wife, saying that Irene probably knew about them anyway, would be thankful to have it in the clear, his face had wavered with fright, like a face seen underwater—rippling, uncontrolled. Berthe had to tell him she hadn't meant it. She could not marry a divorced man. On Louis's face she saw that same quivering dismay. He was afraid of Marie, of her docility, her monogrammed towels, her dependence, her glass-front bookcase. Having seen this, Berthe was not surprised when he gave no further sign of life until the twenty-fifth of June.

During his absence the guilt and darkness of rejection filled every corner of the flat. There was not a room that did not speak of humiliation—oh, not because Louis had dropped Marie but because the Carettes had honored and welcomed a clodhopper, a cheapjack, a ginger-haired nobody. Mme. Carette and Marie made many telephone calls to his office, with a variety of names and voices, to be told every time he was not at his desk. One morning Berthe, on her way to work, saw someone very like him hurrying into Windsor station. By the time she had struggled out of her crowded streetcar, he was gone. She followed him into the great concourse and looked at the times of the different trains and saw where they were going. A trapped sparrow fluttered under the glass roof. She recalled an expression of Louis's, uneasy and roguish, when he had told Berthe that Marie did not understand the facts of life. (This in English, over the table, as if Mme. Carette and Marie could not follow.) When Berthe asked what these facts might be, he had tried to cross her glance, as on that first evening, one man to another. She was not a man; she had looked away.

*

Mme. Carette went on embroidering baskets of flowers, ivy leaves, hunched over her work, head down. Marie decided to find a job as a receptionist in a beauty salon. It would be pleasant work in clean surroundings. A girl she had talked to on the bus earned fourteen dollars a week. Marie would give her mother eight and keep six. She did not need Louis, she said, and she was sure she could never love him.

"No one expected you to love him," said her mother, without looking up.

On the morning of the twenty-fifth of June he rang the front doorbell. Marie was eating breakfast in the kitchen, wearing Berthe's aluminum curlers under a mauve chiffon scarf, and Berthe's mauve-and-black kimono. He stood in the middle of the room, refusing offers of tea, and said that the whole world was engulfed in war. Marie looked out the kitchen window, at bare yards and storage sheds.

"Not there," said Louis. "In Korea."

Marie and her mother had never heard of the place. Mme. Carette took it for granted that the British had started something again. She said, "They can't take you, Louis, because of your eyesight." Louis replied that this time they would take everybody, bachelors first. A few married men might be allowed to make themselves useful at home. Mme. Carette put her arms around him. "You are my son now," she said. "I'll never let them ship you to England. You can hide in our coal shed." Marie had not understood that the mention of war was a marriage proposal, but her mother had grasped it at once. She wanted to call Berthe and tell her to come home immediately, but Louis was in a hurry to publish the banns. Marie retired to the bedroom and changed into Berthe's white sharkskin sundress and jacket and toeless white suede shoes. She smoothed Berthe's suntan makeup on her legs, hoping that her mother would not see she was not wearing stockings. She combed out her hair, put on lipstick and earrings, and butterfly sunglasses belonging to Berthe. Then, for the first time, she and Louis together walked down the front steps to the street.

At Marie's parish church they found other couples standing about, waiting for advice. They had heard the news and decided to get married at once. Marie and Louis held hands, as though they had been engaged for a long time. She hoped no one would notice that she had no engagement ring. Unfortunately, their banns could not be posted until July, or the marriage take place until August. His parents would not be present to bless them: At the very day and hour of the ceremony they would be on their way to Rome.

The next day, Louis went to a jeweler on Rue Saint-Denis, recommended by Mme. Carette, but he was out of engagement rings. He had sold every last one that day. Louis did not look anywhere else; Mme. Carette had said he was the only man she trusted. Louis's mother sent rings by registered mail. They had been taken from the hand of her dead sister, who had wanted them passed on to her son, but the son had vanished into Springfield and no longer sent Christmas cards. Mme. Carette shook her own wedding dress out of tissue paper and made a few adjustments so that it would fit Marie. Since the war it had become impossible to find silk of that quality.

Waiting for August, Louis called on Marie every day. They rode the streetcar up to Avenue Mont Royal to eat barbecued chicken. (One evening Marie let her engagement ring fall into a crack of the corrugated floor of the tram, and a number of strangers told her to be careful, or she would lose her man, too.) The chicken arrived on a bed of chips, in a wicker basket. Louis showed Marie how to eat barbecue without a knife and fork. Fortunately, Mme. Carette was not there to watch Marie gnawing on a bone. She was sewing the rest of the trousseau and had no time to act as chaperone.

Berthe's office sent her to Buffalo for a long weekend. She brought back match folders from Polish and German restaurants, an ashtray on which was written "Buffalo Hofbrau," and a number of articles that were much cheaper down there, such as nylon stockings. Marie asked if they still ate with knives and forks in Buffalo, or if they had caught up to Montreal. Alone together, Mme. Carette and Berthe sat in the kitchen and gossiped about Louis. The white summer curtains were up; the coal-and-wood range was covered with clean white oilcloth. Berthe had a new kimono—white, with red pagodas on the sleeves. She propped her new red mules on the oven door. She smoked now, and carried everywhere the Buffalo Hofbrau ashtray. Mme. Carette made Berthe promise not to smoke in front of Uncle Gildas, or in the street, or at Marie's wedding reception, or in the front parlor, where the smell might get into the curtains. Sometimes they had just tea and toast and Celentano pastry for supper. When Berthe ate a coffee éclair, she said, "Here's one Louis won't get."

The bright evenings of suppers and card games slid into the past, and by August seemed long ago. Louis said to Marie, "We knew how to have a good time. People don't enjoy themselves anymore." He believed that the other customers in the barbecue restaurant had secret, nagging troubles. Waiting for the wicker basket of chicken, he held Marie's hand and stared at men who might be Greeks. He tried to tell her what had been on his mind between the third and twenty-fifth of June, but Marie did not care, and he gave up. They came to their first important agreement: Neither of them wanted the blue-willow-pattern plates. Louis said he would ask his parents to start them off with six place settings of English Rose. She seemed still to be listening, and so he told her that the name of her parish church, Saint Louis de France, had always seemed to him to be a personal sign of some kind: An obscure force must have guided him to Rue Saint-Hubert and Marie. Her soft brown eyes never wavered. They forgot about Uncle Gildas, and whatever it was Uncle Gildas had said to frighten them.

*

Louis and Marie were married on the third Saturday of August, with flowers from an earlier wedding banked along the altar rail, and two other wedding parties waiting at the back of the church. Berthe supposed that Marie, by accepting the ring of a dead woman and wearing the gown of another woman widowed at twenty-six, was calling down the blackest kind of misfortune. She remembered her innocent nakedness under the robe of frieze. Marie had no debts. She owed Louis nothing. She had saved him from a long journey to a foreign place, perhaps even from dying. As he placed the unlucky ring on her finger, Berthe wept. She knew that some of the people looking on—Uncle Gildas, or Joseph and Raymond Driscoll, amazing in their ginger likeness—were mistaking her for a jealous older sister, longing to be in Marie's place.

Marie, now Mme. Driscoll, turned to Berthe and smiled, as she used to when they were children. Once again, the smile said, "Have I done the right thing? Is this what you wanted?" "Yes, yes," said Berthe silently, but she went on crying. Marie had always turned to Berthe; she had started to walk because she wanted to be with Berthe. She had been standing, holding on to a kitchen chair, and she suddenly smiled and let go. Later, when Marie was three, and in the habit of taking her clothes off and showing what must never be seen, Mme. Carette locked her into the storage shed behind the kitchen. Berthe knelt on her side of the door, sobbing, calling, "Don't be afraid, Marie. Berthe is here." Mme. Carette relented and unlocked the door, and there was Marie, wearing just her undershirt, smiling for Berthe.

Leading her mother, Berthe approached the altar rail. Marie seemed contented; for Berthe, that was good enough. She kissed her sister, and kissed the chosen husband. He had not separated them but would be a long incident in their lives. Among the pictures that were taken on the church steps, there is one of Louis with an arm around each sister and the sisters trying to clasp hands behind his back.

The wedding party walked in a procession down the steps and around the corner: another impression in black-and-white. The August pavement burned under the women's thin soles. Their fine clothes were too hot. Children playing in the road broke into applause when they saw Marie. She waved her left hand, showing the ring. The children were still French Canadian; so were the neighbors, out on their balconies to look at Marie. Three yellow leaves fell—white, in a photograph. One of the Driscoll boys raced ahead and brought the party to a stop. There is Marie, who does not yet understand that she is leaving home, and confident Louis, so soon to have knowledge of her bewildering ignorance.

Berthe saw the street as if she were bent over the box camera, trying to keep the frame straight. It was an important picture, like a precise instrument of measurement: so much duty, so much love, so much reckless safety—the distance between last April and now. She thought, It had to be done. They began to walk again. Mme. Carette realized for the first time what she and Uncle Gildas and Berthe had brought about: the unredeemable loss of Marie. She said to Berthe, "Wait until I am dead before you get married. You can marry a widower. They make good husbands." Berthe was nearly twenty-four, just at the limit. She had turned away so many attractive prospects, with no explanation, and had frightened so many others with her skill at cards and her quick blue eyes that word had spread, and she was not solicited as before.

Berthe and Marie slipped away from the reception—moved, that is, from the parlor to the bedroom—so that Berthe could help her sister pack. It turned out that Mme. Carette had done the packing. Marie had never had to fill a suitcase, and would not have known what to put in first. For a time, they sat on the edge of a bed, talking in whispers. Berthe smoked, holding the Buffalo Hofbrau ashtray. She showed Marie a black lacquer cigarette lighter she had not shown her mother. Marie had started to change her clothes; she was just in her slip. She looked at the lighter on all sides and handed it back. Louis was taking her to the Château Frontenac, in Quebec City, for three nights—the equivalent of ten days in Old Orchard, he had said. After that, they would go straight to the duplex property, quite far north on Boulevard Pie IX, that his father was helping him buy. "I'll call you tomorrow morning," said Marie, for whom tomorrow was still the same thing as today. If Uncle Gildas had been at Berthe's mercy, she would have held his head underwater. Then she thought, Why blame him? She and Marie were Montreal girls, not trained to accompany heroes, or to hold out for dreams, but just to be patient.

FORAIN

About an hour before the funeral service for Adam Tremski, snow mixed with rain began to fall, and by the time the first of the mourners arrived the stone steps of the church were dangerously wet. Blaise Forain, Tremski's French publisher, now his literary executor, was not surprised when, later, an elderly woman slipped and fell and had to be carried by ambulance to the Hôtel-Dieu hospital. Forain, in an attempt to promote Cartesian order over Slavic frenzy, sent for the ambulance, then found himself obliged to accompany the patient to the emergency section and fork over a deposit. The old lady had no social security.

Taken together, façade and steps formed an escarpment—looming, abrupt, above all unfamiliar. The friends of Tremski's last years had been Polish, Jewish, a few French. Of the French, only Forain was used to a variety of last rites. He was expected to attend the funerals not only of his authors but of their wives. He knew all the Polish churches of Paris, the Hungarian mission, the synagogues on the Rue Copernic and the Rue de la Victoire, and the mock chapel of the crematorium at Père Lachaise cemetery. For nonbelievers a few words at the graveside sufficed. Their friends said, by way of a greeting, "Another one gone." However, no one they knew ever had been buried from this particular church. The parish was said to be the oldest in the city, yet the edifice built on the ancient site looked forbidding and cold. Tremski for some forty years had occupied the same walk-up flat on the fringe of

Montparnasse. What was he doing over here, on the wrong side of the Seine?

Four months before this, Forain had been present for the last blessing of Barbara, Tremski's wife, at the Polish church on the Rue Saint-Honoré. The church, a chapel really, was round in shape, with no fixed pews—just rows of chairs pushed together. The dome was a mistake—too imposing for the squat structure—but it had stood for centuries, and only the very nervous could consider it a threat. Here, Forain had noticed, tears came easily, not only for the lost friend but for all the broken ties and old, unwilling journeys. The tears of strangers around him, that is; grief, when it reached him, was pale and dry. He was thirty-eight, divorced, had a daughter of twelve who lived in Nice with her mother and the mother's lover. Only one or two of Forain's friends had ever met the girl. Most people, when told, found it hard to believe he had ever been married. The service for Tremski's wife had been disrupted by the late entrance of *her* daughter—child of her first husband—who had made a show of arriving late, kneeling alone in the aisle, kissing the velvet pall over the coffin, and noisily marching out. Halina was her name. She had straight, graying hair and a cross face with small features. Forain knew that some of the older mourners could remember her as a pretty, unsmiling, not too clever child. A few perhaps thought Tremski was her father and wondered if he had been unkind to his wife. Tremski, sitting with his head bowed, may not have noticed. At any rate, he had never mentioned anything.

Tremski was Jewish. His wife had been born a Catholic, though no one was certain what had come next. To be blunt, was she in or out? The fact was that she had lived in adultery—if one wanted to be specific—with Tremski until her husband had obliged the pair by dying. There had been no question of a divorce; probably she had never asked for one. For his wedding to Barbara, Tremski had bought a dark blue suit at a good place, Creed or Lanvin Hommes, which he had on at her funeral, and in which he would be buried. He had never owned another, had shambled around Paris looking as though he slept under restaurant tables, on a bed of cigarette ashes and crumbs. It would have taken a team of devoted women, not just one wife, to keep him spruce.

Forain knew only from hearsay about the wedding ceremony in one of the town halls of Paris (Tremski was still untranslated then, had a job in a bookstore near the Jardin des Plantes, had paid back the advance for the dark blue suit over eleven months)—the names signed in a register, the daughter's refusal to attend, the wine drunk with friends in a café on the Avenue du Maine. It was a cheerless place, but Tremski knew the owner. He had talked of throwing a party but never got round to it; his flat was too small. Any day now he would move to larger quarters and invite two hundred and fifty intimate friends to a banquet. In the meantime, he stuck to his rented flat, a standard émigré dwelling of the 1950s, almost a period piece now: two rooms on a court, windowless kitchen, splintered floors, unheatable bathroom, no elevator, intimidating landlord—a figure central to his comic anecdotes and private worries. What did his wife think? Nobody knew, though if he had sent two hundred and fifty invitations she would undoubtedly have started to borrow two hundred and fifty glasses and plates. Even after Tremski could afford to move, he remained anchored to his seedy rooms: There were all those books, and the boxes filled with unanswered mail, and the important documents he would not let anyone file. Snapshots and group portraits of novelists and poets, wearing the clothes and haircuts of the fifties and sixties, took up much of a wall. A new desire to sort out the past, put its artifacts in order, had occupied Tremski's conversation on his wedding day. His friends had soon grown bored, although his wife seemed to be listening. Tremski, married at last, was off on an oblique course, preaching the need for discipline and a thought-out future. It didn't last.

At Forain's first meeting with Barbara, they drank harsh tea from mismatched cups and appraised each other in the gray light that filtered in from the court. She asked him, gently, about his fitness to translate and publish Tremski—then still at the bookstore, selling wartime memoirs and paperbacks and addressing parcels. Did Forain have close ties with the Nobel Prize committee? How many of his authors had received important awards, gone on to international fame? She was warm and friendly and made him think of a large buttercup. He was about the age of her daughter, Halina; so Barbara said. He felt paternal, wise, rid of mistaken ideals. He would become Tremski's guide and father. He thought, This is the sort of woman I should have married—although most probably he should never have married anyone.

Only a few of the mourners mounting the treacherous steps can have had a thought to spare for Tremski's private affairs. His wife's flight from a brave and decent husband, dragging by the hand a child of three, belonged to the folklore, not the history, of mid-century emigration. The chronicle of two generations, displaced and dispossessed, had come to a stop. The evaluation could begin; had already started. Scholars who looked dismayingly youthful, speaking the same language, but with a new, jarring vocabulary, were trekking to Western capitals—taping reminiscences, copying old letters. History turned out to be a plodding science. What most émigrés settled for now was the haphazard accuracy of a memory like Tremski's. In the end it was always a poem that ran through the mind—not a string of dates.

Some may have wondered why Tremski was entitled to a Christian service; or, to apply another kind of reasoning, why it had been thrust upon him. Given his shifting views on eternity and the afterlife, a simple get-together might have done, with remarks from admirers, a poem or two read aloud, a priest wearing a turtleneck sweater, or a young rabbi with a literary bent. Or one of each, offering prayers and tributes in turn. Tremski had nothing against prayers. He had spent half his life inventing them.

As it turned out, the steep church was not as severe as it looked from the street. It was in the hands of a small charismatic order, perhaps full of high spirits but by no means schismatic. No one had bothered to ask if Tremski was a true convert or just a writer who sometimes sounded like one. His sole relative was his stepdaughter. She had made an arrangement that suited her: She lived nearby, in a street until recently classed as a slum, now renovated and highly prized. Between her seventeenth-century flat and the venerable site was a large, comfortable, cluttered department store, where, over the years, Tremski's friends had bought their pots of paint and rollers, their sturdy plates and cups, their burglarproof door locks, their long-lasting cardigan sweaters. The store was more familiar than the church. The stepdaughter was a stranger.

She was also Tremski's heir and she did not understand Forain's role, taking executor to mean an honorary function, godfather to the dead. She had told Forain that Tremski had destroyed her father and blighted her childhood. He had enslaved her mother, spoken loud Polish in restaurants, had tried to keep Halina from achieving a French social identity. Made responsible, by his astonishing will, for organizing a suitable funeral, she had chosen a French send-off, to be followed by burial in a Polish cemetery outside Paris. Because of the weather and because there was a shortage of cars, friends were excused from attending the burial. Most of them were thankful: More than one fatal cold had been brought on by standing in the icy mud of a graveyard. When she had complained she was doing her best, that Tremski had never said what he wanted, she was probably speaking the truth. He could claim one thing and its opposite in the same sentence. Only God could keep track. If today's rite was a cosmic error, Forain decided, it was up to Him to erase

Tremski's name from the ledger and enter it in the proper column. If He cared.

The mourners climbed the church steps slowly. Some were helped by younger relatives, who had taken time off from work. A few had migrated to high-rise apartments in the outer suburbs, to deeper loneliness but cheaper rents. They had set out early, as if they still believed no day could start without them, and after a long journey underground and a difficult change of direction had emerged from the Hôtel de Ville Métro station. They held their umbrellas at a slant, as if countering some force of nature arriving head-on. Actually, there was not the least stir in the air, although strong winds and sleet were forecast. The snow and rain came down in thin soft strings, clung to fur or woolen hats, and became a meager amount of slush underfoot.

Forain was just inside the doors, accepting murmured sympathy and handshakes. He was not usurping a family role but trying to make up for the absence of Halina. Perhaps she would stride in late, as at her mother's funeral, driving home some private grudge. He had on a long cashmere overcoat, the only black garment he owned. A friend had left it to him. More exactly, the friend, aware that he was to die very soon, had told Forain to collect it at the tailor's. It had been fitted, finished, paid for, never worn. Forain knew there was a mean joke abroad about his wearing dead men's clothes. It also applied to his professional life: He was supposed to have said he preferred the backlist of any dead writer to the stress and tension of trying to deal with a live one.

His hair and shoes felt damp. The hand he gave to be shaken must have chilled all those it touched. He was squarely in the path of one of those church drafts that become gales anywhere close to a door. He wondered if Halina had been put off coming because of some firm remarks of his, the day before (he had defended Tremski against the charge of shouting in restaurants), or even had decided it was undignified to pretend she cared for a second how Tremski was dispatched; but at the last minute she turned up, with her French husband—a reporter of French political affairs on a weekly—and a daughter of fourteen in jacket and jeans. These two had not been able to read a word of Tremski's until Forain had published a novel in translation about six years before. Tremski believed they had never looked at it—to be fair, the girl was only eight at the time—or any of the books that had followed; although the girl clipped and saved reviews. It was remarkable, Tremski had said, the way literate people, reasonably well traveled and educated, comfortably off, could live adequate lives without wanting to know what had gone before or happened elsewhere. Even the husband, the political journalist, was like that: A few names, a date looked up, a notion of geography satisfied him.

Forain could tell Tremski minded. He had wanted Halina to think well of him at least on one count, his life's work. She was the daughter of a former Army officer who had died—like Barbara, like Tremski—in a foreign city. She considered herself, no less than her father, the victim of a selfish adventure. She also believed she was made of better stuff than Tremski, by descent and status, and that was harder to take. In Tremski's own view, comparisons were not up for debate.

For the moment, the three were behaving well. It was as much as Forain expected from anybody. He had given up measuring social conduct, except where it ran its course in fiction. His firm made a specialty of translating and publishing work from Eastern and Central Europe; it kept him at a remove. Halina seemed tamed now, even thanked him for standing in and welcoming all those strangers. She had a story to explain why she was late, but it was far-fetched, and Forain forgot it immediately. The delay most likely had been caused by a knockdown argument over the jacket and jeans. Halina was a cold skirmisher, narrow in scope but heavily principled. She wore a fur-and-leather coat, a pale gray hat with a brim, and a scarf—authentic Hermès? Taiwan fake? Forain could have told by rubbing the silk between his fingers, but it was a wild idea, and he kept his distance.

The girl had about her a look of Barbara: For that reason, no other, Forain found her appealing. Blaise ought to sit with the family, she said—using his first name, the way young people did now. A front pew had been kept just for the three of them. There was plenty of room. Forain thought that Halina might begin to wrangle, in whispers, within earshot (so to speak) of the dead. He said yes, which was easier than to refuse, and decided no. He left them at the door, greeting stragglers, and found a place at the end of a pew halfway down the aisle. If Halina mentioned anything, later, he would say he had been afraid he might have to leave before the end. She walked by without noticing and, once settled, did not look around.

The pale hat had belonged to Halina's mother. Forain was sure he remembered it. When his wife died, Tremski had let Halina and her husband ransack the flat. Halina made several trips while the husband waited downstairs. He had come up only to help carry a crate of papers belonging to Tremski. It contained, among other documents, some of them rubbish, a number of manuscripts not quite complete. Since Barbara's funeral Tremski had not bothered to shave or even put his teeth in. He sat in the room she had used, wearing a dressing gown torn at the elbows. Her wardrobe stood empty, the door wide, just a few hangers inside. He clutched Forain by the sleeve and said that Halina had taken some things of his away. As soon as she realized her error she would bring them back.

Forain would have preferred to cross the Seine on horseback, lashing at anyone who resembled Halina or her husband, but he had driven to her street by taxi, past the old, reassuring, unchanging department store. No warning, no telephone call: He walked up a curving stone staircase, newly sandblasted and scrubbed, and pressed the doorbell on a continued note until someone came running.

She let him in, just so far. "Adam can't be trusted to look after his own affairs," she said. "He was always careless and dirty, but now the place smells of dirt. Did you look at the kitchen table? He must keep eating from the same plate. As for my mother's letters, if that's what you're after, he had already started to tear them up."

"Did you save any?"

"They belong to me."

How like a ferret she looked, just then; and she was the child of such handsome parents. A studio portrait of her father, the Polish officer, taken in London, in civilian clothes, smoking a long cigarette, stood on a table in the entrance hall. (Forain was admitted no farther.) Forain took in the likeness of the man who had fought a war for nothing. Barbara had deserted that composed, distinguished, somewhat careful face for Tremski. She must have forced Tremski's hand, arrived on his doorstep, bag, baggage, and child. He had never come to a resolution about anything in his life.

Forain had retrieved every scrap of paper, of course—all but the letters. Fired by a mixture of duty and self-interest, he was unbeatable. Halina had nothing on her side but a desire to reclaim her mother, remove the Tremski influence, return her—if only her shoes and blouses and skirts—to the patient and defeated man with his frozen cigarette. Her entitlement seemed to include a portion of Tremski, too; but she had resented him, which weakened her grasp. Replaying every move, Forain saw how strong her case might have been if she had acknowledged Tremski as her mother's choice. Denying it, she became—almost became; Forain stopped her in time—the defendant in a cheap sort of litigation.

Tremski's friends sat with their shoes in puddles. They kept their gloves on and pulled their knitted scarves tight. Some had spent all these years in France without social security or health insurance, either for want of means or because they had never found their feet in the right sort of employment. Possibly they believed that a long life was in itself full payment for a safe old age. Should the end turn out to be costly and prolonged, then, please, allow us to dream and float in the thickest, deepest darkness, unaware of the inconvenience and clerical work we may cause. So, Forain guessed, ran their prayers.

Funerals came along in close ranks now, especially in bronchial winters. One of Forain's earliest recollections was the Mass in Latin, but he could not say he missed it: He associated Latin with early-morning hunger, and sitting still. The charismatic movement seemed to have replaced incomprehension and mystery with theatricals. He observed the five priests in full regalia sitting to the right of the altar. One had a bad cold and kept taking a handkerchief from his sleeve. Another more than once glanced at his watch. A choir, concealed or on tape, sang "Jesu, bleibet meine Freude," after which a smooth trained voice began to recite the Twenty-fifth Psalm. The voice seemed to emanate from Tremski's coffin but was too perfectly French to be his. In the middle of Verse 7, just after "Remember not the sins of my youth," the speaker wavered and broke off. A man seated in front of Forain got up and walked down the aisle, in a solemn and ponderous way. The coffin was on a trestle, draped in purple and white, heaped with roses, tulips, and chrysanthemums. He edged past it, picked up a black box lying on the ground, and pressed two clicking buttons. "Jesu" started up, from the beginning. Returning, the stranger gave Forain an angry stare, as if he had created the mishap.

Forain knew that some of Tremski's friends thought he was unreliable. He had a reputation for not paying authors their due. There were writers who complained they had never received the price of a postage stamp; they could not make sense of his elegant handwritten statements. Actually, Tremski had been the exception.

Forain had arranged his foreign rights, when they began to occur, on a half-and-half basis. Tremski thought of money as a useful substance that covered rent and cigarettes. His wife didn't see it that way. Her forefinger at the end of a column of figures, her quiet, seductive voice saying, "Blaise, what's this?" called for a thought-out answer.

She had never bothered to visit Forain's office, but made him take her to tea at Angelina's, on the Rue de Rivoli. After her strawberry tart had been eaten and the plate removed, she would bring out of her handbag the folded, annotated account. Outdone, outclassed, slipping the tearoom check into his wallet to be dissolved in general expenses, he would look around and obtain at least one satisfaction: She was still the best-looking woman in sight, of any age. He had not been tripped up by someone of inferior appearance and quality. The more he felt harassed by larger issues, the more he made much of small compensations. He ran his business with a staff of loyal, worn-out women, connected to him by a belief in what he was doing, or some lapsed personal tie, or because it was too late and they had nowhere to go. At eight o'clock this morning, the day of the funeral, his staunch Lisette, at his side from the beginning of the venture, had called to tell him she had enough social-security points for retirement. He saw the points as splashes of ink on a clean page. All he could think to answer was that she would soon get bored, having no reason to get up each day. Lisette had replied, not disagreeably, that she planned to spend the next ten years in bed. He could not even coax her to stay by improving her salary: Except for the reserve of capital required by law, he had next to no money, had to scrape to pay the monthly settlement on his daughter, and was in continual debt to printers and banks.

He was often described in the trade as poor but selfless. He had performed an immeasurable service to world culture, bringing to the West voices that had been muffled for decades in the East. Well, of course, his thimble-size firm had not been able to attract the leviathan prophets, the booming novelists, the great mentors and tireless definers. Tremski had been at the very limit of Forain's financial reach—good Tremski, who had stuck to Forain even after he could have moved on. Common sense had kept Forain from approaching the next-best, second-level oracles, articulate and attractive, subsidized to the ears, chain-smoking and explaining, still wandering the universities and congresses of the West. Their travel requirements were beyond him: No grant could cover the unassuming but ruinous little hotel on the Left Bank, the long afternoons and evenings spent in bars with leather armchairs, where the visitors expected to meet clever and cultivated people in order to exchange ideas.

Forain's own little flock, by contrast, seemed to have entered the world with no expectations. Apart from the odd, rare, humble complaint, they were content to be put up on the top story of a hotel with a steep, neglected staircase, a wealth of literary associations, and one bath to a floor. For recreation, they went to the café across the street, made a pot of hot water and a tea bag last two and a half hours, and, as Forain encouraged them to keep in mind, could watch the Market Economy saunter by. Docile, holding only a modest estimation of their own gifts, they still provided a handicap: Their names, like those of their characters, all sounded alike to barbaric Western ears. It had been a triumph of perseverance on the part of Forain to get notice taken of their books. He wanted every work he published to survive in collective memory, even when the paper it was printed on had been pulped, burned in the city's vast incinerators or lay moldering at the bottom of the Seine.

Season after season, his stomach eaten up with anxiety, his heart pounding out hope, hope, hope, he produced a satirical novella set in Odessa; a dense, sober private journal, translated from the Rumanian, best understood by the author and his friends; or another wry glance at the harebrained makers of history. (There were few women. In that particular part of Europe they seemed to figure as brusque flirtatious mistresses or uncomplaining wives.) At least once a year he committed the near suicide of short stories and poetry. There were rewards, none financial. A few critics thought it a safe bet occasionally to mention a book he sent along for review: He was considered sound in an area no one knew much about, and too hard up to sponsor a pure disaster. Any day now some stumbling tender newborn calf of his could turn into a literary water ox. As a result, it was not unusual for one of his writers to receive a sheaf of tiny clippings, sometimes even illustrated by a miniature photograph, taken at the Place de la Bastille, with traffic whirling around. A clutch of large banknotes would have been good, too, but only Tremski's wife had held out for both.

Money! Forain's opinion was the same as that of any poet striving to be read in translation. He never said so. The name of the firm, Blaise Editions, rang with an honest chime in spheres where trade and literature are supposed to have no connection. When the minister of culture had decorated him, not long before, mentioning in encouraging terms Forain's addition to the House of Europe, Forain had tried to look diffident but essential. It seemed to him at that instant that his reputation for voluntary self-denial was a stone memorial pinning him to earth. He wanted to cry out for help—to the minister? It would look terrible. He felt honored but confused. Again, summoned to the refurbished embassy of a new democracy, welcomed by an ambassador and a cultural attaché recently arrived (the working staff was unchanged), Forain had dared say to himself, Why don't they just give me the check for whatever all this is costing?—the champagne, the exquisite catering, the medal in a velvet box—all the while hoping his thoughts would not show on his face.

The truth was that the destruction of the Wall—radiant paradigm—had all but demolished Forain. The difference was that Forain could not be hammered to still smaller pieces and sold all over the world. In much the same way Vatican II had reduced to bankruptcy more than one publisher of prayer books in Latin. A couple of them had tried to recoup by dumping the obsolete missals on congregations in Asia and Africa, but by the time the Third World began to ask for its money back the publishers had gone down with all hands. Briefly, Forain pondered the possibility of unloading on readers in Senegal and Cameroon the entire edition of a subtle and allusive study of corruption in Minsk, set in 1973. Could one still get away with it—better yet, charge it off to cultural cooperation? He answered himself: No. Not after November 1989. Gone were the stories in which Socialist incoherence was matched by Western irrelevance. Gone from Forain's intention to publish, that is: His flock continued to turn them in. He had instructed his underpaid, patient professional readers—teachers of foreign languages, for the most part—to look only at the first three and last two pages of any manuscript. If they promised another version of the East–West dilemma, disguised as a fresh look at the recent past, he did not want to see so much as a one-sentence summary.

By leaning into the aisle he could watch the last blessing. A line of mourners, Halina and her sobbing daughter at the head, shuffled around the coffin, each person ready to add an individual appeal for God's mercy. Forain stayed where he was. He neither pestered nor tried to influence imponderables; not since the death of the friend who had owned the cashmere coat. If the firm went into deeper decline, if it took the slide from shaky to foundering, he would turn to writing. Why not? At least he knew what he wanted to publish. It would get rid of any further need of dealing with living authors: their rent, their divorces, their abscessed teeth, not to speak of that new craze in the East—their psychiatrists. His first novel—what would he call it? He allowed a title to rise from his dormant unconscious imagination. It emerged, black and strong, on the cover of a book propped up in a store window: *The Cherry Orchard*. His mind accepted the challenge. What about a sly, quiet novel, teasingly based on the play? A former property owner, after forty-seven years of exile, returns to Karl-Marx-Stadt to reclaim the family home. It now houses sixteen hardworking couples and thirty-eight small children. He throws them out, and the novel winds down with a moody description of curses and fistfights as imported workers try to install a satellite dish in the garden, where the children's swings used to be. It would keep a foot in the old territory, Forain thought, but with a radical shift of focus. He had to move sidelong: He could not all of a sudden start to publish poems about North Sea pollution and the threat to the herring catch.

Here was a joke he could have shared with Tremski. The stepdaughter had disconnected the telephone while Tremski was still in hospital, waiting to die; not that Forain wanted to dial an extinct number and let it ring. Even in Tremski's mortal grief over Barbara, the thought of Forain as his own author would have made him smile. He had accepted Forain, would listen to nothing said against him—just as he could not be dislodged from his fusty apartment and had remained faithful to his wife—but he had considered Forain's best efforts to be a kind of amateur, Western fiddling, and all his bright ideas to be false dawns. Forain lived a publisher's dream life, Tremski believed—head of a platoon of self-effacing, flat-broke writers who asked only to be read, believing they had something to say that was crucial to the West, that might even goad it into action. What sort of action, Forain still wondered. The intelligent fellow whose remains had just been committed to eternity was no different. He knew Forain was poor but believed he was rich. He thought a great new war would leave Central Europe untouched. The liberating missiles would sail across without ruffling the topmost leaf of a poplar tree. As for the contenders, well, perhaps their time was up.

The congregation had risen. Instead of a last prayer, diffuse and anonymous, Forain chose to offer up a firmer reminder of

Tremski: the final inventory of his flat. First, the entrance, where a faint light under a blue shade revealed layers of coats on pegs but not the boots and umbrellas over which visitors tripped. Barbara had never interfered, never scolded, never tried to clean things up. It was Tremski's place. Through an archway, the room Barbara had used. In a corner, the chair piled with newspapers and journals that Tremski still intended to read. Next, unpainted shelves containing files, some empty, some spilling foolscap not to be touched until Tremski had a chance to sort everything out. Another bookcase, this time with books. Above it, the spread of photographs of his old friends. A window, and the sort of view that prisoners see. In front of the window, a drop-leaf table that had to be cleared for meals. The narrow couch, still spread with a blanket, where Halina had slept until she ran away. (To the end, Barbara had expected her to return saying, "It was a mistake." Tremski would have made her welcome and even bought another sofa, at the flea market, for the child.) The dark red armchair in which Forain had sat during his first meeting with Barbara. Her own straight-backed chair and the small desk where she wrote business letters for Tremski. On the wall, a charcoal drawing of Tremski—by an amateur artist, probably—dated June 1945. It was a face that had come through; only just.

Mourners accustomed to the ceremonial turned to a neighbor to exchange the kiss of peace. Those who were not shrank slightly, as if the touch without warmth were a new form of aggression. Forain found unfocused, symbolized love positively terrifying. He refused the universal coming-together, rammed his hands in his pockets—like a rebellious child—and joined the untidy lines shuffling out into the rain.

Two hours later, the time between amply filled by the accident, the arrival and departure of the ambulance, the long admittance procedure, and the waiting-around natural to a service called Emergency, Forain left the hospital. The old lady was too stunned to have much to say for herself, but she could enunciate clearly, "No family, no insurance." He had left his address and, with even less inclination, a check he sincerely hoped was not a dud. The wind and sleet promised earlier in the day battered and drenched him. He skirted the building and, across a narrow street, caught sight of lines of immigrants standing along the north side of central police headquarters. Algerians stood in a separate queue.

There were no taxis. He was too hungry and wet to cross the bridge to the Place Saint-Michel—a three-minute walk. In a café on the Boulevard du Palais he hung his coat where he could keep an eye on it and ordered a toasted ham-and-cheese sandwich, a glass of Badoit mineral water, a small carafe of wine, and black coffee—all at once. The waiter forgot the wine. When he finally remembered, Forain was ready to leave. He wanted to argue about the bill but saw that the waiter looked frightened. He was young, with clumsy hands, feverish red streaks under his eyes, and coarse fair hair: foreign, probably working without papers, in the shadow of the most powerful police in France. All right, Forain said to himself, but no tip. He noticed how the waiter kept glancing toward someone or something at the far end of the room: His employer, Forain guessed. He felt, as he had felt much of the day, baited, badgered, and trapped. He dropped a tip of random coins on the tray and pulled on his coat. The waiter grinned but did not thank him, put the coins in his pocket, and carried the untouched wine back to the kitchen.

Shoulders hunched, collar turned up, Forain made his way to the taxi rank at the Place Saint-Michel. Six or seven people under streaming umbrellas waited along the curb. Around the corner a cab suddenly drew up and a woman got out. Forain took her place, as if it were the most natural thing in the world. He had stopped feeling hungry, but seemed to be wearing layers of damp towels. The driver, in a heavy accent, probably Portuguese, told Forain to quit the taxi. He was not allowed to pick up a passenger at that particular spot, close to a stand. Forain pointed out that the stand was empty. He snapped the lock shut—as if that made a difference—folded his arms, and sat shivering. He wished the driver the worst fate he could think of—to stand on the north side of police headquarters and wait for nothing.

"You're lucky to be working," he suddenly said. "You should see all those people without jobs, without papers, just over there, across the Seine."

"I've seen them," the driver said. "I could be out of a job just for picking you up. You should be waiting your turn next to that sign, around the corner."

They sat for some seconds without speaking. Forain studied the set of the man's neck and shoulders; it was rigid, tense. An afternoon quiz show on the radio seemed to take his attention, or perhaps he was pretending to listen and trying to decide if it was a good idea to appeal to a policeman. Such an encounter could rebound against the driver, should Forain turn out to be someone important—assistant to the office manager of a cabinet minister, say.

Forain knew he had won. It was a matter of seconds now. He heard, "What was the name of the Queen of Sheba?" "Which one?" "The one who paid a visit to King Solomon." "Can you give me a letter?" "B." "Brigitte?"

The driver moved his head back and forth. His shoulders dropped slightly. Using a low, pleasant voice, Forain gave the address of his office, offering the Saint Vincent de Paul convent as a landmark. He had thought of going straight home and changing his shoes, but catching pneumonia was nothing to the loss of the staunch Lisette; the sooner he could talk to her, the better. She should have come to the funeral. He could start with that. He realized that he had not given a thought to Tremski for almost three hours now. He continued the inventory, his substitute for a prayer. He was not sure where he had broken off—with the telephone on Barbara's desk? Tremski would not have a telephone in the room where he worked, but at the first ring he would call through the wall, "Who is it?" Then "What does he want? ... He met me *where*? ... When we were in high school? ... Tell him I'm too busy. No—let me talk to him."

The driver turned the radio up, then down. "I could have lost my job," he said.

Every light in the city was ablaze in the dark rain. Seen through rivulets on a window, the least promising streets showed glitter and well-being. It seemed to Forain that in Tremski's dark entry there had been a Charlie Chaplin poster, relic of some Polish film festival. There had been crates and boxes, too, that had never been unpacked. Tremski would not move out, but in a sense he had never moved in. Suddenly, although he had not really forgotten them, Forain remembered the manuscripts he had snatched back from Halina. She had said none was actually finished, but what did she know? What if there were only a little, very little, left to be composed? The first thing to do was have them read by someone competent—not his usual painstaking and very slow professional readers but a bright young Polish critic, who could tell at a glance what was required. Filling gaps was a question of style and logic, and could just as well take place after translation.

When they reached the Rue du Bac the driver drew up as closely as he could to the entrance, even tried to wedge the cab between two parked cars, so that Forain would not have to step into a gutter filled with running water. Forain could not decide what to do about the tip, whether to give the man something extra (it was true that he could have refused to take him anywhere) or make him aware he had been aggressive. "You should be waiting your turn...." still rankled. In the end, he made a Tremski-like gesture, waving aside change that must have amounted to 35 percent of the fare. He asked for a receipt. It was not until after the man had driven away that Forain saw he had not included the tip in the total sum. No Tremski flourish was ever likely to carry a reward. That was another lesson of the day.

More than a year later, Lisette—now working only part-time—mentioned that Halina had neglected to publish in *Le Monde* the anniversary notice of Tremski's death. Did Forain want one to appear, in the name of the firm? Yes, of course. It would be wrong to say he had forgotten the apartment and everything in it, but the inventory, the imaginary camera moving around the rooms, filled him with impatience and a sense of useless effort. His mind stopped at the narrow couch with the brown blanket, Halina's bed, and he said to himself, What a pair those two were. The girl was right to run away. As soon as he had finished the thought he placed his hand over his mouth, as if to prevent the words from emerging. He went one further—bowed his head, like Tremski at Barbara's funeral, promising himself he would keep in mind things as they once were, not as they seemed to him now. But the apartment was vacated, and Tremski had disappeared. He had been prayed over thoroughly by a great number of people, and the only enjoyment he might have had from the present scene was to watch Forain make a fool of himself to no purpose.

There were changes in the office, too. Lisette had agreed to stay for the time it would take to train a new hand: a thin, pretty girl, part of the recent, non-political emigration—wore a short leather skirt, said she did not care about money but loved literature and did not want to waste her life working at something dull. She got on with Halina and had even spared Forain the odd difficult meeting. As she began to get the hang of her new life, she lost no time spreading the story that Forain had been the lover of Barbara and would not let go a handsome and expensive coat that had belonged to Tremski. A posthumous novel-length manuscript of Tremski's was almost ready for the printer, with a last chapter knitted up from fragments he had left trailing. The new girl, gifted in languages, compared the two versions and said he would have approved; and when Forain showed a moment of doubt and hesitation she was able to remind him of how, in the long run, Tremski had never known what he wanted.

AVAILABLE AND COMING SOON FROM PUSHKIN PRESS CLASSICS

The Pushkin Press Classics list brings you timeless storytelling by icons of literature. These titles represent the best of fiction and non-fiction, hand-picked from around the globe – from Russia to Japan, France to the Americas – boasting fresh selections, new translations and stylishly designed covers. Featuring some of the most widely acclaimed authors from across the ages, as well as compelling contemporary writers, these are the world's best stories – to be read and read again.

MURDER IN THE AGE OF ENLIGHTENMENT
RYŪNOSUKE AKUTAGAWA

THE BEAUTIES
ANTON CHEKHOV

LAND OF SMOKE
SARA GALLARDO

THE SPECTRE OF ALEXANDER WOLF
GAITO GAZDANOV

CLOUDS OVER PARIS
FELIX HARTLAUB

THE UNHAPPINESS OF BEING A SINGLE MAN
FRANZ KAFKA